O9-AIF-043

"I WOULD HAVE YOU KNOW, MY LORD, THAT I THOUGHT YOU WERE QUITE WON- DERFUL. Very cool under fire, as they say. You got us free of the mob and I assure you I shall never forget the way you handled those two footpads. For that, my thanks," Victoria said.

"Your thanks," he repeated in a considering tone. "I am not certain that is sufficient reward under the circumstances."

"My lord?" she whispered, startled.

"No," he said, as if having reached a conclusion. "Your paltry thanks are not enough for what I have been through and what I undoubtedly have yet to endure."

Without any warning Lucas's hands closed around her shoulders and in one smooth, swift motion he had backed her up against the garden wall.

Victoria froze, held still by the warmth of his muscled thigh alongside hers. Her eyes widened in the moonlight as she looked up into Stonevale's starkly etched face.

"You are a hotheaded, reckless hoyden; a little shrew who is badly in need of taming. If I had any sense I would end this here and now," Lucas rasped.

Victoria licked her dry lips. "End what, my lord?"

"This." His mouth came down on hers with a fierce, plundering heat. . . .

Bantam Books by Amanda Quick

*Ask your bookseller for
the books you have missed*

AFFAIR
DANGEROUS
DECEPTION
DESIRE
DON'T LOOK BACK
I THEE WED
LATE FOR THE WEDDING
MISCHIEF
MISTRESS
MYSTIQUE
RAVISHED
RECKLESS
RENDEZVOUS
SCANDAL
SEDUCTION
SLIGHTLY SHADY
SURRENDER
WICKED WIDOW
WITH THIS RING

Sale of this book without a front cover may be unauthorized. If this book is coverless, it may have been reported to the publisher as "unsold or destroyed" and neither the author nor the publisher may have received payment for it.

Surrender is a work of fiction. Names, characters, places, and incidents are the products of the author's imagination or are used fictitiously. Any resemblance to actual events, locales, or persons, living or dead, is entirely coincidental.

2010 Bantam Books Mass Market Edition

Copyright © 1990 by Jayne A. Krentz

All rights reserved.

Published in the United States by Bantam Books, an imprint of The Random House Publishing Group, a division of Random House, Inc., New York.

BANTAM BOOKS and the rooster colophon are registered trademarks of Random House, Inc.

Originally published in hardcover in the United States by Bantam Books, an imprint of The Random House Publishing Group, a division of Random House, Inc., in 1990.

ISBN 978-0-553-59375-4

Cover art: © Brian Bailey

Printed in the United States of America

www.bantamdell.com

2 4 6 8 9 7 5 3 1

Prologue

The hall clock struck midnight. It was a death knell.

The beautiful, old-fashioned, terrifyingly heavy dress that did not fit her properly because it had been made for another woman, hampered her frantic flight down the corridor. The fine wool fabric tangled itself around her legs, threatening to trip her with every desperate step. She pulled the skirts higher, higher, almost to her knees, and risked a glance back over her shoulder.

He was closing on her, running her down the way a hound, maddened with blood lust, runs a deer to earth. His once demonically handsome face, the face that had lured an innocent, trusting woman first into marriage and then to her doom, was now a mask of fear and murderous, burning rage. With wild eyes that bulged from his head and hair that stood on end, he stalked her. The knife in his hand would soon be at her throat.

"*Demon bitch.*" His shout of rage echoed down the upstairs hall. The light of a flickering taper glinted on the evil-looking blade he clutched. "You are dead. Why cannot you leave me in peace? I swear I will send you back to hell where you belong. And this time I will make certain the deed is done right. Hear me, you accursed specter. *This time I will make certain.*"

She wanted to scream and could not. All she could do was run for her life.

"I will watch your blood flow through my fingers until you are drained," he cried out behind her, much closer. "This time you will stay dead, demon bitch. You have caused me trouble enough."

She was at the top of the stairs now, gasping for breath. Fear clawed at her insides. Holding the thick skirts even higher, she started down the staircase, one hand on the banister to keep herself from falling. It would be a bitter irony to die of a broken neck rather than a slashed throat.

He was so close, so very close. She knew there was every chance she would not make it back to safety. This time she had gone too far, taken one risk too many. She had played the part of a ghost and now she was very likely to become one. He would be on top of her before she reached the bottom step.

She had finally gotten the proof she had sought. In his rage he had confessed. If she lived, she would have justice for her poor mother. But it was fast becoming apparent that her quest would cost her her life.

Soon she would feel his hands on her, grabbing at her in a dreadful parody of the sexual embrace he had threatened her with when she was younger. Then she would feel the knife.

The knife.

Dear God, the knife.

She was halfway down the stairs when her pursuer's hideous scream rent the shadows.

She looked back in horror and realized that for the rest of her life, midnight would never be quite the same again. For her, midnight would mean nightmare.

1

Victoria Claire Huntington knew when she was being stalked. She had not reached the advanced age of twenty-four without learning to recognize the sophisticated fortune hunters of the ton. Heiresses were, after all, fair game.

The fact that she was still single and mistress of her own sizable inheritance was proof of her skill at evading the slick, deceitful opportunists who thrived in her world. Victoria had determined long ago never to fall victim to their attractive, superficial charms.

But Lucas Mallory Colebrook, the new Earl of Stonevale, was different. He might very well be an opportunist, but there was definitely nothing slick or superficial about him. Amid the brightly plumed birds of the ton, this man was a hawk.

Victoria was beginning to wonder if the very qualities that should have warned her off, the underlying strength and the implacable will she sensed in Stonevale, were exactly what had drawn her to him. There was no denying she had been fascinated by the man since they had been introduced less than an hour ago. The attraction she felt was deeply disturbing. In fact, it was quite dangerous.

"I believe I have won again, my lord." Victoria lowered her elegantly gloved hand and fanned her cards out across the green baize table. She smiled her most dazzling smile at her opponent.

"Congratulations, Miss Huntington. Your luck is certainly running strong this evening." Stonevale, whose gray eyes made Victoria think of ghosts hovering in the dead of night, did not look in the least dismayed at his loss. He appeared, in fact, quietly satisfied, as if a carefully devised plan had just come to fruition. There was a sense of cool anticipation about him.

"Yes, my luck has been amazingly strong tonight, has it not?" Victoria murmured. "One might almost suspect it had some assistance."

"I refuse to contemplate such a possibility. I cannot allow you to impugn your own honor, Miss Huntington."

"Very gallant of you, my lord. But it was not *my* honor which concerned me. I assure you I am well aware that I was not cheating." Victoria held her breath, knowing she had stepped out onto very thin ice with that remark. She had practically accused the earl of playing with marked cards in order to ensure her win.

Stonevale's eyes met and held hers across the table. His expression was unnervingly calm. Frighteningly calm, Victoria thought with a small shiver. There should have been some flicker of emotion in that cool, gray gaze. But she could read nothing in his face except a certain watchfulness.

"Would you care to clarify that remark, Miss Huntington?"

Victoria quickly decided to step back onto more solid ground. "Pray, pay me no heed, my lord. It is simply that I am as astounded as you should be at my luck with cards this evening. I am only an indifferent player at best. You, on the other hand, have a reputation as a skilled gamester, or so I have been told."

"You flatter me, Miss Huntington."

"I don't believe so," Victoria said. "I have heard tales of the ability you display at the tables of White's and

Brooks's as well as at certain other clubs here in town that are of a, shall we say, less reputable nature."

"Greatly embroidered tales, I imagine. But you make me curious. As we have only just met, where did you hear such stories?"

She could hardly admit she had asked her friend Annabella Lyndwood about him the moment he entered the ballroom two hours before. "I am certain you are aware of how such rumors fly, my lord."

"Indeed. But a woman of your obvious intelligence should know better than to listen to gossip." With a smooth, effortless motion Stonevale gathered up the cards into a neat stack. He rested his graceful, long-fingered hand on top of the deck and smiled coolly at Victoria. "Now, Miss Huntington, have you given any thought to collecting your winnings?"

Victoria watched him warily, unable to repress the excitement that was bubbling within her. If she had any sense, she would end this here and now, she told herself. But tonight it was difficult to think with the sort of cold, clear logic she usually employed in such circumstances. She had never met anyone quite like Stonevale.

The hum of conversation and laughter in Lady Atherton's card room receded, and the music from the ballroom seemed faint and distant now. The Athertons' huge London house was filled with well-dressed members of the ton as well as countless servants, but Victoria suddenly felt as if she were completely alone with the earl.

"My winnings," Victoria repeated slowly, trying to school her thoughts. "Yes, I shall have to do something about them, won't I?"

"I believe the wager was for a favor, was it not? As the winner, you are entitled to request one of me. I am at your service."

"As it happens, sir, I do not need any favors from you at the moment."

"Are you quite certain of that?"

She was startled by the knowing expression in the

earl's eyes. This was a man who always knew more than he ought. "Quite."

"I fear I must contradict you, Miss Huntington. I believe you do need a favor of me. I am given to understand that you will require an escort later this evening when you and Miss Lyndwood have your little adventure at the fair."

Victoria went very still. "What do you know of that?"

Stonevale gently riffled the cards with one long finger. "Lyndwood and I are friends. Belong to the same clubs. Play cards together occasionally. You know how it is."

"Lord Lyndwood? Annabella's brother? You've been talking to him?"

"Yes."

Victoria was incensed. "He promised to be our escort this evening and he gave us his word he would keep quiet on the matter. How dare he discuss this business with his cronies? This is too much by half. And men have the nerve to accuse women of gossiping. What an outrage."

"You must not be so hard on the man, Miss Huntington."

"What did Lyndwood do? Make a general announcement at one of his clubs that he would be taking his sister and her friend to the fair?"

"It was not a general announcement, I assure you. He was most discreet. After all, his sister is involved, is she not? If you must know the truth, I believe Lyndwood confided in me because he was feeling the strain of the situation."

"Strain? What strain? There is absolutely nothing about any of this that should make him anxious. He is simply going to escort Annabella and me to the park where the fair is being held. What could be simpler?" she snapped.

"As I understand it, you and his sister applied a certain degree of pressure on Lyndwood to get him to agree to your plans. The poor boy is still green enough to be manipulated by such feminine tactics. Fortunately, he is also wise enough to regret his weakness and smart enough to seek assistance."

"Poor boy, indeed. What nonsense. You make it sound as though Annabella and I coerced Bertie into this."

"Didn't you?" Stonevale shot back.

"Of course not. We merely impressed upon him that we have every intention of going to the fair tonight and he insisted on accompanying us. Very gallant of him. Or so we thought."

"You left him little choice as a gentleman. He could hardly agree to let you go on your own and you knew it. It was blackmail. Furthermore, I suspect it was largely your idea, Miss Huntington."

"*Blackmail.*" Victoria was now furious. "I resent that accusation, my lord."

"Why? It is little more than the truth. Do you think Lyndwood would have willingly consented to escort you and his sister to such a disreputable event unless you threatened to go on your own? Miss Lyndwood's mama would have a fit of the vapors if she got word of this little escapade tonight, and so, I imagine, would your aunt."

"I assure you, Aunt Cleo is far too sturdy to indulge in a fit of the vapors," Victoria declared loyally. But she knew Stonevale was perfectly correct about Annabella's mama. Lady Lyndwood would indeed have hysterics if she discovered her daughter's plans for this evening. Proper young ladies of the ton did not go to the fairgrounds at night.

"Your aunt may be a sturdy character. I will take your word for it, as I have not yet had the honor of meeting Lady Nettleship. But I sincerely doubt she would approve of your plans for this evening," Stonevale said.

"I shall throttle Lord Lyndwood when I see him. He is no gentleman to have betrayed a confidence in this manner."

"It was not entirely his fault he confided in me. I spent enough years as an officer to know when a young man is agitated about something. It was not that difficult to press him for the details."

Victoria narrowed her eyes. "Why?"

"Let us say I had a great curiosity about the matter. When Lyndwood discovered I was only too happy to come to his assistance tonight, he confessed all and pleaded for a companion."

"You have not answered my question. Why was your curiosity so great?"

"My reasons are not particularly important," Stonevale's long fingers rippled easily through the deck of cards again. "It seems to me we have a more immediate problem."

"I see no problem." Other than getting rid of you, Victoria added silently. Her first instincts had been correct. She should have run when she had the chance. But it was beginning to appear as though she'd never had the opportunity in the first place. Everything suddenly seemed to be proceeding according to some master plan that had been set in motion and over which she had less and less control.

"We should go over the details of the evening's adventure, don't you think?"

"The details have already been taken care of, thank you." Victoria did not like the feeling of not being in charge.

"Please understand. Perhaps it is the ex-soldier in me or perhaps it is mere curiosity, but I like to know exactly what is involved in a venture before it begins. Would you be so good as to outline the schedule of events more clearly for me?" Stonevale asked innocently.

"I do not see why I should. I did not invite you along."

"I merely wish to be of assistance, Miss Huntington. Not only is Lyndwood grateful for my help tonight, but you, yourself, might also find it very convenient to have an extra escort on hand. The mob can become very boisterous and rowdy at night."

"I'm not in the least concerned with the rowdy crowds. That is part of what will make the entire venture exciting."

"Then I'm sure you will at least be grateful for my continued silence on the matter should I happen to be introduced to your aunt this evening."

Victoria studied him mutely for a short, taut moment. "It would seem that Lord Lyndwood is not the only one in danger of being blackmailed. It appears I am also slated to become a victim."

"You wound me, Miss Huntington."

"Not fatally, unfortunately, else I would be rid of my problem, wouldn't I?"

"I urge you to look upon me as a solution rather than a problem." Stonevale smiled his slow smile. It did not affect the ghosts in his eyes. "I ask only to serve you in the capacity of escort this evening when you venture out into the dangerous streets of the city. I am most anxious to discharge my gaming debt."

"And if I decline to collect my winnings by accepting your escort, you will tell my aunt what is planned, is that it?"

Stonevale sighed. "It would be most unpleasant for all concerned if Miss Lyndwood's mama or your aunt discovered your scheme for tonight, but one can never tell what topics of conversation will arise in the course of an evening, can one?"

Victoria snapped her closed fan against the table. "I knew it. This *is* blackmail."

"A nasty word for it, but, yes, I suppose in a manner of speaking, it is blackmail."

Fortune hunter. That was the only explanation. She had never before encountered one quite so bold and aggressive. The type generally tended to be extremely well mannered and gracious, at least initially. But Victoria trusted her instincts. She locked eyes with Stonevale for an instant, fascinated by the waiting, expectant gleam in his hard, gray gaze. When she started to rise from the card table, the earl got to his feet to assist her.

"I shall look forward to seeing you later this evening," he murmured in her ear as she rose.

"If you are fishing for a fortune, my lord," Victoria drawled, "cast your lures elsewhere. You are wasting your time with me. I will grant that your technique is a novel one, but I do not find it at all attractive. I assure you, I have resisted far more agreeable bait."

"So I have been told." ·

He paced beside her as they moved into the glittering, crowded ballroom. Victoria became aware again, as she had earlier, of Stonevale's curiously balanced, but uneven stride. The elegant black evening clothes, finely tied cravat, close-fitting breeches, and polished boots did not disguise the limp that marred the movement of his left leg.

"What, precisely, have you been told, my lord?" Victoria demanded.

He shrugged. "It is said you have little interest in marriage, Miss Huntington."

"Your sources are wrong." She smiled thinly. "I do not have even a little interest in the married state. I have absolutely *no* interest in it, whatsoever."

Stonevale slanted her a considering glance. "A pity. Perhaps if you had a husband and a family to occupy your time in the evenings, you would not be obliged to amuse yourself with risky adventures such as the one you have planned for tonight."

Victoria's smile widened. "I am certain that the sort of adventure I have planned for this evening will be vastly more entertaining than the evening duties of a wife."

"What makes you so certain of that?"

"Personal history, my lord. My mother was married for her fortune and it destroyed her. My dear aunt was also married for her money. Fortunately for her my uncle had the grace to die early on in a hunting accident. But since I cannot count on similar good fortune, I have chosen not to take the risk of marriage."

"You do not fear that you might be missing an important part of a woman's life?" he ventured.

"Not in the least. I have seen nothing of marriage to recommend it." Victoria opened her gilded fan to conceal a shudder. Memories of her stepfather's casual little cruelties and drunken acts of violence toward her mother were never far below the surface. Even the bright lights of the ballroom could not entirely banish them.

She fanned herself languidly once or twice, hoping Stonevale would gain the impression that she was acutely bored with the direction of the conversation. "Now, if you will excuse me, my lord, I see a friend I must speak to."

He followed her glance. "Ah, yes, the intrepid Annabella Lyndwood. She is no doubt anxious to discuss the evening's plans, too. It appears, since you are determined not to be cooperative, that I shall be left to discover the details on my own. But never fear, I am very good at games of strategy." Stonevale inclined his head briefly over Victoria's hand. "Until later, Miss Huntington."

"I shall pray you find something more entertaining to do with your time tonight than to accompany us."

"Not likely." The earl's faint smile flared into a brief, wicked grin that momentarily displayed his strong white teeth.

Victoria turned away from him with an elegant swirl of her golden yellow silk skirts, refusing to give the man the satisfaction of a backward glance. This man was not only potentially dangerous, he was insufferable.

Victoria stifled a small groan as she swept through the crowd. She ought to have known better than to have allowed the earl to entice her into the card room tonight. It was, after all, not quite the thing for a lady to play cards with a man at an affair such as this. But she'd always had a hard time resisting adventure and the damnable man had seemed to sense that almost at once. *Sensed it and used the weakness.* She must remember that.

It was not as if she'd had any warning. Stonevale had, after all, been properly introduced to her by Jessica Atherton, no less.

Everyone knew Lady Atherton was entirely above reproach, a paragon, in fact. Slender, dark-haired, and blue-eyed, the viscountess was not only young, delicate, and quite lovely, she was also becomingly modest, unfailingly gracious, eminently respectable, and a stickler for the proprieties. In other words, she would certainly never have introduced a known rake or fortune hunter to one of her guests.

"Vicky, I've been looking everywhere for you." Annabella Lyndwood hurried over to her friend's side.

She flicked open her fan and proceeded to use it to shield her lips as she spoke in a whisper. "Were you actually playing cards with Stonevale? How very naughty of you. Who won?"

Victoria sighed. "I did, for all the good it did me."

"Did he tell you Bertie has invited him to accompany us tonight? I was furious about that, but Bertie insists we should have another man along for protection."

"So I was given to understand."

"Oh, dear, you are angry. I am so sorry, truly I am, Vicky, but there was no help for it. Bertie promised he would say nothing about our plans, but apparently Stonevale tricked him into revealing all."

"Yes, I can see how that might happen. Probably poured hock down Bertie's throat until the truth emerged. It is certainly a pity your brother could not keep his mouth shut, but don't fret, Bella. I am determined we shall enjoy ourselves regardless."

Annabella's sky blue eyes gleamed in obvious relief. Her fair curls bounced enticingly as she nodded her head and smiled. Annabella Lyndwood was held by certain high sticklers to be just the slightest bit too well rounded for fashion. But that tendency toward a full figure had certainly not put off her many suitors. She had recently turned twenty-one and had confided to Victoria that she would undoubtedly be obliged to accept one of the several offers she had received this Season. Annabella had gotten a late start in the marriage mart because of the untimely death of her father, but she had proven enormously popular when she had finally made her appearance in London.

"What do you know of him, Bella?" Victoria asked quietly.

"Who? Stonevale? Not much, to be perfectly truthful. Bertie says he's respected in the clubs. He just recently acceded to the title, I believe. The previous earl was a distant relative of some sort. An uncle or something. Bertie mentioned estates in Yorkshire."

"Did Bertie have anything else to say about him?"

"Let me think. According to Bertie, the family line

has almost died out. It came close to dying out entirely, I gather, when Lucas Colebrook was badly wounded on the Peninsula a year or so ago."

Victoria felt her stomach tighten in an odd manner. "The limp?"

"Yes. It was the end of his career in the military, apparently. Still, that career would have ended regardless once he inherited. His first duty is to his title and estates now, of course."

"Of course." Victoria did not want to ask the next question, but she could not resist. "How did it happen?"

"The injury to his leg? I don't know the details. Bertie says Stonevale never talks about it. But according to my brother, Wellington, himself, mentioned the earl in several of the dispatches. The story is that during the battle in which he was wounded, Stonevale managed to stay in the saddle and lead his men on to take their objective before he collapsed and was left for dead on the field."

Left for dead. Victoria felt sick. She pushed the queasy sensation aside, reminding herself that Lucas Colebrook was not the sort of man for whom she could afford pity. Furthermore, she seriously doubted that he would welcome it. Unless, of course, he could figure out some way to use it to his advantage.

It occurred to her to wonder if Stonevale had suggested the card game earlier so that he would not be obliged to endure a set of country dances. The limp probably kept him off the floor.

"What do you think of him, Vicky? I have seen the Perfect Miss Pilkington eyeing him all evening and so have several other ladies in the room. Not to mention their mamas. Nothing like a little fresh blood on the scene to whet the appetite, is there?" Annabella teased lightly.

"What a perfectly disgusting image." But Victoria laughed in spite of herself. "I wonder if Stonevale knows he's being looked over like a prize stallion?"

"I don't know, but thus far you are the only one he is looking over in return. No one could help but notice that it was you he coaxed into the card room."

"I suppose he's hanging out for a fortune," Victoria said.

"Really, Vicky, you always believe men are after your inheritance. You are positively single-minded to the point of idiocy on the subject. Is it not possible that some of your admirers are seriously interested in you, not your money?"

"Bella, I'm nearly twenty-five years old. We are both aware that men of the ton do not make offers to women of my advanced years unless they are lured by practical reasons. My fortune is a very practical reason."

"You speak as if you are on the shelf, and that is simply not true."

"Of course it's true, and to be honest, I prefer it that way," Victoria said evenly.

Annabella shook her head. "But, why?"

"It makes everything so much simpler," Victoria explained vaguely, unconsciously scanning the crowd in search of Stonevale. She spotted him at last talking to his hostess near the door that opened onto the vast Atherton gardens. She studied the intimate manner in which he stood towering over the angelic Lady Atherton, who was a vision in pink.

"If it makes you feel any better, Bertie has said absolutely nothing to imply that Stonevale is a fortune hunter," Annabella said. "Quite the contrary. It's rumored the old earl was an eccentric who hoarded his wealth until the day he died. Now it all belongs to our new earl. And you know Bertie. He would not dream of inviting anyone to accompany us tonight unless he approved of him."

That much was true, Victoria conceded. Lord Lyndwood, only two years older than his sister, took the duties of his recently inherited title quite seriously. He was highly protective of his flirtatious, exuberant sibling and he was always pleasant to Victoria. He would not expose either woman to a man whose background or reputation was questionable. Perhaps Annabella was right, Victoria thought, perhaps she was a bit overanxious on the subject of wily fortune hunters.

Then she recalled Stonevale's eyes. Even if he were

not a fortune hunter, he was still more dangerous than
any man she had ever met with the possible exception
of her stepfather.

Victoria sucked in her breath at the thought and then
discarded it angrily. No, she told herself with sudden
fierceness, regardless of how dangerous Stonevale might
be in his own right, she would not put him into the
same category as the brutal man who had married her
mother. Something deep within her was very certain
the two men were not of the same mold.

"Well, congratulations, Victoria, my dear. I see you
have captured the attention of our new earl. Stonevale
is an interesting specimen, is he not?"

Startled out of her thoughts by the familiar, throaty
voice, Victoria glanced to her left and saw Isabel Rycott
standing nearby. She forced herself to smile. The truth
was, she did not particularly care for the woman, but
she did feel a trace of envy when she was around her.

Isabel Rycott always reminded Victoria of an exotic
jewel. She was in her early thirties and had about her
an air of lush, feminine mystery that seemed to attract
men the way honey enticed bees. The sense of exoti-
cism was enhanced by Isabel's catlike grace, her sleek
black hair, and faintly slanted eyes. She was one of a
handful of other women in the room besides Victoria
who had defied the current style by wearing a strong
color rather than demure white or pastel tonight. Her
riveting deep emerald green gown shimmered brilliantly
in the light of the ballroom.

But it was not Isabel's unusual looks that made Victoria regard her with a certain wistful envy. It was the
freedom conferred upon her by her age and her status
as a widow that Victoria secretly admired. A woman in
Lady Rycott's position was far less subject to the close
scrutiny of the ton than Victoria was. Lady Rycott was
even free to indulge in discreet affairs.

Victoria had never met a man with whom she had
wanted to have an affair, but she would have liked very
much to have had the freedom to do so if she chose.

"Good evening, Lady Rycott." Victoria looked down

at the woman who stood several inches shorter than she. "Are you acquainted with the earl?"

Isabel shook her exquisitely shaped head. "We have not yet been introduced, unfortunately. He has only recently entered Society, although I hear he has been active at the gaming tables in the clubs for some time now."

"I heard the same thing," Annabella said. "Bertie says the man is an excellent gamester. Very coolheaded."

"Really?" Isabel glanced across the room to where the earl was still standing with Lady Atherton. "He's not at all in the way of being handsome, is he? Still, there is something quite intriguing about him."

Handsome? Victoria could have laughed aloud at the notion of using such an insipid word to describe Stonevale. No, he was not handsome. His face was strong, harsh even, with a sharp blade of a nose, an aggressive jaw, and an unrelenting awareness in those gray eyes. His hair was the color of a moonless night sky, shot with silver at the temples, but none of it added up to handsome. When one looked at Stonevale, one saw quiet, controlled, masculine power, not a fine dandy.

"You must admit," Annabella said, "that he certainly wears his clothes well."

"Yes," Isabel agreed softly. "He wears his clothes exceedingly well."

Victoria did not like the assessing look Isabel was employing as she surveyed the earl, but there was no denying that Stonevale was one of those rare men who was not dominated by the elegant tailoring that was so fashionable. His powerful shoulders, flat waist, and strongly molded thighs needed no padding or camouflage.

"Perhaps he will turn out to be rather amusing," Isabel said.

"Yes, indeed," Annabella agreed cheerfully.

Victoria glanced again at the tall, dark figure beside Lady Atherton. "Amusing may not be quite the right word." Dangerous was the right word.

But Victoria was suddenly willing to experiment with this dash of danger; the social whirl of the ton, which lately she depended upon more and more to fill up the long hours of the night, was no longer enough. She needed something else to help her hold the restless nightmares at bay.

The Earl of Stonevale might be just the tonic for which she had been searching.

"Dearest Lucas, what did you think of her? Will she do?" Lady Atherton gazed up at Stonevale with an anxious expression in her beautiful, gentle eyes.

"I think she will do nicely, Jessica." Lucas sipped champagne from the glass in his hand, his eyes moving across the crowd.

"I know she is a bit old."

"I, myself, am a bit old," he pointed out dryly.

"Nonsense. Thirty-four is an excellent age for a man intent on marriage. Edward was thirty-three when I married him."

"Yes, he was, wasn't he?"

Jessica Atherton's eyes were instantly filled with a heart-wrenching contrition. "Lucas, I am so sorry. How clumsy of me. You must know I did not mean to hurt you."

"I'll survive." Lucas finally spotted Victoria in the crowd. He kept his gaze on the tall figure of his quarry as she stepped out onto the dance floor with a plump, elderly baron. Victoria obviously enjoyed dancing, although she appeared to restrict her partners to very young, socially awkward males or those much older than herself. She probably viewed such men as harmless.

He regretted he did not dare risk asking her out onto the floor. It would be interesting to see if she followed him there as easily as she had followed him into the card room. But he was not certain how well she would tolerate the lack of grace in his damned left leg, and at this juncture he could not take any chances.

He sensed no streak of cruelty in her, though. She definitely had a temper, but he knew she would not stoop to insults or cutting remarks about his limp. Nevertheless she might very well trod quite forcefully on his toes if he managed to goad her as he had in the card room. The image made Lucas smile.

"It was quite outrageous of her to accompany you into the card room, of course," Lady Atherton said. "But, then, I fear that is our Miss Huntington. She does have a tendency to come very close to the edge of what is considered proper. But under a husband's guidance, I am certain that regrettable element of her nature could be controlled."

"An interesting notion."

"And she does have a noticeable predilection for that rather overbright shade of yellow," Lady Atherton added.

"It's clear Miss Huntington has a mind and a will of her own. But I must allow that the yellow looks attractive on her. Not many women could wear it successfully."

Lucas studied Victoria's tall, willowy figure in the high-waisted gown. The yellow silk was a ray of honeyed sunlight in the crowded room. It gleamed with a warm richness amid the array of classical white and watery pastels.

The only real problem with the gown as far as he was concerned was that the bodice was cut far too low. It revealed entirely too much of the gentle, high slopes of Victoria's breasts. Lucas had an almost irresistible urge to borrow some matron's shawl and wrap it firmly around Victoria's upper torso. Such an impulse was so out of character for him that he was momentarily astonished.

"I fear she has a reputation for being something of an Original. Her aunt's doing, no doubt. Cleo Nettleship is most unusual in her own right," Lady Atherton said.

"I would much prefer a lady who is out of the common run. Makes for more interesting conversation, wouldn't you say? One way or another, I suspect I shall have to endure a good many conversations with the woman I eventually marry. No getting around it."

Jessica sighed softly. " 'Tis unfortunate, but there simply is not a large selection of heiresses around this Season. But, then, there rarely is. However, there is still Miss Pilkington. You really should meet her before you make up your mind, Lucas. I vow she is a very admirable female. Always perfectly correct in her behavior, whereas, I fear, Miss Huntington has a certain tendency to be somewhat headstrong."

"Never mind Miss Pilkington. I'm quite content with Miss Huntington."

"If only she weren't very nearly five and twenty. Miss Pilkington is only nineteen. Younger women tend to be more amenable to a husband's influence, Lucas."

"Jessica, please believe me when I tell you Miss Huntington's age is not a problem."

"You are quite certain?" Lady Atherton eyed him uneasily.

"I would far rather deal with a woman of a certain age who knows what she's about than a young chit straight out of the schoolroom. And I would have to say that Miss Huntington does, indeed, know what she is about."

"You mean because she has managed to stay single so long? You are probably right. She's made it very clear she has no interest whatsoever in turning over her inheritance to a husband. Everyone but the most desperate of fortune hunters has quite given up on her."

Stonevale flashed a crooked smile. "Which narrows the field for me."

"Don't misunderstand me. She is an engaging creature, rather refreshing in some ways, like her aunt. Victoria does have her share of admirers. But they all seem to be relegated to the status of friends."

"In other words, they have all learned their places and they stay in them."

"If they overstep themselves, she drops them immediately. Miss Huntington is known for being kind for the most part, always has a smile and a charming word. Quite willing to dance with the less attractive men in the room. But she is very firm with all of the gallants who hang around her," Jessica added.

That did not surprise him. Miss Huntington would not have remained her own mistress this long unless she had learned the trick of manipulating the males in her orbit. He was going to find himself walking a very narrow line during this courtship.

"She is well educated, I take it?" Lucas asked.

"Some would say extraordinarily so. I've heard that

Lady Nettleship assumed most of the responsibility for educating her niece and one can certainly see the results. Miss Huntington would undoubtedly have come to grief in Society long ago were it not for the fact that her aunt's position is unassailable."

"What happened to Miss Huntington's parents?"

Lady Atherton hesitated, then spoke evenly. "Dead. All of them. Quite sad, really. But the Lord giveth and the Lord taketh away."

"He certainly does."

Lady Atherton cast him an uncertain glance and then cleared her throat. "Yes, well, the father died when Miss Huntington was a small child and her mother soon remarried. But Caroline Huntington was killed in a riding accident a little over eighteen months ago. Then Miss Huntington's stepfather, Samuel Whitlock, died less than two months after his wife. A terrible accident on a flight of stairs, I am given to understand. Broke his neck."

"A strange list of tragedies, but it does have the net effect of leaving Miss Huntington free of parents who might feel obliged to inquire deeply into my finances. The useful rumor of my uncle's hoarded wealth would not hold up under close scrutiny."

Jessica pursed her lips in disapproval. "I fear there's no getting around the fact that Miss Huntington spent the minimal amount of time in mourning after her stepfather's death. She made it quite clear she mourned only her mother, and even that ended as soon as it was seemly to do so."

"You reassure me, Jessica. The last thing I want is a woman who enjoys such entertainments as extended mournings. Life can be very short and it's a shame to waste it in a lot of useless grieving for what one cannot have, don't you think?"

"But one must learn to endure the tragedies thrust upon us. Such things build character. And one must also be conscious of the proprieties," Jessica admonished, looking faintly hurt. "In any event, Lady Nettleship, the aunt, is an excellent female with fine connections, but there is no denying she is a trifle odd in some ways.

I fear she has allowed her niece to run a bit wild. Do you think you can tolerate Miss Huntington's rather unusual manners?"

"I think I can manage Miss Huntington very well, Jessica." Lucas took another swallow of champagne, his attention on Victoria, who was still dancing with her middle-aged baron.

She was not what he had expected, Lucas reflected with a curious sense of relief. He had been prepared to do his duty to his name, his title, and the many people for whom he was now responsible, but he had not expected to be able to enjoy himself in the process.

Definitely not what he had expected.

For one thing, he had not anticipated this near-violent rush of physical attraction. Jessica had informed him that Victoria Huntington was presentable enough, but that was as far as the description had gone.

She was taller than he had been led to believe, much taller than the majority of the women around her. But Lucas was a tall man and it was good to find a woman who's head would rest nicely on his shoulder instead of somewhere down around the middle of his chest.

Not what he had expected.

And she moved with a long, graceful stride that had not a trace of the customary mincing quality women so often affected. She also danced well, he realized, not without a small pang of annoyance. He knew he could not even compete with the middle-aged baron when it came to partnering her.

Lucas watched as Victoria's baron guided her effortlessly under a glittering chandelier. The massed lights revealed the golden highlights in her rich, tawny brown hair. She wore the thick stuff cut entirely too short for Lucas's taste. But the short, artfully careless style did reveal the delicate, enticing line of her nape and framed her fine amber eyes. The lady definitely knew what she was about when it came to fashion.

Not what he had expected.

Jessica had warned him that although there was nothing truly objectionable about Miss Huntington's features, she was not an outstanding beauty. Studying the lively, animated quality of Victoria's face from a distance, Lucas supposed Jessica was correct in one sense. But he decided that the warm golden eyes, so full of challenge, the arrogant yet feminine nose, and that flashing smile went together very nicely. There was a fascinating, vivid element about Victoria that caught and held the eye. It hinted at an underlying passion that was just waiting to be set free by the right man.

Lucas took another glance at the smile Victoria was giving her baron and decided he would very much like to taste Victoria's mouth. Soon.

"Lucas, dearest?"

Reluctantly Lucas turned away from the sight of his heiress. *His heiress,* he thought, amused as he ran the phrase through his mind again.

"Yes, Jessica?" He looked inquiringly down at the beautiful woman he had once loved and lost due to the lack of a title and a fortune.

"Will she do, Lucas? Truly? It is not too late to meet Miss Pilkington, you know."

Lucas reflected on how Jessica, bowing to the dictates of her family, had married another man to secure both a title and a fortune. At the time he had not really comprehended or forgiven her. Now, having acquired the title but still lacking the fortune he desperately needed, Lucas finally understood the position Jessica had been in four years earlier.

He knew now that marriage was not a matter of emotion; it was a matter of duty. Duty was something Lucas understood very well.

"Well, Lucas?" Jessica prompted again, beautiful eyes full of grave concern. "Can you bring yourself to marry her? For the sake of Stonevale?"

"Yes," Lucas said. "Miss Huntington will do very well."

2

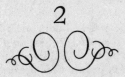

"Is my aunt at home, Rathbone?" Victoria inquired as she hurried into the front hall of the town house. Carriage wheels clattered on the street outside as Annabella and her elderly aunt, who had accompanied Victoria to the ball, took their leave.

Victoria was rather glad to be out of the close confines of the vehicle. Annabella's aunt, who had acted as a chaperon for the younger women, had felt obliged to read her charges a lengthy lecture on the subject of the rather doubtful propriety of females playing cards with men at fashionable parties.

Victoria hated lectures of that sort.

Rathbone, a massive, distinguished-looking man with thinning gray hair and a nose that would have graced any duke, solemnly indicated the closed door of the library. "I believe Lady Nettleship is engaged with several members of her Society for the Investigation of Natural History and Horticulture."

"Excellent. Pray, do not look so glum, Rathbone. All is not lost. Apparently they have not yet managed to set fire to the library."

"Only a matter of time," Rathbone muttered.

Victoria grinned as she sailed past him, stripping off her gloves as she went toward the library door. "Come now, Rathbone. You have been in the service of my aunt ever since I first came to visit as a small child, and never once has she burned the place down around our ears."

"Begging your pardon, Miss Huntington, but there was that time you and she conducted the experiments with the gunpowder," Rathbone felt obliged to point out.

"What? You mean to tell me you still recall our pitiful little attempt to manufacture our own fireworks? What a long memory you have, Rathbone."

"Some moments in our lives are indelibly etched in our recollections, as sharp today as on the day they occurred. I, personally, shall never forget the look on the first footman's face when the explosion occurred. We thought for one horrifying instant that you had been killed."

"But, as it turned out, I was only slightly stunned. It was the fact that I was covered in ashes that gave everyone pause," Victoria noted.

"You did look as gray as death, if you don't mind my saying so, Miss Huntington."

"Yes, it was a rather spectacular effect, was it not? Ah, well, one cannot reflect too much on past glories. There are far too many new and intriguing wonders of the natural world waiting to be explored. Let us see what my aunt is up to this evening."

Rathbone watched a footman open the door of the library, his expression making it clear he was prepared for virtually any sight which might await.

But as it happened, there was nothing at all to be seen immediately. The library was in utter darkness. Even the fire on the hearth had been extinguished. Victoria stepped cautiously inside, trying in vain to peer through the deep gloom. From the depths of the room she heard the sound of a handle being cranked.

"Aunt Cleo?"

The response was a brilliant arc of dazzling white

light. It blazed forth from the center of the darkness, casting the group of people gathered into a small circle inside the room into stark relief for one flaring instant. The small crowd gasped in amazement.

A second later the giant spark vanished and a resounding cheer went up.

Victoria smiled toward the open door where Rathbone and the footman stood. "Nothing to worry about tonight," she assured them. "The members of the society are merely playing with Lord Potbury's new electricity machine."

"Vastly reassuring, Miss Huntington." Rathbone answered dryly.

"Oh, Vicky, dear, you're home," a voice sang out of the gloom. "Did you enjoy yourself at the Athertons' rout? Do come in. We're right in the middle of the most fascinating series of demonstrations."

"So it would seem. I regret I missed some of them. You know how much I enjoy electricity experiments."

"Yes, I know, dear." The shaft of light from the open door revealed Victoria's aunt Cleo as she came forward to greet her niece. Lady Nettleship was almost as tall as Victoria. She was in her early fifties and her tawny hair was elegantly streaked with silver. She had lively eyes and the same vivid, animated quality in her features which had historically characterized the women in Victoria's family.

That quality lent an impression of beauty, even to a woman of Aunt Cleo's years, where an objective eye could discover little true perfection. Cleo was dressed in the height of fashion, as always. Her gown of ripe peach was styled to reveal her still-slender figure.

"Rathbone, do close the door," Lady Nettleship said briskly. "The effect of the machine is far more impressive in darkness."

"With pleasure, madam." Rathbone nodded to the footman, who shut the door in obvious relief, and the library was once more plunged into thick darkness.

"Come in, come in," Cleo said, taking her niece's arm and guiding her through the gloom to where the small group still clustered around the electricity machine. "You know everyone, here, do you not?"

"I believe so," Victoria said, relying on her memory of the brief glimpse of faces she'd had a moment earlier. A murmur of greetings rumbled from the shadows. Visitors to Lady Nettleship's house were accustomed to such inconveniences as being introduced in the middle of a Stygian darkness.

" 'Evening, Miss Huntington."

"Your servant, Miss Huntington. Looking lovely tonight. Quite lovely."

"Pleasure, Miss Huntington. You're just in time for the next experiment."

Victoria recognized these three masculine voices at once. Lords Potbury, Grimshaw, and Tottingham comprised her aunt's faithful circle of admirers. They varied in age from fifty in Lord Potbury's case to Lord Tottingham's nearly seventy years. Grimshaw, Victoria knew, was somewhere in his early sixties.

The three had danced attendance on her aunt for longer than Victoria could remember. She did not know if they had initially been as interested in scientific explorations as their lady was, but over the years they had certainly developed a similar passion for experimentation and collection.

"Please, do carry on with your demonstrations," Victoria urged. "I can only stay for one or two and then I must be off to bed. Lady Atherton's rout was really quite exhausting."

"Of course, of course," Cleo said, patting her arm. "Potbury, why don't you let Grimshaw work the crank this time?"

"Don't mind if I do," Potbury said. "Bit tiring, I must say. Here you go, Grimshaw. Put some push into it."

Grimshaw muttered a response and a moment later the sound of the hand crank rumbled forth once more. Cloth rubbed rapidly against a long glass cylinder until a sizable charge built up. Everyone waited expectantly, and in due course another searing flash of light crackled and danced in the shadows. Gasps of satisfaction and delight again filled the room.

"Heard there's been some efforts to reanimate a couple of corpses with electricity," Potbury announced to the small group.

"How fascinating," Cleo said, clearly enchanted with the notion. "What was the outcome?"

"Got a few twitches and such from the arms and legs but nothing permanent. Tried it myself with a frog. Easy enough to get a few jerks out of the limbs but still stone dead when all was said and done. Don't think there'll be much gained from that line of inquiry."

"Where did the experimenters obtain the corpses?" Victoria asked, unable to stifle her morbid curiosity.

"From the hangman's noose," Grimshaw said. "Where else? A respectable experimenter can't exactly go about robbing graves, y'know."

"If the corpses were those of villains, then it's just as well they stayed dead, I suppose," Lady Nettleship stated. "No point spending all that time and energy hanging thieves and cutthroats only to have them spring up again good as new a day or two later because someone wanted to experiment with electricity."

"No." Victoria felt a little queasy at the thought of such a possibility. Such things were disturbingly close to the contents of her dreams lately. "I quite agree with you, Aunt Cleo. No point getting rid of villains if one cannot count on them staying dead."

"Speaking of the difficulty of obtaining corpses for experimentation, I must say some people are certainly making a nice livelihood robbing graves." The darkened room did not conceal the shudder in Lady Finch's words. "I heard the resurrectionists struck again the other night at a little churchyard on the outskirts of town. Took two bodies that had just been buried that morning."

"Well? What do you expect?" Potbury asked in prosaic tones. "Doctors at Edinburgh and Glasgow Schools of Surgery have got to have something to cut up. Can't expect to train good surgeons without something to practice on. The resurrectionists may be illegal but they are filling a need."

"Excuse me," Victoria whispered to her aunt as the

conversation about the traffic in dead bodies threatened to grab everyone's attention. "I believe I will go on to bed."

"Sleep well, my dear." Cleo patted her hand affectionately. "Remind me in the morning to show you the wonderful collection of beetles Lady Woodbury brought by. Found them all on her last trip to Sussex. She's very kindly agreed to let us study them for a few days."

"I shall look forward to seeing them," Victoria said, not without genuine enthusiasm. An interesting collection of insects was almost as intriguing as a new exotic plant from China or America. "But now, I really must be off to bed."

"Good night, dear. Mustn't exhaust yourself, you know. Perhaps you've been going it a bit strong lately. Just as well you're in before dawn for once."

"Yes. Perhaps it is." Victoria let herself out of the darkened library, blinking a few times in the glare of the brightly lit hall before she started up the red-carpeted stairs. As she reached the landing, her gathering sense of excitement was almost overpowering.

"You may go, Nan," she informed her young maid as she entered her airy, yellow, gold, and white bedroom.

"But your lovely gown, ma'am. You'll need help getting it off."

Victoria smiled in resignation, knowing she would only create questions where there were none if she refused assistance. But she dismissed the abigail as soon as possible and then turned back to the depths of her wardrobe.

From beneath a pile of shawls she pulled a pair of men's breeches and from under a stack of blankets she removed some boots. She found the jacket where she had stored it inside her large, wooden chest and set to work.

Within a short while Victoria was standing in front of her dressing glass examining her appearance with a critical eye. She had been quietly gathering the masculine clothing for weeks, and this was the first time she had tried on the entire outfit.

The breeches fit a bit too snugly, tending to outline

the flare of her hips and the feminine shape of her calves, but there was no help for it. With any luck the tails of her dark blue coat and the night itself would hide the most obvious hints of femininity. At least her breasts, being rather on the small side, were easily concealed beneath the finely pleated shirt and yellow waistcoat.

When Victoria set the beaver hat at a rakish angle on her short hair, she was pleased with the overall effect. She was certain that, at least at night, she could safely pass as a young dandy. After all, people saw only what they expected to see.

Anticipation welled up deep inside her and she realized she wasn't as excited about the forthcoming expedition to the fair as she was anxious about seeing Stonevale again.

It was true, as Annabella had said, Stonevale must be a gentleman or Lady Atherton and Bertie Lyndwood would not count him among their acquaintances. But a woman, especially an heiress, could not depend upon any man's sense of gentlemanly honor. She had learned that lesson well from her stepfather. Still, Victoria knew she would be safe enough tonight so long as she stayed in control of the situation.

She relaxed, allowing herself a small, assured smile. She'd had a great deal of experience controlling situations that involved men.

Victoria crossed the deep blue carpet to the yellow velvet armchair near the window and settled in it. In a little while it would be safe to leave the house.

Tonight there would be no time to worry about the creeping restlessness that frequently threatened her in the long, dark hours of the night; no time to dwell on that sense of something dangerous left unfinished; no time to fret about bizarre notions such as the possibility of bringing the dead back to life with electricity.

Best of all, it was nearly midnight already. With any luck she would be awake most of the night, so there would be less time for the nerve-shattering dreams that increasingly invaded her nights as of late. She had come to fear those nightmares. A small shiver went through her even now as she pushed the memory of the last one to the farthest corner of her mind. She could still see the knife in his hand.

No, there would be little opportunity for those nightmares to strike tonight. With any luck she would not be home before dawn. She could deal with the daylight hours. It was the darkness she had learned to fear.

Victoria gazed out into the shadowed garden and wondered what Stonevale would think when he saw her dressed as a man.

The cheerful anticipation of his stunned expression was enough to banish the small, tattered remnant of horror that still hovered at the edge of her mind.

Lucas leaned forward on the carriage seat and scowled out into the shadows of the dark street. He was not in a good mood. "I don't care for this nonsense. Why are we not fetching Miss Huntington from her front steps?"

"I've told you," Annabella Lyndwood protested. "Her aunt is a very understanding person, but Victoria is afraid that even she would have a few doubts about our plans for this evening."

"I'm glad somebody besides myself has the sense to have doubts," Lucas growled. He turned toward the other man in the carriage. "Lyndwood, I think we should have a few contingency arrangements made in case we become separated in the crowd this evening."

"Excellent idea," Lyndwood agreed with alacrity. He was clearly relieved to have Lucas along. "Perhaps we ought to arrange for the carriage to wait at a specific location somewhat removed from the activity?"

Lucas nodded, thinking swiftly. "It will be difficult to maneuver the carriage near the park. At this time of night the crowds will be large and unpredictable. Tell your coachman that if he does not find us waiting for him at the same place where he sets us down, he should drive two streets over from the grounds and wait there near a small tavern called the Hound's Tooth."

Lyndwood nodded, his handsome, concerned features in deep shadow. "I know the place and so does my coachman, I'll wager. Don't mind telling you again I appreciate your joining us tonight, Stonevale. When the ladies take a notion to have an adventure, ain't much a man can do to stop them, is there?"

"That remains to be seen," Stonevale said.

Annabella, dressed in a stylish blue walking dress with a matching blue pelisse, giggled. "If you believe you can stop Victoria from doing anything she pleases, you have a surprise in store for you, my lord."

"Miss Huntington gets up to these tricks frequently, I take it?"

Annabella chuckled again. "Victoria is never dull, I assure you, but this is a first for her, I believe. She told me she has been planning this for some time."

"It would seem Miss Huntington has gone ungoverned by a husband for far too long," Lucas observed, and glowered at Annabella as the giggles turned into outright laughter. "I have said something amusing?"

"Miss Huntington intends to go the entirety of her life without such governance," Annabella informed him.

"I understand she fears being married for her fortune," Lucas said carefully. He wanted information but he did not want to raise too many questions about his motives.

"She fears marriage altogether," Annabella replied, her laughter fading. "She has seen nothing but very sad examples of the wedded state in her own family. And of course the business of being constantly pursued for her inheritance for so many years has only inclined her more than ever away from any desire for matrimony. Sometimes, I confess I wonder if she isn't right in her thinking. What good is marriage for a woman?"

"Damme, Bella," her brother broke in sharply. "What a mutton-headed thing to say. Don't go taking any foolish notions into your brain about following Miss Huntington's example in life. Mama would have hysterics. To be perfectly truthful, as charming as Victoria is, if her aunt wasn't such a good friend of Mama's, I should think twice about allowing you to go about with her. Only look at the situation I am in tonight because of that woman's influence on you. The sooner you are married, the better. Thank God, Barton has almost come up to scratch."

Annabella smiled demurely in the darkness. "I know

you cannot wait to rid yourself of the responsibility of supervising my behavior, but I fear you must contain your enthusiasm for a while longer, Bertie. Upon due reflection I have decided to have you refuse Lord Barton's offer, if and when it comes."

"Upon due reflection probably means you discussed the matter with Miss Huntington," Lyndwood said morosely.

"I do recall a conversation on the subject," Annabella said. "She was kind enough to give me her opinion as to the sort of husband Lord Barton would make."

Lucas broke in on the fraternal wrangling, his interest sharpened by Annabella's last remark. "How was Miss Huntington able to form an opinion about Barton?"

"Oh, I believe he pursued her quite industriously for several months last year. During that time she had an opportunity to learn a great deal about him."

"Did she?" Lucas was aware of the chill in his own words. "Just what did she learn?"

"A number of small items such as the fact that Barton has apparently fathered a babe or two on his mistress, that he has been known to get so deeply into his cups that he has had to be carried into his house by his coachman, and that he has a passion for gaming hells," Annabella answered.

"Here now," Lyndwood muttered, "can't hold a few insignificant peccadilloes against a man."

"Really?" inquired a familiar, husky female voice from the open window of the carriage. "Would Viscount Barton be equally prepared to overlook a similar list of *insignificant peccadilloes* in his prospective wife?"

Lucas turned his head sharply toward the carriage window, aware that the mere sound of Victoria's voice had immediately reactivated the desire he had first experienced in Jessica Atherton's card room. He concealed his eagerness with the cold control he had learned years ago, prepared to greet his heiress with proper formality.

But instead of a striking woman in an elegant gown and bonnet, he found himself staring at a figure dressed to the nines in men's clothes. Laughing eyes met his through the shadows, challenging him.

"Good God," he said through his teeth, "this is insanity."

"No, my lord, this is amusing."

Lucas recovered himself as he heard the groom start to clamber down from the driver's seat. He shoved open the door before the man could arrive to open it properly, and reached out and caught hold of Victoria's wrist before she realized his intent. He had been expecting a lady with a taste for some mild adventure, not this outrageous creature.

"Get in here, you little baggage, before someone recognizes you."

His urgency brought Victoria through the door far more quickly than she intended. She gasped as she landed heavily on the seat beside Lucas and grabbed her beaver-trimmed hat to keep it in place. He saw she was clutching an expensive-looking inlaid walking stick in her hand.

"Thank you, my lord," she said with heavy sarcasm.

Lucas ignored her. "Let's get out of here, Lyndwood."

Lyndwood obliged by tapping his stick against the roof of the carriage. "To the park, if you please," he called out.

Annabella smiled at Victoria as the carriage clattered into motion. "You look very well turned out this evening, Vicky. Do I detect Brummell's influence in your choice of blue? He is particularly fond of the color, I'm told. But you have always preferred yellow."

"I decided a yellow coat might be a bit too striking for the occasion," Victoria conceded.

"So you limited yourself to a yellow waistcoat. I congratulate you on your sense of restraint. And, pray tell, who tied your cravat? I warrant I haven't seen such a clever design in ages."

"Like it, do you?" Victoria fingered the carefully arranged neckcloth. "Invented this particular fold myself. Call it the *Victoire.*"

Annabella gave a peal of laughter. "Vicky, I swear you sound just like one of the dandies on Bond Street. You've got the whole tone exactly right. Just the proper sense of affected boredom. I declare you could trod the boards and make your living as an actress."

"Why, thank you, Bella. That is high praise indeed."

Lucas lounged back in the seat and surveyed the striking figure beside him with a critical eye. His initial shock was giving way to annoyance and a certain uneasiness that was new to him. It was clear Victoria Huntington was fond of mischief, and this brand of mischief could land her in serious trouble.

"Do you go about like this often, Miss Huntington?" Lucas was aware he had automatically used the tone of voice that in the past he had reserved for young officers under his command who had landed themselves in trouble. He could not help himself. He was irritated.

"This is my first experiment with men's clothes, sir. But to be truthful, I shall probably be strongly tempted to try it again in the future. I find that the masculine attire affords me far more freedom than I have when I wear women's clothes," Victoria admitted.

"It certainly affords you a far greater opportunity for bringing down a wave of humiliation and social disaster on your lovely head, Miss Huntington. If it got out that you have a taste for running around London at night dressed as a man, your reputation would be in shreds within twenty-four hours."

Victoria wrapped her fingers even more firmly around the handle of her walking stick. "What an odd thing for you to say, sir. Do you know, your attitude quite takes me by surprise. I would have thought you less of a prig. I suppose the card game at the ball misled me. Don't you have any taste for adventure? No, I suppose you don't. You are, after all, a good friend of Lady Atherton's are you not?"

The woman was deliberately baiting him. Lucas wished very strongly that they were alone in the carriage. "I do not know what you are implying, Miss Huntington, but I assure you, Lady Atherton is above reproach."

"Well, yes, that is just the point. Everyone knows Jessica Atherton would never in a million years allow herself to be found in this carriage on her way to the fair tonight," Victoria declared.

Annabella giggled again. "That is certainly the truth."

"Are you implying Lady Atherton is a prig?" Lucas demanded.

Victoria shrugged, the movement surprisingly sensual in the well-cut jacket. "I mean no offense, my lord. Just that she isn't the sort of female who enjoys adventure. One naturally has to assume that her friends are equally limited in their choice of entertainment and equally disapproving of those who have broader tastes."

"And you are a woman who enjoys adventure?" Stonevale baited.

"Oh, yes, my lord. I enjoy it very much."

"Even though it carries with it the risk of ruining yourself in Society?"

"There would be no real adventure if there were no real risk, would there, my lord? I would have thought a successful gamester such as yourself would understand that."

Her words made him more uneasy than ever. "You may be right, Miss Huntington. But I have always preferred risks in which the odds were at least somewhat in my favor."

"How very dull your life must be, sir."

Lucas instinctively started to react to the goading remark but caught himself in time. His self-control reasserted itself, along with his sense of reason. The last thing he could afford now was to have his quarry declare him a priggish bore. His instincts told him Victoria would respond to a challenge or even an all-out battle of wills, but she would ignore him entirely if he managed to bore her.

A priggish bore. Good God. The thought of that label stuck on him was enough to make him laugh. It was certainly not the usual description applied to his character. But around Miss Huntington, Lucas discovered, he was rapidly developing a most uncharacteristic regard for the proprieties. He was still in shock from the sight of her in men's clothes.

Victoria was no longer paying any attention to him, however. She was smiling at Annabella. "So you decided to turn down Barton's offer, did you? I am happy to hear it. The man would have made you a perfectly horrid husband."

"I am convinced you are right," Annabella shuddered delicately. "I might have been able to overlook Barton's interest in hazard but just imagine marrying a man who has actually fathered two bastards on some poor woman to whom he will not give his name."

"It certainly casts a nasty reflection on his honor," Victoria agreed grimly.

Lucas studied her profile in the dim light. "Just how did you come to discover the business of Barton's illegitimate offspring? I cannot believe that gossip reached your ears on the dance floor of a hostess such as Lady Atherton."

"No, it did not, as a matter of fact. I hired a runner to discover what he could about Barton and he was the one who turned up the news of the two children and the mistress."

Lucas felt a chill clutch his insides. "You hired a Bow Street runner?"

"I thought it the most efficient approach to the problem."

"It was a brilliant approach," Annabella declared.

Lyndwood groaned. "Good Lord, if Mama only knew. Poor Barton. D'ya know, I think he rather cared for you, Bella."

"I doubt that," Victoria said briskly. "His family has told him they expect him to marry and he is simply in the process of casting about for a wife who will suit his father. He tried me last year until I managed to make him see I would not do at all and then he moved on to try his luck with the Perfect Miss Pilkington. Evidently she, too, had the good sense to see that he was the lowest sort of fortune hunter. Then he spotted Bella, here, and decided to have a go at her. Nothing more to it than that."

"The Perfect Miss Pilkington?" Lucas glanced from one woman to the other. "Why do you call Miss Pilkington perfect?"

"Because she is," Annabella explained reasonably.

"Never puts a foot wrong. A model of feminine perfection. A paragon, in fact."

"You will understand about Miss Pilkington, my lord," Victoria said, "when we tell you that she is a protégée of Lady Atherton's."

"I see." No wonder Jessica had wanted to introduce him to the other heiress. It was a good bet that if he had decided to pursue Miss Pilkington, he would not now be sitting in a carriage with a young lady dressed outrageously in masculine attire. Lucas wondered for half a second if he had made a serious mistake earlier in the evening. And then he decided that whatever the risks, the night was going to be infinitely more interesting with Miss Huntington.

"I thought you would, my lord," Victoria said.

"Well, one thing is certain," Lucas pointed out dryly, "because of your interference, Miss Lyndwood will never have a chance to find out precisely how Barton does feel about her, will she? And Barton, himself, will never know he was done in by a paid runner and a certain Miss Huntington. The man will never even have a chance to defend himself."

"Could he defend himself?" Victoria retorted, her eyes clashing with his in the shadows. This time there was no mischief or humor in her steady, challenging gaze. "Are you saying that what the runner discovered was untrue?"

Lucas held his ground, speaking evenly. "I am saying that it was none of your business to interfere in the matter. There might very well be mitigating circumstances."

"Hah. I doubt that very much," Victoria said.

"So do I," chimed in Annabella. "Just imagine that poor woman tucked away with Barton's children."

Lyndwood bestirred himself on the other side of the coach. "Neither of you two ladies ought to know a deuced thing about any of Barton's offspring who happen to have been born on the wrong side of the blanket. T'ain't right for you even to be discussing such matters, is it, Stonevale?"

"Such conversation is certainly not the mark of well-bred ladies of the ton," Lucas muttered, grimly aware he sounded exactly like the boring prig Victoria had insinuated he was.

Victoria's smile was triumphant. "Lord Stonevale, allow me to point out that if you find my conversation too offensive for your delicate sensibilities, there is an easy remedy for you. Simply open the carriage door and depart."

Lucas realized in that moment that Victoria Huntington had the power to slice through his iron-willed self-control as no one else had been able to do in years. Furthermore, she accomplished the trick quite effortlessly. This lady was dangerous. He was going to have to work hard at staying in command of the situation.

Lucas cleared his throat. "My sensibilities will survive your indelicate manners, Miss Huntington. And I could not possibly exit now. My honor still requires that I pay my gaming debts."

"Hah. This is no honorable gaming debt, sir. This is blackmail, pure and simple."

"I assure you," Stonevale returned, "I am fast discovering that blackmail is neither pure nor simple, not with you cast in the role of the victim."

Her eyes gleamed with mischief at that sally and Lucas felt his whole body react with sharp desire. He folded his arms across his chest and leaned back against the cushions, his gaze holding hers in the shadows. In that moment he wanted nothing more than to be alone with this bewitching creature. He longed to pull her down onto the carriage seat and show her the extent of the risks she was running when she challenged him so openly.

For an instant a charged silence hung between them. When Victoria finally blinked and allowed her gaze to slide away from his own, he knew she had discerned his thoughts.

But Lucas's small sense of victory was short-lived. It was dawning on him rapidly that this courtship he had embarked upon was going to be even more hazardous than he had first thought. With Jessica Atherton's help and his own skill at getting by on his wits and his ability at the card table, he had hoped to conceal the true state of his finances from Society long enough to achieve his objective. He had made his plans with his usual care.

But if his intended bride took a notion to hire a runner to look into his affairs, it was all too likely the full truth would come out. The rumor of his nonexistent inheritance would not hold up for long. It was becoming clear that the task of stalking this particular heiress would be the most exacting hunting he had ever done. One wrong move, one miscalculation on his part, and he would lose the game.

"How long do you intend to spend on your adventure this evening, Miss Huntington?" Lucas kept his tone detached.

"Is time a problem for you? Do you have another engagement planned?" she asked far too sweetly.

He knew intuitively that she was fishing to find out if he had a mistress expecting him later. "No, I do not. Lyndwood and I must secure arrangements to have all of us taken up by his carriage at a specific location, and to do that efficiently in the crowd, we need to decide upon a definite departure time."

"Oh. Yes, I can see that. I would suggest two hours would be ample time to enjoy the fair."

Annabella sighed. "I am afraid I cannot stay out that long, Vicky. Mama will be coming home from the Milricks' soirée in another two hours and she will expect me to be in by then."

Lucas hid his relief. "An hour then?"

"An hour's long enough for me," Bertie Lyndwood said quickly.

"That's probably all the time I should allow," Annabella said with regret.

"Oh, very well." Victoria sounded mildly irritated but resigned. "An hour it is. We shall have to hurry, though, if we are to see everything."

Lucas said nothing, but privately he considered that the next hour was undoubtedly going to be one of the longest of his life.

Half an hour later he was confirmed in his belief. The huge park was ablaze with lanterns that illuminated a seemingly unlimited array of stalls selling meat pies and ale, booths featuring acrobats and rope dancers, and packed tents featuring puppet shows and games.

The crowd was a mix of the high and the low. Servants who had snuck out of their masters' houses, shopkeepers and their wives, apprentices and shopgirls, dandies out for a lark, a few daring members of the nobility, prostitutes, pimps, pickpockets, young boys from flash houses, military men and dockworkers all rubbed elbows together as they sought the after-dark thrills of the fair.

"My lord," Victoria murmured as they stopped to buy a custard tart, "I know you are concerned about calling attention to my disguise."

"Concerned is quite an understatement, Miss Huntington. Those damned breeches fit you like a second skin," Lucas muttered, eyeing the smooth line of her hips.

"I shall be happy to give you the name of my tailor. In the meantime, perhaps it would be best if you released my arm. A certain man across the way is staring."

"Bloody hell." Lucas dropped her arm as if he had been burned. He felt himself turning a dull red as he realized what a stranger would think to see him holding another gentleman's arm the way a man holds the arm of a woman. "This silly getup of yours is bound to cause trouble."

"No one will think twice about it unless they see you treating me as though I were a female." Victoria took an enthusiastic bite of her tart.

"It isn't just the way I treat you, it's the way you look in those breeches."

Victoria fingered her collar. "I thought the coat hid my figure rather well."

"I have news for you. It doesn't."

"You're determined to be difficult tonight, aren't you, my lord? Kindly remember that it was you who insisted on inviting yourself along on this venture. I am merely the innocent victim of your blackmail scheme."

Lucas grinned ruefully. "Innocent victim, Miss Huntington? Somehow I feel that description could never be applied to you. Whatever else you are, you will never be anyone's innocent victim."

Victoria surveyed him, considering his words for a moment. "I should probably take offense at that but I am having far too much fun. Oh, look, the acrobats are starting another performance. Let's go watch them."

Lucas glanced around. "I don't see Lyndwood and his sister."

"Bertie wanted more beer. They'll be back in a moment. Stop fretting, sir."

"I am not fretting, Miss Huntington, I am trying to exercise a measure of prudence. No one else on the scene appears inclined to do so."

"That's because there's little sport to be had in exercising prudence. Come, let's hurry or we won't be able to see the acrobats."

A short while later Lucas had just begun to relax and even convince himself they might all survive the hour at the fair unscathed when disaster broke out with no warning.

It might have been the particularly extravagant fireworks display which started the small fire. Or perhaps it was the fight that occurred between two prostitutes who were demanding payment for their favors from a soldier. Or it could simply have been the normal propensity of any large London crowd to turn itself into a mob on the slightest pretext.

Whatever the reason, the conversion of the throng of cheerful fair-goers into a wild, unruly human wave bent on causing trouble happened in less than a moment. Fireworks burst overhead, people screamed, curses filled the air.

Horses reared and plunged. A gang of boys took advantage of the opportunity to steal a tray of pies, causing the pie seller to run after them, hurling insults into the evening air. There were more screams and another flash of fireworks. Flames leapt up as a nearby booth caught fire and then all was chaos; dangerous, terrifying chaos; a chaos in which people would be trampled, assaulted, and robbed. Some might even be killed.

Lucas reacted automatically the instant he felt the mood of the crowd shift. For the second time that night he clamped his fingers in a viselike grip around Victoria's fine-boned wrist.

"This way," he ordered, pitching his voice to be heard above the din. "Follow me."

"What about Annabella and Bertie?" Victoria cried.

"They're on their own, the same as we are."

Victoria did not attempt to argue further, for which Lucas was profoundly grateful. Apparently the lady was capable of displaying some common sense when it was called for.

Chaining her to his side with his grip on her wrist, Lucas hauled her through the melee toward the uncertain safety of the narrow alleys and streets that bordered the park.

He had known from the start the lady was going to be nothing but trouble.

3

The danger, which had coalesced out of thin air, left Victoria stunned. In that moment the only promise of safety in the entire world lay in the iron grip on her wrist. She followed Lucas blindly, relying instinctively on his strength and the savage manner in which he wielded his stick to forge a way for them through the crowd.

Victoria felt a hand claw at her coat and realized someone was trying to pick her pocket. Another hand tried to grab the inlaid walking stick she carried. Without thinking, she lashed out with the stout length of wood, slashing at the grasping hands.

There was a scream from one of her assailants which brought Lucas's head around briefly. With one quick glance he saw that the would-be thieves had already released their intended victim.

"Good girl." He immediately turned his attention back to forging ahead through the mob.

He did not try to work his way back against the driving force of the crowd. Instead, Victoria realized, he chose to ride the human flow, as if guiding a boat through a strong current. He kept maneuvering steadily toward the edge of the wild, churning river, his pace controlled and strong in spite of his limp. He did not break out into a mad dash and thereby jeopardize his balance and hers. It was obvious he had long since learned to compensate for the weakness in his left leg.

Lucas's cool self-mastery amid the chaos made it clear to Victoria that he was one of those rare men who did not become rattled under pressure. She felt safe with him, even though the mob roiled around her like a violent sea.

As they reached the fringes of the mass of shouting, staggering, shoving humanity, the crowd thinned. Lucas made a calculated bid to escape it altogether; he had apparently been watching for his chance. In what seemed like an instant, he yanked Victoria into a tunnel of darkness between two buildings.

Victoria stumbled after him into the relative safety of the pitch black alley. Her boots skidded on slime and she caught her breath against the terrible stench that welled up from the confines of the narrow stone walls.

She thought the danger was over until she heard the crude drunken shouts from the alley entrance.

" 'Ere now, mate. Bring that light in 'ere. I saw 'em go inter this little 'ole, I tell ye. Two of 'um. Rich coves, by the look of 'em."

"Damn." Lucas swore with deadly softness. "Get behind me and stay down, Victoria."

Not waiting for her to obey, Lucas flung Victoria behind him with such force that she fetched up against the brick wall of the alley. She caught her balance and glanced anxiously toward the entrance just as a lantern appeared. In its pale light she saw the faces of two young ruffians armed with knives. They spotted their quarry and moved forward expectantly.

"What'er ye waitin' for, Long Tom?" the second man asked his pal in an urgent tone. " 'Urry up and spice the swells. There be plenty o' work out 'ere for the likes o' us tonight."

Stonevale stood his ground, shielding Victoria. As

she watched she saw him remove a small, shiny object from his greatcoat pocket.

"Bloody 'ell. 'E's got a pop," the first man cursed as the lamplight fell on the pistol lodged in Stonevale's hand.

"An excellent observation, gentlemen." Stonevale sounded faintly bored. "Which of you would like to test the accuracy of my aim?"

The first young man into the alley slithered to a halt and his companion piled into him. They both toppled into the muck. The lantern fell to the ground, glass shattering in a shower of small sparks. The weak flame continued to flicker a moment longer, casting strange, menacing shadows over the tense scene.

"Bloody damn 'ell," the first man said again, clearly frustrated. "Ye try to make a decent livin' and look at what 'appens." He found his balance and scrambled back toward the alley entrance.

The other would-be footpad needed no further encouragement. There was a clatter of boots on stone, muffled curses, and a few seconds later Victoria and Lucas had the alley to themselves.

But Lucas wasted no time. His long fingers clamped around Victoria's wrist once more and he hauled her through the dark alley into the next street.

The mob had not yet spilled over in this direction, and they were met with blessed silence. Victoria tried to slow her step in order to catch her breath but Stonevale refused to stop, and she stumbled obediently after him, panting.

"Lucas, I must say, that was very well done of you back there in the alley."

Lucas tightened his grip on her wrist. "It would have been entirely unnecessary if you had not taken it into your head to attend the fair tonight."

"Really, Lucas, must you—"

"We can only hope Lyndwood's coachman followed orders," Lucas interrupted as he continued pulling Victoria along at a rapid pace.

"I'm worried about Annabella and Bertie," Victoria got out between sharp, strained breaths.

"Yes. So you should be."

Victoria winced, aware he had no compunction about pointing out her guilt in the matter. The worst of it was he was right; this had all been her idea.

Mercifully, Stonevale said no more as he guided her around the corner and into the street where the coachman had been told to wait in case of emergency. Victoria saw the familiar lines of the Lyndwood coach pulled up in front of the tavern and she heaved a sigh of relief when she spotted two people inside.

"They're here, Lucas. They're safe." Victoria flushed as she realized she had unthinkingly been using Stonevale's given name since the excitement started.

"Yes. It appears we are to be favored with some luck tonight, after all." He said nothing else as they neared the carriage.

"Good God, we were worried about you," Lyndwood said, pushing open the carriage door. "Thought for certain you'd been run down by the mob. Hurry. We don't want to hang out in this street for long. No telling when the crowd might take a notion to come this way."

"Rest assured, Lyndwood, I have no intention of dawdling." Lucas tossed Victoria up into the carriage and followed quickly, slamming the door behind him.

The carriage took off at once and none too soon. In the distance the shouts of the mob filled the night air.

Victoria looked anxiously at Annabella. "Are you all right, Bella?"

Annabella clasped her friend's hand. "I'm fine. Bertie and I were on the fringes of the crowd when the trouble broke out. We managed to get out of the way almost at once. But I was so worried about you two. You were right in the heart of the throng, were you not?"

"It was a near thing," Victoria said. A wave of euphoria was washing over her now, rapidly replacing the tension that had gripped her a moment earlier. "We were accosted in an alley by two men intent on robbing us. But Stonevale produced a pistol and stopped them instantly. He was magnificent."

"Good heavens," Annabella whispered, shocked.

"Damme, Stonevale." Lyndwood frowned with obvious concern. "A near thing, is right. Neither of you was hurt, I take it?"

"We are both perfectly fit, Lyndwood, as you can see." Lucas dismissed the inquiry with a deceptively neutral tone. "Although Miss Huntington's disguise appears to have suffered somewhat."

Victoria belatedly checked her hair and realized something was amiss. "Oh, dear, I've lost my hat."

"You are extremely lucky not to have lost more than a hat, Miss Huntington." Again Stonevale's voice seemed far too calm.

Victoria slanted a sidelong glance at his hard profile and realized that Lucas was in a blazing fury. For the first time since the riot had erupted around her, she felt a trickle of genuine fear.

Lucas glanced out at the empty side street as the carriage drew to a halt. "You intend to be set down here, Miss Huntington? We are nowhere near your front door."

"It will do," she said calmly, collecting her handsome walking stick.

"And how do you intend to get into the house if not through the front door?" Stonevale asked, annoyed.

"I shall go over the garden wall and back through the conservatory, the same way I left earlier. Don't worry, my lord, I know my way." Victoria was already stepping down from the carriage as the door was opened. She hoped he wouldn't feel obliged to follow.

"Good night, Vicky," Annabella called softly. "It turned out to be a most interesting adventure, did it not?"

"It certainly did," Victoria replied.

Lucas followed Victoria through the carriage door. "Wait here, Lyndwood," he instructed over his shoulder. "I shall return as soon as I have escorted our reckless little dandy back over the garden wall."

Victoria turned toward him in alarm. "There is no need to see me home, my lord. I assure you, I am perfectly capable of finding my own way."

"I wouldn't hear of it, Miss Huntington." He must have spotted the new uneasiness in her because he smiled knowingly. "Excellent," he murmured, grasping her arm and propelling her into the shadows. "I see you understand me well enough now to realize that I am not in a good temper. It is always best not to argue with me when I am in this mood."

"My lord," she began, her chin lifting imperiously, "if you think to hold me accountable for what happened this evening, you can think again."

"But I do hold you accountable, Miss Huntington." He glanced up at the high stone wall covered with thick ivy. "How do we get inside the garden?"

She tried to retrieve her arm. When he took no notice of her small struggle, she gave up and nodded toward the far end of the walk. "There is a way over there."

He hauled her along in the indicated direction until she pointed out the heavy vines which concealed a few chinks in the bricks. Without a word, Victoria wedged the toe of her boot into the first opening and grabbed a vine.

Beneath her, Lucas shook his head in grim disapproval as he watched her climb the garden wall. Victoria felt awkward and clumsy under his close scrutiny. She had not as yet had much practice scaling garden walls. She could only hope the fitful moonlight hid the shape of her snugly clad derriere as she went over the top.

Behind her, Lucas grabbed a trailing bit of ivy, found the chink in the wall with the toe of his boot, and followed.

On the other side of the wall, Victoria dropped lightly to the ground and looked up to see that Lucas was almost on top of her. She stepped back quickly as he dropped down in front of her. She noticed he took most of his weight on his strong right leg and did not stumble as he caught his balance.

"My lord," she hissed, "you should be getting back to the carriage. The Lyndwoods will be waiting."

"I have one or two things to say to you first." He stood in the midst of the fragrant, deeply shadowed garden, a tall, lean, menacing figure as dark and dangerous as the night.

Victoria summoned up her courage. "I must tell you, Stonevale, that I have no wish to endure a lecture for what happened this evening. I am already quite aware that none of us would have been in jeopardy if I had not insisted upon going to the fair."

"In that, Miss Huntington, you are correct."

The total lack of emotion in his voice was far more unnerving than a scolding would have been. But Victoria suddenly remembered the way he had defended her in the alley. Impulsively she touched his sleeve.

"I know I am deeply indebted to you, my lord, but I must tell you quite truthfully that up until the moment the crowd turned violent, I was having a fine time. I cannot remember when I have enjoyed an outing more." She took a deep breath when there was no response and rushed on. "I would also have you know, my lord, that I thought you were quite wonderful. Very cool under fire, as they say. You got us free of the mob and I assure you I shall never forget the way you handled those two footpads in the alley. For that, my thanks."

"Your thanks," he repeated in a considering tone. "I am not certain that is sufficient reward under the circumstances."

Victoria looked up at him, suddenly aware that Aunt Cleo's botanical garden was a very dark and lonely place at this hour of the night. She wondered for one awful moment if Stonevale was going to lose his grip on the reins of his temper, and then she started wondering what she should do if he did. Belatedly she took a step back.

"My lord?"

"No," he said, as if having reached a conclusion. "Your paltry thanks are not enough for what I have been through and what I undoubtedly have yet to endure."

Without any warning Lucas's hands closed around her shoulders, and in one smooth, swift motion he backed her up against the garden wall.

Before Victoria could react, Lucas moved in close, so close that the hard, unforgiving length of his body pressed against her much softer frame.

Lucas's booted foot slid between her legs. Victoria froze for an instant, held still by the shock of his muscled thigh alongside her own leg. Her eyes widened in the moonlight as she looked up into Stonevale's starkly etched face.

"You are a hotheaded, reckless hoyden; a little shrew who is badly in need of taming before she lands in serious trouble. If I had any sense, I would end this here and now," Lucas rasped.

Victoria licked her dry lips. "End what, my lord?"

"This." His mouth came down on hers with a fierce, plundering heat that made her fully aware, at last, of the true extent of his dangerous mood.

She had been prepared for his anger but nothing could have readied her for the masculine arousal that poured over her in a searing conflagration.

Stonevale wanted her.

Victoria was momentarily stunned by the sensual assault. She had been kissed a few times by daring or desperate suitors and once or twice because her own curiosity had gotten the better of her. But she had never known anything like the rough, deep, demanding kiss that held her now.

She trembled and her fingers clenched around Lucas's upper arms. He responded with a husky groan and then he was crushing her into the ivy, his thigh forcing her legs further apart. Victoria felt the small jabs of the vines and inhaled the fragrance of crumpled leaves and the musky scent of Lucas's body. Her head spun as if she were being whirled about on a dance floor.

When she felt Lucas's tongue slide along her lower lip, she opened her mouth for him in the same instinctive, unquestioning manner in which she had earlier followed him to safety.

She flinched when his hands circled her waist, but she did not struggle as she knew she should, not even when she felt his thumbs glide up to rest just under the weight of her small breasts.

"My lord," she managed in a ragged voice as he freed her mouth to catch the lobe of her ear between his teeth. "My lord, I don't know . . . that is, you ought not to be doing this."

"I want you to have good cause to remember me, Victoria," Lucas whispered.

Victoria swallowed hard, trying to collect herself. "I assure you, I am not likely to forget you."

"Excellent."

His teeth grazed her tender earlobe, causing no real pain but leaving her with a disquieting sensation of vulnerability. The odd caress left Victoria feeling shaken to the depths of her being. Her insides turned warm and her pulse quickened.

Without stopping to think, she moved her hands up to twine her arms around Lucas's neck. She liked the scent of him, she realized. She also liked the feel of his strong shoulders under her hands. She was acutely aware of the heavy, masculine bulge outlined by his tight breeches.

"This," Lucas whispered, "is going to prove a most interesting association." The anger seemed to evaporate from him in that moment, leaving only the desire—his eyes alive and glittering with it.

"Do you think so?" Victoria was feeling very daring now as she looked up at him. The recent rush of euphoric relief engendered by the close brush with danger was meshing with another kind of thrill, a new and unfamiliar thrill, a thrill of deep sensuality. She felt oddly weak and realized she was clinging to Lucas.

"You don't realize it yet, but you have handed me the keys to the citadel. I know your secrets now, and I give you fair warning, I will use them to court you."

"*Court me?*" Victoria woke from her dazed, sensual reverie.

"I mean to court you, woo you, seduce you. I will make you mine, Victoria. Only the bravest, most determined of suitors would endure what I shall be obliged to endure in order to win you, but in the end I will have you." His smile was slow, dangerous, and infinitely compelling in the moonlight.

"What makes you think I will ever surrender to you, my lord?"

"You will surrender to me because you will not be able to help yourself. You will never find another man who is willing to give you what you want," Lucas told her. "When all is said and done, you won't be able to resist me. Now that I know what you desire, I have you in the palm of my hand."

"What is it you think I want, my lord?"

"Adventure." He kissed the tip of her nose. "Excitement." He kissed her eyelids. "And a companion to share it all with you. The fair tonight was a tame event compared to the sights I can show you. I can take you places where no lady would ever dare allow herself to be seen. I can show you the side of life no respectable woman of the ton ever knows."

"The risks," she heard herself whisper.

It was as though he read her mind. "You can explore that other world with me and no one will ever be the wiser. You would not want to jeopardize your aunt's position or your own in Society by getting caught."

It dawned on her slowly just what he was offering. The bait he dangled was irresistible and he obviously knew it. "But, Lucas, if anyone ever found out, it would be disastrous."

"What we choose to do in the dark hours between midnight and dawn will be a secret only you and I will share. I'm offering you a bargain, Victoria; one I do not think you can ignore. I mean to satisfy your curiosity concerning the wilder side of life."

"You must spell out the agreement more clearly than that, my lord. What precisely would you have of me in return?"

Lucas shrugged. "Very little. A lady by day, a companion in adventure by night."

"I am not so foolish as to believe it will truly be that simple. You say you would court me, woo me, but I will tell you clearly once more that I do not intend to marry."

"Very well, we will not talk of marriage," he said soothingly. "I, as do you, seek a companion for my nights. I am at your service. We will spend those nights as you wish. All I ask is that you save your adventures for our nights together."

"You are quite certain that is all you will require of me in exchange for your midnight protection and escort?"

"That is all I ask at the moment. The rest is in the hands of fate. We will play games together, Victoria. Dangerous games. Games unlike any you have ever played."

She looked up at him, fascinated by the hooded assurance of his eyes, mesmerized by the dark promise of his words. Victoria knew then she should flee, but she could no more have run from the lure he was dangling than she could have flown to the moon.

She was still aware of the edge of his hand under her breasts and she suddenly ached to know how it would feel if he moved his long fingers upward and touched her nipples. She shivered.

Again Lucas seemed to read her mind. He moved his hands slowly upward until he was cupping her breasts. She could feel the heat of his palms through her waistcoat and shirt, and, biting back a small cry, she clutched him.

Before she could summon the strength to protest, Lucas's hands had slipped downward again to clasp her waist. She was left feeling breathless, filled with an urgency, a longing for more of the forbidden touch.

"Well, Victoria? Is it agreed? Will you play the lady by day and my companion in adventure at night? Will there be other evenings such as the one we just spent together?"

"I thought you did not approve of the sort of thing we did tonight."

"I will admit I was astonished initially at your boldness and daring, but I have since recovered myself and it has occurred to me that nights spent with you will be far more amusing than any I might spend at my clubs or in the company of the boring young ladies on the marriage mart," Lucas assured her.

She hesitated, but she could feel herself slipping over the edge of a very high cliff. "It must be our secret," she cautioned. "No one must ever know. If my aunt discovered what I was doing, she would be beside herself with worry. Nor could I allow her to be publicly humiliated by my actions. She has been too good to me and I owe her more than I can ever repay."

"Your secrets will be safe with me. You have my word," Lucas agreed.

She believed him then. Victoria knew without any need for proof that this man's word was his bond. He would not gossip in the clubs or the drawing rooms. He would not treat her with anything more than proper courtesy at the routs and soirées where they would meet socially. "Oh, Lucas, I would so love to explore the night with you."

He brushed his mouth against hers. "Say yes, Victoria. Say you will take what I am offering."

"I must think about it. This is such an important decision. I must have time to reflect properly on it."

"May I call upon you and your aunt tomorrow? You can give me your final decision then."

She drew a deep breath, knowing this was the start of it. "You do not waste any time, my lord."

"I have never been the type to waste time."

"Very well. You may call upon us." She tightened her arms briefly around his neck, already knowing what her final answer would be. Then she released him, feeling abruptly nervous and even a little shy. She glanced up at the darkened windows of the house. "I must go in. And you must hurry back to the Lyndwoods' carriage. They will be wondering what has happened to you."

"I will simply tell them there was some difficulty getting over the garden wall," he said casually.

He bowed gracefully over her hand. When he raised his head, the moonlight revealed his faint, slashing smile. And then he turned, strode to the wall, and unerringly found the hidden toeholds. In another moment he had vanished into the night. Victoria hesitated a moment longer, wondering just what she had done, and then she let herself into the dark conservatory.

Some time later she lay awake thinking there had been far too much satisfaction and triumph in Stonevale's parting smile.

I mean to court you, woo you, seduce you.

She would have to tread warily, Victoria told herself, but she could deal with her midnight lord. She would learn to handle him because she had no choice; she could not resist what he was offering. She needed what he was offering.

For the first time in many months, Victoria enjoyed an untroubled sleep.

Ten minutes after making his exit from the garden, Lucas alighted from the Lyndwoods' carriage, said his good nights, and stalked up the front steps of the town house he had recently inherited. His butler, who, along with the rest of the small staff had been engaged for Lucas by Jessica Atherton, opened the door.

"Send everyone to bed, Griggs. I have some matters to attend to in the library," Lucas ordered.

"Very good, my lord."

Lucas walked into the library, which contained the few good pieces of furniture that were left in the house, and poured himself a liberal measure of port. His damned leg was aching again. All that idiotic running about at the fair followed by climbing that damned garden wall had set it off.

He swore silently and took a long swallow of the port, knowing from past experience it would ease the dull throb in his upper thigh.

It was not just his leg that ached. Another part of him was left throbbing as a result of the garden meeting with Victoria. He could still feel the softness of her as he crushed her up against the garden wall. The sweet, spicy scent of her still lingered in his head, mingling with the fragrance of the rich port.

His eyes fell on the portrait that hung over the mantel. Slowly Lucas made his way across the faded carpet to stand in front of the unsmiling face of his uncle.

Maitland Colebrook, the previous Earl of Stonevale, had not had much to smile about in his last years. Plagued by ill health and depressed spirits, he suffered from an abiding resentment against everything and everyone. Maitland's unpredictable temper had often flared into uncontrolled violence, a violence that was frequently loosed on whoever happened to be in the vicinity, leaving Stonevale always wanting of servants.

In his younger days Maitland Colebrook had been

given to debauchery, drink, and gaming on a wild scale. He had disappeared from Society after going through the bulk of his inheritance, an inheritance which had already been thinned out by his father.

He had become an eccentric recluse, cutting off all communication not only with his London acquaintances, but with his relatives. He had retired to the country to drain what little was left from his estates. He had never married, and when the end had come several months ago, he had grudgingly summoned his heir, a nephew he barely knew.

Lucas remembered the interview well. The gloomy master bedroom with its decaying draperies and shabby furnishings looked pleasant compared to Maitland Colebrook, who, withered and pasty-faced, was propped up in the ancient oak bed, a bottle of port and a bottle of laudanum at his side.

"It's all yours, nephew, every last cursed inch of Stonevale. If you have any sense, you'll walk away and let it rot into the ground. No good has ever come of these lands," he wheezed, wrapping his bony fingers around a dingy blanket and glaring coldly at Lucas.

"Probably because no one in recent history has bothered to put any time and money into them," Lucas had pointed bitterly. Any fool could see that Stonevale had potential. The land was good; it could be made productive again.

Money was the key to reviving Stonevale; money and a lord who cared about his people and estates.

"No point pouring money into Stonevale. Place is cursed, I tell you. Ask anyone around here. Been that way for generations. Bad soil, lazy farmers, undependable water supply. Not a damn thing that's worth saving. Should have sold the whole bloody place. Don't know why I didn't," the old man continued, his voice dry and raspy.

At that point the dying earl had leaned over to yank open a drawer in the night table. His shaking fingers had fumbled around inside for a moment, then closed over an object he could retrieve by the touch. Then he had hurled the thing at Lucas, who had automatically reached out to catch it.

When he opened his fingers, Lucas found himself staring down at a circular amber pendant dangling from a thin chain. There were two figures carved on the pendant rendered in such a finely crafted manner that they appeared to be two miniature humans frozen for all time in the translucent yellow-gold stone. The images were clearly of a knight and his lady.

"What is this, sir?" Lucas demanded, his fingers again closing tightly around the pendant.

"Damned if I know. A gift from my father just before he died. Claimed he'd found it in the old maze in the center of the south garden. Local folks think it represents the legend."

Lucas studied the stone. "What legend?"

Maitland turned purple with sudden fury. "The legend that makes this godforsaken estate so useless, the one responsible for ruining my life, for denying me a son of my own. The legend of the Amber Knight and his lady."

"What is the truth behind the legend?"

"Go ask one of the old witches in the village if you want to know the tale. I've got better things to do than tell you stories."

And with that, Maitland had lapsed into a fit of coughing. Lucas had quickly poured a glass of port and offered it to the pale, thin lips. His uncle had taken a long swallow and quietened.

"It's no good, you know," Maitland Colebrook continued. "None of it. Never was; never will be. Bad luck, the whole wretched place. Take my advice and let it go, boy. Don't try to save it."

Lucas looked down at the amber pendant, possessiveness and sudden resolve flaring in him. "Do you know, Uncle, I believe I will ignore your advice. I am going to save Stonevale."

Maitland Colebrook looked up at him with bloodshot, weary eyes. "And just where do you think you'll get the blunt? I've heard you've some skill at the gaming tables, but you cannot win enough to supply yourself with the sort of steady income you would need to save this estate. I know. I tried that in my younger days."

"Then I'll have to find another way to get the money, won't I?"

"Only other way is to snare yourself an heiress, and that's easier said than done. No decent woman of the ton who has money of her own will look twice at a penniless earl. Her family will be able to do better by her than you."

Lucas met his uncle's glare. "Perhaps I should look a little lower than the ton."

"You'd be wasting your time. Hell, I know the talk in the clubs. There's always a lot of speculation about offering one's title in exchange for some merchant's daughter who comes equipped with an inheritance. But fact is, it don't work that way very often. Money marries money and that's as true among the Cits as it is in the ton."

His uncle's words rang again in Lucas's head tonight as he stood gazing up at the dour portrait of Maitland Colebrook. He smiled grimly and raised his glass in a small toast.

"You were wrong, Uncle. I've found my heiress and I've set my snares well tonight. She's going to lead me a damned merry dance but in the end she will be mine."

And that end could not come fast enough to suit him, Lucas decided as he tossed down the rest of his port. He wanted Victoria's fortune, but he had learned tonight that he also wanted Victoria.

Lucas set down his glass, aware of the amber pendant warm against his chest. He had worn it around his neck, concealed under his clothing, since the night Maitland Colebrook had tossed it at him.

As Lucas stood alone in the library contemplating his future it occurred to him that the rich, tawny glow of the amber was an exact match for the color of Victoria's eyes.

4

Lucas walked up the steps of Lady Nettleship's town house with a sense of keen anticipation mixed with icy determination. He was in a mood not unlike the one that came over him when he sat down to a gaming table. Everything in him was focused now on winning, and Lucas knew he was very good at winning.

He had learned long ago that for a man who must live by his wits, there was no substitute for careful planning and strategy. He knew the value of a cool head and the ability to push aside all emotion in the midst of battle or a card game. Cold-blooded logic was the key to survival and Lucas knew it.

He was well aware that the reason he was able to survive and even flourish at the tables of the clubs and gaming hells of London was simply that he never allowed his emotions to interfere with his play. Unlike the wildly impulsive young bucks, the flamboyant, drunken lords, or the foolish dandies who loved to throw their money away in melodramatic style, Lucas never allowed himself to act out of either exuberance, false pride, or desperation.

When one's luck was running poorly, one simply quit the table and waited for another time and place. Lucas had always found another time and place.

But as successful as he was at the gaming tables, his uncle had been right; there was little chance of winning enough blunt to save Stonevale. Lucas knew he could waste a lifetime attempting to accomplish that feat. The lands and people of Stonevale could not wait that long.

It did not, however, take a lifetime's winnings to keep up appearances here in London. If a man was very clever and watched his expenditures, he could survive from one night's winnings until the next. Polite Society might speculate upon, but it never openly inquired into, a man's financial situation as long as he had the appearance of wealth. Having the title and access to Jessica Atherton's social connections also helped.

Lucas glanced over his shoulder at the expensive black curricle and the beautifully matched grays he had driven here this morning. His tiger was at the horses' heads, calming the high-spirited creatures and preparing to walk them until the master had finished his morning call.

The entire rig had cost far more than Lucas had wanted to spend, but he had reluctantly laid out the necessary just as he had done at his tailor's. When a man went hunting for an heiress, he had to camouflage himself well; especially when said heiress was given to hiring Bow Street runners.

Lady Nettleship's front door opened just as Lucas was mentally running through the day's strategy one last time. Lucas handed the butler his card.

"The Earl of Stonevale to see Lady Nettleship and her niece."

The butler peered down a very long nose. "I will see if Lady Nettleship is receiving this morning."

For one grim moment Lucas wondered what he would do if Victoria had changed her mind about allowing him to pay a call this morning. It was entirely possible that in the clear light of day she had sensed danger.

He should have resisted the hot urge that had driven him to kiss her last night. He had never intended to do so, not this early in the game. But for a short, perilous time there in the dark garden he had broken his own cardinal rule and allowed his emotions to dominate his actions. Lucas vowed he would be more cautious in the future.

The butler returned, and a moment later Lucas experienced relief which melted into triumph when he was shown into the stately drawing room. With the discipline of long practice, he made certain neither emotion was visible in his expression, but reminded himself that the first hurdle was behind him; he had been admitted into the home of his quarry.

An instant later his triumph turned to irritation when he did not immediately spot Victoria in the sunny room. He realized he had not expected her to lose her nerve this morning. But the lady who had followed him fearlessly into that alley last night had apparently had a few second thoughts about meeting him in the light of day. Lucas forced himself to give his full attention to the striking middle-aged woman seated on the elegant sofa.

"Your servant, Lady Nettleship," he murmured as he bowed over the beringed hand. "I see now that Victoria's fine eyes are a family trademark."

"Very charming, my lord. Do sit down. We've been expecting you. Victoria, do put down those beetles, my dear, and come greet your guest." Victoria's aunt turned her head slightly in the direction of her niece and smiled.

Satisfaction soared in him. The little baggage had not changed her mind after all. Lucas straightened with a smile and turned to see Victoria standing quietly near the window at the far end of the room. No wonder he hadn't spotted her at once. She was dressed in a yellow and white dress that tended to blend with the gold drapery behind her.

Her very motionlessness told him that she had deliberately chosen her position so that she would be able to study him unobserved for a few minutes as he entered the room. Lucas's brows rose faintly in amused acknowledgment of her tactics. There was no substitute for getting a close look at one's opponent before facing him. It was clear he was not the only one who knew something about strategy.

"Good morning, Miss Huntington. For a moment I feared you had discovered you had a conflicting social engagement today."

She came forward smoothly, her soft slippers making no noise on the carpet. She was carrying a flat box in her hands and her eyes were alight with mischief. "How could you possibly think I would forget your visit to us this morning, my lord?"

"One can never be completely certain of a lady's memory." Lucas inclined his head over the hand she gracefully extended. Her fingers felt cold and he knew then that she was not as composed as she appeared. This pleased him.

"I assure you my memory is excellent."

"Unfortunately for a man, it is not always a lady's memory that fails. Sometimes she simply changes her mind," Lucas said.

Victoria tilted her head and studied him. "Not without good cause. Please sit down, as my aunt suggested. Are you at all interested in beetles?"

"Beetles?" For the first time Lucas glanced into the box and found himself viewing an array of dead insects pinned inside. They were carefully arranged in rows according to size, with the largest, a true monster, at one end. "To be perfectly truthful, Miss Huntington, I have never paid much heed to beetles."

"Oh, but these are very excellent beetles, are they not, Aunt Cleo?"

"A fine collection," Lady Nettleship agreed enthusiastically. "Lady Woodbury, a member of our little society, collected them."

"Fascinating." Lucas sat down slowly, his eyes on Victoria as she took a place on the sofa next to her aunt. "One wonders how Lady Woodbury managed to kill so many large insects."

"In the usual manner, I presume," Cleo said. "Pinched them under the wings or used camphor or a length of wire."

"Do you collect insects, Miss Huntington?" Lucas asked.

"No, I fear I have not the stomach for it." She glanced down into the box. "The poor things do not always die quickly, you know."

He watched her profile. "The will to survive can be amazingly strong."

"Yes." She put the lid on the box of beetles.

"I fear my niece is a bit too softhearted for certain areas of intellectual inquiry," Cleo said with smile.

"I will admit I prefer botany and horticulture to the study of insects."

"Your interests appear to be quite varied, Miss Huntington," Lucas observed.

"Did you think them limited?" She glanced at him through her lashes, her eyes gleaming with a mocking innocence.

Lucas recognized a trap when he saw one. "Not at all. In the course of our brief association it has become quite clear to me that you are a woman with a most unusual mind."

Cleo glanced at him with interest. "Are you a student of horticulture and botany, sir?"

"As you may have heard, I have only recently acceded to my title. I find that coming into my inheritance has greatly expanded my range of interests. It seems to me that I shall need to learn something about horticulture and similar subjects if I am to implement improvements on my estate," Lucas said.

Cleo looked pleased. "Excellent. Then you will no doubt be interested in Victoria's watercolors and her drawings of plants."

Victoria turned a bright shade of pink, which amazed Lucas. "Aunt Cleo, I'm sure his lordship would not be in the least interested in my dabbles."

"I assure you, I would be most interested," Lucas said quickly. Anything that could make Victoria blush was bound to be fascinating.

"She has a wonderful ability." Lady Nettleship said as she jumped to her feet and went to a nearby table to fetch a sketchbook. "Take a look at these."

"Aunt Cleo, really . . ."

"Now, no false modesty, Vicky. Your work is lovely and so wonderfully true to life. I have been telling you for ages that you should get some of it published. Here you are, my lord. What do you think of these?" Cleo thrust the book into Lucas's hands with an air of expectant triumph.

Aware that Victoria was watching him in a resigned silence, Lucas took his time examining the sketchbook. He opened it expecting to find the usual assortment of amateurish artwork a man associated with females. It was considered quite fashionable for young ladies to learn to sketch and paint flowers.

But Lucas was startled at the clarity and liveliness of Victoria's work. Her plants bloomed on the pages of the sketchbook, glowing with exuberant energy. They were not just artistically beautiful, they were precise in every detail.

Lucas was fascinated as page after page full of roses, irises, poppies, and lilies came to life in front of him. Each one was labeled in a fine hand with its formal, botanical name: *Rosa provincialis, Passiflora alata, Cyclamen linearifolium.*

He looked up to find Victoria still watching him with an oddly anxious expression. He realized then that her art was a vulnerable subject for her. He closed the sketchbook. "These are excellent, Miss Huntington, as I'm sure you've been told. Even to my untrained eye these sketches and watercolors are beautiful."

"Thank you." She smiled suddenly, very brilliantly, as if he had just told her that she, not her art, was beautiful. Her amber eyes were almost gold. "You're very kind."

"I am rarely kind, Miss Huntington," he told her quietly. "I am merely telling you the truth. I will admit, however, that I don't recognize all of these plants. Where did you get your subjects?"

"From the conservatory," Cleo explained. "Together, Victoria and I have established what I like to believe is a most creditable botanical garden. Nothing on the scale of Kew, of course, but we're rather proud of it.

Would you care to view the conservatory? Victoria would be happy to give you a short tour."

Lucas nodded. "I should very much like to see it."

Victoria rose gracefully. "This way, my lord."

"Run along, then," Cleo said. "Perhaps you will join us for a dish of tea when you have finished viewing the plants, my lord?"

"Thank you." Lucas smiled to himself as he followed Victoria out into the hall and down a short passageway that led to the back of the house. Matters were going well, he decided as she led him into a large glass gallery filled with plants and the rich, humid scent of soil. Already he was alone with his quarry.

He looked around and realized that today he would be doing his hunting in a real jungle. He examined the view through the glass. Beyond the conservatory windows was a large, charming garden with a familiar-looking brick wall covered in ivy.

"I wondered what the garden looked like by day," Lucas remarked.

Victoria's brows snapped together in an admonishing frown. "Hush, my lord. Someone might overhear you."

"Not likely. We appear to have the place to ourselves." He examined the lush greenery and the array of exotic blooms that filled the glass room. "You and your aunt are, indeed, interested in horticulture, aren't you? This is amazing."

"My aunt had the conservatory built some years ago," Victoria said as she started down one green-shrouded aisle. "She has friends who travel all over the world and send us cuttings and small plants. Recently Sir Percy Hickinbottom, one of her many admirers, sent a new variety of rose he discovered on an expedition in China. He named it Cleo's Blush China in her honor. Wasn't that sweet? Last month he sent the most beautiful chrysanthemum plant. We are quite hopeful it will survive. Are you at all familiar with chrysanthemums, my lord?"

"No, but I do know what it means when a person suddenly becomes excessively chatty. Relax, Victoria. There is no need to be so anxious."

"I am not at all anxious." Her chin lifted proudly as she paused beside a large tray of strange, lumpish-looking plants that were covered in thorns. "Do you care for cacti?"

Lucas glanced down curiously at the assortment of spiny plants that were unlike anything he had ever seen. Experimentally he touched one of the thorns and discovered it was needle sharp. He glanced up and met Victoria's gaze.

"I am always interested in an adversary's defenses,' Lucas said.

"Is that because it is your instinct to find a way past those defenses?"

"Only when the prize promises to be worth the battle." He was going to enjoy fencing with her, Lucas thought. She was no coward.

"How can you estimate the value of the prize in advance of the battle?"

It had not been a mistake after all to kiss her last night, Lucas decided. He knew from the way she was watching him that she had been thinking a great deal about the embrace they had shared. "Sometimes one is allowed a small sample of the goods. The bit I was allowed to taste last night was very promising."

"I see. And do you go around sampling a great many potential prizes before you determine which ones you will pursue?" She glared at him.

His mouth quirked as he saw the hauteur flash in her eyes. "One must have some basis for comparison."

The hauteur changed almost imperceptibly into disgust. She turned away and started down the aisle again. "I rather suspected that might be the case."

Lucas was suddenly annoyed. She had started this. He reached out and clamped a hand around her wrist, drawing her to a sudden halt. She swung around to fix him with a defiant gaze.

"What is it, Victoria? You don't like the fact that there have been other prizes in my life? They have not been very important."

"I do not like the fact that you may have been very

indiscriminate in selecting and pursuing those prizes, nor the fact that you have been casual about the matter."

"I assure you, I have never been indiscriminate and rarely casual. In truth, there have not been all that many prizes. I have spent most of my life in the army, and one does not keep expensive mistresses on an officer's pay." He deliberately exerted enough pressure on her wrist to draw her closer. "What about you? You fence very skillfully. Is it because you have had a great deal of experience at this game?"

"I have had a great deal of practice at playing the role of cactus, my lord."

"And tell me," Lucas said smiling, "has anyone ever gotten past the spines?"

"That is none of your affair, is it?"

He saw the bright warmth in her cheeks but her eyes never wavered. "Forgive me. I cannot help but entertain a certain curiosity under the circumstances. After all, I fully intend to get past the thorns and claim the treasure for myself. I told you that much last night."

"You are not subtle, are you, Stonevale?" she said.

"I am when subtlety is required, but I think I can be completely honest about my intentions in this case. You're not a silly young girl straight out of the schoolroom. I do not think you are the type to be easily frightened by an honest man's intentions."

Victoria straightened and peered at him. "Speaking of honesty, just what are your intentions, my lord? You were not quite clear on that subject last night. I must know."

"I thought I had made myself very plain. You must be aware by now that I want you. I will do what I must to claim you."

"Last night—" she began urgently, and then broke off, hunting for the right words. "Last night I warned you not to think in terms of marriage."

"I heard your warning. You issued it several times in a variety of ways, as I recall."

"You do understand, then, that I am not playing a game when it comes to that subject? I have no interest in marriage."

"I understand." Lucas smiled faintly at the earnest expression in her eyes. She might not think she was playing a game, but that fact would not save her from losing it. "You do want to play other games, though, do you not, Victoria? Midnight games?"

She was silent for a moment, but Lucas noticed that her fingers trembled ever so slightly as she reached up absently to touch a broad leaf that draped over her shoulder. "You were right last night, my lord. I would dearly love a companion to share my evening adventures. Someone I can trust to keep his silence, someone who can take me into the sort of places I cannot go alone or even with friends such as Annabella Lyndwood and her brother. I admit that what you offered in the garden last night is very tempting. What worries me most is that you seem to be aware of just how tempting I find it."

"You hesitate because you are not certain you can take what I offer and get away without paying for it. Is that the problem, Victoria?"

She nodded, her mouth curving wryly. "You are quite correct, my lord. You have gone straight to the heart of the matter. I am not at all certain you will remain satisfied with whatever payment I choose to bestow."

Lucas drew a long breath and folded his arms across his chest. "The problem, it would seem, is mine. As long as I am satisfied with the bargain, why should you worry?"

"Because, quite frankly, my lord, I do not see you remaining content with a few stolen kisses taken in the garden, and I promise you that is all you will get from me by way of payment. There. Have I made myself perfectly clear?"

"Perfectly."

She waited for him to argue, and when he politely examined the unusual cacti instead, she lost a measure of her self-control, just as Lucas had known she would. The lady was swimming far out of her depth and she did not yet realize it.

"There will be no talk of marriage?" she demanded.

"None." He tested the spine of another of the curious cactus plants and found it as sharp as the first. "But I feel compelled to warn you that my guarantee not to speak of marriage does not mean I will not do my best to lure you into my arms. You are right, Victoria. I would like more than a few stolen kisses from you."

"You are far too bold, my lord."

"I see no need to dance around the truth. You know what I want in exchange for my companionship at midnight."

"Then the price is too high. I will never pay it," she said.

"I said you would know the price I seek, I did not say I will force you to pay it." He looked at her, enjoying the storm of emotion and curiosity that lit her eyes. "You need have no fear of me, Victoria. You have my word of honor I will not force your surrender."

"Pray, do not use that word again," she said through her teeth.

Lucas shrugged. "Surrender? Very well. Use whatever word you wish to describe my goal, but do not deceive yourself about the nature of that goal."

Her mouth pursed with strong disapproval. "Your *goal*, my lord, is a most dishonorable one."

"You leave me little choice. You have forbidden me to speak of a more honorable one."

"It seems to me you agreed very quickly not to speak of it," she pointed out tartly. She toyed thoughtfully with the leaf that hung over her shoulder. "One would almost think, my lord, that you are not interested in marriage, after all."

"Not every man is, Victoria. Why should a sane man rush to sacrifice his freedom if he can claim the woman he wants without giving her his name?" he pointed out dryly.

"Assuming he can claim her without doing so."

Lucas grinned. "It happens all the time. Surely you have been out in the world long enough to know that, Victoria."

"I know it." She sighed, sounding exasperated. "Don't misunderstand me. I am well aware that most men do not go into marriage out of a feeling of love. They generally go into it out of necessity, either to ensure themselves of an heir or to get their hands on a fortune or both."

"I have always found love to be a very vague and totally insufficient reason for doing much of anything."

She studied him through narrowed lashes. "You sound very cynical, my lord, but I suppose that is only to be expected from a man who is proposing to try for what is nothing more than a sordid, scandalous affair."

Lucas shook his head ruefully. "I fear you are confused, Victoria. You forbid me to talk of the honorable estate of marriage and then in the same breath accuse me of being cynical when I speak of having an affair with you."

Victoria bit off what sounded like a very unladylike oath. "You are right," she conceded. "It's this business of being an heiress that confuses matters. Annabella tells me I am extremely skittish on the subject; too wary by half."

Lucas smiled gently, taking pity on her obvious dilemma. "Always looking for danger in the nearest hedge?"

"I suppose so," Victoria said.

"Not a bad policy, all things considered."

"It has certainly been a very practical policy for me," Victoria acknowledged.

"Because it has seen you safely into spinsterhood?"

"Beast." But her mouth curved back into an amused smile. "You are quite right, however. I am a spinster and glad of it. Furthermore I intend to keep things that way."

Lucas's attention wandered from the cacti to a spectacular yellow-gold bloom he did not recognize. The flower, touched here and there with deep purple, flared like a crown from the green stalk that held it. He moved toward it, drawn by the shade of gold which reminded him of Victoria's eyes. He cupped the regal bloom in one hand and studied it. "After what happened between us in the garden last night, you will never convince me that you intend to live your entire life without exploring your own passions, Victoria You are too much like this flower, lush and sweet and full of passionate promise."

She grinned. "Really, my lord, you needn't get carried away by a flower. I understand your background is in the military world, not the literary one."

"Sometimes a man can learn more of life when he is surrounded by death than he can from all the poetry of the ancients. Even if you did manage to ignore your womanly passions for the rest of your days, I doubt that you could ignore your own intellectual curiosity."

"*Curiosity.* You think you can talk me into an illicit affair by appealing to my intellectual curiosity? How very original."

"It makes perfect sense to me. Any woman who can work up an admiration for beetles and cacti must certainly entertain a few scientific questions concerning her own physical nature." He inclined his head in a small, elegant bow. "I offer myself to you in the interest of intellectual inquiry, Miss Huntington. I'm hoping you will not be able to refuse."

Outraged, Victoria stared at him for a few tense seconds and then the mirth appeared in her eyes. In a moment she was laughing so hard she had to grab a post for support.

Lucas watched her, his hand still cupping the yellow-gold bloom. He was fascinated by her wholehearted amusement. She did not giggle in that annoying way young woman so often did, as if trying to imitate tinkling bells and rippling brooks. Victoria's laughter was full of life and warmth. It made him want to pull her into his arms and kiss her until he converted the humor in her into the passion he had tasted last night.

He could do it, Lucas thought. He knew from the way she had responded in the garden that he could make her feel desire. And he would use that knowledge, along with her quest for adventure, to seduce her. In the end she would be powerless to resist him. As he had told her in the garden, she would not easily find another man who could offer the bait he was holding out.

And once he had her locked safely in his arms, it

would be only a short step to marriage. Victoria might speak daringly of engaging in an illicit liaison, but he knew that she would find it difficult to actually conduct an affair that threatened her aunt's as well as her own position in Society. She was, after all, a young woman of excellent breeding and she knew both the rules and the risks that governed the world in which she lived.

Society required that young women of her background save their illicit affairs until after they were wed and had given their husbands an heir. After that, many wives felt free to pursue their own romantic interests so long as they were discreet. Their husbands, who generally kept mistresses before and after marriage, did the same, not always so discreetly.

But as Lucas watched Victoria's laughter fade slowly back into a glowing smile, it struck him quite forcefully that he did not intend to let his unsuspecting future bride trod the usual social path from altar to marriage bed to a string of discreet affairs.

He had always known that he would never be one of those men who overlooked his wife's infidelities. It was not in his nature to share the woman he considered his own. But the possessiveness he felt was far beyond what he had expected to feel toward the woman who would one day bear his name.

Once she was his, Lucas decided, Victoria would remain his and his alone. Social conventions be hanged. He was not going to share this half-wild, unpredictable creature with any man.

"My lord, you are impossible. Utterly impossible." Victoria wiped the moisture from her eyes and shook her head, still grinning. "Imagine offering yourself in the spirit of intellectual inquiry. How very altruistic. How very noble. You are far too generous."

"I shall do what it takes to win you."

"And just how am I to be won, my lord?"

"With adventure and excitement and passion. I will give you all of those things, Victoria."

She looked at him, her decision in her eyes. "I will pick and choose among them, taking only as much of any of them as I wish and paying for them as I wish."

He inclined his head in acquiescence, quietly satisfied with the victory. "That is your prerogative."

She hesitated and then impulsively took one step forward, reaching out to touch his sleeve. "Lucas, do you mean it when you say you want me, just *me*, not my money?"

He lifted a hand to stroke the fine line of her jaw. "I want you."

"I cannot promise you anything," she said with grave honesty. "I enjoyed your kisses last night, but that is as far as it should go and we both know it."

He covered her fingers as they lay on his sleeve. "I understand. Don't concern yourself with promises now. Together we will find out just how far this liaison of ours will go."

She did not move for a moment. She just stood there gazing up at him with a barely suppressed longing that made him want to pull her into his arms. It was not the promise of either passion or reckless excitement he saw in her beautiful amber eyes now, but something else, something sweet and vulnerable, an altogether heart-wrenching look of hopeful expectation.

"If you're very sure this is what you want, if you're sure this will be enough," Victoria said, "then I accept your offer to be my midnight companion."

Lucas exhaled deeply. "Then the bargain is sealed." He leaned down and brushed his mouth lightly across hers. She trembled at the touch and Lucas wanted simultaneously to soothe her and pull her down onto the tile floor and make passionate love to her. Before he could deal with the conflicting emotions, she was slipping out of reach and thrusting a small piece of paper into his hand.

"What's this?" he asked, frowning at the elegant writing on the paper. "A gaming hell? A brothel? A race meeting? A gentlemen's club?"

"Those are the first items on my list," she informed him.

"What list?" Then it hit him. He had seriously underestimated his opponent, a mistake he rarely made. "Bloody hell. You expect me to take you to a gaming hell and a brothel? Good God, Vicky, be reasonable. A nighttime visit to a fair or the dark walks of Vauxhall Gardens is one thing. It is quite another matter to sneak you into a brothel or take you to a gaming hell. You cannot be serious."

"You are wrong, my lord. I am very serious," Victoria said, unyielding.

He looked at her and saw that she was. "Damn it, Vicky. This wasn't quite what I had in mind."

Victoria dismissed the protest. "Thursday night would be an excellent time for our next adventure. I will no doubt see you at the Kinsleys' ball earlier in the evening and we can make our final plans. In the meantime—"

Cleo Nettleship's voice broke into Victoria's instructions. "Vicky, dear, are you still out there? Don't get too carried away or you will bore Lord Stonevale. Not everyone enjoys an extended tour of the conservatory, you know."

Lucas turned to see Lady Nettleship standing in the doorway, beaming at him. "I assure you, madam, I have never been less bored in my life."

"One rarely is around Victoria."

Lucas glanced at Victoria's satisfied expression and then he looked once more at the yellow-gold bloom he had been examining earlier. "Before we leave the conservatory, Miss Huntington, I would appreciate it if you would tell me the name of this strange plant."

"*Strelitzia reginae.* Everyone was thrilled when the first one flowered at Kew. Aunt Cleo and I were very fortunate to have this one bloom, too. Magnificent, isn't it?" Victoria said excitedly.

Lucas looked at her. She was glowing with life in her yellow-gold gown. Her amber eyes were brilliant. "Yes," he said. "Magnificent."

5

One week later Victoria put on her new yellow-trimmed brown riding habit, adjusted the dashing little military-style hat with its yellow feather at a rakish angle over one eye, and called for her favorite horse and groom. It was five o'clock and nearly everyone would be riding in the park.

Everyone today had better include the Earl of Stonevale. Last night, during the five minutes she'd had with him at the Bannerbrook rout, Victoria had given him very strict instructions to put in an appearance. She had a few things to say to him.

The problem in dealing with Lucas, Victoria had discovered, was that although he appeared unfailingly obedient when it came to receiving her instructions, he had a nasty habit of carrying them out in his own way. Enough was enough.

Cleo was crossing the hall into the library when Victoria came down the stairs. She peered at her niece in mild astonishment. "Going riding this afternoon, my dear?"

"Yes, I am. I feel in need of a little exercise." Victoria

paused briefly to kiss Cleo's cheek before hurrying toward the door. "Don't worry, I shall be home in plenty of time to dress for Grimshaw's little lecture on recent agricultural improvements in Yorkshire."

"Excellent." Cleo smiled benignly. "I am quite looking forward to it and so is Lucas."

Victoria halted on the threshold and whirled around. "I beg your pardon?"

"I merely said I was quite looking forward to Grimshaw's lecture."

"You said Lucas was looking forward to it."

"Oh, yes, I did, didn't I? And so he is. Told me so himself. Well, it's only natural he'd be interested, isn't it? His estates are, after all, somewhere in Yorkshire, I believe. I invited him on Wednesday when I was showing him my new dahlia plants. I must say the earl seems to be developing more than a passing interest in horticulture and related matters," Cleo remarked.

Yes, the earl did seem to be developing more than a passing interest in the subject, Victoria thought grimly, adjusting her small hat with a quick yank. Lately, in fact, his interest in matters of horticulture and agriculture had begun to border on the keen. She was beginning to feel she was running a poor second to such fascinating topics as methods of manuring and crop rotation.

For a man who only a week ago had seemed bent on seduction, he had certainly veered off course recently. Victoria did not know whether to be incensed or relieved.

A few minutes later she entered the park at a brisk trot, her groom following discreetly behind her on a pony. The public trails were thronged with elegantly attired riders, curricles, and small, open carriages. At this time of day the social world went into the park to see and be seen, not to actually ride for pleasure or exercise. That sort of riding was done in the early-morning hours.

Victoria automatically smiled and greeted her myriad acquaintances while keeping an eagle eye out for Lucas. She was beginning to think he had deliberately avoided the meeting altogether and was wondering what his excuse would be, when he materialized at her elbow on a spectacular chestnut. For a moment she forgot her annoyance.

"What an excellent animal, Lucas. He's beautiful."

Lucas smiled faintly. "Thank you. I'm rather fond of old George, myself. We've been through a lot together, haven't we, George?"

Victoria wrinkled her nose. "Did you name him after the king?"

"No. I named him George because George seemed a simple enough name for me to remember."

"No one's likely to forget a horse like that, regardless of his name. Have you any colts by him?" Victoria asked.

"Not yet, but George has big plans for the future."

At this, she grinned. "I see. You expect him to sire a dynasty?"

"Why not? The male of the species has certain obligations when he bears the sort of bloodlines old George here bears. We men do what we must, don't we, old boy?" He patted the stallion's neck and the horse ducked his head and blew through his nose.

Victoria's grin faded. She was sorry she had raised the topic of dynasty founding. Lucas occasionally made an oblique reference to the little matter of his future obligations to his name and title and she had discovered she preferred to avoid the subject. The idea of the present Earl of Stonevale someday taking a wife and getting himself an heir was becoming strangely unpalatable.

"Well, he's a lovely animal, but that is not what I wish to discuss with you, Lucas," she said quickly.

"I regret to hear that. I enjoy talking about horses." Lucas nodded politely toward a middle-aged man and woman in a handsome carriage. They smiled back and glanced pointedly at Victoria.

Victoria summoned up a regal smile for Lord Foxton and his lady and urged her horse to a slightly faster pace. Lucas and George promptly fell behind. She glanced back over her shoulder and scowled.

"Really, Lucas, do stop dawdling. I told you I specifically wish to speak to you today."

"Then don't rush ahead without warning like that."

"I was trying to avoid having to speak to Lady Foxton. She was giving me a very knowing look. And she's not the first to do so. That's one of the things I wanted to discuss with you, Lucas. People are starting to notice our, uh, association."

"What did you expect? You know as well as I do that if two people dance more than twice together at a ball, someone will wonder if there's a marriage offer brewing," Lucas said.

"But we do not dance together."

"Details. We've been paired off at a few routs and that's enough." He tipped his hat to another elderly lady, who smiled archly.

"Never mind that. It can't be helped. I specifically asked to speak to you today because I was afraid I would not get another chance tonight to speak to you privately and I have a few matters I want to clarify."

"I was afraid of that."

"There's no need to adopt the attitude of a martyr. You agreed to our adventuring. In fact, you insisted on accompanying me on our midnight tours. This bargain between us was made at your instigation, Lucas," Victoria said.

Lucas narrowed his eyes. "I sense a complaint about my performance to date. I'm crushed. Haven't you enjoyed yourself on the two occasions I risked life and limb to climb your garden wall?"

"Don't look at me like that. You know very well I found those two occasions this past week quite interesting. But they weren't what I expected, Lucas."

"What did you expect to find when you went spying on a man's world?"

Victoria chewed her lower lip thoughtfully. "I'm not sure, precisely. More adventure, I think. More excitement."

"Didn't you get adventure and excitement enough on Wednesday night?"

"The late-night supper at the restaurant was amusing, I'll admit. At least I found it so until those two young men got sick all over the skirts of their little opera dancers." Recalling the scene she had witnessed and how it had completely put her off her own food, Victoria made a face.

"I hate to disillusion you, Vicky, but the unfortunate truth is men don't do very edifying things when they get together late at night and start drinking. How about the excursion to Vauxhall? You liked that, didn't you?"

"For heaven's sake, Lucas, you cannot fob me off with trips to Vauxhall. Much too tame. Too respectable. I could have gone there with Annabella or any of my other female acquaintances and no one would have thought it amiss."

"Be fair. Dressed as a man, you saw a whole different side to the place."

"You are missing my point, Lucas," Victoria said firmly. "Deliberately, I think."

"What is your point?"

"My point is that thus far you have not taken me to any of the places on my list."

"Ah, yes, the famous list. I was afraid this conference today was going to focus on that damned list."

"You promised, Lucas. You said you would take me wherever I wanted to go. Instead, you've been deliberately trying to give me a disgust with the whole notion of adventuring, haven't you? Don't think I can't see right through your plan. You've been hoping that such revolting incidents as that business of witnessing those young men drinking until they became ill and viewing that boxing match at Vauxhall will put me off the entire scheme," Victoria accused.

"I was only trying to show you what you were getting into without putting you at undue risk in the process. You know you did not care for all the blood at the boxing match."

"Ah-hah, I knew it. You are trying to fob me off with mild adventures. Well, it won't work," Victoria declared. "I demand that you live up to your part of this bargain. Tomorrow night I insist we go to a brothel or a gaming hell." She brightened, considering the prospect. "I think I should prefer the latter. Yes, let us go to a real gaming hell."

"You won't like it, Vicky."

"That is for me to judge. Now, do we have an agreement or must I find someone else to take me?"

Lucas smiled and inclined his head to yet another curious middle-aged woman passing in a carriage. Outwardly, he was the picture of polite gallantry, but his voice, when he responded to Victoria's threat, was suddenly ice cold.

"Do not issue an ultimatum you cannot possibly carry out, Vicky."

Victoria was learning that when he used that particular tone, it was best to back off and find another path to her goal. It irked her that the man tended to turn utterly implacable when she pushed too hard, but he did have a point. Where was she going to find another companion who would show her the night?

There was, too, another aspect to the situation. She was becoming increasingly enthralled by the farewell kisses Lucas gave her before he departed from her garden after an adventure. There had been two more such embraces since the night they had gone to the fair and Victoria was already anticipating the next occasion when he would take her in his arms.

"Lucas, you seem to be overlooking the fact that I am in charge of this adventuring project. Must I remind you that I am the one who makes the decisions? Now, as to our next venture . . . Oh damn." Victoria broke off with a somewhat forced smile as a familiar couple in a curricle pulled abreast of her horse. She looked across into Isabel Rycott's amused eyes.

Isabel glittered like the small, perfect jewel she was in a rich shade of ruby. Seated next to her, holding the reins, was her current escort, Richard Edgeworth. Victoria had been introduced to him the previous evening and had not been much impressed. In fact, she wondered what Isabel, who could have her pick of men, saw in him.

On the surface there was certainly nothing wrong with the man. Edgeworth was fair-haired and handsome by most standards. He was in his early thirties, but Victoria did not think his looks would last into his forties. There was an unpleasant hint of sullen discontent in his eyes, as if Edgeworth had always felt himself victimized by life. There was, too, a curiously weak, dissolute quality about his mouth that implied a certain lack of inner strength.

Victoria wondered briefly if she was being too hard on the man. She was, after all, starting to use Lucas as her standard of comparison.

"Good afternoon, Vicky, dear," Isabel said. "So nice to see you again."

"Your servant, Miss Huntington," Edgeworth murmured. His gaze slid toward Lucas and away again. "Stonevale."

"Edgeworth."

Sensing the coldness between the two men, Victoria glanced at Lucas's enigmatic face but could read nothing of his thoughts. She turned quickly back to Isabel Rycott. "What a stunning hat, Lady Rycott. You must give me the name of your milliner."

"I will be happy to do so. She has a shop in Oxford Street. Perhaps we'll have a moment to chat tonight at Lady Atherton's small party?"

"I'm afraid I won't be there," Victoria said, remembering that she had declined the invitation earlier in the week. She wondered if Lucas had accepted. "I have other plans. Perhaps another time."

"Perhaps." Lady Rycott shot Lucas a mysterious smile and signaled to her companion that she wished to move on down the path. To this, Edgeworth gave the reins a small snap, his fine gray gloves giving the gesture an elegant touch.

"You don't care for Lady Rycott, do you?" Lucas observed casually as their carriage moved out of hearing range.

"And I got the impression you're not a particular friend of Mr. Edgeworth's," Victoria said.

"A small matter of a gaming debt, I'm afraid."

Victoria slid him a sidelong glance. "You played cards with him?"

"Only once. The man cheats."

Victoria was horrified. "Edgeworth is a cheat? How astonishing. Why is he still allowed to play in the clubs?"

Lucas watched the carriage roll out of sight behind a crop of trees. "Because he's never been caught. He is quite good at it."

"What happened the night you played with him?" Victoria asked, her interest piqued.

Lucas grinned briefly. "Halfway through the game, after losing rather heavily, I somehow managed to drop the entire deck of cards on the floor. Naturally a new pack had to be fetched immediately."

"An unmarked deck. How very clever of you." Victoria was delighted. "And Edgeworth started losing?"

"Yes. Heavily."

"Excellent. You see, Lucas, that is just the sort of excitement I wish to witness firsthand."

"There wasn't much to see. A few cards on the floor. A few glares from Edgeworth. Me mentally on my knees thanking the powers that be that I'd figured out what the devil was going on before I played too deep."

"There you go, trying to discourage me from exactly the sort of adventure I am anxious to experience." She frowned. "Was that card game the only time you and Edgeworth have encountered each other?"

"What makes you ask that?"

"I don't know. Something about the way the two of you reacted to each other a moment ago. I almost had the impression you had known each other for some time. Never mind. To get back to my original subject—"

"Why don't you like Isabel Rycott?"

Victoria's jaw tightened. "Is it that obvious?"

Lucas nodded to another couple on the path. "Only to someone who knows you well. And I am getting to know you very well, my dear."

"I have no real reason to dislike her. She was introduced to me a few weeks ago and immediately claimed a past acquaintanceship with my mother and stepfather," Victoria explained cautiously.

"Your stepfather was a man named Samuel Whitlock?"

"Yes."

"You have never spoken much of your family, other than your aunt Cleo," Lucas pointed out.

"It is not a subject I care to discuss. How did you know my stepfather's name, Lucas?"

"I believe Jessica Atherton mentioned it."

"Yes, of course." Her voice turned brittle.

"Now what's amiss?" Lucas asked gently.

"Nothing."

"Vicky, I'm your friend, remember? One of these days I intend to be your lover. You can talk to me."

She looked around sharply, aware of the heat rising in her cheeks. "Really, Lucas, what a thing to say in public. And neither of us is at all certain about the course of our future relationship. Kindly do not go about presuming too much."

"You don't like the idea that I discussed you with Lady Atherton, do you?"

"No, I do not."

"You don't much care for her, either?" Lucas asked.

"I do not dislike Jessica Atherton. I have explained once before that she and I do not have a lot in common, but I have nothing against her. Who can have anything against a paragon?" Victoria paused. "How long have you known her, Lucas?"

"Jessica Atherton? Several years. I was acquainted with her before her marriage to Atherton."

There was more to it than that, Victoria decided, listening to the clipped note in his words. She did not know how to ask for further details, however, so she changed the subject.

"I cannot imagine what Lady Rycott sees in Edge-worth," Victoria observed. "She probably does not know about his card-playing habits."

"Probably not."

"It is certainly convenient being a widow, is it not?" Victoria mused.

That got Lucas's attention. "What the devil are you on about now?"

"Do you realize that as a widow in command of her own financial affairs, Lady Rycott has considerably more freedom to go about with an escort of her choice than I do?"

"I had not given the matter much thought," Lucas muttered repressively.

"I have. Considerable thought. As a woman who has never been married, I am far more restricted than Lady Rycott. I must always be conscious of what people will say. I am still at an age when I must have a care for my reputation. But Isabel Rycott can ride in an open carriage with Edgeworth and dance with him tonight and let him take her home after the Athertons' party, and no one will pay any heed. It's not fair, Lucas. Not fair at all."

"Pray don't take a notion to marry me and then murder me in my bed so that you may enjoy the freedoms of wealthy widowhood."

Victoria laughed softly. "I would not think of it. Even the prospect of being a free and wealthy widow is not enough of an inducement to lure me into marriage."

Lucas eyed her thoughtfully. "If our interview is finished, we had best part. We've been riding together for some distance and we certainly wouldn't want anyone to speculate unduly on our association."

"No, you are quite right." But for a moment Victoria longed to have the freedom Isabel Rycott did. She was not in the least anxious to say good-bye. "One moment, Lucas. About our next adventure. I really must insist on something a little more exciting than Vauxhall or another restaurant. I shall be waiting in my aunt's garden tomorrow night after the Chillingsworth party and I shall be expecting to be taken to a gaming hell at the very least."

Stonevale's brows rose at her tone of authority. "Your wish is my command, Vicky. But in the meantime, I shall look forward to seeing you this evening when I attend Grimshaw's lecture."

Victoria grinned. "Are you really interested in agricultural improvements in Yorkshire?"

"Is that so amusing?"

She shrugged her shoulders. "No. I suppose not."

Lucas tipped his hat to her. "Be warned, Vicky. You still don't know everything there is to know about me.

Good afternoon." Before she could respond, he had turned George's head and was cantering down the path. Victoria stared after him until Annabella Lyndwood called to her from a short distance away. Shaking off an odd emotion she could not identify, Victoria went to greet her friend.

The night after Grimshaw's lecture Victoria slipped cautiously through the darkened town house and out into the conservatory. Pale moonlight pierced the windows, turning the array of exotic plants into a strange and forbidding world.

Victoria was growing accustomed to the eerie jungle that was the conservatory at night. She hurried down one aisle and let herself out into the garden. The night air was chilled and the grass was damp beneath her booted feet. She hesitated, searching the shadows for Lucas. As usual, she did not spot him until he moved.

Lucas stepped away from the shelter of the wall, a dark and forbidding figure dressed chiefly in black. His Hessians gleamed faintly in the moonlight. His face was in shadow. Victoria caught her breath at the sight of him and anticipation rushed through her veins, leaving her trembling with excitement.

Lucas held out his hand. Smiling in welcome, she put her fingers trustingly into his. As she did so, Lucas tipped up her chin with his other hand and kissed her; a quick, hard, possessive kiss. It was just the sort of kiss she knew she ought to protest but which instead always left her hungering for more. These stolen moments of fleeting, sultry passion were creating a sense of strong frustration within her.

"The carriage I hired for the evening is waiting around the corner," Lucas said as he dropped lightly down beside her on the street side of the wall. "Hurry. I don't want anyone to see us near your aunt's garden."

"You worry too much, Lucas." Nevertheless, she made haste to where the dark carriage was waiting and quickly leapt inside.

Lucas was right behind her, taking his weight, as usual, on his right leg as he came through the door. In the dim moonlight she saw him wince as he took the seat across from her. His hand went to his thigh and absently rubbed it.

"Does your leg hurt?" Victoria asked, concerned.

"Let's just say that I am aware of it occasionally."

"And this is one of those occasions?"

"Yes. Don't fret about it, Vicky."

She bit her lip. "I heard from a friend that you were wounded on the Peninsula. Is it true?"

His eyes met hers in the shadows. "I feel much toward that subject the way you do toward your stepfather."

"Meaning you don't discuss it?" she said.

"Precisely."

"Dear God, Lucas, it must have been terrible for you."

"I said I do not discuss it." He stopped massaging his leg. "Now do me a favor and pay attention. You are going to get your heart's wish this evening. We're going to a certain establishment that can only be classified as a gaming hell. I do not dare try to get you into one of my clubs. There's too much chance someone would recognize you, even in your disguise. In any event, I would certainly be obliged to explain you and I can't."

A thrill shot through her. "A gaming hell. Lucas, this is wonderful. How exciting. I cannot wait."

Lucas sighed. "I wish I could share your enthusiasm. Vicky, these places are run with only one object in mind and that is to separate the client from his blunt. To that end there is a great deal of drinking and wenching."

"Will it be dangerous?" she demanded, growing more excited by the minute.

Lucas gave her a disapproving look. "Things do not often turn violent inside the establishment, largely because it would be bad for business, but there are occasionally problems when one leaves."

"What are you talking about?"

"It is not unknown for someone who has suffered heavy losses to attempt to recover them with the aid of a knife or pistol. It is also not uncommon for the management to employ a certain type of debt collector who meets one outside in an alley," he explained.

Victoria's eyes widened. "Oh."

"What I am trying to say is that we must take care. I must have your word that you will do exactly as I instruct at all times. We will take absolutely no chances," Lucas ordered.

"Lucas, you are far too anxious about all this. Try to relax and calm yourself. I assure you, I will behave sensibly." She smiled brilliantly.

Lucas studied her smile for a moment and groaned. "Something tells me I am going to regret this night."

"Nonsense. We'll have a marvelous time."

"One of these days, Vicky, we really must discuss my end of this bargain."

She stilled, suddenly very alert. "You said you would be content with whatever I chose to pay."

It was Lucas's turn to smile. Victoria shivered and turned her attention to the view outside the carriage. The streets may have been dark, but they certainly were not empty. They were filled with an endless line of carriages carrying the members of the ton to and from their interminable round of parties. The streets would be busy until dawn when the elegant vehicles would be replaced by farmers' carts and milk wagons.

Twenty minutes later Victoria felt the rented carriage draw to a halt. She peered out excitedly and saw a dingy, unpromising establishment with a broken sign hanging over its front door. She glanced at the faded lettering on the swinging sign.

"The Green Pig?"

"The name does not exactly whet one's enthusiasm, does it?"

"Do not sound so hopeful. I am not about to change my mind at this juncture."

"Somehow I didn't think you would. Well, onward then, if you're determined to go through with this."

If the outside of the Green Pig could be described as dingy, the inside could only be called sordid. Everything appeared to have been decorated in red at one time, but the red velvet drapes and carpets had turned dark and sooty and indelibly stained from years of rough wear and tear. The roaring blaze on the hearth cast an evil light over the entire scene, making the interior glow like the hell it was called.

Victoria stared about in amazement as she followed Lucas toward the bar. She had never seen anything like this in her life. The shadowy room teemed with men from every walk of life, all intent on the next roll of the dice or turn of the card. Dandies and coachmen and professional boxers rubbed shoulders as they crowded around the tables. The tinkle of dice and the accompanying shouts of triumph or groans of despair created a continuous din. Tension, nervous excitement, and male sweat thickened the air, especially around the green baize tables where players stood three and four deep. Barmaids circulated through the throng, using ale and overflowing bosoms to coax reluctant players back into a game.

Lucas thrust a tankard into Victoria's hand. "Camouflage," he muttered. "It will look odd if you are not drinking. But have a care. The Pig is notorious for the strength of its ale."

"Do not fret, Lucas. I shall not get so foxed that you will be obliged to carry me out of here," Victoria assured him.

"Good God, I should hope not."

Victoria took in the scene around her as she stood sipping at the contents of the tankard. Her eye was caught by a rather depressed-looking man being led upstairs by a sympathetic serving girl. When he returned a short time later, the gamester appeared eager to return to the fray, all signs of depression vanquished.

Victoria was fascinated. "This is amazing, Lucas. Quite unique. Totally different from anything I have ever witnessed before."

Lucas eyed the crowd. "I am not so certain of that. It bears a certain striking resemblance to that crush at the Bannerbrooks the other night, don't you think?"

Victoria nearly choked on her laughter and a sip of ale. "If Lady Bannerbrook overheard that remark, I swear it would be weeks before you received another invitation from her."

"If Lady Bannerbrook knew where you were tonight, you would wait until the crack of doom for another invitation from her. What's more, you wouldn't get one from anyone else in Society, either."

"Now, do not try to terrorize me or depress me, Lucas, I am having a wonderful time. This is much better than the restaurant and a thousand times better than Vauxhall. Tell me, why on earth do those men keep trotting upstairs with the barmaids?"

Lucas glanced briefly toward the narrow staircase at the far end of the room. "Those are losers who are being consoled and encouraged to try their luck again."

"Consoled?"

"There are several small bedrooms upstairs, Vicky."

She blinked, aware of the heat rising in her cheeks. "I see." She turned to peer more closely at the newest couple on the stairs. The man was staggering drunkenly and had to be supported by his companion. Victoria frowned. "I do hope you have never had occasion to climb those stairs, Lucas."

His teeth flashed in a rare, quick grin around the rim of his tankard. "Never, I give you my word. I told you once I have always been extremely discriminating in certain matters. In any event, the stairs are primarily for losers."

"And you always win," Victoria concluded with a sense of satisfaction. "Really, Lucas, I cannot wait to throw the dice. My aunt and I taught ourselves how to play hazard when we were investigating a certain area of mathematics that relates to chance. Quite a fascinating game. Did you know that it is far easier to throw some numbers than others?"

"I am aware of that." Lucas's tone was exceedingly dry.

"Oh, yes, of course you would be aware of such things, wouldn't you? Well, then, let us find ourselves a table."

"Control your enthusiasm, my dear. You do not want

to throw the dice here. There isn't an honest pair in the house."

"Nonsense. You are merely saying that to put me off. I came here to have fun and I intend to play. I am quite a skilled gamester, if you will recall."

"Victoria, you are not quite as skilled in such matters as you believe."

Her eyes widened innocently. "But I must be very good at gaming because I won the night we played cards."

"Victoria . . ."

"The only other possible explanation for your losses that evening is that you did not play fair. But I hesitate to insult you by making such an odious accusation."

"Wise girl," Lucas said coolly.

"If I did insult you, would you call me out?" Victoria asked.

"Hardly. I have a great dislike for pistols at dawn or any other time."

"An odd thing for an ex-soldier to say."

"The only reasonable thing for an ex-soldier to say if you ask me."

"You carry a pistol," Victoria pointed out softly.

He shrugged. "This is London and you will insist on dragging me out into the streets at night. I don't have much choice."

Victoria took another sip of ale and then, feeling deliciously bold, she leaned closer. "Did you cheat that night we played cards, Lucas? I have been dying of curiosity ever since."

"It does not signify."

"Hah. If you are going to be that way, I shall find another fashion in which to amuse myself." Victoria started toward the nearest table.

"Victoria, wait. . . ."

But Victoria was already making a place for herself near the action. Half-crushed by the press of hot, sweaty masculine bodies, she leaned forward to peer at the play. She was aware of Lucas moving into a position behind her but she paid no heed. The dice were already being handed to her. They clicked in her palm as she shook them and then hurled them lightly down onto the green baize.

"The young nob's got 'imself a main o' seven," someone called. Instantly bets were placed on Victoria's next roll.

Victoria felt a thrill go through her. Seven was an excellent number for a main, she recalled. She could almost ignore the smell of the male bodies that crushed her now. Knowing Lucas was at her back gave her a heady sense of invulnerability. She was quite safe and having a wonderful time. She rolled the dice again.

"Eleven, by God," a man yelled gleefully. "The cull's nicked it." Shouts of triumph went up around the table.

Under cover of the din, Victoria turned to whisper to Lucas. "Nicked it? What's that mean? I thought I'd won."

"You did win. That's what 'nicked it' means. Collect your stakes, Vicky. You've had enough play," Lucas announced.

"But I am winning. I cannot possibly leave now."

A swaying, red-faced man in a threadbare coat and a dirty cravat overheard Victoria's remark. He rounded on Lucas, eyes glaring. "Here now, the boy's got a right to play. You can't be draggin' him off."

"The man is perfectly correct, Lucas. I have a right to play."

Lucas ignored the man and leaned closer to Victoria. He was clearly annoyed now. "Vicky, the management will let you win for a while until you're hooked and then you'll start losing. Heavily. Trust me, I know what I'm talking about."

"Well, I shall just play as long as I am winning," she assured him cheerfully, and turned back to the table. She thought she heard Lucas swear softly and succinctly as she returned to the fray, but the shouts of her enthusiastic fellow players drowned out the words.

Ten minutes later her excellent luck turned with a vengeance, just as Lucas had predicted. Victoria watched in shock as she lost all her accumulated winnings in one throw of the dice. Angrily she turned to whisper again to Lucas.

"Did you see that? How could that happen? I was winning, Lucas. I cannot believe my luck would suddenly alter in such a fashion."

Lucas led her away from the table. "That's the thing about luck, especially in a place such as this. I did warn you."

"You needn't look so smug, you know. I *was* winning. Furthermore, I . . ."

But Lucas was no longer paying any attention to her. His gaze, which had been unobtrusively scanning the room, stopped abruptly on a group of card players in the corner. "Damn it to hell."

"What's wrong?" Victoria glanced at the card table.

"I chose this place because I was fairly certain we would not run into any of your acquaintances here, but it appears I was wrong. We must leave at once."

"Lucas, do stop fretting so. No one will recognize me. One sees only what one expects to see and no one I know will expect to see me here dressed as a man," Victoria argued.

"I am taking no chances. Come along, Vicky." Lucas started toward the door.

Reluctantly she followed, casting one last, annoyed glance at the card table. "Good grief, that's Ferdie Merivale, isn't it?"

"None other."

"He appears quite drunk, Lucas. Look at him, he's barely able to sit in his chair and yet he is trying to play cards," Victoria noted, concerned.

"So he is. With Duddingstone, no less. Which means that Merivale will no doubt part with a large portion of the fortune he recently inherited. Stop dawdling, Vicky."

"What do you know of this Duddingstone?"

"He's an excellent player, a brilliant cheat, and completely without conscience. He's not above taking advantage of a young fool like Merivale. Does it quite regularly, in fact."

Victoria halted abruptly. "Then we must do something."

"I am trying to do something. I am trying to get you out of here before Ferdie Merivale recognizes you."

"He is in no shape to recognize me or anyone else.

Lucas, we cannot leave him in Duddingstone's clutches.
I am friends with Ferdie's sister, Lucinda. I simply
cannot stand by and let poor Ferdie be fleeced by a
notorious player. He's a nice boy."

"We are not going to stand by and watch. We are
going to leave at once."

"No, Lucas. I must insist we do something."

Lucas turned around and glowered at her. "What,
exactly, do you suggest we do?"

Victoria considered the problem. "You will simply
have to interrupt the play and persuade Ferdie to leave."

"My God. You don't ask much, do you? What if
Ferdie doesn't wish to leave?"

"You must make him do so."

"Impossible. That will cause a scene and that is the
last thing we can afford."

"Do not worry about me, Lucas. I shall wait here
near the door. Ferdie will never see me. All you have
to do is fetch him out of here and put him in a carriage
and send him home."

"You are the one I intend to put into a carriage and
send home," Lucas said through gritted teeth. "I knew
this was going to be a mistake. I should never have
allowed you to talk me into bringing you here."

"Hurry, Lucas. They are about to begin another round
of play. You must rescue Ferdie."

"Now listen to me, Victoria. . . ."

"I am not leaving here until you have rescued poor
Ferdie. He's a very sweet boy and he does not deserve
to get chewed to pieces by this Duddingstone person.
Go on. Save him." She gave Lucas a slight push in the
direction of the card table. "I promise to stay out of
sight."

Lucas swore softly, but like any good soldier, he
appeared to recognize defeat when he saw it. Without a
word he turned on his heel and started back into the
crowd.

Victoria could see very little of what was happening,
but a few minutes later Ferdie Merivale emerged from
the throng, Lucas directly behind him. Victoria noticed
that one of Ferdie's arms appeared to be twisted at an

odd angle behind his back. The young man did not look happy as he preceded Lucas out into the street.

Victoria caught Lucas's commanding glance and followed the two men at a discreet distance. Outside she could clearly hear Ferdie Merivale complaining loudly in a slurred voice.

"Damme, Stonevale, you can't do this. My luck was about to turn. Just a few more hands and I'd have had the man."

"A few more hands and you would be obliged to leave town tomorrow to rusticate indefinitely in the country. You would not care for that, Merivale. You are a city creature. How much had you already lost to Duddingstone?"

Ferdie muttered something indistinct and Lucas shook his head grimly. "I know you don't much appreciate this at the moment, Merivale, and I am not particularly enjoying myself, either, but neither of us has much choice. Perhaps tomorrow you will be grateful." Lucas signaled a passing coach.

"Bloody damn, Stonevale, I don't want rescuing. I can handle the play," Ferdie wailed drunkenly.

"Do us both a favor. Next time you decide to throw away your inheritance, do it someplace where I am not likely to witness it. You have been a greater nuisance than you know tonight." Lucas tossed the young man into the coach and gave instructions to the driver.

The coach rattled off down the street and Lucas stepped back. He turned to look at Victoria.

"Satisfied?"

"That was very well done of you, my lord." Laughing with relief and pride in his rescue efforts, Victoria stepped off the sidewalk to join him. "I swear, you have my undying gratitude even if you do not have Ferdie's."

She saw him open his mouth to say something in response, saw the startling change in his expression as his eyes went to a point behind her, and then she heard the clatter of horses' hooves on stone and the rattle of carriage wheels.

The wheels sounded much too close. Victoria turned

around to see just how close and saw a black carriage drawn by two black horses bearing down upon her.

At that moment the safety of the walkway seemed miles away, and the scream that began in her throat disappeared into the pounding hooves and the screeching wheels of a carriage.

Then something heavy struck her, carrying her back out of the path of the hurtling carriage. She sprawled under Lucas's full weight as hooves and wheels went past scant inches from her booted foot.

6

"Some drunken idiot showing off his lamentable driving skills, no doubt," Victoria said from the opposite side of the carriage.

"No doubt."

She tried to see Lucas's expression in the shadows. She was still somewhat shaken from the near miss, but mostly she was bubbling over with the excitement of the entire affair. Her main concern now was for her companion.

Lucas had uttered barely a word since he had helped her up from the pavement and tossed her into a carriage. She could feel the angry tension in him. He was absently rubbing his leg and she wondered if he had hurt it rescuing her.

"You were very quick, Lucas. I vow I would have been run down if you had not moved so fast."

Nothing.

"Does your leg pain you very much?"

"I'll survive."

Victoria sighed. "It is all my fault, isn't it? If I had not insisted on going to that gaming hell tonight, you would not have hurt your leg."

"That is certainly one way of looking at the incident," Lucas said.

"I'm so sorry, Lucas."

"Sorry?"

"Well, not about going to the Green Pig, precisely," she admitted candidly. "For I did have a marvelous time. But I am terribly sorry you got hurt." Impulsively she slipped across the short distance between them and sat down next to him. "Here, let me massage it for you. I am quite good with horses, you know."

"Is that a recommendation?"

She smiled, relieved to hear the unwilling humor in the question. "Of course. One needs to learn how to soothe a spirited animal after a bruising ride."

"You're the one who probably got bruised. You were on the bottom. You are certain you're not hurt?"

"Oh, I am quite all right. One of the useful things about men's clothing is that it provides much more protection for the body than an evening gown. If only you had not twisted your leg when you threw yourself toward me the way you did."

As she talked she put her hands on his thigh and probed experimentally. She was instantly aware of the strong sinew and muscle under her fingers. The snug-fitting breeches hid nothing of his natural contours. It was almost like touching his bare skin, she thought as she cautiously began to knead his leg.

Lucas made no move to stop her. He simply sat there looking down at her as she worked over him. Victoria concentrated fiercely, anxious to bring him some relief from his obvious discomfort.

There was very little give in him, she thought, squeezing the solid muscle. Hard as stone.

"I really do appreciate what you did for Ferdie Merivale." Victoria found herself speaking quickly in an effort to fill what seemed to her a highly charged silence. Her fingers dug deeper into his thigh.

"I'm glad you do because I doubt that Merivale does."

Lucas sucked in his breath. "Easy, if you please, Vicky. That is my injured leg, you know."

"Oh, yes, of course." She lightened her touch, glancing up to see his expression. "Is that better?"

"Much better." He was silent for a moment longer and then he said, "You do have excellent hands. I envy your horses."

This time when she looked up into his shadowed face, she realized he was smiling slightly, a piercingly sensual smile that sent a rush of heated awareness through her. She could feel the tension in his leg changing in some indefinable fashion and she found herself running her palm along the inside of his thigh.

He lifted a hand and drew his slightly rough fingertip slowly down the line of her throat to the nape of her neck. Victoria held her breath, sensing he was going to kiss her. She'd learned to recognize that glittering gaze. She'd seen it on the occasions when she'd stood with him in her aunt's garden after an evening's escapade. The anticipation alone was enough to set fire to her senses.

"Lucas?"

"Tell me, Vicky, do you like my good-night kisses?"

"I . . ." The words seemed to get caught in her throat. "Yes. Yes, I do."

"One of the things I like about you, my dear, is that you can be so delightfully honest at the most interesting times." He threaded his fingers through her hair and then his hand tightened on the back of her head, urging her close. "I wonder if you have any idea of how it affects me."

She went to him willingly, tumbling across his lap as the coach swayed and jounced. With a soft little sigh of pleasure she wrapped her arms around his neck and lifted her face for his kiss. There was no doubt about it, she thought, her appetite for this sort of thing had been well and truly whetted by those previous kisses in the garden.

Lucas's mouth came down on hers, his tongue sliding along the edge of her lower lip, seeking admittance.

Eager now for the heat and excitement she always

found in his good-night embraces, Victoria nestled closer. His arms were strong and hard around her, and when his hand moved to the buttons of her waistcoat, she made no move to resist.

All the pent-up excitement of the evening was flowing through her and this was the most thrilling moment of all. Victoria barely felt her cravat being loosened, but when his fingertips glided down her throat, she tightened her arms around his neck.

Lucas laughed softly against her mouth as his fingers went lower to part her waistcoat and shirt. "There is something rather strange about unfastening men's clothes on you, sweetheart."

Victoria could not respond because he was suddenly cupping her bare breast in his hand. She gasped instead and went taut. Then, instead of protesting, as she knew she ought, Victoria turned her hot face into his shoulder and clutched him tightly.

"Do you like the feel of my hand on you, Vicky?"

She nodded jerkily. "*Yes.*" She could feel her nipple tighten under the touch of his thumb.

"So honest. Can you feel what you're doing to me?"

She could. He was growing hard beneath her buttocks. His thighs parted slightly, making her even more aware of the solid shape of his manhood beneath the tight breeches.

"Lucas, your poor leg."

"I assure you it is not paining me in the least right now."

"We must stop."

"Do you really want me to stop touching you?" Lucas whispered.

"Please don't ask me such a question." Breathlessly she dug her fingers into the muscles of his shoulders and strained against his hand. She was growing hotter and she could feel a warm dampness between her legs.

As if he, too, knew about the moist heat between her thighs, Lucas moved his hands down to the fastenings of her breeches. Victoria completely lost her voice just when she knew she should be raising it to its loudest level in a fierce demand for him to halt. Instead she was suddenly fascinated with the masculine scent of his body and the sensual tension in him. Her fingers clenched and unclenched on his shoulders.

"You are damp and ready for me, aren't you?" Lucas slid his hand inside the open breeches and found her secret warmth. "Your body is already preparing its welcome."

"*Lucas.*"

"Do not be embarrassed, my sweet. I am glad to know you want me as much as I want you. When the time comes, we are going to deal very well with each other."

Dazed, she managed to lift her head long enough to look up at him. "When the time comes?"

"Not tonight. I would much prefer a bed instead of a carriage seat for our first time together. And I want all the time in the world, not the few minutes we have left before we reach your home."

"Lucas, we must stop. We must." He had never touched her like this and she did not know how to handle her own emotions. A delicious sense of eagerness was gripping her.

"Are you sure you want to stop, little one? You feel so good, darling." His mouth was on hers again and then on her throat as his fingers slipped lower, parting soft petals to seek out the tiny bud of desire. "So damned good. And you want me. Say it, Vicky. Give me the words at least."

Victoria sucked in her breath as the wondrous sensations made her tremble in need. She wanted to tell him again that he must cease touching her so intimately, but she knew she could not. Not yet, at any rate. She wanted more of this exotic feeling and she sensed that only Lucas could provide her with what she desired.

"The words, sweetheart. Is that so much to ask?" His voice was gentle, coaxing, intimate. "All I'm asking is for you to tell me what you are feeling. Does this feel good?"

"Yes, oh, Lucas, *yes.*" She squeezed her eyes shut so she would not have to meet the gleaming satisfaction she knew she would find in his intent gaze. She twisted helplessly against his probing hand.

"Keep talking to me, sweetheart. Keep telling me how you feel when I touch you like this." He slid one finger gently into her warmth.

She cried out and muffled the sound against the fabric of his jacket.

"And this . . ."

She flinched and suddenly she could not get enough of his long, sensitive fingers. She lifted her hips, silently pleading for more but not knowing what it was she sought. "Lucas, do that again. Please touch me again."

"Like this, my sweet?" His fingers worked magic in the hot, damp area between her legs. "God, you are beautiful, Vicky. You respond to me as though you had been made for me."

"Please." She could barely speak as she arched her hips and writhed again beneath his touch. "I don't know . . . I can't . . . *Please.*"

"Yes. I know. I will. Just give yourself up to it, darling. Do you want me?" he asked again.

"Oh, yes, yes, *yes.*" And then she was beyond thought, beyond speech. Something tight and vibrant that lay coiled within her suddenly released itself without warning, reverberating through her body until she was shivering. The small convulsions made her tremble from head to toe, but she was not cold, nor did she know any fear. She had never felt so joyously alive in her life.

And then she collapsed in an exhausted little heap against Lucas's hard chest.

"So beautiful. Such a sweet, hot passion." Lucas dropped light, reassuring kisses all over her face and throat as he withdrew his hand from between her thighs and hastily refastened her breeches. "I will go out of my mind waiting for you. But I do not think you will make me wait too long, will you, sweetheart? You would not be so cruel."

Victoria hesitated until she could breathe normally before lifting her head away from his shoulder. The

carriage was already slowing. She looked up at him, still
dazed. He was smiling faintly, a warm, knowing expression in his eyes.

"That was . . ." She licked her lips and tried again.
"That was very strange."

"Think of it as an experiment in natural history."

"An experiment?" In spite of her odd mood, the
laughter welled up inside her, revitalizing her and flush-
ing away some of the sensual lethargy that had held her
in thrall. "You are utterly impossible, my lord."

"Not at all." His smile was gentle, but there was a
disturbing heat in his eyes. "The things I want to do
with you are all quite possible. Some may be improb-
able, but not impossible."

She was staring wordlessly into his eyes when she
suddenly became aware that the carriage had stopped.
She gave herself a small shake and her fingers flew to
her untied cravat. "Good heavens, we're here. I must
get out or the coachman will think we've fallen asleep."

She scrambled about the carriage, collecting her walking stick and coat. As she pushed open the door she
realized that Lucas was moving far more cautiously than
usual. She frowned at him as she jumped down. "Are
you all right?"

"No."

"Oh, dear, your leg."

"It is not my leg that is bothering me." He stepped
down beside her and adjusted his coat with great care.

"Then what is it, Lucas?" Victoria prodded.

"Nothing you can do anything about tonight, but rest
assured I will look forward to you resolving the problem
in the near future." He rapped on the side of the
coachman's seat with his stick. "Be so good as to wait a
few minutes. I shall return shortly."

The coachman tipped his hat with a bored air and
reached for the flask he kept under his box.

"But Lucas, what is it? What is the matter?" Victoria
asked again as they hurried around the corner and
through an alley to the garden wall.

"Think back on all your studies of natural history,

particularly the details of reproduction among the male of the species and I'm sure the answer will come to you."

"Oh dear." She swallowed, aware that her face was burning. She was not precisely certain what he meant, but she was at last getting an inkling of the probable source of his discomfort. "Heavens. I had no idea. Are you, uh, very uncomfortable, my lord?"

"Don't look so contrite," he said with a quick, fleeting grin. "I am well pleased with the results of the experiment. They were worth any minor discomfort I am now experiencing." He gave her an assist up the garden wall. "And I did offer myself in the spirit of intellectual inquiry, did I not?"

"I do wish you would stop talking about the whole thing as an experiment." Victoria dropped down into the fragrant, shadowed garden and stood back as he lowered himself down beside her.

"I think it will be easier for you to think of it that way for a while." He kissed her nose and stood back. "Good night, Victoria. Sleep well."

She stood watching for a moment as he vanished back over the wall and then, reluctantly, she turned toward the conservatory door. She abruptly longed for the privacy of her room so that she could think about what was happening between her and Lucas.

The feelings he was arousing in her were startling in their intensity and a little frightening. For a few minutes there in the coach she knew she had surrendered a large measure of her self-control to him. She had put herself literally in his hands and he had shown her the power of her own body.

She frowned in thought as she approached the conservatory door. She must not let matters get out of control. She had to be careful. But Lucas was so different from any other man she had ever met. It was becoming increasingly difficult to think logically about him. More and more she was reacting on the basis of emotion, and that, she knew, was dangerous.

Damn it, she thought resentfully, it simply was not

fair that a widow such as Isabel Rycott was free to
indulge in a discreet romantic liaison while a dedicated
spinster was not granted the same privilege. At least
not a spinster who was only twenty-four. Perhaps in
another ten years she would be able to behave as she
wished, but who wanted to wait ten years to discover
the mysteries Lucas was now revealing to her?

And who knew where Lucas would be ten years from
now, Victoria thought in sullen disgust. He would undoubtedly be off in the country, attending to his estates, a wife, and several children.

It simply was not fair.

Victoria knew now that if she was ever going to
experiment with this particular aspect of natural history, she wanted that experiment to take place with
Lucas. Perhaps she should do as he said and regard this
entire matter from a scientific point of view.

She was mulling over the pros and cons of that angle
when she spotted the white silk neck scarf fluttering
from the handle of the conservatory door.

One of the servants must have left it here when he or
she went into the garden to collect herbs for supper,
she thought. But surely she would have noticed it earlier when she had left the house to meet Lucas.

Curious, she lifted the scarf away from the handle.
She felt the monogram beneath her fingers but could
not read it in the pale moonlight.

Victoria hurried indoors, paused in the conservatory
to listen for any sound, and then decided her aunt had
probably not yet returned from the Crandalls' ball. The
Crandalls' affairs were famous for lasting until dawn.

Victoria went upstairs and into her room and immediately lit a candle. Then she held the end of the scarf
near the glow of light and deciphered the monogram. It
was in the shape of an elaborately worked "W."

Victoria's fingers shook as she carefully folded the
scarf. She had seen similar monograms before. They
had been embroidered on the handkerchiefs and neck-
cloths of her dead stepfather, Samuel Whitlock.

The morning light poured through the conservatory

windows, illuminating the spectacular spray of *Plumeria rubra* that Victoria was endeavoring to capture with her watercolors. She frowned at the emerging flower portrait on her easel, knowing her attention was not completely on her work and wondering if she should simply abandon the project. Normally when she was engaged in her sketching or painting, her concentration was complete.

But this morning her thoughts churned, writhed, and danced with memories of her passion in Lucas's arms the previous night. She had been unable to get the images out of her head although she had spent several fitful hours trying to calm herself. She knew she would turn herself into a candidate for Bedlam if she did not sort out her confusion and make some decisions.

"There you are, Vicky, dear. I have been looking for you." Cleo Nettleship rounded the corner of the aisle of plants and headed toward her niece. She was wearing a delightful morning dress of pale coral. "Such a lovely day, is it not? I should have known I'd find you out here." She paused briefly, her attention caught by a small plant on a tray. "Good heavens, did you notice the new American iris we got from Chester last month? It's blooming beautifully. How exciting. I must remember to tell Lucas."

Victoria gave a small start and a drop of pink splashed on the page. "Damn."

"I beg your pardon, dear?"

"Nothing, Aunt Cleo. I just had a small accident with my paint. Do you think Lucas will be interested in the iris?"

"Certainly. Haven't you noticed how enamored he has become of horticulture? He is learning everything he can about such matters in preparation for taking over his estates. But he is particularly fascinated with the new species of plants that are arriving in this country from America. I imagine that at the rate he's going, his gardens at Stonevale will one day be a great attraction," Cleo said.

Victoria concentrated on putting a faint shadow on the pink blossom. "He does seem to have developed a strong interest in the subject, doesn't he? Does that strike you as odd, Aunt Cleo? The man has been a soldier most of his adult life."

"I don't find it in the least odd. Only think of Plimpton and Burney. Two ex–military men who have settled down on their estates and produced magnificent results both in their gardens and in their crop production. Perhaps there is something in the business of gardening and horticulture that appeals to men who have witnessed a great deal of violence and bloodshed."

Victoria recalled Lucas's refusal to discuss the circum-stances surrounding the injury of his leg. "I wonder if you might be right about that, Aunt Cleo."

"Speaking of Lucas, dear." Cleo paused again to examine another plant that was putting forth shoots.

Victoria caught the slight change in her aunt's inflection and braced herself. Cleo rarely lectured, but when she did, Victoria had learned to pay attention. For all her scattered scientific interests and her unending social life, Cleo Nettleship was a wise and intelligent woman.

"What about him, Aunt Cleo?"

"I hesitate to say too much, Vicky, dear. You are, after all, a grown woman and you have always given every indication of knowing precisely what you are about. But I must confess I have never known you to spend quite so much time in the company of any one man. Nor have I heard you mention a particular male acquaintance quite as frequently as you seem to mention Stonevale. And one cannot help but notice lately that he seems to be underfoot a great deal of the time."

Victoria's fingers tightened around her brush. "I thought you liked Lucas."

"I do. Very much. That is not the point, Vicky, and I think you know it." Her aunt spoke gently as she poked a finger into a bedding tray to check for moisture.

"If Lucas seems to be underfoot much of the time, I expect it is because you are constantly inviting him to attend lectures and demonstrations you think will interest him," Victoria declared defensively.

"True, I have extended a number of invitations and he has always accepted." Cleo looked thoughtful. "But it is not just at our natural history and horticulture meetings that he appears, is it? Lately he seems to have put in an appearance at nearly every soirée you have attended."

Victoria swallowed uneasily. "He is a friend of Lady Atherton's. She has introduced him into her circle."

Cleo nodded again. "Very true. And Lady Atherton's circle of acquaintances does include us, does it not? But all the same, I think perhaps you should consider exactly what it is you wish to have happen next, Vicky."

Victoria set down her brush and looked at her aunt. "Why don't you come out and tell me what it is that's worrying you, Aunt Cleo?"

"I am not worried so much, dear, as concerned that you understand your position vis-à-vis the earl. You have always insisted you do not wish to marry."

Victoria stiffened. "That has always been true and still is."

Cleo's face softened as she regarded her niece's stubborn expression. "Then, Vicky, you have a certain obligation, one might even say your female honor requires that you do not give false hope to your male acquaintances. Do you comprehend what I am trying to say?"

Victoria stared at her aunt in outraged astonishment. "You think I have been leading the earl on? Allowing him to believe an offer of marriage might someday be welcome?"

"Not for a moment do I think you have done such a thing deliberately," Cleo said hastily. "But lately, my dear, I have begun to wonder if Stonevale might interpret some of your interest in him as a signal that you might be willing to entertain an offer. He could hardly be blamed if he had."

Victoria bristled. "And what about your interest in him? How is he supposed to interpret all your various invitations, Aunt Cleo?"

"It is not at all the same thing, dear. If he is misinterpreting my invitations, it is only because you always choose to attend the same lectures and demonstrations he chooses to attend," she explained evenly.

"There is hardly anything to remark upon in that. I have always attended the most interesting of the lectures and talks given by your friends."

"I cannot help but note, dear, that until recently you rarely attended the talks on crop rotation, orchard management, and viticulture," Cleo pointed out dryly. "Your interests have always focused more on animals, electricity, and exotic plants."

Victoria felt her face growing very warm. "I assure you, Aunt Cleo, Stonevale is very well aware of my opinions on marriage. I am certain he would not misinterpret our friendship."

"What about you, Vicky?" Cleo came closer and smiled down at her niece. "Is there any possibility you may not be quite so certain of your own feelings on the subject of marriage as you once were?"

"Believe me, my opinions on marriage have not changed in the least," Victoria said with absolute conviction.

"Forgive me for asking, my dear, but is it possible that you are toying with the notion of another sort of liaison with Stonevale?"

Victoria's eyes collided with her aunt's. "You think I am contemplating a . . . an affair with Lucas?"

Cleo held her niece's gaze and spoke very firmly. "I am not blind, Vicky. Nor am I lacking in intelligence. Furthermore, I am a woman who has been out in the world for a good many years. I have seen the way you look at Stonevale when you don't think he is aware of your regard. Add to that his obvious interest in you and the fact that you are a normal, healthy young female who does not wish the chains of marriage, and I fear we must conclude you are treading on treacherous ground. I would be extremely remiss in my duty as your aunt if I did not warn you."

Victoria's hand clenched into a small fist in her lap. She stared blankly at the half-finished flower in front of her. "I appreciate your concern, Aunt Cleo."

"No, you don't, you resent it, and I cannot entirely blame you for that. But we must face facts and it is not only your own reputation you must consider here. Stonevale's is in jeopardy as well," Cleo said.

Victoria's head snapped up. "Stonevale's reputation?"

"You know very well, my dear, that a man of his position has an obligation to his name and title. Someday he must marry a socially acceptable woman from a good family. He cannot afford to be known as a seducer of respectable, innocent young females. Such a reputation would immediately ruin his chances for a proper marriage and cast him out of Society. Nor would he wish for such a nasty reputation. He is a decent man, Vicky."

"It is all so very unfair."

"What is unfair? That your status as a young, unmarried woman of good breeding makes it completely impossible for you to even consider a romantic liaison with Stonevale? Yes, it is most unfair. But Society is very strict about such matters and you must heed most of the unwritten laws if you wish to survive in our world. You flout enough of the rules as it is. Be patient. And as you grow older you will be able to get away with disregarding more and more of them."

"I am four and twenty. Quite on the shelf and you know it, Aunt Cleo."

Cleo smiled and shook her head. "You know as well as I do that is not completely true. Society still views you as eligible and the size of your inheritance guarantees that you will remain so for a few more years. You must be careful."

"If I were widowed like Isabel Rycott, I would be free," Victoria muttered tightly.

Cleo grinned, breaking the tension. "Are you by any chance contemplating marriage to the earl and then doing him in so that you can gain the freedom Isabel Rycott enjoys?"

Victoria's answering grin was reluctant. "Stonevale asked me very particularly not to consider that course of action."

Cleo stared at her in astonishment and then burst into a gale of delighted laughter. "I am pleased to learn that Stonevale is every bit as quick and intelligent as I had thought. Obviously the two of you have arrived at some sort of mutual understanding. You do not need my advice, after all, Vicky. Please forgive my intrusion into your affairs."

Victoria relaxed slightly. "I appreciate your concern, truly I do. And I will treat what you have said with the utmost consideration."

"Do that. Society will tolerate a great deal but there are limits, as we both know, especially for females. I should hate to see you ruined socially at such an early age, my dear. You take far too much pleasure in your friends to risk losing them," Cleo warned gently.

"That is certainly true enough." A small jolt of alarm went through Victoria. She would be heartbroken if she thought she could never entertain Annabella or some of her other friends again.

Cleo nodded in satisfaction. "Precisely, my dear. Now, if you will recall, we are engaged to talk to our man of affairs this morning. Something to do with that ship we invested in last year. Apparently it has returned safely with a lovely cargo from China. We are several thousand pounds richer as of this morning. Isn't that nice?"

Victoria was immediately distracted. She loved the more exciting sort of business ventures such as investing in shipping. A bit of risk always added an element of interest to the deal.

"Marvelous!" Victoria exclaimed. "We must thank Mr. Beckford for recommending that particular ship to us. Oh, Aunt Cleo, wait, there is something I wanted to ask you about." Victoria reached under her chair and picked up the monogrammed silk scarf she had found on the conservatory door the previous night. "Do you recognize this?"

Cleo examined the monogram with a slight frown and handed it back to her niece. "No. It's obviously not one of mine. Wherever did you find it?"

"In the garden. I asked the servants if one of them

knew anything about it and they all said they did not recognize it. Perhaps it belongs to one of the members of your natural history society?" Victoria said, running her finger over the elegantly woven "W."

"Hmmm. Perhaps. It is a man's scarf. Let me think. Who do we know who has a name beginning with 'W'? There's Wibberly and Wilkins for starters. I must remember to ask both of them the next time I see them if either lost this. Is that all, Vicky?"

"Yes, Aunt Cleo. That is all I wanted to ask. Let's go talk to Mr. Beckford about our latest business success. Perhaps he will have something else to recommend."

7

Victoria hated to admit it but the notion of going to a brothel had been a serious mistake.

She clutched her glass of champagne and sat tensely in the shadows, partially concealed by a garishly gilded screen. There were several such discreetly shadowed areas around this room and the adjoining one. All the lamps had been turned very low. Drunken giggles and other sounds of a very unsettling nature emanated from behind most of the screens. Victoria shuddered to think of what was going on upstairs.

It was very late, well after three in the morning. Lucas had dictated the time of their arrival. He had said he wanted to take no chance of running into anyone who might be sober enough to recognize Victoria. He had also specified this particular house because it catered to those who favored some modicum of privacy. Hence the screens and subdued lighting.

Everyone around her except Lucas appeared to be staggeringly drunk. Some men, snoring heavily, lay sprawled on pink velvet sofas. The room was too loud, too hot, and choked with smoke from rich cigars. There was another sort of smoke coming from two or three odd pipes scattered here and there around the pink and gold chamber.

Victoria was beginning to feel a little sick. A moment earlier she had watched Lucas casually wave off two young women whose gowns were cut so low as to reveal the tops of their rouged nipples.

"We just came to observe the activities tonight," he'd explained smoothly when one of the women had protested being sent away.

"But it's ever so much more fun to join in the play," the other cooed. Her eyes had moved over Lucas in a glance that made Victoria want to dump the contents of a chamber pot on her head.

"What about the young gennelman?" the first woman asked with a beckoning smile aimed at Victoria. "Wouldn't you like to come upstairs with me? My, you're a pretty boy. I have a lovely-looking glass on the wall o' my room. You can watch *everything* in it. And you should see my collection of rods and whips. Every bit as fine as the ones they use on young lordlings in school."

Victoria had shaken her head quickly and edged a bit deeper into the shadows. Lucas had shot her a sardonic glance and sipped his champagne, offering little help. She could almost hear him saying "I told you so."

In addition to acknowledging that the brothel idea was a bad one, she was also fast arriving at the conclusion that men's clothing was not always very comfortable. Her flawlessly tied cravat was much too high and much too tight around her throat tonight, for example. The top folds were halfway up her ears and covered her chin. She was practically drowning in the thing and it was all Lucas's fault. He had retied it for her in the carriage because he'd claimed he wanted her features better concealed.

He had also insisted she keep her hat on and pulled down low over her eyes until she'd found a secluded spot to sit. As a further precaution, Lucas had deliberately chosen a house that was not patronized by the males of the ton. He had wanted to take as few risks as possible.

Her stomach grew more queasy. She *had* to get out of here. She did not think she could take much more of the appalling display.

She was about to lean forward and inform Lucas that she was bored and quite ready to leave when a cheer went up at the far end of the shadowed, crowded chamber. Then a sudden hush fell over the throng of drunken men and provocatively dressed women.

The middle-aged mistress of the brothel, dressed in a billowing, low-cut gown, walked into the center of the garishly decorated room. The bawd's face was a mask of white face powder and rouge in the style that had been popular several years earlier. Her dress was made of expensive pink velvet that matched the chairs, but it lacked the elegance of simplicity which was the hallmark of fashion in polite circles. The gown was as cheap looking and overblown as the woman herself.

"Gather 'round, all you fine gentlemen who are so anxious to prove your mettle this evening. The house invites you to inspect the lovely bit of goods we have on offer tonight. Guaranteed as clean and virgin as the day she was brought into this world. Fresh from the country and not yet thirteen years of age, I present our newest recruit to our noble profession, little Miss Molly."

Victoria stared past the edge of the screen in horror as a dazed-looking young girl dressed in a thin white shift was pushed into the center of the room. Molly gazed around at the leering men and laughing women and hugged herself tightly. The laughter increased.

Molly's frightened gaze moved from one face to another until her eyes somehow collided with Victoria's. The girl did not look away. Victoria clutched the arm of the chair as the sick feeling in her stomach grew more intense.

"Now, then, let us begin the bidding. Sweet young things such as our Molly do not come cheap," the madam said.

"I think it's time we left," Lucas muttered as voices rose loudly in the room. He flicked one last, disgusted glance at the brothel owner and started to get to his feet.

"No." Victoria shook her head, unable to look away from the terrified Molly. "No, Lucas, we cannot leave. Not yet."

"Damn it, Vicky, you don't want to see this."

"They are bidding on her, Lucas. As if she were a cow or a horse."

"And the winner will take her upstairs and introduce her to her new profession," Lucas concluded roughly. "Perhaps he won't even bother with privacy. Perhaps he will do the business right here in front of an audience. Surely you do not wish to witness such a thing."

"Of course not. Lucas, we must save her."

Lucas stared at her in amazement as he sank slowly back into his chair. "Save her? How do you propose we do that? It is a common enough occurrence here in town. The young women from the country step off the hay wagons straight into the arms of ruthless old abbesses such as this one. The girls are doomed and there is nothing that can be done."

"Well, there is certainly something that can be done about this one," Victoria stated. "I shall buy her."

Lucas sucked in his breath. "You don't know what you're doing, Vicky."

But Victoria was already watching the bidding frenzy. She had the advantage of knowing she was undoubtedly wealthier than anyone else in the room and she intended to use that fact.

"Thirty pounds," a man on the other side of the room shouted.

The brothel mistress regarded him with acute scorn. "For a certified virgin, sir? Come now, you cannot expect me to listen to such a ridiculous offer. Let us hear from some more noble sports."

"Who's to say she's still virgin?" hooted another. "I'll risk fifty pounds and no more."

"Interestin'," the bawd approved, "but not nearly good enough. Come now, I expected better from this crowd. You spend more on a horse."

"You can ride a horse longer than you can a virgin," someone called out, snickering.

"Nonsense. Our Molly will give you a fine ride, won't

you, Molly, dear?" The madam stroked Molly's blond
hair in a mockingly affectionate gesture. The girl
shuddered.

"Not pretty enough to go for more than eighty pounds.
And I'll want my money back if you've lied about her
condition."

Molly started to weep and the laughter in the room
grew even more raucous. Victoria looked straight at the
girl, willing her to stay strong as she bided her time.

The bidding crept higher but not at a very great rate
after the initial rush. The miserliness of the bids veri-
fied what Victoria had already concluded. Not everyone
in the room was convinced that poor Molly was worth a
huge sum nor were there any men of great wealth here
tonight. Men of vast wealth preferred to keep fashionable mistresses and only ventured into brothels such as
this one for casual entertainment.

Victoria waited a few more minutes until the bidding
stopped at ninety pounds. Then she casually raised her
hand from behind the screen. "Three hundred pounds."

Lucas groaned.

The middle-aged woman turned a beaming countenance toward the shadowed screen. "Why, sir, you
have excellent taste, whoever you be. Excellent, indeed. I do believe little Molly is yours to do with as you
please this evening." She patted the young girl's hand.
"What a lucky girl you are, my dear. Such a nice,
discreet gentleman he is. Run along now and mind you
don't make a fuss or it'll be the worse for you."

"You do not have three hundred pounds on you,"
Lucas reminded Victoria between set teeth. "You can
hardly give the old bawd your personal marker, can
you? She'll realize who you are."

Victoria blinked. "You are quite right. Very well, you
will have to pay the woman. Say it is on my behalf as I
am rather shy. Hurry, Lucas."

"Bloody, hell," Lucas murmured as he got slowly to
his feet. "Don't think I won't collect from you for this."

"I assure you, I'm good for the blunt," Victoria said
sharply.

He stood up and strode toward the bawd, ignoring

the shouts and ribald comments. When he reached the center of the room, he gave Molly a small push toward the screen where Victoria hovered. "Go on, girl. Move."

Molly looked up at him in terror and then responded automatically to the tone of command. She made her way through the laughing crowd to where Victoria waited.

"Hush, now, and all will be well," Victoria murmured as she took the girl's shaking hand and led her toward the door, cramming her hat down low over her eyes as she tugged the girl out into the hall.

Molly was too frightened to even protest. Perhaps being led out into the night appeared a better alternative to being taken up the stairs. The girl staggered a bit and Victoria realized she had undoubtedly been given several glasses of wine or perhaps an opium concoction to keep her dazed.

"Well, well, and just where d'ye think ye be goin' with the new piece? Ye ain't allowed t' take the merchandise off the premises." A very big, coarse-faced man loomed in Victoria's path. He was supposed to be the brothel's butler, but Victoria could see he had another job as well.

"My walking stick, if you please," she said imperiously.

"I just told ye, ye cannot be takin' the girl off the premises," the man boomed.

"I'm not going to take her off the premises," Victoria said in an utterly bored tone. She remembered what one of the prostitutes had said about rods and whips. "But I do have certain tastes I like to indulge. And I have found that my walking stick makes a very fine rod for my purposes. It has just the right heft and balance, if you take my meaning."

Little Molly stifled a scream but the big man looked somewhat mollified. It was obvious he was accustomed to such bizarre things.

"So that's the way of it, is it?" He leered at Molly. "Yer in for a fine time tonight, Molly, my girl."

Victoria waited tensely, glancing back over her shoulder once more for Lucas. He was still nowhere in sight. When the butler appeared with her walking stick, she

decided she had to act on her own and find a way to the
door directly behind the big man.

"Now, I believe I would prefer the comfort of my
own carriage for what I have in mind," she said coolly.
She started forward, yanking Molly with her.

The man narrowed his eyes and crossed his beefy
arms across his chest. "I told ye, ye ain't takin' the little
piece off the premises."

Victoria did the only thing she could think of. She
lunged forward suddenly, ramming the end of the walking stick straight at the large man's crotch.

The butler shrieked and fell back, cursing and clutching himself. Victoria raced for the door, hauling Molly
along in her wake.

"Hell," said Lucas from somewhere behind her. "I
should have guessed something like this would happen."

There was a roar from the butler and then a solid,
sickening thud. Victoria looked back from the doorway
and saw the big man sprawled on the floor and Lucas
calmly reaching for his coat and gloves.

"Go on," he ordered. "Get into the carriage."

In all the commotion Molly had clung to Victoria,
and now pale and nervous, she began to babble in fear.

Victoria patted her shoulder as she steered her out
into the night. "Do be quiet, dear. No one's going to
hurt you."

The dozing coachman who had driven Lucas and
Victoria to the brothel flapped the reins on the horses'
rumps and moved the vehicle into position when he
saw his customers emerge. He leered at poor Molly as
Victoria thrust her up into the cab.

"I want t' go home," Molly wailed as Victoria climbed
in behind her. The girl threw herself, sobbing, against
Victoria's shoulder. "Please sir, just let me go home to
Lower Burryton. My ma will be ever so scared. I
should never 'ave left but I was told there were plenty
o' good jobs 'ere in Town and my family needs the
money so."

"Hush, hush, 'tis all right. You will go home, I promise." Victoria was still comforting the sobbing girl when

Lucas emerged through the carriage door. He eyed the crying Molly.

"Well, she's yours now, what do you propose to do with her?" Lucas asked as he signaled the coachman to pull away. "You can hardly take her to your aunt's house. You cannot possibly explain her presence. Everyone will know what you've been up to tonight."

"Once again you have the right of it, Lucas. How very perceptive of you. She cannot go home with me, so we must send her home with you. Your housekeeper can see to her welfare tonight and get her on the northbound stage in the morning."

"Bloody hell," said Lucas. But he looked resigned to the inevitable.

Silence, broken only by Molly's sobs, reigned for a few minutes.

"Had enough of brothels?" Lucas finally inquired calmly.

Victoria shuddered. "Quite enough. I never want to see such a place again as long as I live. It was sickening, Lucas. That those poor women should be reduced to being forced to survive by selling themselves to those awful men goes against all decent sensibility."

"Allowing you to witness such a scene goes against all decent sensibility, too," said Lucas. "I have only myself to blame for having indulged you in such a foolish fashion. I begin to think our night games have gone far enough."

Victoria was suddenly alarmed by his unexpectedly grim tone. "Surely you do not mean to put a halt to our adventures."

Lucas glanced meaningfully at the still-sobbing Molly. "We had best discuss this at another time."

"But, Lucas . . ."

"By the bye, you owe me three hundred pounds." Lucas leaned his head back against the seat cushions and closed his eyes. "Plus whatever it costs to get her out of town tomorrow morning."

Victoria sniffed. "Really, Lucas. If you're going to be that way about it, I shall see that you are repaid immediately."

"There is no great rush, Vicky. I can wait to collect."

She bit her lip. "But you do intend to collect?"

Lucas opened his eyes and looked at Victoria. "Oh yes, my dear," he said, "you may be certain of that."

Lucas plucked a glass of champagne off a passing tray and turned to greet Jessica Atherton, who was making her way determinedly toward him through the glittering crowd. She looked as lovely as always in her ball gown of blush rose, and her hair was fashionably ornamented with two combs studded with rubies.

But the expression on Jessica's face was that of a woman on a holy mission. It occurred to Lucas that more and more he was beginning to notice a certain pinched look about the woman he had once loved and lost.

What he had once interpreted as an expression of becoming modesty now seemed to border on perpetual disapproval. And there was something about her eyes that bothered him, something eternally distant and sadly aloof, as if she had looked out at the world and found that it did not live up to her high standards and never would.

Lucas contemplated his problem with the look in Jessica's eyes for the three or four minutes it took her to reach him. Just as she arrived at his side he finally realized exactly what it was about her that bothered him now. There was no fire in her, he thought suddenly, only the uncomfortable chill of angelic righteousness and a touch of female martyrdom. Thank God he did not have to look forward to getting into bed beside this untouchable, ethereal creature tonight or any other night.

It occurred to Lucas that during the brief time he had been engaged in the unconventional wooing of Victoria Huntington, he had become addicted to fire.

"Dearest Lucas, I have been anxiously waiting for you to arrive." Jessica smiled achingly up at him as if she had been afraid he had dropped off the earth sometime during the past few days. "Is everything going well with you?"

"Very well, thank you, Jessica." Lucas took the smallest of sips from his champagne and scanned the crowd for Victoria.

Jessica lowered her voice in a melodramatic fashion. "I have been extremely concerned to know if our plans were proceeding smoothly. There has been some gossip, nothing substantial, you understand."

Lucas did not like the way she said *our plans,* as if Jessica were somehow intimately involved in this courtship. But he could hardly deny that she had set the entire business in motion. If it had not been for Jessica, he might never have met Victoria. "What sort of gossip are you talking about Jessica?"

"Simply that you are seen frequently with Miss Huntington at parties and soirées and that you have ridden together more than once in the park. It is one thing to attend lectures and such events with her in the company of her aunt, but quite another to meet Miss Huntington in the park. I must ask if all this is leading up to our desired goal, Lucas."

Lucas set his back teeth at the way Jessica had used the word "our" again. "Kindly refrain from worrying about me. I am quite satisfied with the status of my association with Miss Huntington."

"Really, Lucas, you needn't act so churlish. I am only concerned for your success in this important matter of marrying an heiress. I know it is required of you and I am doing my best to assist you. There is still Miss Pilkington, you know."

Lucas stifled an oath and tried to appear properly grateful. "Thank you, Jessica. I appreciate your efforts. You have been most helpful."

She was somewhat mollified. "It is the least I could do in view of our past connection. I do hope you realize that I shall always think fondly of you, Lucas."

Fondness was about the limit of whatever affection Jessica Atherton would ever feel for anyone, Lucas decided. *No heat in her at all.*

He smiled to himself as he finally caught sight of Victoria on the far side of the room. She was in animated conversation with her friend Annabella Lyndwood.

When Victoria fell in love, she was going to burn like wildfire, he decided.

As if she sensed his gaze on her, Victoria looked up and saw him. She said something to Annabella and started through the crowd.

Lucas studied her as she moved toward him. Her height as well as the egg-yolk yellow silk gown made it easy to follow her progress. She looked vivid, regal, and almost unbearably provocative tonight. The gown was cut much too low again, of course. All her gowns seemed to be cut too low. This one made him long to grab her, take her out into the gardens, and pull the small bodice straight down to her waist. Her breasts were a constant source of delight to him; high, softly curved, and perfectly suited to the palm of his hand.

As she moved toward him, pausing politely to chat with friends en route, he remembered the hot, slick feel of her on his fingers the other night in the carriage. His body tightened just at the thought. Capturing his heiress was proving to be a very taxing business.

He was getting damned tired of denying himself what lately he had sensed Victoria was more and more eager to offer.

But with this particular female, strategy was everything and Lucas had plotted very carefully even as she had shivered in his arms with her first feminine climax. Forcing himself to think in strategic terms had been the only way to keep a tight rein on his own raging desire. Lucas did not think he could endure too many such "experiments," however.

He grinned a little when he saw Victoria pause in the crowd to cast a critical, assessing eye on Jessica Atherton. Then he watched her paste a very engaging smile on her lips and continue forward. Beside him, Jessica continued talking in confidential tones.

"You know, Lucas, I have had a few second thoughts about Victoria's suitability. It is true that her social connections are excellent and she does have a sizable inheritance, but I am not at all certain you would find her easy to manage."

"Don't fret, Jessica. I believe I can manage Miss

Huntington." Lucas inclined his head toward Victoria as she closed the distance between them and continued smoothly, "Good evening, Miss Huntington. What a coincidence running into you here at the Ridleys'. Is your aunt with you?" Beside him, he felt Jessica stiffen and close her mouth instantly.

"Yes, of course," said Victoria. "I left her talking to Lady Ridley. Good evening, Jessica. What a charming gown. I trust you are well?"

Jessica turned around quickly and smiled with a determined graciousness. "Very well, thank you, and yourself?"

"I have been slightly indisposed for the past day or two," Victoria said with a warning glint in her eye as she slid a quick glance at Lucas.

"I am so sorry to hear that," Jessica said.

"Oh, 'tis nothing significant, mind you, merely a small problem with my digestion. I fear my appetite is often affected by my mood and I confess I have been in a rather ill humor lately. Do you have the same reaction to ill humors, Jessica?"

"As a matter of fact, I do. It is not at all uncommon for me to lose my appetite completely when I am in distress. I am often a victim of the headache, too," Jessica agreed.

"Precisely. You are always so understanding, Jessica. So perceptive. Unlike some people." Victoria smiled pointedly at Lucas.

Lucas managed to pretend he noticed nothing amiss. "I hope you are feeling better, Miss Huntington."

"Oh, I will feel infinitely better just as soon as I have occasion to settle a small matter that has been plaguing me recently."

"I know what you mean," Jessica put in helpfully. "One's digestion is often improved when one's peace of mind is restored."

"How very true." Victoria's smile would have outshone the sun. She aimed it straight at Lucas. "Lord Stonevale, I was wondering if I might have a word with you?"

"I am at your service, of course, Miss Huntington."

But he made no move to escort her out of Jessica's hearing. Instead he placidly took another minuscule sip of champagne. "What is it you wished to speak to me about?"

Victoria cleared her throat meaningfully and glanced at Jessica. "A small matter, my lord. It concerns a forthcoming lecture. You know how interested you are in lectures."

"It depends. Is this lecture of a scientific nature?"

"Definitely. I believe it might be described as a matter of *intellectual inquiry.*"

"Then I am naturally interested to learn more." He drew his watch from his pocket. "Unfortunately, however, I have promised to meet a friend at my club and I fear I am late. Please tell your aunt that I am always happy to receive invitations to her society's lectures and shall look forward to this one, whatever it is. If you will excuse me, Miss Huntington? Lady Atherton?"

Lucas inclined his head politely to both women and made his escape from the ballroom.

This was not his first such escape in the past few days. Lucas grinned as he hailed a carriage. He had been studiously avoiding Victoria's increasingly pointed attempts to speak to him in private.

Strategy.

He was certain he knew what the topic of discussion would be when he finally allowed his heiress to pin him down.

He was almost positive that what Victoria was working herself up for was a request for more of the sort of *intellectual inquiry* that he had introduced her to that night in the carriage after the visit to the Green Pig.

Lucas cautioned himself for the thousandth time that he must not give in easily. After all, he thought wryly as the carriage halted at the steps of his St. James Street club, he wanted the lady to continue to respect him in the morning.

But there was another, far more serious consideration. Vicky was his responsibility. As her future lord and husband, it was his duty to protect her. Once he had made love to her, a new risk arose. There was every possibility she would get pregnant.

He supposed he should look upon that possibility as another useful tactic. Perhaps, back at the beginning of this strange courtship he might have done so. Now, however, it occurred to Lucas that he would far rather have Vicky come to him of her own free will. He wanted her to want him, he realized. He wanted her to want him enough to take the risk of surrendering completely. He wanted her to marry him because she loved him, not because she had to.

Lucas shook his head ruefully. Something about the wooing of Victoria Huntington was threatening to turn his clear-headed, cool-thinking soldier's brain into romantic mush.

The club's gaming room was far different in outer appearances than the gaming hell where Lucas had taken Victoria. Here, only gentlemen of respectable birth and reputation were allowed. The atmosphere around the green baize tables was far more subdued and aristocratic in tone. But the stakes were higher here in St. James than in the stews, and the potential for disaster enormous.

The potential for profit was correspondingly higher, too, however, and since the games were far more likely to be honest in this environment, such clubs were where Lucas habitually came to make his living.

"I say, Stonevale, been wanting to speak to you." Ferdie Merivale got to his feet and hastened forward as he saw Lucas walk into the room.

Lucas picked up a bottle of claret and poured himself a glass. He cocked a brow at the young man and wondered if he was about to be called out for his rescue efforts at the Green Pig. Then he thought of how he would explain such a situation to the lady who had gotten him into the mess in the first place. *Oh, by the bye, Vicky, the young pup you insisted I rescue has decided to try to kill me tomorrow morning.*

At least Molly the farm girl was safely out of town and not likely to come back anytime soon.

"What is it, Merivale?"

Ferdie flushed and ran a finger under the extremely

high fold of his neckcloth. But his gaze was determined and direct. "I wished to thank you, my lord."

Lucas narrowed his eyes in muted surprise. "Do you, indeed? For what?"

"For your interference the other night," Merivale plowed on gamely. "Don't believe I was properly appreciative at the time. Had a few glasses of claret before I got into the game, you know."

"Glasses or bottles?"

"Bottles," Ferdie admitted ruefully. "At any rate, I had no way of knowing what sort of reputation Duddingstone had. I've since learned that respectable men don't sit down to cards with him."

"*Intelligent* men don't sit down to cards with him," Lucas corrected. "I am glad you realize what he is. I will not bore you with a lecture on your responsibility to your name and estates, but I would urge you to think twice about risking more than you can afford to lose in a card game with anyone, respectable or otherwise."

Merivale grinned. "Are you quite certain you're not going to bore me with a lecture? Completely unnecessary, you know. I swear I have had three or four from my mother."

Lucas grinned. "Sorry. I fear I spent too long in the army. One gets accustomed to issuing warnings to green officers. And spare me your thanks, Merivale. To tell you the truth, I had no real intention of rescuing you that evening. I had other things on my mind at the time."

"Then why did you bother, sir?" Merivale asked.

"My, uh, companion took pity on you and suggested I do something. I obliged. That was all there was to it."

"I do not believe that for a moment, sir. You were kind enough to get me out of a situation in which I could have lost a great deal and I want you to know I am in your debt." Ferdie Merivale bowed slightly and went back to join his friends at the bar.

Lucas shook his head in silent amazement. Victoria had been correct. Ferdie Merivale wasn't such a bad lot after all. If he continued to grow up at this pace, the young man might very well become a credit to his title and his family.

None of that, however, made up for the fact that because he had been occupied with stuffing Merivale into a carriage, Victoria had nearly been run down. Every time he recalled the terrible scene, Lucas's insides went cold.

Deliberately he shook off the chill. He had business to do tonight. He picked up the claret bottle and went across the room to see who was playing cards. He needed to augment his financial reserves. It cost a staggering amount to move in Victoria's social circles.

The one truly irksome thing about this courtship was that the money he was spending on the social trappings he needed for camouflage was money that could not be sunk into the hungry lands of Stonevale.

Lucas consoled himself with the knowledge that one sometimes had to take risks in order to secure a greater profit.

He soon found what he was looking for—a game of whist where the play would be deep enough to suit his current financial needs. He was invited to sit down at once. Lucas did so, putting the bottle on the table.

In reality, he would actually drink very little this evening. He had learned long ago that a clear head gave him a distinct advantage in a game where his opponents usually preferred to fortify themselves with endless bottles of claret and port. The bottle of claret sitting at his elbow was simply more camouflage.

A long time later, after nearly four hours of steady play, Lucas finally decided he had enough to placate his tailor and his bootmaker as well as sufficient to keep his small staff satisfied for a few more weeks. He excused himself from the game and went to collect his hat and coat.

He realized he was tired. The intensity and concentration he brought to his card playing often left him feeling exhausted. But he knew it was precisely that intensity and concentration that helped him win on a reliable basis.

It was the fashion among the men of the ton to play wildly and without much thought or analysis. Gaming was just one more way of displaying one's wealth and style, a method of enhancing one's sense of power and masculinity and impressing one's companions with one's sangfroid.

Huge losses were handled with casual disdain as if money meant nothing. But it was no secret that some men went home and put a pistol to their own heads after a disastrous night at the tables.

Lucas much preferred winning and he took great care to do so. Indeed, a man who was good at strategy could prosper at the gaming tables.

He was halfway to the door when he spotted Edgeworth watching him from the hearth. The other man's sullen dislike was palpable, but Lucas was not particularly concerned. The feeling was mutual. He had not minded in the least relieving Edgeworth of a sizable sum a fortnight ago. Lucas also had no intention of ever getting into another game with the man.

"Good evening, Stonevale. Enjoying your outrageous little heiress?" Edgeworth spoke just loudly enough to catch Lucas's attention. "A very interesting young lady, is she not?"

Lucas contemplated Edgeworth's taunting expression and wondered if he could simply ignore the man. Probably not. Young Merivale and his friend had overheard the remark. They were already turning their heads to see how Lucas would respond.

"I do not discuss respectable women with your sort, Edgeworth," Lucas said mildly. "Now that I think of it, I do not believe I would discuss women of any kind with you."

" 'Tis said the lady in question has no intention of ever marrying," Edgeworth continued, ignoring the clear warning in Lucas's voice. "Since matrimony is not a possibility, may we assume you have other goals in mind for Miss Huntington? After all, the two of you are seen together so frequently one cannot help but speculate on the nature of your association."

This was what came of having a reputation for being slow to anger, Lucas thought ruefully. The fact that he had made no accusation against Edgeworth the night of their infamous card game had obviously emboldened the man.

Meditatively Lucas sipped the claret, aware of his audience. Merivale and his companion were frowning now, waiting to see how Lucas would handle what bordered on a thinly veiled insult to Victoria's virtue.

"One would be wise to resist the temptation to speculate too much on Miss Huntington's social activities," Lucas said. "Unless, of course, one is prepared to present oneself at dawn in Clery Field accompanied by a pair of seconds."

The small tableau of Edgeworth, Merivale, and Merivale's friend went abruptly still.

Edgeworth eyed Lucas through narrowed lids. "Just what is that supposed to mean, Stonevale?"

Lucas smiled his thinnest, coldest smile. "Precisely what it sounds like. I am, as you well know, prepared to let a little matter such as cheating at cards go unremarked. I am not, however, quite so sanguine when a slur is cast on an innocent young woman's name. I leave the decision up to you, Edgeworth."

Edgeworth straightened away from the mantel, his face turning an angry shade of red. "Damn you, Stonevale. God damn you to hell, you bastard. Do you think your luck will hold out forever?" He turned on his heel and walked swiftly out of the room.

Merivale and his companion watched with open mouths as Edgeworth departed. Lucas swallowed a far larger amount of claret than he'd had all evening. He considered himself fortunate that Edgeworth did not care to play any game in which the deck was not marked.

"Good God," Ferdie Merivale said, mopping his brow with a linen handkerchief. "Thought for a moment there I was going to get my first invitation to act as a second. I must say, you handled him very well, sir. Certainly cannot have Miss Huntington's name bandied about in such a manner."

"I should say not," Merivale's companion put in. "Miss Huntington is a very decent sort of female. Danced with me at my first ball when I was damn sure I would make a complete ass of myself on the floor. After a couple of dances with her, I felt much more confident, and after being seen with her, I had no trouble getting other dances, I can tell you."

"She was extremely good to my sister," Merivale

added. "Poor Lucinda was stricken with the most awful case of shyness when she made her debut a year ago. Frozen with fear, you might say. But Miss Huntington took her under her wing and showed her how to go on in Society. Mama was excessively grateful, I can tell you. As a friend of Miss Huntington's, Lucinda soon got some excellent invitations."

"Edgeworth backed right down, didn't he?" the other young man observed eagerly. "But, then, lately I have heard rumors the man don't much care for a fair game of any kind."

"I believe, sir," Merivale said slowly, "that Edgeworth is a bit annoyed with you because of that little scene at the card table a while back. Everyone knows you're much too good a player to drop an entire deck on the floor by accident. After you called for a new deck and began to win, people started wondering at Edgeworth's incredible luck in the past. He's finding it harder and harder to get into a game these days. Wouldn't be surprised if there's some talk of kicking him out of his clubs soon."

"Interesting." Lucas nodded briefly at the two young men. "If you will excuse me, I must be going."

A moment later Lucas walked down the front steps of the club and hailed the nearest carriage. Inside, he sprawled back against the seat and exhaled deeply. He needed to think.

Idly he rubbed his jaw and stared out into the night. This game he was playing with Victoria was getting increasingly risky. Aside from the very real physical dangers of their midnight adventures, there was now a genuine risk to her reputation. Killing Edgeworth in a duel would not be enough to silence the gossip, once it had started.

He could not allow Victoria to get hurt, Lucas told himself grimly. The thing had reached a very serious stage. They were courting an increasing risk of discovery with every midnight outing, and every time they were seen together at parties or in the park, tongues wagged.

Lucas knew Victoria well enough now to realize that even if he refused to escort her on any more midnight adventures, she would probably find some way of going about on her own. She had grown extremely confident in her flimsy masculine disguise.

There was another possibility, too, Lucas reflected. If he stopped providing escort, she might very well find another man who would. And that was the most intolerable thought.

Lucas absently massaged his leg while he examined his own logic. It was clear that the dangerous courtship had to end and soon. The only solution was to marry Victoria as quickly as possible.

His nerves would not tolerate too much more of this wild, reckless, midnight wooing.

Two days later Lucas folded his arms across his chest and sent an amused scowl at Victoria, who was shifting restlessly again in the neighboring seat. She pretended not to notice his admonishing look as she readjusted her skirts.

Next to Victoria sat Cleo Nettleship, paying rapt attention to the speaker, a certain Sir Elihu Winthrop, who was delivering a stimulating lecture entitled "An Enumeration of the Principles of the Cultivation of Buckwheat."

Lucas, at least, was finding the subject stimulating. He was already making plans to put some of Stonevale's fields into buckwheat. The stuff made excellent fodder for cattle and sheep and, according to Winthrop, was frequently consumed by humans over on the continent. Of course, everyone knew that people on the continent would eat virtually anything. Still, there were periodic shortages of wheat throughout England and buckwheat might provide a good emergency grain for his people.

Victoria began to tap her foot impatiently. Lucas knew he should probably not be too hard on her. She obviously had other things on her mind this afternoon and he was quite certain he knew what was making her so fidgety.

Lucas hid a quick smile of satisfaction. He had absolutely no intention of making it easy on the lady. Now that he had her hooked, she was going to have to work a little more at getting herself landed.

For a moment he allowed himself a few glittering

memories of her sweet passion and then, when he realized what it was doing to the region of his groin, he gave his full attention back to the speaker. Winthrop was now deep into a discussion of various methods of manuring buckwheat.

"Most educational," Lady Nettleship declared at the end of the lecture. "Although I confess I have a much stronger interest in lectures on exotic plants. Still, one should certainly be aware of the newest techniques employed in domestic agriculture. Did you enjoy it, Lucas?"

"Very much. Thank you again for letting me know the lecture was going to be held today."

"Anytime, anytime. Are you ready to leave, Victoria?"

"Yes, Aunt Cleo. Quite ready." Victoria was on her feet, collecting her bonnet and reticule.

"Well, we mustn't rush out of here. I see one or two people I should speak to first." Cleo glanced around the room with enthusiasm. "I will be right back."

Victoria shot Lucas a meaningful look from beneath her lashes as they started toward the doors of the lecture hall. He looked down at her, enjoying the sight of her in a charming little yellow spencer jacket worn over a white muslin walking dress. She looked very lovely, he thought with a sense of possessive pride. He ushered her politely toward the exit, nodding at several of the society's members with whom he was becoming friends.

The departure from the hall took some time as several people stopped to talk. Lucas could feel Victoria simmering with impatience beside him.

"Is something wrong?" he finally inquired quite casually as they stood in the entryway waiting for Lady Nettleship.

"No, but Lucas, I must talk to you."

"Then something *is* wrong?"

"Nothing is wrong. I simply wish to speak to you in private and I have not had an opportunity to do so since the night we—" She broke off, turning pink. Then she gamely cleared her throat and finished the sentence, "Since the night we went to the Green Pig."

"Speaking of which, I ran into Ferdie Merivale the

other evening at my club. You will be happy to know
he was not nearly as annoyed with me as I had expected. Even thanked me for rescuing him. It seems he's
come to his senses and feels he had a rather close call."

Victoria's eyes brightened for a moment. "I'm so
glad. I have always liked Ferdie and his sister."

"Too bad I cannot tell him he owes the lesson to you,
not me. I'd have left him to his fate, I'm afraid."

"Only because you were so concerned with protecting me," Victoria said with a touching loyalty. "Otherwise, I am certain you would have done something on
your own for the boy. And you were very helpful with
little Molly, too."

Lucas smiled wryly. "Will you be at the Foxtons'
tonight?"

"Yes, but you know how difficult it is to find any
privacy at a crush like that. Lucas, why do you not ride
in the park tomorrow afternoon? I shall arrange to be
there, also."

"As much as I would wish to do so, I'm afraid I have
another engagement."

Victoria's face fell. "You do? Are you very sure you
cannot make it? Even for a few minutes around five?"

He took pity on her. The poor woman was obviously
so far out of her depth now that she could not possibly
swim to shore by herself. Lucas contemplated just how
he would save her. "I dislike riding in the park in the
afternoons, Vicky. Too crowded."

"Yes, I know, but I simply must speak to you. If you
won't join me in the park, you must come to the garden
tonight. We can talk there." Victoria lowered her voice.
"This is very important, Lucas."

"I fear I had not planned on one of our little adventures tonight. These things do take planning, you know."

"Damn it, Lucas," she hissed softly, "I am not planning an adventure. But I do want to see you. I would
greatly appreciate it if you could fit me into your busy
schedule."

Lucas looked at her in mild surprise. "You sound
upset, Miss Huntington."

Victoria fidgeted. "I am upset, Lord Stonevale. You are being exceedingly difficult."

"I am only thinking of your reputation, Victoria. We must be very, very careful these days," Lucas warned, glancing about to prove his point.

"Hang my reputation. I must talk to you."

He was startled and rather warmed by her insistence. She was obviously at the end of her tether. Lord knew he was more than ready for the next phase of this business, himself. It was time to end her frustration and his own.

"Very well," Lucas said, as if considering the matter carefully, "I will check my engagement book and see if I can spare a few minutes with you in your garden later this evening around midnight. Will that suffice?"

"You are far too kind, my lord."

He winced as the knife edge of her tongue took a slice out of his hide. "Not at all."

"I begin to believe you are toying with me, Lucas."

His brows rose. He must never forget the woman was extremely astute. "I will do my best to be in your garden tonight at the usual time. Now, if you will excuse me for a moment, I see Tottingham over in the corner. He promised to loan me his copy of White's *Natural History and Antiquities of Selborne*. I have been wanting to read it since he mentioned it to me."

"You need not bother Tottingham with your request, my lord," Victoria said icily. "If you manage to keep your appointment with me tonight, I will allow you to borrow my copy."

He grinned. "Victoria, my sweet, are you by any chance trying to bribe me?"

She turned an even brighter shade of pink and whirled around to go in search of her aunt.

8

Lucas saw her waiting for him in the shadows of a tree as he came over the garden wall. She was an elegant ghost hooded and cloaked in a maroon velvet cape lined with yellow satin. The same cape she had worn earlier that evening to the Foxtons' ball.

He eased himself carefully to the ground, catching his weight on his right foot and using his left primarily for balance. But even taking care, the short drop sent a sharp twinge through his bad leg. He had no business climbing garden walls.

Lucas straightened, idly massaging the old wound, and wondered how he had come to find himself dancing on the end of Victoria's string for so long. He had let the lady run him in circles.

It was high time to take her to bed and make her his own. He would have much preferred to marry her first, but barring that possibility, he would take what he could get. Just the thought of being able to spend a comfortable night in a bed with Victoria instead of racketing around in hired carriages and flirting with disaster was enough to make his leg feel better and assured himself that bed was bound to lead to marriage.

"Lucas?" Her voice was the softest of whispers as she came forward through the damp grass. She lifted her cloaked face and looked up at him with a sweet, vulnerable expression that wrenched his heart.

He groaned and thrust his hands under the hood to frame her face. Without a word he lowered his head to drink hungrily of her mouth. When he finally released her, his whole body was tight with desire.

"Damn, but it was hard to watch you dance with one man after another tonight at the Foxtons'," he muttered against her throat.

"Lucas, please, you must not kiss me like that tonight. There is no time. My aunt will be home shortly. I told her I had the headache when I left the Foxtons. She will probably go straight to my room to check on me when she comes home."

"What is it that was so important we are once again risking your reputation, Vicky?"

She clutched the velvet cloak more tightly around her, meeting his eyes bravely in the flickering moonlight. "I thought this would be easy to say, but I am discovering it is not easy at all."

He wanted to fold her close against his chest and assure her she did not have to say anything, but he resisted the temptation. She must take this step herself. *Strategy*, he reminded himself bleakly.

Strategy and a desperate wish not to be blamed later for having seduced her. Far better for both of them that she engineer her own fall into bed with him.

"I am listening, my sweet."

She lifted her chin determinedly. "I have done a great deal of thinking lately, my lord."

"Not always a good thing. I have found that sometimes too much thinking can disturb one's peace of mind."

"Well, mine is already disturbed." She stepped away from him and turned to pace back and forth in the wet grass. She seemed unaware of the way the toes of her satin evening slippers were growing damp. "I have gone through this problem many times in my own mind. For reasons I am certain you will understand, it is a subject that is almost impossible to discuss openly with anyone else, even my aunt."

"I understand," he said gravely. "There are some things we cannot discuss, even with those who are close to us."

"Yes, precisely." She turned and paced in the opposite direction. "I believe I have told you that I do not wish to marry."

"On several occasions."

"Lately I have discovered, however, that I am not entirely opposed to a . . . a romantic liaison with a man."

"I see."

"I am glad, because this is very hard to put into words." She swung around and stalked back the way she had come. "Do you, uh, recall what happened the other night in the carriage after we left the Green Pig?"

"Very clearly."

She ducked her head deeper inside the hood. "I was astonished to learn that the connection between a man and a woman can be quite so . . . so intense."

He hid his amusement. "I am pleased you found the experience pleasant."

"*Pleasant.*" She halted and spun to face him, her eyes huge in the pale light. "It was vastly more than pleasant, my lord. It was rather unnerving in some respects but very, very exciting. Quite astonishingly delightful, in fact."

Her delicious honesty on the subject entranced him. "You flatter me."

"Not at all." She resumed her pacing. "Lucas, I have given this much thought and I have decided I wish to repeat the experience. In fact, I have decided I would like to discover the full range of that particular sort of experience. As a matter of intellectual inquiry, you understand."

"Intellectual inquiry," he repeated slowly. "Rather like collecting beetles, I imagine."

"I suppose one could say that."

"Will you put me on display in a box when you've finished your inquiries?"

Victoria scowled at him from inside her cloak. "Lucas, don't you dare tease me. I am perfectly serious about this."

"Yes, I can see that."

"To be quite blunt, I would like to establish a romantic connection with you of the sort Isabel Rycott enjoys with her friend Edgeworth."

"Good God, I sincerely hope not."

Victoria stopped and turned toward him with a shocked, embarrassed expression. "You do not want me?"

Instantly he realized how she had interpreted his words. He moved forward and pulled her roughly into his arms, covering her mouth with his own in a kiss of such fierce possession that she trembled in response. When he finally released her, he captured her face between his hands and looked down at her, knowing the full force of his need was probably blazing in his eyes.

"I want you more than I have ever wanted anything else on the face of this earth. Don't ever forget that, Victoria. No matter what happens, promise me you will never forget that."

She circled his wrists with her fingers, smiling tremulously. "And I want you, Lucas. I have never known anything like this need I feel for you. Please, will you make love to me?"

"*Vicky*. Oh, Vicky, my sweet, wayward, passionate hoyden." He crushed her against his length, light-headed with a strange combination of passion, tenderness, and relief. "I will make love to you until you go up in flames and then I will join you and we will burn together."

"That does not sound particularly comfortable, my lord," she remarked, her voice muffled against his coat.

He grinned. "Wait until you try it."

She laughed softly and her arms went around his waist. She hugged him tightly. "Lucas, I am so excited."

"So am I," he whispered, and then added deliberately, "It is almost as if you had just agreed to marry me."

She went rigid. "Lucas . . ."

"Almost, but not quite. Calm yourself, Vicky. I don't
mean to frighten you, but you cannot help but know by
now that I would not be averse to something more than
a romantic connection with you. Would you care to
discuss marriage rather than a romantic liaison?" He
held his breath, praying she would say yes and everything would suddenly become very simple.

"Thank you, Lucas. That is very nice of you, you
know. Entirely unnecessary, but very nice. I do appreciate the offer, because you certainly were not obliged
to make it," she said, beaming.

"But the answer is no?"

"You know it is, but thank you again for asking." She
raised her head to brush her mouth lightly against his
own. Then she smiled brilliantly up at him. "Now, let
us get on to making our plans."

Her rather casual dismissal of his proposal irritated
Lucas. The little baggage thought she could have it all
without paying the price. Perhaps it was time to gently
point out that this was not going to be quite as simple
and straightforward as she had anticipated.

"Very well. When?"

She blinked. "When what, my lord?"

"When shall we arrange our first meeting as lovers?
And how? Have you given any thought to that? It needs
some consideration. Also, there is the matter of where,
isn't there? We cannot just hire a carriage to drive us
around London for several hours while we make love
on the cushions. Most uncomfortable and I don't want
the coachman making a guess about what is going on
inside," he explained roughly.

Her expression moved from startled to appalled. "I
thought . . . I thought you would take care of those
little matters. That is, I assumed you knew how to
make the arrangements for this sort of thing, Lucas."

"Not likely. I've never formed a romantic connection
of such an intimate nature with a young lady of your
sort before in my life. It generally is not done, Victoria.
At least, not by men who consider themselves gentlemen. You put me in something of an awkward situation,
you see."

She groaned. "Aunt Cleo warned me that it is not only my own reputation I am toying with, but yours also."

"Did she really?" Lucas was not particularly surprised to hear that Lady Nettleship had guessed in which direction the wind was blowing. He wondered what Cleo's real views on the matter were. "Lady Nettleship is a very perceptive woman. She obviously does not like the notion of you playing ducks and drakes with your reputation."

"Or yours. Lucas, I understand this is not easy for you and there certainly are dangers involved. I am not so blind that I do not comprehend that."

"That speaks well for your intelligence, Vicky."

She bit her lip and slanted him a sidelong glance. "I suppose it really is not fair of me to ask you to do this."

"As you said, one cannot deny there are risks involved."

She sighed, a very tragic-sounding sort of sigh. "You are quite right. I have no business jeopardizing your reputation as well as my own, do I? Perhaps we should simply forget it."

"My offer presents a possible alternative," he began cautiously.

She patted his arm affectionately as if he were a well-meaning puppy. "Your offer of marriage was very sweet, Lucas. But I fear the only real alternative for me is to wait a few more years until I am well and truly established as a spinster. Perhaps then no one will care too much if I choose to follow in Lady Rycott's footsteps. Do forgive me, Lucas. I am sorry I ever brought up the subject."

Alarm swept through him as he realized she was already backing away from the affair. What's more she was considering spinsterhood rather than marriage as the only alternative. If he let her go completely, he might never get her back. Even worse, she might find another man who would not have any hesitation at all in letting her take all the risks she wished.

Lucas reached out a little roughly and caught her chin between thumb and forefinger. "Victoria, if a romantic liaison is truly what you want, then it will be my privilege to give it to you."

Her sudden smile was much too luminous and her eyes glowed with what looked suspiciously like feminine triumph. "In the spirit of intellectual inquiry, my lord?"

Somewhere inside Lucas a warning bell belatedly clanged. He studied Victoria's delighted, cheerfully smug expression and a nasty notion was born in him that he'd just been well and truly outmaneuvered.

"I have always been a great believer in the benefits of intellectual inquiry," he said grimly.

"Oh, Lucas, how can I ever thank you?" She threw her arms around his neck and hugged him fiercely. "You are always so good to me."

Swearing silently, he succumbed to the allure of her obvious delight. He was beginning to realize that it would always be difficult to refuse Victoria whatever she happened to want. He would do well in the future to remember his weakness in that regard.

Reluctantly Lucas pulled her arms from around his neck, kissing her reassuringly on the tip of her nose. "Then 'tis settled. Now, my sweet, you had better get back into the house. I think I hear a carriage coming down the street."

"Oh, dear, that must be Aunt Cleo. I must go." She turned swiftly, the cloak whirling around her sadly dampened slippers. Then she swung back with a quick frown of concern. "Do be careful of your leg when you go back over the wall, Lucas. I worry about all this climbing about. It cannot be good for you."

"I'm inclined to agree." The damned leg was already aching from his first assault on the wall this evening. Now he must repeat the process. "I look forward to the night when this wall climbing is no longer necessary. Good night, Vicky."

"About our plans for our first, uh, liaison . . ." She glanced anxiously toward the conservatory door as she, too, heard the carriage in the street.

"Don't fret, Vicky. I will arrange everything."

"You will?"

He paused, straddling the garden wall, and looked down into her upturned face. He bit back an oath. "Yes, Vicky, I will. That's my job, is it not?"

"You will let me know just as soon as you have got the details worked out?" she called out hopefully.

"Believe me, my dear, you will be the first to know." He cleared the wall and dropped down into the alley. His thigh protested strongly and his limp was more pronounced than usual as he made his way back toward the street where he had left the carriage. One way or another he definitely had to put a stop to this wall climbing.

Lucas checked the street and saw no one. He crossed it and started around the corner. He very nearly walked straight into the man holding the knife.

The footpad appeared equally surprised at the suddenness of the encounter. He had obviously been lounging in the shadows, waiting for his quarry, and had not heard Lucas approach. But he reacted immediately, lunging forward with the blade held low.

Lucas was already diving to the side, cursing as he felt his bad leg give away. He landed hard on the knee of his injured leg and forced himself to ignore the pain while he reached up and grabbed for his attacker's knife arm.

The man yelled in rage and surprise as Lucas rolled onto his back and tugged hard. The assailant slammed into the brick wall of the darkened house on the corner and the knife clattered to the paving stones.

Lucas kept rolling, moving up onto his knees. Then he staggered to his feet, bracing himself with one hand against the brick wall. Raw agony tore through his left leg.

The footpad was already thudding away into the darkness, footsteps echoing harshly in the night. He did not stop to retrieve his knife.

"'Ere, now," the coachman yelled, pounding up the street as he belatedly realized his passenger was in trouble. "What's goin' on? What 'appened, m'lord? Are ye hurt?"

"No." Lucas glanced down at his expensive Weston

jacket and swore again. He had just paid a fortune for
the damn thing and now he would have to purchase a
new one.

"Some footpad lookin' to prig a gennelman's purse,"
the coachman declared, reaching down to scoop up the
knife. "Wicked-lookin' thing. The cove meant business,
didn't 'e?"

"Yes," said Lucas. "But I am not certain just what
sort of business he had in mind."

"Streets ain't safe for man nor beast," the coachman
remarked. "You 'andled him right proper m'lord. Saw
the way you sent 'im flyin'. Learn that sort of thing at
Gentleman Jackson's academy, did ye?"

"No. I learned that sort of thing the hard way." Lucas
started toward the coach and sucked in his breath as his
left leg nearly collapsed again. He summoned up a
vision of the bottle of port waiting in his library. "Let's
be off, if you don't mind. It is not my intention to
amuse myself standing around the streets at this hour."

"Certainly, sir. But I'd just like to say I never met a
member o' the fancy could 'andle 'imself as well as you
just did in a street fight. Most of the nabobs I run
across would o' ended up with their gullets slit."

Victoria stepped back into her room and closed the
door quietly behind her. Then she shut her eyes and
leaned back against the wooden panels. Her heart was
racing and she felt as though her legs were going to melt.

She had done it.

It had taken more raw courage than she had dreamed
it would, more than she had even believed she pos-
sessed, but she had done it. She was going to have an
affair with Lucas Mallory Colebrook, the Earl of
Stonevale.

Her hands were trembling as she came away from
the door and walked a little unsteadily across the room
to stare out of the window into the darkness.

Now that she had accomplished her goal after days of
agonizing over the matter, she discovered she was weak
with reaction. There were so many dangers, both for
herself and for Lucas.

But the chance to discover passion in Lucas's arms was worth any risk.

Such an admirable man. He was not a silly, foppish dandy or a callous rakehell. He cared about her reputation yet he accepted her desire to avoid marriage. He was not after her fortune, it seemed, only her.

"Dear God, listen to me. I sound as if I am in love with the man." Victoria caught her breath as the realization momentarily swamped her. "I *am* in love with him."

She hugged herself with the wonder of this latest adventure. To be in love and yet to be free. What more could a woman ask?

She stood at the window for a long time, trying to see the future in the darkness. But everything seemed cloudy and without solid form. After a long while, she went to bed.

At dawn she came awake suddenly, sitting bolt upright against the pillows.

Demon bitch. I will send you back to hell.

The knife.

Dear God, the knife.

She did not remember much about the nightmare that had jolted her from sleep, but she did not need to recall the details. She'd had similar dreams often enough during the past few months and they always ended the same way, leaving her restless and disturbed, filling her with a sense of dark, brooding menace that could not be logically explained away.

At least she had not cried out this time, she thought in relief. Occasionally she screamed in the middle of the terrible dreams and poor Nan would come running to check on her.

Victoria got out of bed. She knew from experience that daylight would banish the disquieting sensation. In the meantime there was not much point in trying to go back to sleep.

She reached for her wrapper. It was a clear day and soon the morning light would be streaming into the conservatory. A perfect day for painting. When all else failed, she could frequently find peace of mind by losing herself in her art.

Dressing quickly, she hurried downstairs. The household was just beginning to stir. She could hear cook clattering the pans in the kitchen.

Her easel, paintbox, and sketchbooks were just where she had left them. Victoria stood looking around the lush conservatory for a moment and then her eyes fell on the glorious blooms of *Strelitzia reginae*.

In the morning sunlight the flower was a wonderful cross between gold and yellow, a fabulous shade of amber touched with highlights of royal blue.

She quickly set about shifting all her equipment to a new vantage point where she would have a clear view of *Strelitzia*. She remembered how Lucas had admired it that first day in the conservatory.

She was going to paint it for him, she decided on a sudden impulse. He had appeared genuinely pleased by her botanical watercolors and sketches and there was no doubt about his new enthusiasm for horticulture. Perhaps he would like *Strelitzia reginae* as a memento of their first night together as lovers. It would be her gift to him on that memorable night.

Almost like a wedding gift, came the unbidden thought. She banished it quickly and sat down to go to work.

She saw the snuffbox inside her paintbox the moment she raised the lid.

For a few seconds she simply stared at it, astonished, and wondered why anyone would deposit a perfectly good snuffbox in her paintbox. It was as odd to find such an object here as it had been to discover the monogrammed scarf on the conservatory door a few nights earlier.

With a small, niggling sense of dread, Victoria picked up the tiny snuffbox and examined it carefully. It was a nicely worked box but not particularly distinguished except for the letter "W" engraved on the inside of the lid.

For a minute she was short of breath. She reminded herself violently that she did not believe in ghosts. But the thought that someone might be playing a macabre game with her was even more chilling than the prospect of a phantom.

And even more impossible, she told herself, taking several deep breaths to calm her nerves. She had to be sensible. This could not be her stepfather's snuffbox any more than the scarf could possibly have belonged to him.

This was all some sort of bizarre coincidence. One of her aunt's numerous acquaintances had been on a visit to the conservatory and had left the scarf and snuffbox behind. The scarf had been found immediately but the snuffbox had been set down and forgotten only to be discovered much later. By her.

It was the only possible explanation because no one, *no one* except herself knew what had really happened on that dreadful night when her stepfather had died at the foot of a flight of stairs.

Four days later Victoria looked around the Middleships' glittering ballroom at the sea of fashionably dressed guests and realized she was as nervous and excited as a bride at her own wedding party. *This was the night.*

As this was as close as she ever intended to get to a genuine wedding celebration, she had best enjoy it, she decided.

Three days ago Lucas had calmly told her that he had made all the arrangements for their first night together. The plans were contingent on Lady Nettleship accepting a long-standing invitation to a weekend house party in the country, he had warned. But that had been no problem. This morning Cleo had set off cheerfully for the nearby country home of one of her dearest friends.

"You are quite certain you do not mind staying here alone for one evening?" Aunt Cleo had demanded for the third time as she tied her bonnet and prepared to follow several bags into her traveling coach.

"Hardly alone, Aunt Cleo. I have all the servants including Nan. I shall do very well. You will recall that I am invited to the Middleships' ball tonight and their soirées never end before dawn. I shan't be home until sunrise and you will be back in the afternoon."

"Well, you are nearly twenty-five. I daresay no one can remark upon you staying here in your own home for one night without having me, and you will be ac-

companied by Lady Lyndwood and her daughter when
you attend the ball, so all is well. Take care, Vicky."
Cleo had given her a good-bye peck on the cheek
before settling into the coach for the trip.

Victoria had waved from the steps and then felt her
stomach do a series of strange little flips as anticipation
set in with a vengeance.

This was the night. There was no turning back now.
This was what she wanted; Lucas was the man she
wanted. She was on the brink of a romantic liaison with
the man she loved. The dazzling prospect of this sort of
intellectual inquiry was enough to take away her breath.

The time had come. Victoria began to edge through
the crowd, making her way unobtrusively toward the
door. Lucas would be waiting.

"Off so soon, Victoria?" Isabel Rycott seemed to ma-
terialize out of nowhere.

"I fear I have a number of engagements this evening," Victoria said politely. "I promised a friend I
would drop in at the Bridgewaters' for a while and then
I have to go on to yet another rout after that."

Isabel tapped Victoria's gloved wrist admonishingly
with her fan and smiled her mysterious smile. "I understand completely, my dear. You will slip from one party
to another until you happen across your earl, will you
not?"

Victoria flushed. "I have no idea what you are talking
about, Lady Rycott."

Isabel laughed softly but with a strange touch of
bitterness. "Don't be embarrassed, my dear. It is not so
very unique to find oneself attracted to an interesting
man. It is part of the female condition. But a wise
woman takes care to remain in command of her emotions and the situation at all times. She is careful to
choose men who are not particularly strong, men who
can be easily managed."

"Really, Lady Rycott, I must be off."

"Yes, of course. But do keep my words in mind. As
Samuel's and Caroline's friend, I want only the best for
you." Isabel's eyes glittered with sudden harshness.
"And you needn't act so superior, damn you."

Victoria was shocked. "I assure you, it is not my intention to offend you in any way."

Isabel's mouth twisted in a smile that was not in the least charming or even particularly mysterious. "Yes. You are noted for your kindness, are you not? But I know what you think of my friend Edgeworth. I saw it in your eyes the day we met in the park. You find him sadly lacking when you compare him to your precious earl."

Victoria started. "I never said—"

"You did not have to say anything. I saw it in your eyes. Such arrogance. You think I have landed the spavined, broken-down pony while you have got the fine-blooded stallion. But you will be sorry for your choice," Isabel hissed.

"Please, Lady Rycott, do not upset yourself."

"I am not in the least upset. I will tell you something, my dear. I will take an Edgeworth over a man like Stonevale any day, and if you were smart you would do the same. Your failure to do so will probably be your downfall."

Victoria was nonplussed by the bizarre conversation. She wondered how many glasses of wine Lady Rycott had consumed. The gem-hard glitter in Isabel's beautiful eyes was almost frightening. "Please excuse me, Lady Rycott." She made to move away, but Isabel's fingers reached out to grip her bare arm.

"You think you have chosen the more exciting, more interesting man, but you are a fool. The plain truth is that men are of little use to a woman if they cannot be manipulated. Don't you understand? We are trapped by Society into being dependent on men for so much. Our only defense is to be stronger than they are in all the ways that count. When a strong woman allies herself with a weak, manageable man, she can have everything she wants. *Everything*."

"Lady Rycott, you are hurting my arm."

Isabel glanced down at her own fingers, registering surprise. She instantly removed her hand from Victoria's arm, quickly regaining total control of herself. "Never mind. It is undoubtedly too late for you anyway. But you should have been shrewd enough to know by now that a strong man is very dangerous. If you'd had any sense, Vicky, you would have picked an Edgeworth, not a Stonevale."

Isabel turned away and disappeared into the crowd, but not before Victoria thought she glimpsed the brightness of tears in her exotic eyes.

Victoria stood staring after the other woman for a moment, utterly at a loss. Her happy anticipation was briefly dimmed by the startling encounter. But by the time she had collected her cloak and pulled the hood up over her head to conceal her features, she was back in the grip of excitement. She hurried down the steps of the town house.

The closed carriage was waiting for her, just as Lucas had promised. The coachman sat on the box, heavily shrouded in his top hat and enveloping cape. She shot him a quick, laughing glance and then allowed one of the Middleships' footmen to assist her into the carriage.

A few minutes later the vehicle was making excellent progress through the streets of London, and within a short while they had reached the quieter, outlying areas of the city. The noise of passing traffic faded and the buildings grew more sparse. Moonlit meadows, fields, and farms came into view.

Then, without any warning, the carriage came to a halt in an inn yard. Victoria's mouth went dry. The time had come and she was suddenly awash in a sea of contradictory emotions. Anticipation and excitement and longing did battle with anxiety, uncertainty, and a few second thoughts. She was forced to wonder once more if she was doing the right thing.

But she was four and twenty, she reminded herself, not a silly little seventeen-year-old chit fresh out of the schoolroom. She knew her own mind and she had already made her decision. She would not back out now.

She glanced out at the courtyard, listening to her "coachman" give directions to the young boy who came out of the inn to assist with the horses. No matter what sort of orders he was issuing, Lucas always sounded so very much in command.

A moment later the carriage door opened and Lucas stood looking at her. He had removed the hat and coachman's cape. Without a word he held out his hand.

"Are you very certain this is what you want, Victoria?" he asked quietly.

"Yes, Lucas. I want this night with you more than I have ever wanted anything in my life."

His smile was enigmatic but tender. "Then you shall have it. Come with me."

A short time later Victoria found herself sitting in front of a pleasant fire in a comfortable upstairs room, sipping tea the landlord's wife had brought her on a tray. There was a decanter of sherry next to the teapot. The good woman had addressed her as "my lady" and Victoria knew it was because Lucas had informed the innkeeper that she was his wife. No one had thought to question two obvious members of the Quality who claimed such a relationship.

"I've told the innkeeper that you are weary and we plan to rest for a few hours, but that we are in a hurry and must be on our way before dawn," Lucas announced as he walked into the room and shut the door behind him. "That will give me time to get you safely back to the last party on your list of invitations tonight before most of the guests have taken their leave. You will be able to go home with Annabella Lyndwood and her mother, just as you had planned. No one will be the wiser."

"Except, perhaps, myself?" Victoria smiled tremulously over the rim of her cup.

Lucas's eyes gentled as he looked down at her. "I think both of us are going to learn a great deal tonight." He walked over to the chair that stood across from hers near the hearth. His eyes were gleaming as he sat down and poured two glasses of sherry. "Here's to intellectual inquiry, Vicky."

She put down her teacup and took one of the sherry glasses from his hand, aware that her fingers were trembling slightly. "To intellectual inquiry," she murmured, lifting her glass in a small toast.

Lucas raised his glass in an answering salute, his eyes

never leaving hers. They finished the sherry in a charged silence and then Lucas removed the glass from Victoria's fingers and set it down alongside his.

Victoria remembered her gift and stood up abruptly. She hurried to where she had hung her cloak and reticule.

"Vicky? What's wrong?" Lucas called after her.

"Nothing is wrong. I have something for you. A small present." She turned back toward him, clutching the little parcel in both hands. It suddenly seemed like a rather paltry gift. "It is not much, really. I thought, *hoped* you might like it." She smiled wistfully. "It seemed like the sort of night one might want to remember with a gift."

He stood up slowly. "It is exactly that sort of night. I only wish I had a gift for you. My lamentable military mind, I fear. I was so concerned with the practical aspects of this evening that I failed to think about other, perhaps more important matters." He came toward her and took the parcel out of her hands. Then he led her back to her seat by the fire and sat down to open his present.

Victoria sat tensely as Lucas reverently removed the paper wrapping and stared thoughtfully down at *Strelitzia reginae*. She realized she was in an agony of suspense. It really was not much of a present, she thought. Just a painting of a flower.

But when Lucas looked up again, revealing a rare, intense emotion in his eyes, she took a deep breath and relaxed slightly. He was pleased.

"Thank you, Vicky. It is beautiful and I will hang it where I shall be able to look at it daily. And whenever I do look at it, I will remember this night."

"I am glad you like it. Not every man would care for a picture of a flower, you know."

"Just as well. I'd as soon you didn't go around giving any other man your paintings under similar circumstances." He reached out and took her hand.

"Lucas?"

"Your fingers are cold," he observed, cradling her palm. He turned her hand in his and bent his head to kiss her bare wrist. Her fingers curled. "You are very tense."

"I am nervous, if you must have the plain truth," she admitted.

"Would it make you feel any better to know that I, too, am anxious about what lies ahead?"

"That I refuse to believe, my lord."

"Then you sadly overestimate my fortitude. I want you very much, Vicky, but I do not want to hurt you or frighten you or somehow spoil the magic with clumsiness or a lack of self-control," Lucas said quietly.

Victoria looked up at him in surprise and was suddenly overwhelmed with a need to reassure him. "I should have realized this would be as awkward for you as it is for me. We are very much alike in many ways, are we not?"

Lucas nodded. "I like to think so."

"You are doing this because I asked it of you. I have forced you to go against your own code of honor."

He smiled faintly and his hand tightened around her fingers. "Do not credit me with too many fine scruples and sensibilities, Vicky. You cannot know how much I have wanted to hold you naked in my arms and feel you shiver when I enter you, how much I have longed to have you cling to me and draw me deep inside you. I am here tonight because you have made it clear that this is the only way I will ever learn how hot you will burn and I cannot live the rest of my life without discovering the answer to that question."

Victoria stared at him, unable to look away from the intensity of his gaze. She felt the heat of the flames on her skin, but it was nothing compared to the warmth that was pooling within her. She knew her fingers were trembling within his.

"Lucas, I have something to tell you."

"What is that, my sweet?" His voice was indulgent as his fingers trailed along the inside of her arm.

"I . . . I think I have fallen in love with you," she blurted.

"Only think?" He glanced up, eyes gleaming.

"Oh, *Lucas*."

He tugged her gently out of her chair and down onto his thighs, where he held her tightly against his chest. He speared his fingers through her curls, gripped her head, and kissed her.

Victoria thought she would drown under the impact of his mouth. At the touch of his tongue against her lips all her qualms and fears vanished as if he had waved a magic wand. Of course he wanted her. There could be no doubt of that. And she wanted him. Dear God, how she wanted him.

The next few minutes were a haze of small movements and tender, stroking caresses that somehow combined to remove Victoria's gown and petticoats along with most of her remaining inhibitions. It occurred to her that she ought to be feeling at least somewhat embarrassed. But all she could really feel was her own stirring passion and a sense of wonder that this man should want her so much that he would risk his reputation to please her.

"You are very good to me." She touched his cheek with gentle fingers. "You give me so much. All those nights of adventure and now this very special night."

"Just remember that from now on all your adventures must be with me." His hand stroked her slowly from breast to thigh until she moaned against his shirt. The heat in his eyes sent flames through her.

He set her on her feet and then led her over to the bed. When they reached it, she snuggled under the covers, watching in fascination as he doused the candles. When only the flames of the small fire lit the room, Lucas sat down on the edge of the bed, putting a considerable dent into it. A moment later one highly polished Hessian hit the floor. The second soon followed.

Victoria unconsciously clenched the sheet in her hands as she watched Lucas undress. The firelight turned his skin to bronze and underscored the smoothly muscled contours of his broad shoulders. His belly was hard and flat. Something gleamed in the mat of dark curls on his chest and Victoria looked more closely.

"What is that pendant, Lucas? Is it made of gold?"

He touched it absently. "Amber. There's a small carving on it. It's been in the family for years, I was told."

"And you wear it always?"

He shrugged. "I have worn it constantly since it was given to me by my uncle." Lucas smiled. "I like to think it brings me good luck, and it must work, otherwise I would not be here with you." His fingers suddenly tightened around it. "But I think it would suit you better than it does me."

He removed the chain from around his neck and moved closer.

"No, Lucas, I could not possibly take your pendant. It is a family heirloom. You cannot give it away."

"I can do anything I want with it." He placed it carefully around her throat and nodded in satisfaction. The amber glowed like honey-colored fire against her skin. The small figures of the knight and his lady were visible in all their exquisite detail. "It looks right on you. I want you to have it, Vicky. 'Tis a symbol of what we will share between us tonight. As long as you wear it, I will know you care for me and that you *think* you might be in love with me."

She answered his gentle, sensually teasing smile with one of her own. "In that case, I will never have cause to remove it. I cannot imagine not feeling about you the way I do now."

"Remember that, hmmm?" He brushed his knuckles lightly across her cheek before reaching down to open his breeches.

He stepped out of the remainder of his clothes, revealing a hard, aroused male body. But Victoria noticed nothing else about him in that moment except the wide, ragged scar on his thigh.

"Dear God," she whispered.

"Does it bother you?" He stood waiting, his breeches still in his hands, his eyes unreadable.

She reached out to touch the ruined flesh with gentle, soothing fingers. "Bother me? Of course it does not bother me. Not in the way you mean." She looked up at him, stricken. "But how it must have hurt you. I cannot bear the thought that you suffered such agony, that you came so close to death."

"Hush, Vicky. Do not fret about it. It was a long time

ago and I assure you right now it is not bothering me in the slightest. I have far more important things on my mind and none of them have anything to do with death. They are all matters of life." He caught her fingers in his hand and kissed them. "Do you know I didn't think it would upset you too much. There are women who would have recoiled in shock and revulsion. But somehow I rather thought you would not be put off by it. You are a most unusual woman, Victoria."

"Not really, but I—" She broke off as she finally noticed the rest of him. "Oh, my." Victoria gazed at him, mesmerized. He was hard and swollen in a state of full arousal and his masculinity appeared overwhelming to her inexperienced eyes.

"Well, at least your mind is off that damned scar," Lucas observed with wry humor as he tossed his breeches over a chair.

"You are very . . ." Her tongue seemed to grow awkward in her mouth. She moistened her lips and tried again. "You are quite magnificent, my lord. Rather large, in fact. Bigger than I had imagined." She felt herself turning red as he quirked a brow. "Not that I was quite certain just what you would look like, but I am . . . that is, the plain fact is that I was not expecting quite so much of you."

Lucas muttered an exclamation that was half laugh and half groan as he came down beside her and slid under the covers. "Vicky, my darling, you say the most delightfully honest things at the most amazing times. God, but you are sweet. I wonder how I waited this long to have you near me like this."

He pulled her close, his hand closing around her bare buttocks to urge her against his strong thighs. He used his foot to gently pry apart her legs and she suddenly realized she had been clamping them together. Fully intending to force herself to relax, she wound up squeezing her knees even more tightly shut.

Lucas's smile was deeply sensual. "I must tell you, sweetheart, that this particular aspect of our intellectual inquiry cannot proceed much farther if you keep your knees locked together."

The comment broke through her nervousness and elicited a small gurgle of laughter from her. Victoria put her arms around his neck and smiled up at him. "Is that right, my lord? I would never have guessed. I shall rely upon you to keep me informed of the small details of this experiment."

"Very well, here is one small detail that most certainly must not be overlooked." He bent his head and sipped one nipple carefully between his strong, white teeth.

"*Lucas.*" Victoria gasped and closed her eyes at the thrill that shot through her. Instinctively she arched herself so that he could take her more completely into his mouth.

Lucas obliged her, and when she was dazed with the sensations pouring through her, Victoria felt his leg slide effortlessly between her thighs. This time she offered no resistance at all, opening herself completely to his touch.

"So soft. So sweet and soft and welcoming." Lucas's voice was husky with his passion. His long, elegant fingers moved over her, exploring, searching, setting her on fire, just as he had promised.

As she adjusted to the exquisite delights unfolding in and around her, Victoria slowly grew more bold. When she stroked his shoulders and then traced the line of his spine down to his hips, Lucas encouraged her with dark, heated words.

"You feel so good, Vicky. Your touch is like none I have ever known."

He brushed himself lightly against her thigh, letting her feel the fullness of his manhood but not forcing her to accept him yet.

Without stopping to think, Victoria reached down to glide her fingertips across the broad tip of his engorged shaft. She gasped a little and drew back when she encountered a bead of moisture.

"Please," Lucas rasped against her breast. "Do it again." He thrust himself back into her palm, asking silently for another caress.

This time Victoria stroked him tentatively with quivering fingers and was delighted with his deep groan of response. She discovered she loved knowing she had such an effect on him.

Slowly he moved on top of her, settling himself between her legs. She felt his hands under her knees, raising them until she was completely open to him. Then he lowered his mouth and kissed her.

"Lift yourself," he urged.

She drew a deep breath and did so cautiously. He was ready and waiting for her. She retreated instantly as she felt him start to enter her. He was very large and solid, she realized. There was no give to him at all. She lifted her lashes and looked up into his stark face.

"I am not at all certain this is going to work," Victoria said tightly.

"It will work. Do not be in such a rush, darling. We have hours yet." He kissed her throat and nibbled tenderly at her ear. "Although I am quite certain I won't be able to wait hours to show you that we will fit together very well indeed. If I did hold off that long, I would be headed for Bedlam in the morning, a ruined man."

She started to laugh nervously at the image, but just as the giggle emerged he slid his palm down over her belly and carefully sought the blossoming petals between her legs with one long finger. Victoria's small giggle turned into a breathless gasp.

Then he was doing the things he had done to her that night in the carriage, the things that would soon make her shiver and cry out against his shoulder. The fabulous spiral of excitement twisted and condensed within her and turned her into a wild, writhing creature of light and energy.

As the storm within her threatened to break, Victoria clutched tightly at Lucas, digging her nails into his shoulders and lifting her hips impulsively against his hand. Her pleas began as small, frantic, cajoling cries of delight and finally were transformed into fierce little feminine demands for release.

"Do you want me now, sweetheart?" Lucas parted her with his fingers and let her feel the broad head of his shaft once more.

This time she did not retreat. "*Yes*. Oh, dear God, yes, my love."

He groaned, his whole body taut with the effort he was exerting to retain his self-control. Slowly he started to sink into her.

Victoria flinched, unprepared for the full force of his intrusion. Much of the dazzling excitement she had been feeling vanished as the pressure built. But she refused to stop now. She had come this far and it was clear that Lucas was at the end of his tether. She could not deny him the same release he had once given so generously to her. She tightened her grip on his arm and braced herself.

"Take it easy, darling, this is not supposed to be an act of martyrdom," Lucas whispered.

"I'm sorry. Please, Lucas, go ahead. I will be all right."

"I want you to be more than all right." His mouth fastened on hers and he withdrew himself from her. He reached down to insert his hand once more between their bodies.

He teased her with his fingers, sliding first one and then another just inside her, stretching her gently, drawing forth the sweet, hot honey. Soon she was once more swept back into the grip of sensual excitement.

This time he waited until she went coiled and taut beneath him, waited until her head tipped back over his arm, waited until she cried out, waited until she began to convulse gently and clutched at him so passionately she left small marks in his skin.

Then and only then did Lucas thrust fully into her in one long, relentless stroke that filled her completely.

He was drinking the last of her soft cries of mingled release and erotic surprise when his own shuddering climax broke over him.

9

Victoria came slowly awake as she realized that the unending pounding she was hearing was the sound of someone knocking forcefully on her door. But that made no sense. Nan would not dream of knocking so impolitely and no one else in the household except her aunt would feel free to barge in on her so early in the morning like this.

But this was not a normal morning. This was the morning after . . .

Victoria's eyes flew open as the full realization of what was happening and where she was struck her. Relief rushed through her as she realized it was still dark outside. She and Lucas were safe. They had time to get back to the ball before dawn. Then she realized she was alone in the bed.

She sat up suddenly, clutching the sheet to her throat, and saw that Lucas was hastily pulling on his breeches near the foot of the bed. He swore softly, grabbed his shirt, and stalked barefoot to the door.

"Lucas, no, *wait*, I have a dreadful feeling you should not open that door."

But it was too late. Lucas had already yanked open the door and was starting to growl ferociously at whoever stood on the other side.

"What the hell is the meaning of this interruption? My wife and I are trying to sleep." There was a shattering pause and then Lucas continued with awful gravity, "I beg your pardon, Lady Nettleship. I certainly did not mean to yell at you. Forgive me. To be perfectly honest, you are the last person I expected to see tonight."

"Yes," Cleo Nettleship said in frozen accents, "I can understand that."

Victoria closed her eyes and lowered her forehead down onto her updrawn knees as the enormity of the disaster struck her.

"If you will give me a few minutes to dress, I will join you downstairs. Under the circumstances you will probably desire a few explanations."

"You are quite correct, sir. But you will answer my first question before I go downstairs. Is my niece all right?"

"Victoria is quite all right, madam. I give you my word."

"Do not be long. It is not yet dawn, but there is very little time to spare. There are decisions that have to be made and acted upon at once, as I am sure you are well aware."

"I understand. I will join you in a few minutes. We will talk while Victoria gets dressed."

Lucas closed the door quietly and turned slowly toward the bed. His face was an unreadable mask in the dim glow of the smoldering fire. "I am sorry, Vicky. As you can see, we have something of a problem."

"Dear heaven, what are we going to do?" She could not seem to get her thoughts in order. It was as if she were swimming in a sea of chaos.

"We will do what must be done, of course." He sat down on the chair and swiftly pulled on his boots. Then he finished dressing with the quick, efficient movements of a military man.

Victoria looked blankly at Lucas. "I do not understand. Why is my aunt here? How could she possibly know about us and this inn? I did not know myself where you would be taking me until we got here. Lucas, none of this makes any sense."

He walked over to the bed and stood looking down at her, his expression grim. "I have no idea what your aunt is doing here or how she found out about us tonight. I assure you, I fully intend to discover the answers. But it makes no real difference now, Vicky. Surely you can see that? We both knew from the outset that there were certain risks involved in this sort of entanglement. We have been caught and there is no way to go back to the beginning. We must deal with the situation as it stands."

She hugged her knees and looked up at him, her eyes wide with uncertainty and a dawning fear. "You sound so very military about all this. And you look like a soldier getting ready for battle. You frighten me, Lucas."

His eyes softened for a moment as he leaned over and caught her face between his rough hands. "This is not how I would have chosen to have had things turn out between us. But now that the dice have fallen this way, all I can do is ask you to put your trust in me. I will take care of you, Victoria. I swear it on my honor."

Before she could think of a reply to that, he was gone, out the door and down the stairs to meet her aunt. Victoria sat perfectly still for a few minutes and then, very slowly, she pushed back the covers and got out of bed.

As she stood up she was chagrined to discover she was sore in places she had never been sore before in her life. She would have given a great deal to have been allowed to relax in a hot bath. But that was impossible.

She felt the unfamiliar weight of the pendant around her throat and reached up to touch the amber figures as if they were a talisman.

Memories of the night sleeted through her mind like silver rain as she made her way to where her clothes waited on a chair. She struggled into her petticoats and gown without nearly as much dexterity as Lucas had demonstrated pulling on his own clothing. She had never before tried to get into a ball gown without the assistance of a maid. It was not easy.

Later, enveloped in her cloak, Victoria drew a deep, steadying breath and went out the door and down the stairs. A concerned-looking innkeeper, who appeared to have been recently rousted from his sleep, showed her to a private parlor.

Victoria stepped through the door, instantly aware of the quiet tension in the room. Lucas stood near the hearth, one arm resting on the mantel, his booted foot propped on a log. Lady Nettleship was seated in a chair at the table. They both looked toward the door as Victoria came into the room.

"Perhaps I have been shown to the wrong parlor," she said wryly. "I seem to have walked in on a funeral."

"I pray you will not consider it such when all is said and done," Aunt Cleo remarked. "Sit down, Victoria."

It had been a long time since her aunt had used that tone. Victoria sat. Her gaze flew to Lucas but she could read nothing in his eyes. There was about him that air of implacable determination which she saw rarely but which never failed to make her feel uneasy.

"Now, then," Cleo said as if calling to order a meeting of her Society for the Investigation of Natural History and Horticulture, "Lucas and I have already discussed what must be done. He is quite prepared to do the proper thing, and you, I trust, are also willing to pay the price of your indiscretion. A marriage by special license can be arranged first thing in the morning. I will attend as a witness so that everyone will know it has my sanction."

Marriage. Victoria's hands clenched together in her lap. All the while she had been struggling into her clothing upstairs she had refused to think about what might happen next. Frantically she tried to calm herself and think rationally.

"There is no need for any of us to overreact," she said cautiously. "I am sorry you had to discover us, Aunt Cleo, but surely if you are the only one who knows about what happened tonight, it can all be hushed up?"

"I did not raise you to be a fool, Vicky. The very fact that I did discover you and Lucas here together means that someone else knows. How do you think I found out?"

Victoria closed her eyes briefly. "Yes, of course. How stupid of me. Forgive me, Aunt Cleo, but how did you find out?"

"A messenger was sent to my friends' house in the country, where I had just finished dinner," Cleo said coldly. "The note was unsigned and merely stated that I would be interested to know that my niece was here at this inn with a man whom I knew to be a friend. I came at once, naturally."

"Naturally." Victoria looked across the room at Lucas. *Marriage*, she repeated silently; marriage to the man she loved. It was not what she would have chosen at the outset, but it did not seem so bad now that she considered it.

Indeed there were certain definite advantages. They would no longer have to conceal their relationship from Society. They could go about freely together in each other's company. They could sleep together every night. No, marriage did not sound so very terrible anymore. "It would take some time to procure a special license," she said.

Lucas met her gaze. "I have one in my pocket. I have been carrying it around for several days."

Her eyes widened in astonishment. "You have? But why on earth would you have one with you?"

"For just such an emergency as this, of course. Why do you think? The risk of discovery has been with us from the moment we met and there were other risks as well. In the event the inevitable happened, I wanted to be prepared to limit the damage as much as possible." He smiled fleetingly. "I learned long ago that it is always wise to have a position to which one can fall back and regroup."

"The military mind at work." Victoria shook her head in unwilling admiration for his strategic planning. "Everyone seems to have considered the potential for disaster except me."

Cleo gave her an oddly pitying glance. "I must confess, Victoria, I am astonished to see that you have precipitated yourself into this sort of situation. It is true you have often flirted with the outrageous in many ways, but you have always been quite cautious in your dealings with men. How on earth could you have let yourself—" She broke off abruptly, glancing at Lucas. "Never mind. I think I know the answer to that. In any event there is no point looking back. We must go forward."

"We cannot move in any direction," Lucas pointed out quietly, "until Victoria has made her decision. She is not a child. She cannot be forced into marriage. I have already offered for her and I would be honored if she will give me her hand in marriage, but I will not coerce her into it."

"Well, Victoria?" Cleo regarded her solemnly. "Lucas is obviously willing to do what must be done. What about you?"

Victoria looked at Lucas, love and longing and guilt and uncertainty twisting themselves into a tight knot in the pit of her stomach. This was all her fault and she knew it. Lucas was in this situation only because he had tried to please her in spite of his better judgment.

It was not only her own honor and her aunt's position in Society she had jeopardized, but Lucas's honor and position as well.

"I am entirely to blame for all that has happened," Victoria said, looking down at her clenched hands. "If Lord Stonevale will do me the great honor of accepting my hand in marriage, then I will give it to him."

There was a taut silence following her words. When Victoria looked up again, she was aware that her aunt had relaxed somewhat, but she only had eyes for Lucas, who was watching her with unwavering intensity.

Without a word he left the hearth and came toward her. He pulled her gently to her feet. "You honor me. Thank you, Vicky. I give you my word I will try to make you happy."

She smiled slowly, a great deal of tension dissolving inside her at the touch of his hands. She loved him and

he obviously cared deeply for her. "I have always considered marriage a fate worse than death, but I believe
that with you I shall view it in an entirely different
light, my lord."

Lucas grinned, his eyes lighting with satisfaction. He
dropped a quick, possessive, little kiss on the tip of her
nose and turned to face Cleo. "Very well, madam, the
worst is over. The lady is resigned to her fate. Now we
must move swiftly and carefully."

Cleo arched her brows. "Somehow I have already
gained the impression that you will see to it we all do
precisely that, Stonevale. I leave everything to you."

Several hours later Victoria conceded with amusement that her aunt's prediction had been absolutely
correct. Matters had moved with blinding speed since
she and Lucas had been married early that morning.
Her aunt's household was in a frenzy as Victoria's bags
were packed in preparation for the hurried departure
for Stonevale. Lucas had decreed and Aunt Cleo had
quickly agreed that leaving for the country was the best
move at this point for all concerned.

"We shall tell everyone that because of your advanced years, neither of you wished for a formal wedding," Cleo had explained to Victoria as she outlined
Lucas's plans. Lucas himself was nowhere around. Directly after the short ceremony he had excused himself
to go home to his own town house to prepare for the
departure.

Victoria had wrinkled her nose at the phrase "advanced years" but she could not quarrel with the rea-
soning. It was a slim excuse for such a hasty marriage,
but it was all they had. There would be plenty of talk as
it was.

"We shall also put it about that Lucas has received
word that there are matters requiring his immediate
attention at Stonevale. The two of you will leave town
this afternoon and spend your honeymoon on his estates while he sees to his lands. With any luck, you will
both be out of town by the time anyone thinks to start
asking questions. When you return in a few weeks, it

will all be a fait accompli, long past the interesting-gossip stage," Cleo explained.

Victoria had inclined her head in demure agreement. The more she grew accustomed to the idea of being married to Lucas Mallory Colebrook, the less burdening and more appealing it all became. As she watched her baggage fill the hall she began to think of the whole thing as a grand adventure, one that would prove even more exciting than her midnight escapades.

Rathbone's announcement an hour later of Lady Jessica Atherton's presence on the doorstep came as a shock.

"She rarely calls on us. She must have gotten word of the wedding. But how could she possibly know about it already?" Victoria demanded of her aunt in dismay.

Cleo exhaled in disgust. "You surely do not need to be told that gossip flows through London like the Thames. It was only a matter of time before Jessica Atherton found out along with everyone else. But I had rather hoped for a bit more time than this. Come, Victoria, it cannot be all that bad. After all, if she were going to cut us dead because of this, she would not be paying a social call, now, would she?" Cleo turned her head toward the drawing-room door.

Jessica Atherton glided swiftly into the room, a vision in pale lavendar, smiling her gracious, condescending smile. She went straight to Cleo and took both the other woman's hands in a gesture of deepest sympathy and understanding.

"Cleo, dear, I was so sorry to hear of this rather hasty business. I knew how you would be feeling, so I came as soon as I heard."

"Very kind of you, Jessica. Pray sit down." Cleo waved her to a nearby chair and slid a chiding glance at Victoria, who was rolling her eyes toward the ceiling. "Just how did you come to hear of Victoria's recent marriage?"

"Why, the news is all over Town, of course." Jessica smiled pityingly at Victoria. "You have always been so impetuous, Vicky. It would have been far wiser to do things in a more proper fashion, but there is no denying this is an excellent match for both you and Lucas and I want you to know you have my heartfelt congratulations."

Victoria forced a grudging smile of gratitude. The problem with dealing with Jessica was that one always had the impression one should be grateful. It was very wearing. "Thank you, Jessica."

Jessica settled deeper into the cushions of her chair. "You are quite welcome. Do try not to worry much about the gossip. There is bound to be some, of course, but it will fade with time. As you can see I have already taken steps to help squelch it by paying this call today. Few will disapprove openly when they learn that I have been here to call upon you and lend countenance to the match."

Cleo's brows rose. "You are quite right, Jessica. How very considerate of you to act so swiftly on Victoria's behalf."

"As you know, Lucas is an old friend of mine and I can do no less than make his bride feel welcome." Jessica reached out and patted one of Victoria's hands.

"My aunt is right," Victoria managed. "You are most thoughtful, Jessica."

Jessica's smile took on the aura of a benign saint's. "Do you know, Lady Nettleship, I have often heard about your impressive conservatory. I wonder if Victoria might take a moment to show it to me since I am here."

"But, of course. Show her the conservatory, Vicky," Cleo said quickly, obviously relieved to get out of the duty of playing hostess. "I am sure Jessica will enjoy the new roses from China."

Victoria got to her feet, trying to hide her reluctance. But as she led Jessica Atherton down the hall toward the conservatory, she chided herself for being churlish. Jessica was going out of her way to do a favor for Lucas and herself. The least she could do was act properly grateful to the woman.

"What a perfectly charming collection of plants," Jessica said as she was shown into the glass-walled room. "Quite delightful."

She started down one aisle, pausing to examine several small items along the way. Victoria followed, offering desultory comments on the various species of roses and irises that passed beneath Jessica's graciously approving gaze.

But as they made their way to the far end of the room, Victoria became aware that Jessica was paying less and less attention to the plants she was admiring. In fact, by the time they reached the end of the aisle, Jessica's expression had changed considerably.

Victoria stifled a groan of dismay as it dawned on her that Jessica had asked for the tour because she wanted to have a few words in private.

Jessica halted abruptly near a blood red parrot tulip. She seemed to gather herself. When she spoke, it was in a soft, urgent little voice. "You will be a good wife to him, will you not, Vicky?" Jessica did not meet Victoria's eyes, pretending to study the tulip instead. "He deserves a good wife."

Victoria's first response to the impertinent, highly personal question was anger. She quelled it. Jessica meant well and it was clear she cared about Lucas's happiness. "I assure you I shall do my best, Jessica."

"Yes, I am sure you will try. It is just that you are hardly his type, are you? I knew it from the beginning, but he kept insisting you would do."

"What type did you think he preferred, Jessica?"

Jessica's eyes squeezed shut for a moment. "A woman who will make him an admirable hostess and see to the management of his home in a proper fashion. A woman who will give him an heir and ensure that his children are raised to take their positions in Society. A well-behaved woman who knows her duty and fulfills it without complaint. A woman who will endeavor to make his life comfortable in every way. One who will not plague him with silly demands nor give him any trouble or cause for embarrassment. Lucas is a very proud man, you know."

Victoria made another bid for her patience. "I assure you again I will do my best. In any event, he seems quite satisfied with the bargain."

"Yes, he has made his decision. Lucas is a man who

knows his own mind and acts accordingly. He is aware of the responsibilities his title has brought him. He told me this marriage would suit him well and I pray he is right."

"Lucas has already spoken to you of our marriage, Jessica?" Victoria was suddenly paying complete attention to her maddening visitor.

"Naturally. Lucas felt he could confide in me right from the start. We have, as I explained, known each other for several years. We understand each other." Jessica's fingers trailed gracefully along a long leaf. "Dear Lucas. I know I hurt him dreadfully when I was forced to refuse his offer of marriage four years ago. But when he found himself in the same position a few months ago, he finally understood why I had done what I did. He felt he could come to me for help."

Victoria swallowed thickly. "I had not realized. . . ."

"Lucas comprehends the notion of duty better than most men and he knows now that I only did what was necessary when I accepted Lord Atherton's offer instead of his. Marriage is a matter of duty and practicality, is it not? One does what one must."

Victoria grew cold. "I was not aware that you and Lucas knew each other quite so well," she finally managed.

"Very well, indeed." A glimmer of moisture appeared at the edge of Jessica's dark lashes and splashed down onto the rose petal where it glistened like a drop of dew. "You cannot imagine how hard it was for me when he sought me out after all this time to tell me he had inherited his uncle's title and would be needing a suitable wife."

Victoria stared at Jessica's lovely profile and watched another teardrop fall to the petals of the rose. "A suitable wife," she heard herself echo, sounding stupid, even to her own ears.

"He asked me to introduce him into the sort of social circles where he could meet the sort of woman he needed."

"How did Lucas describe this woman he sought?" Victoria asked, her mouth going dry.

"Well, his first requirement, of course, was that she be an heiress."

"An heiress." Victoria felt dazed.

"As I am certain you must realize by now, the business about his uncle having died with a fortune hidden under the bed is all rubbish. I put the story about myself so that people would not suspect the true state of Lucas's financial affairs."

Victoria stiffened. "Yes, of course. How very clever of you."

"I did my best," Jessica said with tragic pride. "I could not refuse to help him, not after all we had once meant to each other. But there have been times when I confess it was difficult watching him court you."

"I can imagine." Victoria wanted to pick up the nearest flowerpot and hurl it through one of the glass walls of the conservatory.

"When I got word this morning that you and Lucas had been married so precipitously, I told myself it was best this way. I know Lucas needs this marriage if he is to salvage his estates, and it would be easier on him, as well as me, to get the business done as quickly as possible."

"What about me, Jessica? Or did you consider me at all when you arranged to introduce me to Lucas?"

Jessica turned to her then, briefly considering her words. "You? What have you to complain of? You were in danger of spending the rest of your life on the shelf. Instead you are now a countess. You are married to Lucas. What more could you want?"

"To have been allowed to have spent the rest of my life on the shelf, perhaps?" Victoria's hands tightened into small fists at her sides. "Believe what you wish when you say you were only doing a favor for Lucas but do not lie to yourself about what you have done to me. I assure you, I am not at all grateful for your interference. *How could you have done such a cruel, heartless thing to me?*"

Without waiting for an answer, Victoria whirled on her heel and started down the aisle toward the door.

"Vicky, wait, please wait. You must not be angry. I

thought you understood. You are an intelligent woman. Indeed, you are known for your quick mind. I thought that at your age you would surely realize that your inheritance was your chief attraction. I mean, why else would a man want to offer for a woman who is inclined to such outrageous behavior, such an ungoverned female who has no—" Jessica broke off, looking haunted. "That is to say, I assumed you were as satisfied with the bargain as Lucas is. You have got yourself an earl, after all."

Victoria halted and spun around. "And Lucas has my money. You are quite right, Jessica. It is a bargain we have both made and now we must live with it. But you have done your part. You need not concern yourself further in our lives."

Jessica's eyes widened and more tears glistened and pearled on her lashes. "I am sorry if you are not content. But you are a woman and you must know it is not our lot to be content. Only a schoolgirl expects to marry for love. We all do what we must. If you cannot bring yourself to feel any real affection for Lucas, only think how hard this is on him. This is going to be just as difficult for him as it is for you. After all, he must have an heir from you."

"Thank you for reminding me of my wifely duty."

"Dear heaven, you truly are angry. You do not comprehend at all. I believed you did. Victoria, please, I am sorry. You cannot know how sorry." Jessica dissolved completely into tears, groping frantically for a handkerchief.

Victoria hesitated, torn between fury and a reluctant sympathy she did not want to feel. Jessica's tears were real.

Then, annoyed with herself but unable to ignore the sobbing woman, she went forward and hesitantly touched Jessica's arm.

"You must not do this to yourself, Jessica. You will make yourself ill. Pull yourself together. What is done is done. I do not hold you responsible. I made my own decisions at every point along the way. I have no one but myself to blame for what has happened."

Jessica gulped back her sobs and clutched helplessly at Victoria, who found herself patting her awkwardly.

"Please, I beg you, Vicky, do not hold any of this against Lucas. He only did what he had to do for the sake of his title."

Victoria tried to think of a response that would not further alarm the weeping woman. But there was nothing to be said. The truth was she wanted to do a great deal of damage to the Earl of Stonevale. Even as the images formed in her head, she heard his voice in the hall.

"Vicky? Whr way. Your aunt says you have not yet changed into your traveling dress." His boots rang on the tile of the conservatory as he stepped into the room, looking for her. He glanced briefly around, frowning impatiently, and then his eyes collided with hers over Jessica's heaving shoulders.

Victoria watched dispassionately as Lucas registered just who it was who was crying her heart out in his wife's arms.

"Lady Atherton has come to give us her good wishes, my lord. Was that not kind of her under the circumstances? I understand that you and she are extremely close friends of very long standing and that she has been of great assistance in securing an heiress for you. It appears the rumors of your uncle's hoarded wealth were quite unfounded. Now, if you will excuse me, I believe I shall leave the two of you alone together to make your good-byes. I certainly would not wish to intrude."

Realization dawned in Lucas's gaze. He did not move. "Damn it to hell, Vicky," he said very softly.

She smiled grimly. "My sentiments precisely."

She freed herself from Jessica's grasp and stepped around her, heading toward the door. When she reached the point in the aisle where Lucas blocked her path, she looked up at him and said nothing.

"We will talk later," he promised through his teeth.

"There does not appear to be a great deal left to say. If you will excuse me, my lord?"

He moved reluctantly out of her way, his eyes gleaming with frustrated anger. "Do not be long in dressing for the trip, Vicky. I want to get started as soon as possible. We have a long drive ahead of us."

She did not bother to respond to that. It took all her concentration simply to get through the door without hurling some of the cacti at his head.

Victoria was trembling with fury and raw pain by the time she reached her bedchamber. She walked into the room to discover an excited Nan fussing with several last-minute items.

"Oh, there you are, ma'am. I've almost finished. Albert says the last of the bags is going into the coach now and the horses are ready. You must hurry and change. I hear his lordship just arrived and is impatient to be on his way."

"There is no rush, Nan. I will not be going anywhere today. Please be so good as to leave me in peace until I send for you."

Nan's mouth fell open in shock. "What are you saying, ma'am? His lordship has already given strict instructions that we are not to delay. He will be furious if he hears we're dawdling up here."

"Please go, Nan."

Nan bit her lip. She had rarely seen her mistress in this mood and it was obvious she was not at all certain what to do. She opted to retreat for the moment. "Would a dish o' tea help, ma'am? If yer not feelin' well, I'm sure his lordship would understand a short wait for tea."

"I do not want tea, only some peace."

"Dear me, there will be the devil to pay for this bit o' nonsense," Nan mumbled as she went to the door. "Men don't take kindly to delays when they're waitin' to set off on a trip, especially not them that's used to givin' orders to fightin' men in the field. Accustomed to havin' people jump when they say jump, that type is."

Victoria watched the door close behind her muttering maid and then she went slowly over to the window. Jessica Atherton's elegant carriage was waiting on the street below. As Victoria watched she saw Lucas escort his former love down the steps and put her into the vehicle. He ordered the coachman to be off, turned, and stalked grimly back up the steps into the house.

A moment later she was not surprised to hear hurried footsteps in the hall outside her room and the inevitable knock on her door.

"His lordship wishes to talk to you, my lady." Nan's voice was muffled by the closed door. "He says 'tis terribly urgent."

Victoria crossed the room and opened the door. "Tell his lordship I am indisposed."

"Oh, please, ma'am, don't make me tell him that. He is not in a good temper just now, truly he isn't."

"To hell with his temper." Victoria closed the door in Nan's shocked face. Then she went back to her post by the window to idly watch the last of her luggage loaded into the traveling coach Cleo had insisted on loaning the newly married couple.

The next knock on the door was, predictably enough, Aunt Cleo's. "Vicky, dear, open up at once. What is this nonsense? Your husband wishes to be off without delay. Ex–military men are not very good about unnecessary delays."

Victoria sighed and crossed the room again to open the door. "Tell my husband that he is free to leave anytime he chooses. Tell him not to wait upon me as I shall not be coming with him."

Cleo eyed her severely. "So that's the way of it, is it?" She walked into the room and closed the door. "I thought there was something distinctly odd about Lady Atherton's visit this morning. What in the world did she say to upset you so?"

"Did you know that Lucas once asked her to marry him?"

"No, but I hardly see that it matters. Lucas is thirty-four years old. Stands to reason you aren't the first woman he's asked to marry him. Is that what has upset you? Come now, Vicky, you are far too intelligent to fly up into the boughs over a minor fiddle like that. Whatever happened between those two occurred years ago," Cleo said.

"She was unable to accept his offer of marriage because he did not have either a title or sufficient financial resources to suit her or her family."

"Well, that is her problem, is it not? Lucas has his title now. I fail to see how all this affects you, Vicky."

"Lucas inherited the title," Victoria said coolly. "But there was apparently very little money to go with it. Jessica explained that his lordship came to the conclusion he would be obliged to marry an heiress for the sake of his damned title and he asked his dear friend Lady Atherton to arrange an introduction to a suitable female. Would you care to hazard a guess as to just which female of your acquaintance was thus honored?"

Cleo's brows climbed in their characteristic gesture. "I'd sooner hazard a guess as to just which female of my acquaintance obligingly made herself a bed and now complains because she must sleep in it. If she has half the common sense I trust she has, she will attend to the business of making that bed a comfortable one for both herself and her husband."

Victoria blinked at the unexpected lack of support. She crossed her arms under her breasts and stared at her aunt. "You do not seem unduly shocked by all this."

"Forgive me. I have already had to deal with the shock of finding you in that inn last night. One shock at a time is sufficient at my age."

Victoria felt herself turning an angry red. She looked away. "Yes, of course. I am sorry for that. Far more sorry now than I was when you first discovered us, I assure you."

Cleo's face softened. "Vicky dear, I fear you are letting yourself be unnecessarily upset. I am not surprised to hear that Lucas is not as well off as you had assumed. He told me the truth this morning while we waited for you to dress at the inn."

"He told you he was marrying me for my money?"

"He told me he had asked to be introduced to you because he was, to be blunt, hanging out for an heiress. But he said that he was marrying you because he had become quite fond of you and decided you would make him a very suitable wife in every respect."

"*Fond* of me. How very gracious of him," Victoria said.

"Victoria, I shall be quite blunt with you. I knew from the first that you were probably bound to get into trouble with Stonevale. There is something between the two of you that fairly crackles in the air when you are in the same room together. But I rather liked him and I decided that if you were to risk everything for a man, it might as well be with him."

"I am so glad you approve, Aunt Cleo."

"There is no need to take that tone with me. You are the one who brought yourself to this pass."

Victoria looked down at the pattern of the carpet and then raised her eyes to meet her aunt's sympathetic, but unyielding gaze. "You are right, as usual. Now I must decide how to proceed."

Aunt Cleo softened her tone. "The first thing you must do is change into your traveling clothes. Lucas is determined to be on his way this afternoon and I must say I think he is absolutely correct. The sooner you are out of town, the better."

"I have no intention of going anywhere with Stonevale."

"Vicky, you are being unreasonable. You have no choice but to go with him."

Before Cleo could say more, there was a desperate pounding on the door. Nan's voice came clearly through the wood. "Forgive me, ma'am, but his lordship says to tell you that if yer not so obligin' as to come downstairs immediately, he'll be obliged to come up here and fetch you down."

Lucas would do it, too. Victoria did not fool herself on that score. There was no point in delaying the inevitable interview. She stepped past her aunt and then, her hand on the doorknob, she turned and looked at Cleo. "I have certainly got myself a most charming and gallant husband, have I not? What bride could ask for more?"

10

He was waiting for her in the library, standing near the window that looked out onto the garden where he had so often waited for her at midnight. Victoria walked into the room and heard the door close very softly behind her. A respectful hush seemed to have fallen over the household, as if everyone was holding his or her breath.

The entire staff, including her maid and Rathbone, was moving with great caution, she noticed. Lucas had only been her husband for a few hours and he was technically a guest under her aunt's roof, but he had clearly established himself as a figure of authority. No one wanted to risk his temper. That was left for Victoria to brave.

"You sent for me, my lord?" she asked, taking refuge in an icy, correct politeness.

He watched her come part way into the room and halt. His expression was starkly controlled. "You have not changed into your traveling dress."

It took more courage than she had expected to face him and tell him her decision. "For the very good reason that I will not be joining you. I wish you a good journey, my lord." She swung around on her heel and started for the door.

"If you walk out on me now, Vicky, you will regret it more than you can possibly imagine."

The deadly soft tone stopped her as nothing else would have. She turned back to face him. "I beg your pardon. Did you have something else you wished to say to me?"

"A great deal. But the time grows late and I would rather have this conversation in the coach than here in your aunt's library. For now, however, I will only say that I apologize for Lady Atherton's emotional outburst. I assure you, I had no idea she would fall apart in such an unfortunate manner."

"Yes, her timing was rather poor, was it not? When had you planned to tell me the truth, yourself?"

"What truth would you have me tell you? That I once asked Jessica to marry me? That is old news, Vicky, and need not concern us."

"Damn you," she hissed. "You know very well which truth interests me now. You deliberately set out to form a connection with me because I am an heiress. Do you have the gall to deny it?"

Lucas held her cold glare. "No. You guessed as much at the time, if you will recall. I seem to have a very clear memory of your warning me off. But you wanted what I offered, regardless, didn't you? You played a risky game and you lost, but it was your choice to play. Did you not once inform me that there was no real risk without real danger?"

"Must you throw my stupidity in my face like this?"

"Why not? It is little more than you expect from me, is it not? I am nothing but a heartless fortune hunter who has snagged himself an heiress."

She felt as if she had been punched in the stomach. "And now you expect me to accept my humiliation without protest?"

He crossed the room in a few short strides and gripped her upper arms. His eyes were blazing. "I expect you to show some trust in me, damn you. For the past few weeks you've been willing enough to trust me with your safety and your honor. Now that you are my wife, I expect no less."

"Trust you? After what you have done to me?"

"What have I done that is so wicked? I did not set us up to be discovered last night. I told you the entire plan was dangerous, but you had to have your night of *intellectual inquiry* at all costs, remember?"

"Don't you dare mock me, Lucas."

"I am not mocking you. I am reminding you of how you tried to justify your desire to let me make love to you. You wanted what happened last night as much as I did. Hell, you even told me you loved me."

Victoria shook her head, her eyes moist. "I told you I *thought* I loved you. I was obviously mistaken."

"You gave me the painting of *Strelitzia reginae* and then you gave yourself to me without any reservations. I believed you did love me, madam. When your aunt knocked on the door, my first instinct was to protect you. What would you have had me do? Refuse to offer marriage?"

"Pray do not twist my words. You saw the opening you had been waiting for and you took it. Do not bother to deny it."

"I will not deny that I wanted to marry you. I would not have risked your honor or my own last night if I had not been certain that sooner or later we would be married. It was unfortunate that your aunt discovered us and precipitated this chain of events, but the end result was inevitable."

"There was nothing inevitable about it," she stormed.

"Vicky, be reasonable. You must see that we could not have carried on as we had been for much longer. Things were getting shaky enough even before we went off together last night. People were starting to talk and you were doing nothing to stem the gossip. We were taking dangerous risks to indulge your midnight whims. Sooner or later we would have been discovered, and once that happened neither of us would have had a choice. There was also the possibility you'd get pregnant, did you think of that?"

"Why could you not have told the whole truth before

any of it started?" She could hear her voice climbing toward the hysterical shriek of an enraged fishwife. Frantically she fought to control herself.

"To be perfectly blunt, I told you nothing because I was out to win you and I was afraid that if I went into a great deal of detail about my personal financial circumstances, you wouldn't give me a chance. You were so adamant about not getting married, so skittish on the subject of fortune hunters, that I had no choice but to woo you in the only way you allowed. You will never know how hard the past few weeks have been on me, Vicky. The least you could do is show some consideration and kindness."

She was incredulous. "Kindness? How dare you attempt to make me feel sorry for you now?"

"Why not? You are quite prepared to be kind to everyone else, up to and including Lady Atherton. I saw the way you were trying to offer her some comfort as she wept all over your shoulder in the conservatory." Lucas released her abruptly and ran his fingers through his hair. "Why shouldn't I try to gain a little kindness for myself? After all, I am your husband and God knows that role is not going to be an easy one."

"What have you got to offer in return?"

He took a deep breath. "I will do my damnedest to be a good husband to you. You have my word on it."

"And just how do you interpret the notion of being a good husband to me?" She rubbed her hands over her forearms where his fingers had gripped her tightly enough to leave red marks. "Obviously you will not have to provide financial support. I am the one supplying the capital in this marriage, according to your former love. You do bring me a title. I'll grant you that much, but I have never been overly concerned with titles."

Lucas's mouth tightened. "I also brought you the adventure you had been seeking."

"You mean you tricked me with adventure."

"Vicky, listen to me. . . ."

"There is one thing I must know, Lucas. Do you intend to begin a romantic liaison with Lady Atherton now that you have taken care of the business of getting married?"

"God, no. 'Tis plain you don't think much of my integrity at the moment, but if you knew Jessica as well as you think you do, you would realize the whole idea of a romantic liaison with her is out of the question."

Victoria winced. "Forgive me. Of course it is. Lady Atherton is a paragon of all that is proper. She would not dream of getting involved in an illicit affair with you."

"Quite right."

"She is such a noble creature. She had no qualms at all, apparently, about following the dictates of duty rather than her heart four years ago when she accepted Lord Atherton's offer instead of yours."

"She did what she was obligated to do," Lucas said impatiently.

"How dreadfully understanding you are about the entire matter," Vicky said.

"Four years is a long time," Lucas said with a shrug. "And to tell you the truth, I am greatly relieved now not to be married to Jessica. Lately I have come to realize it would have been a bad match."

Victoria gave him a sidelong glance. "Why do you say that? She seems so very perfect for you. She is obviously the sort who would be a dutiful wife, being, as we have just noted, a paragon of female behavior."

"Sheathe your claws, Vicky." Lucas's mouth quirked faintly. "The fact is, I find her rather dull. I have discovered recently that I prefer a more adventurous sort of female. And after last night, I would have to say that I also prefer a more passionate sort."

"Really?" Victoria's chin rose. "You speak from experience, I presume? You have had an opportunity to compare my performance in bed with that of Lady Atherton's?"

Lucas's smile broadened into a wicked grin. "Don't be a goose, Vicky. Even in your wildest flights of imagination, can you possibly envisage Jessica sneaking off to an inn with me or any other man? I assure you, she was just as prim and proper four years ago as she is today.

She would never have risked her reputation for a man
or a night of the sort of intellectual inquiry we shared at
that inn."

Victoria sighed. "Unlike me."

"Yes. Unlike you. Completely unlike you. In fact, I
have never met a woman who is anything like you. You
are quite unique, Vicky. Which is why I am not always
certain just how to handle you, I suppose. But I assure
you, I fully intend to do my best. Now, we have wasted
far too much time on this pointless discussion. Go upstairs and change at once." He glanced at the clock.
"You have fifteen minutes."

"For the last time, my lord, I am not going anywhere
with you."

She jumped slightly when he moved without any
warning, covering the short distance between them
with his distinctive, oddly balanced stride. He caught
her chin on the edge of his hand and forced her to look
up at him. When she did, she froze. The full, un-
leashed force of his will glittered in his eyes.

Victoria suddenly understood why men had followed
Lucas into battle and why everyone else in the household was walking about with such extreme care.

"Victoria," he said, "it occurs to me that you do not
fully comprehend just how serious I am about leaving
in fifteen minutes. That is no doubt my fault. Until now
I have been so indulgent of your headstrong ways, so
willing to ignore my own better judgment in an effort to
please you, that you are obviously under the impression
you can disregard a direct order from me. I assure you,
that is not the case."

"I do not take orders from you or any other man."

"You do now, Vicky. For better or worse, you have a
husband and he means to leave London in"—he paused
to glance at the tall clock—"thirteen minutes. If you are
not dressed for traveling when he is ready to go, he will
personally put you into the coach in whatever garment
you happen to have on at the time. Is that very clear,
madam?"

Victoria sucked in her breath, realizing he would do
exactly as he said. "You appear to hold the whip hand,

my lord," she drawled in a scathing tone. "And like most men, you do not hesitate to use it."

"I assure you, I would never use a whip on you, Vicky, and you know it. Now stop trying my patience. You have less than twelve minutes left."

Victoria turned and fled.

The journey into the distant wilds of Yorkshire was the longest Victoria had ever endured in her life. She saw very little of her husband along the way. Lucas spent most of his time outside the coach, choosing to ride his stallion, George, alongside the vehicle, rather than deal with Victoria's temper. At night she and Nan shared a room at the inns where they stopped and Lucas took a separate room for himself and his valet. Meals were a series of chillingly polite affairs.

By the time they reached Stonevale, Victoria's mood had not improved one bit and she suspected Lucas's hadn't either, although he seemed content to ignore her as long as she gave him no trouble.

Her first view of the lands surrounding her new home was not inspiring. It did not take even her extensive background in horticulture and botany to detect that this summer's crops would be mediocre at best. There was a generally depressed atmosphere about everything she saw, from the farmers' run-down cottages to the gaunt animals standing listlessly in the fields.

The lack of goods in the village shop windows emphasized the economic gloom that hung over the area like a dark cloud. Victoria frowned at the sight of several children playing in the dirt. Their clothing was as bad as any street urchin's in London.

"This is inexcusable," she muttered to Nan. "These lands have been allowed to wither and die."

"I reckon his lordship has a sizable job ahead o' him," Nan offered cautiously. She was well aware of her mistress's feelings about the earl. "He'll earn his fancy title, he will, if he manages to put some life back into this place."

"Yes, he certainly will," Victoria agreed grimly. And he'll need my money to do it, she added silently. For the first time she began to realize the magnitude of the responsibility Lucas had faced when he had inherited Stonevale. Everyone living in and around the estate depended on the general prosperity and leadership of the great house that dominated the economy. Victoria was well aware that the fortunes and futures of the local tenants and villagers were closely tied to Stonevale.

If she had been handed the task of salvaging these lands, would she have been above marrying for money? She wondered. Probably not. As Lady Atherton had said, damn her, one did what one must.

That acknowledgment did not make Victoria feel any more charitable toward Lucas, however. She might be able to understand his need to marry an heiress; she would never forgive him for choosing her and tricking her into this marriage. Surely he could have found a willing sacrifice if he had been willing to search for one among the ladies of the *ton*. There were those who would have traded a fortune for a landed title.

"It's a lovely house, ain't it, ma'am?" Nan said, leaning eagerly out of the coach window to catch the first glimpse of the great house of Stonevale. "Pity the grounds and garden are so shabby. Not like Lady Nettleship's country place at all."

Victoria found herself leaning forward for a look, although she had vowed she would adopt an air of disdainful aloofness about everything concerning Lucas's home.

Her maid was right. Stonevale was a magnificent house. The stone facade was imposing and well proportioned. The wide front steps descended to a cobbled courtyard and a huge curving drive. A large fountain and pool decorated the middle of the curve. But the pool was full of rubble instead of water. The fountain was silent.

There was the same air of depression and hopelessness about the house as there was about the village and surrounding fields. Victoria stared at her new home with a sense of dismay as the coach halted. It was all a far cry from the luxurious, comfortable, well-gardened world she had known with her aunt.

Lucas turned his mount over to a groom and came forward to escort Victoria up the steps and into the house.

"As you can see," he said quietly, "there is much to be done."

"That is certainly an accurate observation, my lord." She was feeling somewhat dazed.

"I would like us to share the task together, Vicky. We both have a stake in Stonevale. It is your home now as well as mine. It will be our children's home."

She flinched at that, recalling more of Jessica Atherton's words. *If you cannot bring yourself to have any real affection for Lucas, only think how hard this is on him. He must have an heir from you.*

Victoria composed her features immediately, but she knew Lucas had seen her brief expression of anger because his own face hardened. "I will introduce you to the staff, although as yet there is not much of it. The butler's name is Griggs. He's from my London staff. The housekeeper is Mrs. Sneath. She's from the village."

Exhausted from the long trip, depressed by what she had seen of Stonevale, and too proud to give an inch in response to Lucas's small overtures, Victoria picked up her skirts and climbed the stairs to her new bedchamber.

Dinner that night was not an impressive affair. Griggs apologized for the poor quality of the wine and the lack of footmen to serve. The food was limited, both in quality and selection. The surroundings were even less prepossessing than the food. The carpet was threadbare, the furniture scarred and unpolished, the silver tarnished. The chandelier overhead had obviously not been cleaned in years.

But it was the grim silence at the table that really got to Victoria. She was not a creature of long silences and she had almost reached the end of her ability to maintain one. It annoyed her now that Lucas seemed oblivious to her efforts.

"Well, my lord," she began after fortifying herself with a large sip of wine. "Where do you propose to begin spending my money? On the gardens, perhaps?

Or the tenants' farms? Or maybe you would like to refurnish the house itself? It certainly needs it."

Lucas swirled the wine in his glass and regarded her for a moment. "Where would you like to start, Vicky?"

"Why would my feelings on the subject matter to you? Salvaging Stonevale is your project, not mine." She smiled a cold, brittle smile. "And now that you have my money, I am certain you will think of lots of ways to spend it. My stepfather certainly had no problem spending my mother's money on his horses and his women."

"It occurs to me, madam, that you are in this fix in the first place because you lacked a suitable challenge in your life."

She glared at him. "What is that supposed to mean?"

"You are a woman of intelligence and energy who happened to have access to a great deal of money. You used that money to buy your independence and finance your social life, but you did not use it to do anything else particularly useful."

That stung. "I have always given large sums to charities."

"Which demanded very little of your time or skills. Furthermore, you had neither a husband nor a family to absorb your considerable energies. Other than your interest in botanical painting and the occasional scientific lecture, you did not devise anything else of a serious nature to occupy your time and ability. Your only outlet for action was your social life. So you got bored and started looking for adventure. And that, my dear, is what got you into trouble."

Victoria was incensed. "I was not bored with town life, sir, I assure you."

"No? I rather think it was boredom that led you to dream up your midnight escapades."

She paled. "That is not true. You know nothing of why I sought my midnight adventures and I would appreciate it if you refrained from making silly conjectures."

He shook his head thoughtfully. "No, I believe I am correct in my logic. You were initially attracted to me solely because I was willing to give you the adventure you wanted. If you dislike the notion of being married for your money, how do you think I felt knowing that my primary appeal for you was that I could offer you some fleeting excitement? You were perfectly willing to use me for your own ends, were you not?"

"That is not true," she retorted before stopping to think.

"No? Are you admitting your feelings for me went deeper than a frivolous desire to use me to provide you with the adventure you wanted?"

Victoria scowled at him. "Yes, I mean no. Damn it, Lucas, you are twisting my words."

"Either way, you are here now, madam, and there is no going back. You were aware of the risks and you chose to run them. The first rule of gaming, my sweet, is learning how to pay up without whimpering when you lose. If you play, you pay," Lucas said.

"I am not whimpering. I am furious. There is a vast difference."

Lucas leaned back and folded his arms. "You are sulking, Vicky. It is nothing more than that. Having never dealt with you in this mood, I will admit I'm curious to see how long it will last. I had hoped you would be through the worst of it by the time we got here, but it appears I was wrong."

"Yes, it certainly does appear that you were wrong." She was vibrating with the force of her anger. The injustice of his accusations was intolerable. "Completely wrong."

"You should be grateful to me, Vicky. I am offering you a way to avoid future disasters of the sort that led you into this situation. I am pleased to be able to give you a project that will in turn give you something important to do both with your time and your money." Lucas looked at her. "Help me restore Stonevale and its lands."

"How kind of you to refer to it as *my* money."

"Vicky, I want you to be a part of this place. I want you to share it with me. I admit that I can do nothing without access to your inheritance, but I do not intend to spend your money without consulting you. I am more than happy to involve you in every detail. You have a good mind and a vast store of knowledge, thanks to the way you have been raised. You can be a tremendous influence on what happens here at Stonevale. All I ask is that you work with me instead of amusing yourself with a fit of the sulks."

"What you offer is certainly very exciting to say the least," she said in silky tones. "If you are so eager to include me in every little decision, then perhaps you would like to consider giving me a written wedding contract? One in which you guarantee not to touch a penny of my money without my consent?"

His mouth curved ruefully. "I am not a complete fool, madam. It would be the height of idiocy for me to have such a contract drawn up while you are in your present mood. Perhaps we can discuss the matter again when you have decided you are ready to be a true and loving wife to me."

"Hah. You would never give me such a contract and we both know it."

"Even if I did, it would carry little real weight under the law, Vicky. We are husband and wife. That relationship will always give me certain rights."

"It is the principle of the thing."

Lucas smiled briefly. "The hell it is. If I were to give you such a contract right now, you would use it to get even with me for this marriage. Admit it, Vicky. You are not accustomed to being outmaneuvered and all you can think of at the moment is revenge."

"At least the notion of revenge has the undeniable advantage of providing me with something useful to occupy my time and energy, does it not?" She smiled coldly and rose to her feet. "Now, if you will excuse me, my lord, I fear I am not yet done feeling sorry for myself. I believe I shall retire to my bedchamber and sulk for a while."

Griggs scrambled to open the door for her as she swept out of the dining room.

Lucas watched his wife's magnificent exit through hooded eyes and then signaled the butler for the port he had brought with him from London. His leg ached from the long days of riding it had recently endured.

For a considerable length of time Lucas sipped the port and contemplated which he would rather do: strangle Jessica Atherton or turn Victoria over his knee.

On the whole, turning his wife over his knee sounded far and away the more interesting option. He would give a lot right now for another glimpse of her enticingly curved backside.

Lucas slowly and deliberately worked his way through the bottle of port in splendid solitude. The wine was useful for something besides dulling the ache in his thigh. It also took some of the edge off his frustrated desire. Since that hot, sweet night of illicit passion at the inn, he had been plagued with memories that pushed his normally ironclad self-control to the limits.

He could not believe that Victoria was not haunted by the same memories. She had been so responsive, so magnificent in her passion, so welcoming and trusting. Damn it, he thought, she had even told him she thought she was in love with him, and he was quite certain she had never said as much to any other man.

And he knew for a fact that she had never given herself to anyone else. The joy of watching her sensual discovery had been the most erotic experience he had ever known.

The painting of *Strelitzia reginae* was already hanging on the wall upstairs near his dressing table, where he would be able to see it every morning. Lucas had directed that it be among the first of his personal items that were unpacked. He wondered if Victoria had any idea how much the small gift had meant to him.

Probably not. She was not thinking of anything else at the moment except her savaged pride.

He had been startled to find himself so deeply touched by *Strelitzia*. Perhaps it was because it was the first gift any woman had ever given him since his mother had died. He refused to count the keepsake locket with a wisp of dark hair in it that Jessica Atherton had given him four years ago.

She had pressed it into his palm even as she had

tearfully rejected his offer of marriage and explained where her duty lay. He had tossed the locket into a ditch one night on the eve of a battle.

Lucas finished the last of the port and contemplated the empty bottle. Then he contemplated the notion of the empty bed that awaited him.

If matters had not exploded in his face the way they had, he would be back in his London town house preparing to climb a certain garden wall tonight. His reckless, passionate midnight companion would be waiting eagerly for the night's adventure.

But things had changed. He was married to the little baggage now and somehow he had to find a way to deal with her. He refused to spend the rest of his days with a sulking wife and he was even more certain he was not going to spend his nights alone in his own bedchamber.

It was so damn easy for Victoria to be kind to everyone else, Lucas thought in annoyance as he got to his feet. Why could she not spare a little kindness for her husband? Surely she must realize he had not had a lot of choice in his actions lately.

A man in his position had no option but to secure an heiress in any manner he could. Victoria was old enough to understand the realities of marriage. In any event, the deed was done and there was nothing for it but for Victoria to accept the situation with good grace. This sulking business would have to stop. He would not tolerate her ill humor much longer.

Nor would he tolerate a lonely bed for long. He was a married man now and that gave him certain rights and privileges.

With a hardening sense of determination, Lucas stalked out of the dining room and up the staircase. He would make one more effort to talk to Victoria tonight, and if she still refused to listen to him, he swore he would find another way to take the edge off her temper.

His valet, Ormsby, was busy in the master bedchamber, still unpacking. He glanced up with surprise as Lucas entered the room.

"Good evening, sir. Did you wish to retire early tonight?"

"Yes, as a matter of fact, I do. Tell Griggs to send the staff to bed, too. It has been a long trip for everyone."

Ormsby nodded. "Will you be needing anything for your leg, sir? It generally bothers you after long hours in the saddle."

"I have just finished a bottle of port. That should take care of it."

"Very good, sir." Ormsby moved about with soothing efficiency. "Nan told me that Lady Stonevale has also retired for the evening. If this is any indication, it appears we shall all be keeping rather different hours here in the country than we did in Town."

"Just as well. I much prefer country life to the demands of the city." Lucas absently rubbed his bad leg. He was not going to miss climbing that damned garden wall one bit. Nor was he going to miss the nerve-racking business of constantly worrying about protecting his companion's identity and safety while she flitted blithely through the gaming hells, brothels, and back streets of London.

Ormsby took his leave a few minutes later. Lucas waited until the sound of his footsteps had receded before he picked up a candle and went to the connecting door. There was no sound from Victoria's room. She was probably already in bed; perhaps asleep.

He quietly opened the door, telling himself he had every right to walk into his wife's bedchamber. The knob twisted easily in his hand. He wondered if Victoria had tried to lock it against him. He had taken possession of the key earlier just in case.

Her bedroom was shrouded in darkness except for the pale light coming in through the window. Victoria apparently liked to sleep with the drapes open, he noted. A rather unusual quirk.

With the aid of the candle and the moonlight, Lucas could make out the slender shape of his wife as she lay huddled under the covers. His belly tightened.

Unfortunately the candlelight also revealed a little too much of the faded drapes, dirty carpet, and worn furnishings that decorated the bedchamber. Lucas felt a sharp twinge that could have been embarrassment. The new home he had provided for Victoria was definitely not up to her usual standards.

He walked over to the bed, wondering how to announce himself and tell her he had come to claim his right as a husband.

On the way up the stairs he had composed a rather lengthy speech about wifely duties and husbandly rights, but now it all sounded unconvincing. What was he going to do if she simply did not want him anymore, he wondered bleakly?

But even as the cold thought formed in his head the candlelight fell on the warm pool of golden amber that nestled between her breasts.

She was still wearing the pendant.

Relief flooded through Lucas. All was not lost after all, he thought jubilantly.

Even as that realization flared like fire through his veins, Victoria stirred restlessly on the pillow. Her lashes fluttered briefly, and then, without any warning, she opened her eyes, looked straight up at him, and screamed.

"Dear God, no, *no*. Stay away from me."

Lucas stared in shock as Victoria sat bolt upright in bed. She held out a hand as if trying to ward him off. He had been wrong. She could not bear the thought of him coming to her bed. His insides clenched in a sickening fashion.

"Vicky, for God's sake . . ."

"The knife. Merciful heavens the *knife*." She was staring at the candle in horror. "No, please, *no*."

Lucas finally understood that she was still half-asleep. He had evidently awakened her in the middle of a nightmare and she was trapped in the remnants of the dream.

He moved quickly, putting the candle down on the nearest table and grasping Victoria by the shoulders. She opened her mouth to scream again, her eyes focused on something only she could see.

Lucas shook her. "Victoria, stop it."

When there was no sign of any response in her eyes, he did what he had occasionally had to do when con-

fronted by a soldier who had slipped over the edge of
sanity into battle-front hysteria. He drew back one hand,
and with cool calculation, he slapped Victoria quite
hard.

That stopped her. She gasped, blinked in confusion,
and finally focused on his face.

"Lucas," she breathed. "Dear heaven, 'tis you." She
gave a small cry of overwhelming relief and threw herself into his arms. She clutched him as if he were an
angel sent to rescue her from the pits of hell.

There were hurried footsteps in the hall and then
anxious knocking on Victoria's door. "Ma'am? My lady?
'Tis me, Nan. Be everythin' all right?"

Lucas reluctantly disengaged himself from Victoria's
clinging grasp. She whimpered softly in protest and he
soothed her with a touch.

"Hush, darling. I have to go reassure your maid. I
will be right back."

He went to the door and opened it to find Nan
hovering nervously in the hall.

"I was on the stairs, startin' for my bed, when I heard
her ladyship scream." Nan looked up at him, her eyes
faintly suspicious in the glow of the candle she held. "Is
all well?"

"She is fine, Nan. It was my fault. I awakened her in
the middle of a bad dream."

"Oh, I wondered if that might be it." Nan's eyes lost
their trace of accusation. "Poor thing. She's been havin'
some trouble with bad dreams for the past few months.
I think it is one o' the reasons she's taken such a likin'
for the parties and nightlife o' London this Season.
Keeps her busy till dawn. But looks like she'll be sufferin'
with those plaguey dreams again now that we're all
keepin' country hours. Mayhap I should sleep a little
closer to her."

"You needn't worry about her, Nan. She's got a husband now, remember? I will take good care of her. I am
much closer than you are."

Nan flushed and nodded quickly. "Yes, sir. Well, I'll
be off, then." She bobbed a quick curtsy and hurried
back down the hall.

Lucas closed the door and turned back to the bed. Victoria was watching him from the shadows, her arms wrapped around her updrawn knees. Her eyes were huge in the dim light.

"My apologies, Vicky. I did not mean to startle you awake so abruptly," Lucas said.

"What were you doing sneaking about in my room in the first place?" she asked tartly.

He sighed, aware that the few moments of vulnerability had already passed. "I know this will come as something of a shock, Vicky, but you have a husband now and husbands have a right to sneak around their wives' bedchambers." He crossed the room and sat down on the side of the bed, ignoring her hostile gaze. "Your maid says you suffer from bad dreams frequently of late. Is there a particular reason, do you think?"

"No."

"I only ask because I, too, have had the occasional unpleasant dream," he said softly.

"I imagine everyone does from time to time."

"Yes, but my dream is a very specific one and it is always the same. Is yours?"

She hesitated. "Yes." Then, probably in an effort to change the focus of the conversation, she asked quickly, "What do you dream of, my lord?"

"Of being trapped beneath a dead horse in the middle of a field of dead and dying men." Lucas drew a deep breath and looked at the flickering candle. "Some of those men took a very long time to die. Every time I have the dream I have to listen to them in their agony. And I have to live through the torment of wondering whether or not I shall also die, wondering whether one of the human vermin who come out to loot the dead after a battle will simply slit my throat for me and end the matter once and for all."

Her small, anguished gasp and the fleeting touch of her fingers on the sleeve of his dressing gown brought his eyes back to her face.

"How terrible," Victoria whispered. "Dear God, Lucas, how ghastly. Your dream is even worse than mine."

"Of what do you dream, Vicky?"

Her fingers clenched around the sheet and she looked down. "In my dream I am always standing at the top of a staircase. A . . . a man is coming toward me. He holds a candle in one hand and a dagger in the other."

Lucas waited, sensing there was more. Something about the way she had hesitated over the phrase "a man" gave him the impression her nightmare figure had a face she recognized. But it was obvious she did not intend to add to the description of the dream and he was unwilling to jeopardize their new intimacy by prodding her for details.

In fact, Lucas decided, he had already gotten closer to her tonight than he had at any time since the fateful night he had made love to her. If he was wise, he would not push too far, too fast.

Strategy, he reminded himself. In the long run, a man always got farther with strategy than he did with force.

He suppressed a groan and got to his feet. "Are you all right now?"

She nodded quickly, not quite meeting his eyes. "Yes, thank you. I shall be fine."

"Then I will say good night. Call me if you need me, Vicky."

Forcing himself to walk back to his own chamber was one of the hardest things Lucas had done of late.

11

The following afternoon Victoria sought relief from the tension of the ever-so-civilized, now-silent battle raging between herself and Lucas by fleeing into the nearby woods with her sketchbook.

She walked for some time before coming to a halt. Eventually she chose a comfortable spot on a hill beneath some trees where she could sit gazing out over the uninspiring view of the depressed farming community. From here she could see the cottages that needed patching, the rutted lanes that needed repair, and the nearly empty fields. Lucas was out there somewhere in one of those fields, she knew. He'd made plans to ride out on an inspection tour with his steward this afternoon.

There was certainly much to be done here, Victoria was forced to acknowledge. Whatever else one could say about her husband, at least he apparently intended to put her money to good use. There was no evidence yet that he was going to pour it into wine, women, and song.

But, then, Lucas was not a frivolous man, in spite of his reputation as an accomplished gamester.

196

Frowning at her uneasy, chaotic thoughts, she bent her attention to the small plants and grasses around her. With a practiced eye she picked out several familiar species. But then she spotted a rather unusual cluster of mushrooms and her interest was immediately piqued in spite of her mood. She opened her sketchbook.

This was what she needed, she thought. She wanted the temporary peace of mind her sketching and painting could bring her.

Victoria spent a long time detailing the delicate mushrooms, losing herself in her work. Time passed quickly and the pressures of her new marriage faded, at least for the moment.

When she was finished with the mushrooms, she went on to draw several interesting dead leaves that had fallen nearby in a graceful heap. After the leaves she discovered a quite fascinating puffball. Puffballs always presented a serious challenge. It was difficult to get just the right airy appearance without sacrificing the tiny details. Botanical drawing was an exhilarating combination of art and science. Victoria loved it.

Two hours later she finally closed the sketchbook and leaned back against the tree trunk. She discovered she was feeling much better. Calmer and more steadied. The warm afternoon sun felt good and somehow the fields and farms below did not look quite so bleak. There was hope for Stonevale, she thought suddenly. Lucas would be able to salvage these lands. If any man could do it, Lucas could.

With her money, of course.

But even that thought was not as irritating as it had been earlier. An insidious notion occurred to her. Perhaps Lucas had had a point last night at dinner. What had she ever done that was so terribly useful with her money in the past?

Nevertheless, it *was* her money. Victoria scowled at that notion and got to her feet, brushing leaves from her walking dress. She must remember that she was the innocent victim in this situation.

*   *   *

Three days later Victoria made her first trip into the village. She had wanted to ride on horseback, the better to explore her new home, but Lucas had put his foot down immediately.

"I will not have the new Countess of Stonevale make her first public appearance on horseback. A certain amount of propriety is demanded in this instance, madam. You will go in a carriage together with a maid and a groom or you will not go at all," he stated.

As her relationship with Lucas could only be described as precariously balanced at best, Victoria had decided not to argue the point.

In choosing that course of action, she realized she was fast becoming as prudent as the rest of the household. She was learning that it was decidedly easier on both herself and the staff of Stonevale if she refrained from challenging her husband at each and every turn.

It irked her to think she might be surrendering some small stretch of ground to him. But the truth was, it was difficult to maintain her bristling defenses twenty-four hours a day. She was accustomed to being happy with Lucas, not at war with him.

And there were definitely a few distinct benefits to maintaining some semblance of peace in the household, she grudgingly admitted to herself. There was no denying that in response to her newfound discretion, Lucas, in turn, refrained from letting everyone feel the chill of his shockingly cold temper. The man had an air of absolute authority about him, which, when he chose to exercise it, got attention in a hurry.

His capacity for leadership and command was, Victoria had decided, in part a product of his military background. But she also suspected that a good portion of it came very naturally to Lucas. He was a born leader.

And the arrogance of a natural leader was no doubt bred in the bone. Without such arrogance and the accompanying leadership characteristics, Lucas would not have had a chance of salvaging Stonevale and the land around it.

Victoria reflected on that unpalatable notion as the

carriage jolted uncomfortably over the bad road into the village.

She had to admit that she had caught an occasional glimpse of the hard steel core of Lucas's character before her marriage. Indeed, it was probably part of what had drawn her to him. But the truth was, she had rarely been forced to confront that steel directly. Lucas had, after all, been deliberately wooing her. Naturally he had hidden the more unpleasant elements of his nature from her.

"You cannot really be meanin' to shop in this drab place, ma'am," Nan said as the carriage entered the main street of the village. "Hardly the likes o' Bond Street or Oxford Street, is it?"

"No, it certainly isn't. But we aren't here to find a ball gown. My goal is just to have a look around and perhaps meet some of the people with whom Stonevale does business on a daily basis. This is our new home, Nan. We must meet our neighbors."

"If you say so, ma'am." Nan did not look convinced of the wisdom of the idea.

Victoria smiled faintly and decided to make the appeal on a more practical basis. "You have seen the conditions at Stonevale. The house is in a terrible state. Utterly deplorable. His lordship is too busy with his farmers to worry about the running of the household, and being a military man, I doubt he would know how to run it, even if he tried."

"That be true enough, I reckon. Runnin' a household the size o' Stonevale is a lady's job, beggin' your pardon, ma'am."

"Unfortunately, I fear you are correct, Nan. And I appear to be the lady who is stuck with the task. As long as we must live there, we might as well make the place habitable. And if we are going to spend money to make it comfortable, we may as well spend as much as possible here in the village. These people rely on Stonevale for their incomes."

Nan brightened somewhat at this bit of logic. "I see your point, ma'am."

People came out of the shops and the small, decrepit

taverns to watch as the Stonevale carriage made its way
sedately down the rutted street. Victoria smiled and
waved.

There were one or two tentative waves in response,
but the general lack of enthusiasm for the new mistress
of Stonevale was rather daunting. Victoria wondered if
it was her, personally, they found unappealing, or if
their attitude was simply an extension of the local feeling toward Stonevale in general. She could not blame
the villagers for being less than optimistic about their
futures, given the obvious neglect they had endured
from the past master of the great house.

These poor people, she thought, nibbling on her
lower lip. They had suffered a great deal. This was a
place where money could accomplish much.

In the middle of the village, Victoria spotted a tiny
dry-goods shop. "I think here would be an excellent
place to begin our shopping."

Nan managed to keep her mouth shut, although her
opinion of the place was plain.

Victoria was smiling in amusement at her maid's superior attitude when she stepped down from the carriage with the aid of her footman.

The warmth of a bright spring sun fell on her full
force, highlighting the deep amber yellow shade of her
gown and glinting off her honey-colored hair. The amber feather in her tiny, yellow hat bobbed in the small
breeze and the amber pendant she wore around her
throat caught the sunlight and glowed with a life of its
own. Everyone on the street stared as if momentarily
transfixed.

Then a little girl, who had been watching from behind the safety of her mother's skirts, suddenly crowed
in delight and ran out into the street, making a beeline
for Victoria.

"Amber Lady, Amber Lady," the child shouted merrily as she raced forward on bare feet. "Pretty Amber
Lady. You came back. My granny always said you would.
She said you'd have hair the color of gold and honey all
mixed up and you'd be wearin' a golden dress."

"Here now," Nan snapped not unkindly as she moved

to intercept the youngster. "We don't want to get mud all over her ladyship, now, do we? Shoo, child. Go on back to your ma."

The girl ignored her, darting swiftly around the obstacle to grab hold of Victoria's yellow skirts with grubby fingers.

"Hello," Victoria said with a welcoming smile. "What would your name be?"

"Lucy 'awkins," the child said proudly, looking up at her with eyes full of wonder. "And that's my ma. And over there's my big sis."

The woman Lucy had pointed out as her mother was already hurrying forward with a horrified grimace on her worn-looking face. She could not have been more than five years older than Victoria, but she appeared to be at least twenty years her senior.

"I'm so sorry, mum. She's just a child. She didn't mean nothin'. Don't know her manners around her betters. She ain't seen that many of 'em. Betters, I mean."

"It is quite all right. She's done no harm."

"She ain't?" The woman's face held an expression of honest bewilderment. "She dirtied your dress, mum," she pointed out in case Victoria had failed to notice the muddy fingerprints on the fine amber muslin.

Victoria did not bother to glance down at the stains. "I appreciate her warm welcome. Lucy is the first person from the village whom I have had a chance to meet, except for our housekeeper, Mrs. Sneath. Speaking of which, is there any chance your older daughter or one of her friends might be interested in a job in the kitchens? We are in desperate need of staff. I cannot imagine how Stonevale has managed to function at all with so few people working there."

"A job?" The woman's face went blank in open astonishment. "A real job at the big house, yer ladyship? Why, we'd be ever so grateful. My husband ain't worked in ages and neither 'as a lot o' other men around here."

"It is Lord Stonevale and myself who will be grateful, I assure you." Victoria glanced around the ring of curious faces that was starting to gather near the carriage.

"In fact, we shall be needing a number of people. If anyone is interested in working in the gardens or the stables or the kitchens, please present yourselves to-morrow morning. You shall be taken on immediately. Now, if you will excuse me, I thought I would do a little shopping in your charming village."

When Victoria started forward with Nan at her heels, the crowd parted magically. She could still hear Lucy's squeals about the Amber Lady as she stepped over the threshold of the small shop.

Two hours later Victoria sailed into Stonevale's main hall. "Do you by any chance know the whereabouts of his lordship, Griggs? I must see him at once."

"I believe he is in the library with Mr. Satherwaite, madam. His lordship expressly requested that he not be disturbed while he was in conference with his new steward."

"I am certain he will make an exception in my case and I am particularly delighted to catch him with Satherwaite. Very convenient." Victoria smiled and started briskly for the closed door of the library, stripping off one of her fine kid gloves as she went forward.

Griggs sprang for the door. "Forgive me, madam, but his lordship was most particular about his request."

"Don't fret, Griggs. I shall deal with him."

"Begging your pardon, madam, but I have been privileged to be in his lordship's employ for several months now and I pride myself on having learned his preferences. I can assure you he has a strong preference for being obeyed."

Victoria smiled grimly. "Believe me, I understand better than most that Stonevale has a few difficult quirks in his nature. Be so good as to open the door, Griggs. Rest assured I shall take full responsibility for any mayhem which may ensue."

Looking doubtful, but unwilling to contradict his mistress, Griggs opened the door with an expression of deep foreboding.

"Thank you, Griggs." Victoria peeled off her second glove as she went into the room. She saw Lucas glance up, scowling. But the scowl changed to an expression of surprise as he saw who it was who had interrupted him.

"Good afternoon, madam." Lucas rose politely to his feet. "I thought you had gone into the village."

"I did. Now I am returned, as you can plainly see. How fortunate to find you together with your steward." She smiled at Mr. Satherwaite, an earnest-looking young man seated on the other side of Stonevale's desk. The steward dropped the journal he had been holding and sprang to his feet, bowing deeply.

"Your servant, your ladyship."

Lucas eyed Victoria somewhat cautiously. "How can I be of service, my dear?"

"I just wanted to apprise you of a few minor details. I have let it be known in the village that we will be taking on staff. Those who are interested, which I gather will be a sizable number, have been instructed to present themselves in the morning. Mr. Satherwaite can handle them, I am certain. I will be consulting with Griggs and Mrs. Sneath as to the exact number of people we shall require in the house proper. Since I am certain you are busy enough with the tenants' problems, I shall also attend to the staffing of the gardens."

"I see," Lucas said.

"In addition, I should mention that I have made a number of purchases in the village. The tradesmen will be delivering most of them tomorrow morning. Please arrange to have their bills paid at once. It is quite obvious they cannot afford to wait upon our convenience, as is customary."

"Anything else, madam?" Lucas asked dryly.

"Yes, I met the vicar's wife, Mrs. Worth, while I was in the village and have invited her and her husband to tea tomorrow afternoon. We will be discussing the various charity needs of the village. Kindly arrange your schedule so that you may join us."

Lucas inclined his head in grave acknowledgment of the command. "I will consult my schedule to see if I am free. Will that be all?"

"Not quite. We really must do something about that terrible road into the village. Most uncomfortable."

Lucas nodded. "I shall put it on my list of items needing repair."

"Do that, my lord. I think that will be all for now." Victoria smiled warmly again at Mr. Satherwaite, who was looking dumbfounded, turned on her heel, and headed for the door. She paused on the threshold and glanced back over her shoulder at Lucas. "There was one other thing, my lord."

"Somehow I am not surprised," Lucas said. "Pray, continue. You have my full attention, madam."

"What is this nonsense about an Amber Lady?"

Lucas's eyes flicked briefly to the pendant she wore. "Where did you hear the phrase?"

"One of the children in the village called me by that odd title. I simply wondered if you were familiar with it. Apparently it is some sort of local legend."

Lucas glanced at Satherwaite. "I will tell you what little I know of the story later."

Victoria shrugged. "As you wish, my lord." She swept back out of the library and Griggs hastily closed the door behind her. The butler regarded her with an air of acute concern.

"Have no fear, Griggs," Victoria said, grinning with unabashed triumph at her small, successful assault on the sanctity of the library. "My lord has teeth but it takes considerably more than a minor interruption from his wife to make him bite."

"I shall remember that, madam."

In the library Lucas sat down again and reached for the next aging ledger. He realized Satherwaite was watching him with an expression of deep curiosity.

"My wife, as you can see, will be taking an active interest in the estate," Lucas remarked.

"Yes, my lord. She appears to have a rather keen interest in local matters."

Lucas smiled complacently. "Lady Stonevale is a woman of great energy and enthusiasm. She has been needing an interesting challenge to occupy her full attention."

"Shopping in our poor village was certainly an act of gracious mercy on her part. I cannot imagine a lady of her excellent taste finding anything she truly desired in the local shops."

"I believe the point was to do something for the local economy," Lucas mused. "And I am grateful to her. It will take both of us to save Stonevale. As I said, we are facing a challenge."

Satherwaite looked at the stack of journals and ledgers that stood on the desk. "No offense, sir, but rescuing these lands presents enough of a challenge to occupy a regiment." He looked back at his employer with a hint of the sort of hero worship a young man often feels for an older male who has seen combat. "Of course, you have had some experience with military matters, sir."

"Just between you and me, Satherwaite, I don't mind telling you that I find the challenge of making this land productive again infinitely more appealing than the business of war."

Satherwaite, who clearly did not see how anything could be more exciting than the business of war, wisely kept his mouth shut and opened the journal in front of him.

Later that evening Lucas leaned back in his chair, stretched his feet out toward the fire, and indulged himself in the purely masculine pleasure of watching his wife pour after-dinner tea in the drawing room.

It was a small thing, this matter of pouring the tea, but it seemed to symbolize so much. He was not so foolish as to think Victoria had surrendered to the inevitable yet, but he saw the distinctly wifely act as a definite step in that direction.

He suddenly realized that in common with most of his sex, he was not given to a great deal of idle reflection on all the small routines that turned a household into a home. At least, he had not been particularly conscious of them until recently when, having gotten himself a wife, he had discovered he had not automatically gotten all the little niceties that were supposed to come along with one.

For the past three days he had been living in a state of armed truce, a truce that was only an inch away from

open warfare. Nothing in the household had been seen
to beyond such minimal matters as producing meals
and emptying chamber pots. Griggs had been getting
desperate. Mrs. Sneath had threatened to quit because
of overwork.

But as of the moment of Victoria's return from the
village, things had begun to change. Lucas realized he
thirsted mightily for each small sip of the honey of
domestic harmony. Having his tea poured for him by
Victoria was one such golden drop. It was the first he'd
tasted since he'd taken his wedding vows.

"About the legend of the Amber Lady, my lord,"
Victoria said coolly as she handed him his cup and
saucer. "I would like to hear the details now, if you
please."

"I confess I do not know all of the tale." Lucas stirred
his tea, trying to think of ways to stretch out the conversation. Victoria was in the habit of rushing off to bed
early lately. "My uncle mentioned the matter shortly
before he died. It was in conjunction with the pendant
he gave me." He frowned, wishing he had not called
her attention to the amber around her throat. Victoria
appeared totally oblivious of the fact that she wore it
twenty-four hours a day. "I asked for the story, but you
must realize my uncle was a bitter, ill-tempered man.
To top it off, when I saw him, he was on his deathbed
and not particularly inclined to humor me or anyone
else."

"What did he tell you?"

"Just that the pendant had been handed down through
the family for several generations. It apparently belonged to the first lord of Stonevale. My uncle said I
might get more information from the villagers. I asked
Mrs. Sneath about it. As you know, she was about the
only member of the staff left when the old bastard died.
He had turned off everyone else."

"Go on, what did Mrs. Sneath say?"

Lucas looked at her and saw the bright curiosity
shining in her beautiful eyes. "Having met Mrs. Sneath,
you must know she is not the talkative sort. But she did
tell me that the villagers tell an old children's story

about the first lord of Stonevale and his lady. The man had been dubbed the Amber Knight because of the colors he wore into battle."

"So he was a warrior, too," Victoria murmured, staring into the fire.

"Most men who acquired estates the size of Stonevale were," Lucas pointed out dryly.

"They called his wife the Amber Lady?"

Lucas nodded. "According to the legend, the lord and his lady were very much in love and devoted to the land and the people on it. Stonevale grew prosperous under their guidance. Several generations of happily married men succeeded the first and the lands flourished. People began to say that the well-being of the estate and its surrounding lands was contingent on the happiness of the lord and lady who lived in the great house."

Victoria frowned. "A rather precarious thing on which to hang the welfare of this entire region."

"It is just a superstition, Vicky."

"I know, but—"

Lucas interrupted her swiftly. "According to Mrs. Sneath, it became a saying in the village that the Earls of Stonevale must marry for love or the lands would suffer. Given the wealth of the estate, it was very convenient for each succeeding earl to make a love match rather than a business match."

"Very convenient. There was no need to marry for money until the present generation, I take it?"

Lucas hurried on, anxious to skirt the quicksand he sensed waiting for him in that direction. "At any rate, three generations back, the Earl of Stonevale fell in love with a young woman who, it seemed, had already given her heart to another." Lucas paused. "Not only her heart, but everything else, apparently. Her family rushed her into the marriage knowing she was carrying another man's babe, the child of a penniless second son who left for America when he found out she had married the Earl of Stonevale."

"That poor girl. How sad for her to be forced to marry a man she did not love. But her family was not about to lose the opportunity of having their daughter become a countess, I suppose," Victoria murmured with a touch of bitterness.

"Probably not," Lucas agreed. "But as long as you are overflowing with sympathy for the young lady, you might spare some for my ancestor who found himself tied to a woman who was not exactly a virgin on her wedding night."

Victoria's gaze turned even more frosty. "So? I did not come to this marriage a virgin, either, if you will recall.

"It is hardly the same thing, given the fact that I was the one and only man you slept with before the wedding. In any event," Lucas added, feeling a little dangerous now himself, "we haven't even had a *wedding* night, so your point is irrelevant, to say the least."

"Do you know, Lucas, I do not see why your ancestor or you or any other man has any right to expect his wife to be a virgin. You men certainly do not bother to remain in a chaste state until your wedding nights."

"There is the little matter of attempting to ensure one's children are one's own."

Victoria shrugged. "Aunt Cleo one told me that women have been inventing ways to feign virginity for as long as men have been so arrogant as to insist upon it. Even if one is certain one's wife is a virgin at marriage, that still does not ensure her children are not the footman's by-blows, does it?"

"Victoria . . ."

"No, it would seem to me, my lord, that the only way a man can be relatively certain his children are his own is if he truly trusts his wife and knows he can believe her when she tells him they are his."

"I trust you, Victoria," Lucas said softly.

"Well, as you said, 'tis all irrelevant as far as we are concerned, is it not?"

"Not entirely," he muttered. "Victoria, could we please get on with the legend?"

She blinked and occupied herself with the teapot. "Yes, of course. Kindly continue with the story, my lord."

Lucas took a swallow of tea, wondering how in hell he had allowed the conversation to get so wildly off track. "The earl had his suspicions, but no proof, and since he was very much in love with his new wife, he decided to believe what he wanted to believe. That worked until the babe was born dead. His lady was so grief-stricken that she lost her wits. She confessed all, blamed her unhappiness on her husband for having made it impossible to marry her true love, and claimed she was now so miserable she wanted to die. Then she promptly did precisely that."

Victoria's eyes flew to his, deep suspicion in her amber gaze. "How?"

"Pray do not look at me like that. He didn't kill her, you know. She simply never recovered from childbirth. Mrs. Sneath says the legend has it that she willed herself to die and the fever obligingly took her."

"What a tragic story. What did the earl do?"

"He grew bitter and cynical toward all women. There was pressure from the family to produce an heir, so he eventually remarried. But this time not for love. It was strictly a business decision on his part and he and his second wife hardly formed what could be called a happily married couple. In fact, after the required heir was born, the earl and his wife spent very little time together and none at all at Stonevale, apparently."

"Was that when the lands began to go into a decline?"

Lucas nodded. "Yes, according to the tale and to the old ledgers and records. I went through several of them today just out of curiosity and I must admit one can trace the gradual decline of the estate to that disastrous marriage three generations ago."

"Truly?"

"Yes, truly. The next earl, my uncle's father, was not only a cold and bitter man, he was also a rake and a poor gamester. He started the tradition of the Earls of Stonevale spending more time at the gaming tables and less on their lands. He, too, eventually married, but not for love. Once my uncle was born, his father and mother went their separate ways," Lucas said.

"And the lands continued to decline. Hardly surprising, given the lack of interest on the part of the masters. What about your uncle?"

"Maitland Colebrook never even bothered to marry for the sake of the title or anything else, let alone love. He concentrated instead on going through what was left of the family fortune. He bled the estate dry and then retired to the country to rail against his ill fate."

"So that is how the villagers explain their present impoverished situation." Victoria stared thoughtfully into the fire again. "Interesting."

Lucas studied her averted profile, wondering what she would do if he pulled her into his lap and kissed her. Would she melt for him the way she always had in the past or would she use her nails on his eyes and cut him to shreds with her tongue? One thing was for certain, when he eventually got around to taking her into his arms, it would be a real adventure for all concerned.

"The most interesting part is that business of the Hawkins child in the village calling you the Amber Lady," Lucas said quietly.

"Why is that? She had obviously been told the tale, and when she saw me dressed in that particular shade of yellow, she jumped to a child's conclusion."

Lucas watched the firelight bring out the amber and gold in Victoria's tawny brown hair. "I am not so certain she jumped to the wrong conclusion. There is something rather amberish about you, you know. Your eyes, your hair, the colors you choose to wear."

She glared at him. "For heaven's sake, Lucas, do not talk such nonsense."

He held out his cup for more tea. "It is little wonder the child would like to believe you are the Amber Lady. I have not yet told you the last bit of the legend."

She glanced at him warily as she poured tea into his cup. "How does the tale conclude?"

" 'Tis said that one day the Amber Knight and his lady will return to the great house and the lands of Stonevale will once more prosper along with their love."

"What a tidy ending," Victoria said scornfully. "But if the luck of the region depends upon the lord and lady marrying for love, then it is obvious everyone around here will have to wait for another chance at bettering their fortunes. The newest Earl of Stonevale married for money, not love."

"Damn it, Vicky. . . ."

She was already on her feet. "If you will excuse me, my lord, I will bid you good night. I grow weary."

Lucas swore again as he got to his feet. He waited until the door had closed behind her before he put down his teacup and, with cold deliberation, went across the room to pick up the brandy decanter.

Idly he massaged his aching leg. It was going to be a long night.

Three hours later as Lucas lay awake in bed listening to the soft sounds in the room next door, he wondered if he was being a fool to continue to restrain himself. Maybe this waiting game was not such wise strategy after all.

He heard another whisper of movement from the next chamber. It sounded as if Victoria had gotten out of bed. It was obvious she was not yet asleep. Perhaps she was afraid to go to sleep too early for fear of inducing another nightmare.

There was nothing like the sort of passion they could experience together to ward off bad dreams, Lucas told himself. As a concerned husband he owed her what comfort and reassurance he could give her, even if he had to force it on her.

Resolutely he pushed back the covers and reached for his dressing gown. This had gone far enough. One way or the other they had to form a normal marital relationship and it was rapidly becoming clear that his self-imposed restraint was having no effect whatsoever on her recalcitrance.

In other words, he thought ruefully, she was hardly begging for his lovemaking.

He heard the outer door to her bedchamber open and close just as he lifted his hand to knock on the connecting door. Quietly he twisted the knob and stepped into his wife's empty room.

Fury and panic seized him. Surely she was not idiotic enough to run off in the middle of the night. Then he recalled that Victoria was very much accustomed to running about in the dead of night. He had even taught her something about how it was done.

Lucas put down his candle and hastily pulled on breeches, boots, and a shirt. A few minutes later he was moving swiftly down the hall. His instincts told him she would leave via the kitchen door. It was the way he would have gone if he had been trying to sneak out of the house. He hurried after her.

A few minutes later he emerged from the house. He saw Victoria almost at once. She was standing quietly in the dilapidated, sadly overgrown kitchen garden. She was wearing her long, hooded, amber-colored cloak to ward off the chill and she was bathed in moonlight. Memories of all those other nights when he had rendezvoused with her in her aunt's garden swept over him, leaving him filled with a hunger that was sharpened to the point of pain.

This was his wife and he wanted her.

Lucas stepped slowly out into the shadows, making no sound. But she sensed his presence and turned toward him. He sucked in his breath.

"I have missed our midnight meetings in the garden," he said softly.

"You wooed me most cleverly when you promised me adventure in the middle of the night, did you not? I succumbed to that lure as I would have succumbed to no other."

His stomach clenched at the soft bitterness in her voice. "Were you going to seek an adventure on your own tonight, Vicky? I doubt there are any gaming hells or brothels or inns filled with young lordlings and their opera dancers in the village." He walked toward her until he was standing only a short distance away.

"I merely wanted to walk," she said quietly.

"Will you allow me to accompany you?"

"Have I any choice in the matter?"

"No." As if he would allow her to wander around out

here alone at night, Lucas thought. "Where were you planning to walk?"

"I am not certain. I had not really thought about it."

He considered quickly, trying to remember what he had seen during the past few days as he had ridden over his lands. "There is an empty cottage not far from here. I believe it belonged to the gamekeeper back in the days when Stonevale had a gamekeeper. Why don't we walk there and back?"

"All right." She fell silent.

"It is a lovely night, is it not?"

"I find it rather chilly," she told him distantly.

"Yes," Lucas agreed thinking swiftly. There was some old firewood stacked outside the cottage, he recalled. Too bad he had not ordered the place cleaned yesterday when he'd examined it. He stumbled slightly over a nonexistent stone and stifled a small groan.

"What is the matter with you?" Victoria asked, frowning in annoyance.

"Nothing important. My leg is acting up a bit tonight." He tried to sound stoic and brave.

"Really, Lucas, I should think you would have learned by now not to go about in the cold night air when it is paining you."

"You are undoubtedly correct about that, madam. But you seem to favor running about at night and that leaves me with little choice but to accompany you."

"You should have gone after an heiress who is not fond of this sort of sport," she told him. "The Perfect Miss Pilkington would have done nicely for you."

"Do you think so? I admit she was on Jessica Atherton's list, but somehow I could not seem to work up much enthusiasm. There was something a bit boring about the prospect of being married to Miss Pilkington. As you and Annabella said, she was a bit too much like Lady Atherton."

Victoria retreated deeper into the hood of her cloak until her voice was muffled. "You are right on that account. If you think Lady Atherton has grown somewhat dull over the years, you should see Miss Pilkington. Do not mistake me. She is very nice but she's only nineteen and she told me herself, she believes she may have a religious calling."

"I see. We would not have suited each other at all. I cannot imagine taking her to a gaming hell. Nor can I envision her using a walking stick on a brothel butler."

"On the other hand, she probably wouldn't have given you any trouble. I am certain she would have made a most dutiful wife. Speaking of duty . . ."

He sighed. "Yes?"

"Lady Atherton did warn me that I must be prepared to do mine and provide you with an heir."

"I wouldn't mind throttling Lady Atherton."

"She was only trying to help. After all, you did ask her to assist you in finding an heiress."

"You need not remind me."

"Lucas?" Victoria asked shyly.

"Hmmm?"

"Lady Atherton pointed out that if I thought doing my duty was going to be difficult for me, I should only consider how very hard it was going to be on you to have to pretend some degree of affection in the marital bed."

"God damn it to hell and back." Lucas came to a halt and swung her around to face him. He glared down at her incredulously. "You cannot tell me you believed her? After that night we spent together at the inn?"

She faced him staunchly, her eyes glittering within the shadow of the cloak. "I have learned from both my mother and my aunt that men do not seem to have any great degree of difficulty pretending that sort of physical affection when it suits them."

"Men are not the only ones who can manage the trick," Lucas muttered, and then added ruthlessly, "Some would say I have good cause to question the depths of your feelings that night."

Anger flashed in her gaze. "How dare you question my feelings that night? I was painfully honest with you about the depth of my emotions, as I recall."

He shrugged. "If your feelings ran as deep as you imply, I doubt you could have buried them so quickly afterward."

"I buried them quickly because I felt ill-used. Damn you, I had no choice but to suppress my foolish affection. I feel nothing but humiliation whenever I recall my actions that cursed night."

"I must say you have done an excellent job of suppressing your feelings. One would never guess you ever held me in anything but complete dislike."

"Yes, well, that is certainly—" She broke off as he stumbled and winced. "What's wrong now?" she demanded impatiently.

"I told you, my leg is troubling me somewhat this evening."

"There are times, Lucas, when you display very little common sense." She took his arm to steady him. "I suppose we ought to return to the house before you take a bad fall."

"I don't believe I can make it that far. The cottage is closer. If I could just rest inside it for a while, I am certain I will be all right."

"Very well," she muttered irritably. "Here, you had better let me assist you."

"Thank you, Vicky. You are very kind." Leaning rather heavily on her, Lucas allowed himself to be assisted into the dark confines of the small gamekeeper's cottage.

12

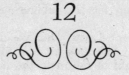

Strategy.

Lucas settled himself on the floor of the cottage, his arm propped on one up-drawn knee, his sore leg stretched out straight. He watched cheerfully as Victoria busied herself building a fire. She had refused to allow him to carry the wood, insisting he rest, instead.

"This is a pleasant little place, is it not?" she asked, glancing about as the fire she had just built blazed into existence and revealed the interior of the cottage. "It looks like someone has lived here fairly recently. The chimney is clear and the floor is not nearly as dusty as one would expect."

"I wouldn't be surprised if some evicted tenant took up residence here until we arrived. My uncle was extremely prone to evictions."

"A nasty man."

"Bear in mind that I descend from a slightly different branch of the family," he pointed out.

Instead of smiling, she took that very seriously. "We are certainly not responsible for the actions of other members of our family. Here, let me rub your leg for you."

Lucas did not protest. His mind was on fire with images of what had happened the first time she had rubbed his throbbing leg. "Thank you. I would appreciate it."

She folded her cloak on the floor and knelt on it. Keeping her eyes focused on his leg, she went to work, massaging gently. Lucas groaned at the first touch of her hands.

"Am I hurting you?"

"No. That feels wonderful." He closed his eyes and leaned his head back against the wall. "You can have no idea."

"It must have been terrible."

Lucas opened his eyes and studied his wife. "What must have been terrible?"

"That day when you were wounded."

"I will admit it was not the highlight of my life. A little higher, please. Yes. Right there. Thank you." Her hand was mere inches from his groin. He wondered how she could be unaware of the rapidly growing bulge in his snug breeches. "That fire feels good."

"Lucas?" There was a short, poignant pause.

Lucas saw the intent look on Victoria's face. "Yes?"

"Did you love her very much?"

He closed his eyes again as he struggled to follow her train of thought. "Who?"

"Lady Atherton, of course."

"Oh, her. Well, I must have thought I did at the time, else why would I have bothered to ask her to marry me?"

"Why, indeed?" Victoria muttered.

"But looking back on it, I find it hard to believe I was that much of an idiot."

"She still loves you."

"She loves the idea of suffering from a star-crossed love and the feeling of being a gallant martyr to duty far more than she'll ever love any man. I do not envy Lord Atherton one bit." Atherton's bed must be a very cold one, Lucas thought.

"Forgive me, my lord," Victoria said wryly, "but that is a remarkably perceptive comment for a man."

He opened one eye. "You think women are the only ones who can make remarkably perceptive comments?"

"Well, no, but . . ."

He closed his eye. "Some of us males are capable of learning from our mistakes and of gaining a measure of perception in the process."

"Is that right?"

Lucas inhaled sharply. "Ah, Vicky, could you possibly go a bit easier on that portion of my leg? Perhaps if you moved your hands a bit higher?"

"Like this?" She slid her fingers up his thigh a few more inches.

Lucas did not trust himself to speak. Her touch was now so intimate he was afraid he would lose his self-control entirely in another moment or two.

"Lucas, are you all right?" Victoria began to sound genuinely worried.

"After that night we spent together at the inn, you should know what your touch does to me, my sweet."

Her hands stilled instantly on his thigh. "Do you want me to stop?" she asked hesitantly.

"Never. Not in a million years. A man could die happy under such torture."

"Lucas, are you by any chance trying to get me to . . . to seduce you?"

He opened his eyes and looked straight at her. "I would sell my soul to get you to seduce me."

She blinked at his bluntness. Then her eyes filled with longing. "I do not think the price would be quite so high, my lord."

He touched her face and then let his fingers slide along the chain of the pendant. "Thank God for your honesty in matters of intellectual inquiry."

"Oh, *Lucas*." With a small cry she threw herself against his chest and nestled there, her arms wrapping around his waist. "I have thought about that night so often. I was so happy with you for those few hours."

"Only your pride is keeping you from being happy in that way again." He stroked her arm, enjoying the weight of her against his chest. "Is your pride worth all this disharmony between us? We are bound together for life now, Vicky. Do you intend to put us both through hell every night?"

She kept her head tucked against his shoulder so that she did not have to look at him. "When you put it like that, it does not make much sense, does it? Aunt Cleo said that I had made my bed and now must lie in it. She said it was up to me to make that bed as comfortable as possible."

"Much as I appreciate your aunt's sentiments, I'd just as soon not have a martyr in my bed. I narrowly escaped that fate once before, as you will recall," Lucas said.

Her shoulders shook with soft, nervous laughter. "Yes, I do recall. Very well, Lucas, I shall view my decision to carry out my responsibilities as your wife as a matter of logic and common sense, not a matter of duty. There is, as you say, no point in putting us both through hell."

"Give me the logical bluestocking rather than the pious martyr any day." Lucas tipped up her chin and kissed her. "At least when the bluestocking talks herself into succumbing to passion, she doesn't have to pretend she cannot enjoy it." His mouth moved slowly on hers.

Victoria seemed to hesitate briefly, as if silently running through her logic one more time to be certain this was the right solution to the problem she had set herself. Then, with a tiny gasp, she responded with the sweet, hot fervor that Lucas always found so enthralling.

Her hands tightened around his back and she parted her lips for him. Lucas let his tongue plunge into her mouth in anticipation of the way he would soon be surging into her body. She pressed herself against him. He could feel her breasts beneath the bodice of her dress and his entire body throbbed with impatience.

"Sweetheart, I have waited so long for our wedding night." He tore his mouth from hers and reached for the amber cloak on which she had been kneeling. He tossed it out deftly with one hand so that it formed a blanket for her to lie on.

"It will get dirty." Her protest was automatic, but without any real heat.

"You have others." He fumbled with her gown, a

part of him appalled by his haste and the unaccustomed clumsiness that accompanied it. So much for strategy. Another part of him was running wild and free now that the torment of waiting was nearly over.

That first time he had prepared himself to hold back until he was certain she was as eager as he was. He had been so intent on not hurting her or alarming her, so intent on pleasing her. But this time he could think only of possessing her once more. He had to reassure himself that she was his again.

This time he could not contain himself.

Victoria looked startled by his urgency, but she went willingly over onto her back as he eased her down onto the cloak. He gave up fighting with her clothes and contented himself with pushing her skirts up to her waist. Then he looked up quickly to see if she was offended by the lack of gallantry. When he saw her luminous smile and the reflected heat of the fire in her eyes, he went to work on his own clothing.

"Damn."

"What is it?" she asked softly.

"Nothing. Merely my own clumsiness." He finally managed to get the breeches open. He decided he could not take the time to remove them or his boots. His need was raging through him.

And then he was falling on her in a white-hot fever. He put his hands on her thighs and she opened them for him, offering herself. He moved between her legs, feeling the moist heat of her as he pushed against her softness. He took one of her nipples into his mouth and bit down with exquisite care as he surged into her tight, hot channel.

She cried out and clung to him. He could feel the initial resistance of her body as he pushed steadily deeper. He reminded himself that this was all still very new to her.

"Lift yourself, sweetheart. Open yourself for me." He slid one hand down under her to cup her lush buttocks and urged her upward so that he could sink himself even deeper into her clinging warmth.

"Lucas."

"Am I hurting you?" His voice was husky, even to his own ears.

"No, not precisely. But the feeling is indescribable. Oh, Lucas."

"I know, I know, darling, I know." He sank himself slowly to the hilt. He felt her thighs shiver as they closed around him and the knowledge that she had willingly made herself so vulnerable to him nearly undid him. "Wrap your legs around my waist. That's it. *Yes.*"

With a soft exclamation, she gave herself to him just as she had that first night. She was clinging to him, whispering his name, pleading with him for the release he promised.

Glittering shards of sensation flickered through his senses. Lucas was aware of the heat of the fire, the alluring scent of Victoria's aroused body, the silky strength of her soft thighs as they tightened around him.

He opened his eyes and saw that hers were tightly closed. She was breathing quickly, her throat arched back over his arm. She was in the grip of her passion and the sight was devastating to his senses. He was utterly fascinated. He moved slowly, deliberately, within her, letting her pull him back every time he had retreated to the entrance of her tight little channel.

"*Lucas.*"

"Yes." He eased back into her again, glorying in her hot, clinging warmth. He was sweating now, his whole body surging toward release. Then he felt the sudden tension in Victoria and knew she was close to her own climax.

He moved his hand on her buttocks, letting one finger glide intimately along the dark cleft to the point where their bodies were joined.

Victoria's eyes flew open and her lips parted on a soft, startled, purely feminine shriek.

"Lucas? Dear heaven, *Lucas.*"

And then she was convulsing gently around him, drawing him even more deeply into her. Lucas heard his own triumphant shout fill the small room as his release swept over him.

Several minutes passed before he felt like stirring. When he did, it was only to roll onto his side and gather Victoria close against him. The fire was still blazing merrily, casting cheerful, dancing shadows on the walls. Lucas felt his wife's leg slide lazily along his as she allowed herself to be cuddled.

"You must admit there are some benefits to marriage, madam. At least this time we do not have to concern ourselves with being discovered and threatened with social ruin." Lucas yawned mightily, aware of a singular contentment. "But do you think that perhaps next time we might try it in the comfort of your bed or mine? That mattress at the inn was lumpy and this floor is damned hard."

"We are having an adventure. Don't you think it might be a bit ordinary to use one of our own beds, sir?"

"This is what I get for marrying a woman with a taste for excitement. She only wants to make love in unusual locations and under novel circumstances." Lucas ruffled her short curls affectionately. "Fear not, madam, your husband will do his best to keep you amused and entertained in your own bed."

"It sounds like a great deal of work on your part," she said.

"Believe me, it will be infinitely easier to dream up interesting things to do with you in the comfort of your bedchamber than it is to chase after you at midnight, wondering what mischief you're up to."

She did not respond to that. Instead she wriggled a bit, quite delightfully, in fact. She made no move to free herself from his arms but her silence continued for some time. Lucas began to worry.

"Lucas?"

"Yes, my sweet?"

"Do you swear to me that you did not arrange for my aunt to discover us that first time at the inn?"

Anger snapped to life within him, driving out much of the contentment he had been enjoying. He pushed himself up on one elbow and scowled down at her. "Damn it, Vicky, I set out to seduce you, not humiliate you. How can you think I would deliberately do such a thing?"

"You said, yourself, you were determined to marry an heiress."

"I was determined to marry *you*," he corrected roughly, "not just any heiress. Furthermore, to be perfectly blunt about it, my dear, I had no need to resort to extreme measures such as arranging for your aunt to discover us in compromising circumstances."

Her brows came together in a swift frown. "What do you mean by that?"

"Only that I was doing a creditable job of seducing you into marriage just fine on my own. I did not require anyone else's assistance. At the rate we were going, it would have been only a matter of time before you talked yourself into marrying me."

"Why, you arrogant beast." She tried to push herself away from him and sit up.

Lucas grinned and threw one leg over her bare thighs. He rolled back on top of her, pinning her wrists to the floor on either side of her head. " 'Tis true and you know it, sweetheart. Admit it. Admit you could not possibly have conducted the sort of torrid love affair you wished for unless we got married. It would have proved impossible."

She glared up at him, struggling futilely. "It would have been possible. It merely required planning."

"I assure you, when it comes to planning and strategy, I am very, very good and even I could not have kept you content or safe for long. Hell, I could not even manage it that one time we tried to seclude ourselves at the inn. And it would have been impossible for you to steal away from a soirée to run off to an inn in a strange coach every time you wanted to make love. Sooner or later someone would have been bound to notice."

"I would have been most discreet," Victoria insisted.

"Is that right? And what would we have done when the Season was over and there were very few large parties from which you could disappear without being noticed?"

She bit her lip in annoyance. "I would have thought of something."

"No, love. We were headed for trouble right from the start."

"And you knew it."

"Of course I knew it. As you are far from being an idiot, you would soon have come to your senses and realized it also. At that point I am convinced you would have started to think seriously about marrying me." He smiled deliberately. "To be perfectly truthful, given your appetite for *intellectual inquiry*, I do not believe I would have had to wait too long."

She went still and looked up at him through her lashes. "You were so sure of me you took to carrying a special license in your pocket."

"I wanted to be prepared. We were playing with fire, love."

Victoria closed her eyes to his satisfied grin. "And I got burned."

"Are the flames so bad?" he asked softly, brushing his mouth across hers. His body reacted immediately and he groaned.

"I have given the situation much thought during the past few days," she said, her expression very serious now. "If the world were a different place, I would never have chosen marriage."

Her insistence on that point began to annoy him. He scowled. "If the world were a different place, I would not have been obliged to capture an heiress."

"True. Lucas, as I said, I have given this much thought. We both did what was required of us by our sense of honor and now we have been forced to seal a bargain. This is something of a business arrangement. I have decided to think of our marriage in that light. I see us as two business associates who have invested in the same enterprise."

Lucas frowned. "I do not like all this talk of going into trade."

She shook her head restlessly. "Think of it how you will; the point is, we are investing together in a future, and as long as we can find a way to work comfortably together, I begin to believe we can be reasonably content together."

"Reasonably content," he echoed, thinking seriously of putting her over his knee. "Is that how you felt a few minutes ago when you were shivering in my arms? Reasonably content?"

The flush on her face was more than just the effect of the fire's warmth. "Really, Lucas. A gentleman would not ask such an intimate question."

"How would you know? You haven't been with any other gentlemen in such circumstances."

"I can hazard a guess," she retorted. "Besides, that is not the issue."

"And what is the issue? You mean to think of our marriage as a partnership? An investment? A business arrangement in which the associates happen to sleep together?" His eyes caught hers in a burning gaze.

"But is that not precisely what it is? Isn't that what you wanted?"

"No, damn it. 'Tis not at all what I wanted."

"I see. Perhaps you do not care for the notion of me being an equal partner? Perhaps you just wanted my money and would prefer I stay out of the matter entirely, except insofar as I am needed to provide your heir."

"Vicky, Vicky, calm yourself. You are twisting my words and getting everything wrong."

"I am trying to do as everyone says I must. I am attempting to find a sensible, intelligent way to deal with this matter. I thought you would be pleased that I am finally being so reasonable about everything."

Lucas fought to quell his outrage. "I don't want a business associate, I want a wife."

"What is the difference, other than the fact that as your wife I shall share your bed occasionally?"

"It will be more than occasionally and the difference is that you love me, madam. You said so yourself."

Her eyes widened. "I did not."

"Yes, you did. That first night at the inn. I heard you."

"I only said I *thought* I was in love with you. In any case, all that is naturally changed by what happened."

"The devil it is." His fingers tightened on her wrists.

"Vicky, stop talking all this nonsense about a business arrangement. We are man and wife."

"Are you saying there is more to our relationship than a bargain?"

"Of course there is."

Her eyes narrowed. "Are you claiming to be in love with me, then, my lord?"

"You would not believe me if I told you I was." He released her and sat up, adjusting his clothing.

"Who knows? Why don't you try it and see?"

He looked at her and did not quite know what to make of the look in her eyes. But she was challenging him, of that much he was certain. "What do you want from me, Vicky?"

"What I imagine every new bride wishes to hear," she said coolly. "A declaration of undying love and a promise of eternal devotion. But I am not likely to get it, am I?"

"Bloody hell." He stood up, sensing the treacherous sand beneath his feet. Women were the very devil with words and a woman like this one would know how to take full advantage of any leverage he gave her. He'd already had ample proof of how skillfully she could maneuver him into going against his own better judgment. Just the memory of those dreadful nights climbing Lady Nettleship's garden wall was enough to start his leg aching again. "You tease me at your peril, madam."

"Does that mean you cannot give me what I want?"

"I do not trust your mood, Vicky, nor whatever is behind your request. I believe you are looking for a way to manipulate me. If I gave you a declaration of undying love and eternal devotion, you would hurl it in my face every time I refused to indulge one of your whims. You would say I had lied about loving you."

"Does that mean you do not love me?"

"It means it was a goddamned mistake to indulge you so much initially in London. You have come to expect that with very little effort you can keep me on a leash," he said through his teeth.

"I see." She got slowly to her feet and concentrated on arranging her clothing.

Lucas stared at her slender, rigidly held back, feeling hunted. A few minutes ago they had been sharing a passion unlike any he had ever known. Now the fragile relationship seemed to have been shattered by mere words. For the life of him he could not figure out where everything had gone wrong.

"Vicky, don't do this to yourself." He turned her around and pulled her into his arms. He thought he heard a small sniff and he immediately felt helpless. He did not like the feeling at all. "You are no green girl, damn it."

She hesitated and then nodded reluctantly against his shoulder, her face buried in his shirt. "You are right. I am behaving like a silly little chit straight out of the schoolroom who cannot face the world as it is." She pulled back and looked up at him with renewed determination. "As I said, Lucas, I do believe this marriage can work if we both agree to act logically and reasonably. I vow I will uphold my end of this bargain."

He looked down into eyes that still shimmered with tears and he did not know what to say. He realized he wanted to hear the sweet, tentative words of love he had heard from her that first night, but he sensed that now was not the time to demand them.

"Vicky?"

"Yes, my lord?"

"Thank you for making up your mind to make the best of this marriage," he heard himself say gently. "I am grateful."

"You are welcome, my lord."

He grimaced a little at the excruciating formality of her tone but managed a reassuring smile. As he stood looking down at her the amber pendant glowed in the firelight and Lucas relaxed slightly.

It would be all right, he decided. She would find the words again in her own good time. "Do not tie yourself in knots trying to dissect your feelings, Vicky. Or mine." He touched the gold chain of the pendant and smiled. "Everything will come right in time. Let's go home."

She nodded in swift agreement and stood back as he shook out her cloak. The garment was dusty but otherwise unharmed. He put it around her, thinking that even though she was tall for a woman, she was still considerably smaller than he was. He was aware again of a fierce need to protect her and keep her safe.

"Lucas," she said thoughtfully as he put out the fire, "if you did not arrange for us to be discovered that night at the inn, who did?"

He shrugged. "Who knows?"

"Lady Atherton, perhaps? In her never-ending zeal to assist you in your quest for an heiress?"

He grinned, relieved to hear the returning edge of impudence in her voice. " 'Tis possible, I suppose. Does it matter? What's done is done." He took her arm and led her toward the door.

"You are quite right," she said slowly. "What's done is done. But there were one or two rather odd things that happened to me recently in Town and combined with the mystery of wondering who had been spying on us, I began to think."

"About what?"

"Never mind. 'Tis just my imagination."

Lucas went cold. He dragged her to an abrupt halt just outside the cottage. "Victoria, what in hell are you talking about? What odd things happened?"

"Really, Lucas, it was nothing, I'm sure."

"I would like an answer, madam."

"Do you know, Lucas, when you talk in that particular tone, there is a strong tendency for everyone in the vicinity to jump through the nearest hoop. Did you learn that in the army?"

He prayed silently for patience. "Enough, Victoria. Tell me what made you ask me about who might have spied on us. Tell me now, wife, or we will stand here until you do."

"It occurs to me that on the two occasions when we have conducted our *intellectual inquiries*, you have not been particularly affectionate afterward. The first time I will grant there was the extenuating circumstance of my aunt's presence. But this time there is no excuse. Is it this way with all men?"

"You cannot resist goading me, can you? One of

these days you really will push too far. Answer me or we are likely to discover that this is the day."

Victoria shrugged. "Very well, but it really does not amount to much. It is just that on two occasions in Town I came across objects that did not belong to me. They were both marked with a 'W.' One was a scarf that had been left on the conservatory door. I found it that night we went to the gaming hell."

"The night you were nearly run down by that carriage." Lucas frowned. "What was the other object?"

"A snuffbox, of all things. I found it in my paintbox."

"And no one ever claimed either object?"

"No." She shook her head and resumed walking back toward the house.

He fell into step beside her, trying to think. "When did you find the snuffbox?"

She muttered a response that he did not quite catch.

He flicked an impatient glance at her averted face. "What was that?"

"I said I found it the morning after our last, fateful interview in my aunt's garden. You may recall the evening, my lord. It was the night I asked you to arrange for us to, uh . . ."

"Oh, yes. That night. Fateful, indeed." He turned her words over in his mind, looking for a pattern that was not there. " 'Tis strange."

"Why do you say that?"

"I was attacked by a footpad that night on my way back to the carriage," he explained briefly. "I wondered at the time if the man might have been deliberately waiting for me, but I dismissed it as unlikely."

Victoria whirled around, her eyes wide with shock. "You were attacked? By a footpad? Why didn't you tell me? For heaven's sake, Lucas, you should have said something."

"Such as?" Her renewed concern for his safety pleased and reassured him.

"Do not be flippant. This is a very serious matter. You could have been hurt. Did he take your money or your watch?"

"No, he did not."

"No, of course not," she agreed quickly. "You would have been much too quick for him."

"You flatter me. I fear the simple truth is that I was lucky." He took her arm again and resumed guiding her back to the house. "The footpad was of no particular consequence, unless one considers the damage done to my coat. But it is a rather interesting coincidence."

"What is? And how can you say the attack on you was of no consequence? It seems to me it could have had very alarming consequences."

"Yes, but the interesting part is the coincidence of each of us having a rather narrow escape just before you discovered those objects with 'W' inscribed on them."

She was stunned into a rare silence. Lucas could almost hear her mind working feverishly. "What do you make of such coincidences?"

"To be honest, I do not know what to make of them. There probably isn't anything at all to be made of them. I will admit it had occurred to me that the footpad might have been hired by Edgeworth."

"Edgeworth. Oh, yes, him. Because of his embarrassing loss at cards? Do you think he would have stooped to that sort of vengeance just because he lost money to you?"

Lucas reflected on his last conversation with Edgeworth. "There was a bit more bad blood between us than just the gaming-table scene. But even if he resorted to such tactics, it still fails to explain the object you discovered in the conservatory."

She frowned. "No. Nor does it tie in with the carriage incident, although I suppose that if that had been a deliberate attack also, we might have been wrong in thinking I was the intended victim."

"You think I was the target?" He was surprised by her insight and took a minute to think about it. "I'm not sure. 'Tis possible. We were not standing very far apart on the street when it happened."

"Edgeworth again?"

Lucas chewed on that. On the night of the carriage incident he and Edgeworth had not yet had their confrontation over Vicky's honor. But there was still the matter of the gaming loss and Edgeworth might have begun to realize his reputation was declining in the clubs. And, of course, there was always that bit of bad business in the past that would forever stand between them.

"Possible," Lucas said finally.

"But what could either of those attacks have to do with my discovering the scarf and the snuffbox?"

"Do you know anyone whose name begins with a 'W'?"

"*No*. I mean, yes, of course. Several people. As I said, none of them had lost either item."

She rushed on, telling him about all the people whose name began with "W" and how her aunt had talked to them all about the missing items, but Lucas was not listening.

His attention had been caught and held by the strange note in her voice when she had first answered the direct question. Once before quite recently he had heard that hesitation, detected that slight distance, as if she did not want to get too close to the question. He reflected for another instant and then he had it. He had heard it the night she described her nightmare.

". . . and she also checked with Lady Wibberly, who takes an inordinate amount of snuff. Lord Wilkins, too, I believe. He wears scarves. And then we asked Waterson, but to no avail."

"Vicky."

"One can never be certain Lord Waterson remembers things all that well, however. It is entirely possible he lost both items and doesn't recall it. Always has his mind on higher things like meteorology, you know. He has built the most impressive instrument for measuring rainfall."

"Victoria."

"As I said, what with my aunt's long list of acquaintances, it is possible we missed someone."

"Vicky, darling, please hush for a minute. I want to ask you a very particular question and I would be very grateful if you gave me a direct answer." He stopped, obliging her to halt also. Then he turned her toward him and caught hold of her shoulders.

"Yes, Lucas?"

"Vicky, is there someone whose name begins with 'W' whom you do not like? Someone who frightens you or whom you feel you cannot trust? Someone who, perhaps, makes you exceedingly anxious?"

"No," she said instantly.

He smiled slightly at the obvious lie. "Try again with your answer, my sweet. And don't be afraid to tell me the truth. I'm your midnight companion in adventure, remember? You can tell me things you would tell no one else."

"Lucas, please, do not press me like this."

He urged her close, pushing her face into his shirt. Her amber cloak swirled around his legs. "Tell me, Vicky."

Her shoulders were stiff, her body unyielding. "You do not understand."

"Try me."

"Lucas, he's *dead*."

Lucas frowned into her soft hair, hearing the desperation in that simple statement. He flipped through the information Jessica Atherton had given him before he began to stalk his heiress. It took him less than a couple of seconds to hit upon a name: Samuel Whitlock. "Are we, by any chance," he asked gently, "talking about your stepfather?"

She jerked her head back, making a visible effort to pull herself together. "I told you it was impossible. He is dead and buried."

"But you did not like him very much, did you?"

Her eyes glittered in the moonlight. "I hated him for what he did to my mother and for what he would have done to me if he'd gotten the chance. My mother saved me from that lecherous bastard by sending me to live with my aunt for most of my life. But she could not save herself. In the end, he killed her."

13

"You believe your stepfather killed your mother?" Lucas's voice sounded amazingly calm, Victoria thought. It was the sort of voice in which he might have asked if she would care for a glass of sherry before dinner. As he spoke he draped an arm around her shoulder and resumed walking toward the house.

"Yes. Yes, I do, although I have never said as much to anyone except my aunt." Victoria felt the heavy weight around her shoulders and was oddly reassured. He was so very strong, she thought fleetingly. Comfortingly so.

She was not certain why Lucas's arm around her had such a soothing effect, but she didn't question it just then. She was too busy reminding herself to be very careful about what she said next. She had already blurted out a great deal more than she had ever intended.

"What does your aunt think?"

Victoria clutched at the edges of her cloak. "That 'tis very possible. She knows the sort of man he was. A cruel drunkard who lacked any shred of decency. She did point out that if he murdered her, it would be interesting to know why Samuel Whitlock waited so many years to do it. Why did he not simply get it over and done soon after he married my mother and had access to her fortune?"

"There may have been no real reason to kill her in the early years," Lucas said reflectively, as though working out a curious puzzle in his mind. "After all, as you said, he did have access to her money. Why should he risk hanging for murder?"

Victoria sighed. "That was Aunt Cleo's point. My mother not only sent me to live with my aunt, she frequently came to stay with us for weeks, sometimes months at a time. After she realized what sort of man she had married, she spent as little time with him as possible. When he got drunk he got violent."

"In other words, in addition to turning her money over to him, she obligingly stayed out of his way. So why kill her after all those years?" Lucas asked.

"Perhaps he simply got tired of her," Victoria said tightly. "Perhaps he got especially angry at her one day and lost his temper. He had a terrifying temper. When he lost it, he lost his self-control completely. He was like a madman." Unlike Lucas, she thought fleetingly, who was always controlled, even when he was angry.

"Your mother died in a riding accident, I believe?"

"Yes. Near his house in the country. She had gone there to entertain his friends that weekend. She had been staying with Aunt Cleo and me for several weeks prior to that, as usual, but Whitlock ordered her to return for a few days to do her duty as a wife, as he put it. My mother was very beautiful, very charming. An excellent hostess, in fact, and Whitlock often used her to impress his friends," Victoria explained.

"A riding accident sounds more like a planned murder, not one done in the heat of anger."

Victoria shrugged. "You may be right. I only know he did it."

"How do you know that?"

Because he told me so, himself, she thought wildly. *He told me even as he plunged forward to his death at the foot of those stairs.*

But she could hardly tell Lucas why she was so certain of her stepfather's guilt. Lucas was entirely too shrewd. Once he had that bit of information, he would probe for more and she had already learned she had a bad habit of becoming altogether too trusting and vulnerable in his arms.

Besides, she reminded herself grimly, while Lucas was a very unusual man in some respects, he was not likely to be so tolerant and understanding as to welcome the news that he was married to a murderess.

"I have no real proof, of course," Victoria said cautiously. "But in my heart I am certain of his guilt."

He let that go. "Riding accidents happen all the time, Vicky."

"My mother was an excellent rider." Victoria hoped this would close the matter, but Lucas, in his inimitable fashion, pushed on.

"Did you confront Whitlock?"

This was getting too close to dangerous territory. "He knew I had no proof. He laughed at me."

Lucas's hand tightened around her shoulders. "What did you do then?"

"There was nothing I could do. He died less than two months later and Aunt Cleo and I decided it was rough justice."

"He was found at the foot of a staircase, I believe?"

She glanced up quickly. "Where did you hear that?"

Lucas's mouth curved wryly. "Jessica Atherton."

"You certainly obtained a great deal of information from Lady Atherton."

"Let us not start that quarrel again. Did your stepfather die that way?"

"Yes." Victoria picked her words carefully. "He had apparently been drinking very heavily that night, which was not unusual for him. He tripped and fell at the top of a long flight of stairs. That was the end of the matter."

"Not quite."

She started. "What do you mean by that?"

"Merely that you are still upset by the sight of his initial embroidered on someone else's scarf or engraved on a strange snuffbox. What's the matter, Vicky? Are you beginning to wonder if there really are such things as ghosts? Did you think Whitlock had come back to haunt you?"

"*Do not say that.*" She got control of herself instantly. "Of course I don't believe in ghosts. What bothered me about the scarf and the snuffbox was that it appeared both had been left where I was the most likely one to find each."

"The location of the scarf is particularly interesting, isn't it? It implies someone knew you would be coming back into the house late via the conservatory door."

"Yes, that is exactly it, Lucas. Looking back on it, it makes one wonder if someone was spying on us the whole time. That same someone apparently was watching so closely that he or she saw me leave the party that night and get into the carriage you had hired," Victoria concluded.

"And followed us to the inn? 'Tis possible."

"It could have been Jessica Atherton."

Lucas's tone lightened. "I cannot envision Lady Atherton climbing the garden wall at midnight."

"You have a point. So that means the scarf and snuffbox were left by someone else. Unless . . ."

"Unless what?"

Victoria was struck by an idea. "Do you suppose she hired a Bow Street runner to follow us around?"

"You, of all people, my dear, would know how easy that is to do."

There was an acute silence following that remark, a silence during which it occurred to Victoria that if she'd been thinking clearly, instead of following her heart, she might have had the good sense to hire a runner herself to obtain some information on the mysterious Lord Stonevale.

"I wondered, myself, how long it would take you to get around to doing just that," Lucas said.

She frowned, afraid he had read her mind. "Doing what?"

His teeth flashed in a wicked grin. "Hiring a runner to have me investigated. It was one of the reasons I wanted to get the courtship over and done as quickly as possible."

"You are perfectly despicable, Stonevale."

"I am also perfectly content with our bargain, madam." He paused outside the kitchen door to brush his mouth lightly over hers. His eyes gleamed. "And while I would not have wanted you put in the awkward position you were in that night at the inn, I cannot say I am particularly sorry things happened the way they did. All in all, considering the risks we were running, we got off lightly."

"I do not see how we could have gotten off much worse."

"Then you lack imagination, madam. I used to lie awake nights thinking about all that could go wrong during our midnight jaunts." He tipped up her chin. "Are you really so unhappy with me, Vicky?"

She wanted to rail at him for not loving her as she loved him. She wanted to accuse him of having manipulated her into this marriage where her emotions threatened to tear her apart while his seemed under perfect control. She longed to bring him to a more forceful realization of his overwhelming guilt, to make him grovel for her forgiveness and proclaim his undying love and devotion.

In short, Victoria realized, she wanted some vengeance for the situation in which she found herself. However, she was realistic enough to know she would probably never get it.

But she had learned her lesson well, Victoria vowed silently. She would keep the secrets of her heart, just as she had learned to keep other, darker secrets. If the Earl of Stonevale was content with his marriage, she would strive to be satisfied also. But she would not give him any more than what he had set out to trap—an heiress who was obliged to accept the fact that she had been married for her money with relatively good grace.

"I believe," Victoria said carefully, "that as husbands go, you are probably not such a bad one."

"You damn me with faint praise, madam," he complained softly. "Surely you can do better than that?"

She licked her lower lip as she looked up at him. He

was a menacing figure by moonlight. Large and powerful, he loomed over her. The stark lines of his face were etched with palest silver and deepest shadow. His eyes glittered with a sensual threat that made her recently sated senses flicker back to life. She ought to be afraid of him, she told herself. Instead, she always felt ridiculously safe in his presence. Damn the man.

Her instinct was to throw her arms around him and confess her love. But her sense of self-protection and her pride stepped in to cut off such a rash and useless course of action. She would not make herself totally vulnerable to Lucas ever again the way she had that fateful night at the inn.

"I believe, my lord, that I have already explained to you I will do my best to live up to my part of our bargain."

Lucas shook his head ruefully and kissed the tip of her nose. "So proud. And so determined not to give an inch more than you must. How can you be so cruel, Vicky?"

"I hardly think 'tis being cruel to say I am willing to accept the situation in which I find myself. What more can you rightfully demand of me, Lucas?"

"Everything."

"You sound as if you talk of my complete surrender, my lord."

"Perhaps I do."

"For that I vow you will have to wait until the world allows women to wear breeches in public," she shot back tartly. "In other words, forever."

"Perhaps not quite so long. But we will come back to the matter later. For now I will be content with the progress we have made tonight." He took her hand and led her into the dark, slumbering house.

The vicar and his wife were nervous. It was painfully obvious they were not accustomed to taking tea in the great house of Stonevale. Victoria decided that if she were to hazard a guess, she would say they had never before been invited into the house for any reason at all, let alone a consultation about the charity needs of the district. That irritated her. It was further proof that the previous earl had not cared about the people who lived on and near his lands.

"I cannot tell you how very happy we are to have you and your lovely lady installed here at the house, Lord Stonevale." The Reverend Worth, a ruddy-faced, solidly built man in his fifties, spoke very earnestly.

"Yes, indeed. We're delighted to welcome you," Mrs. Worth, a sweet-faced little wren of a woman who sat stiffly next to her husband, said tremulously. The teacup in her small hand trembled as she took a very tiny sip. Every now and then she would steal a quick, timid glance around the drawing room, as if she could not quite believe she was inside the great house.

"Thank you," Victoria said gently, smiling at the uneasy woman. "It was very kind of you to arrange to be here on such short notice."

"Not at all, not at all," the woman sputtered, and nearly spilled her tea. "We are ever so grateful for your interest in local matters."

The vicar made a valiant effort to meet his host's eyes in a man-to-man look. "Hope you don't mind my saying so, sir, but your family's lands have been neglected entirely too long. I am delighted to say that I have already heard talk in the village of the improvements you have begun. 'Tis a great relief."

"I am glad you are pleased, Reverend Worth. I couldn't agree with you more about the status of the estate and the surrounding countryside." Lucas put down his cup with a distinct snap that made Victoria hide a quick grin. Her husband was concealing his impatience well, but she knew for a fact that he would have much preferred to have been allowed to escape this particular social function.

He was, he had told her in no uncertain terms that morning, a busy man and he did not have time to waste taking tea with the vicar. Victoria had informed him that he was not going to be let off the hook and in the end she had won, much to the interested surprise of one or two of the new servants who had happened to overhear the discussion in the hall. It was not going

unnoticed that the new Earl of Stonevale had a decided
tendency to indulge his bride.

"There is a great deal to be done," Worth noted.
"The situation around here was getting desperate."

"Your ladyship has made a wonderful impression on
the local people," Mrs. Worth said shyly. "When I
went to visit Betsy Hawkins this morning to take her a
petticoat for her daughter, she told me quite proudly
she wouldn't be needing any more charity. Her daughter had a job up here in the kitchens, she said, and her
husband was going to start work in the stables. She was
so happy, madam. You cannot imagine. That poor lady
has had a hard time of it, as have many others."

"We are grateful to have so many willing workers.
We shall need a great many people to get this place in
shape," Victoria said, meaning every word. It had been
a harrowing chore getting the drawing room in even
halfway decent condition for today's visit. She'd started
the new staff cleaning it at dawn that morning.

"Well, I don't mind telling you that thanks to a
poacher's ghost story, you are off to a fine start as far as
folks around here are concerned." The vicar chuckled
and then caught himself as his wife threw him a horrified look. He hastily picked up his teacup and cleared
his throat. "Beg pardon."

But Lucas was not to be sidetracked. "What ghost
story and what poacher, Reverend?"

The vicar's initial uneasiness became visibly more
noticeable. It was clear he felt he had already said too
much. He coughed slightly. "I fear, sir, that a few of
the local men are not above poaching in the woods,
especially when times are hard, as they have been
lately. Lord knows it's sometimes worth life and limb to
do it, what with the mantraps the previous earl set."

"You needn't worry, vicar. Having served in the army
and thus been obliged to live off the land occasionally
myself, I assure you I am inclined to ignore a little
poaching. I have already made arrangements to destroy
what mantraps the hunters have not already discovered."

The vicar's smile broke like sunshine on a cloudy

day. "I am extremely happy to hear that. Your uncle, as you must know, had an entirely different attitude."

"Now about this particular poacher's ghost story," Lucas prodded quietly.

The vicar exchanged a quick glance with his wife and then sighed heavily. "Yes, well, it was just an amusing tale I happened to overhear this morning. You know how country folk talk. It seems a certain intrepid hunter was taking a shortcut home last night when he caught a glimpse of the Amber Knight and his lady. You have heard the legend, of course?"

"I am aware of it."

Victoria leaned forward intently. "The Amber Knight and his lady were seen in the district?"

The vicar's wife laughed nervously. "Right here on the grounds of the estate, if you please. At least, according to the way the tale was being told this morning. It seems the knight and his lady were spotted walking home through the gardens sometime after midnight. Is that not a delightful notion?"

"Fascinating," Victoria said as the truth began to crystallize in her head. She pictured how she and Lucas might have appeared to a startled poacher in the dead of night, her amber cloak swirling around her. "Walking home through the gardens, you say?" She felt Lucas's quelling glance but chose to ignore him. This was far too amusing. "What would they have been doing running around at that time of night, do you suppose?"

Lucas cleared his throat. "Would you pour me another cup of tea, my dear? I seem to find myself rather thirsty."

"Yes, of course." Victoria laughed at him with her eyes as she dutifully poured the tea. He gave her a severe glare in return, which only inspired her to fresh mischief. "You were saying, Mrs. Worth?"

"Was I? About what they might have been doing running around at midnight? Oh, dear." The good woman's smile was tentative. "Well, they are ghosts, you know. I suppose that is the only time they are allowed to run around. And according to legend, the pair was very much prone to midnight trysts. It seems the two had a habit of riding the lands at night and returning to the house shortly before dawn."

The vicar cleared his throat. "That's quite enough speculation about ghosts, my dear. You'll have Lord Stonevale and his lady thinking we deal in nothing but village gossip."

"Never," declared Victoria. "I find it all most interesting, don't you, Stonevale?"

"I find it all a lot of nonsense," Lucas said repressively.

"You must understand," the vicar's wife said hurriedly, "the villagers were thrilled to hear the story. They want to believe it because they want to believe that things really have begun to change for the better around here. According to the legend, Stonevale will prosper again only when the Amber Knight and his lady return. I pray you won't begrudge the people their small tale of hope, my lord."

"Yes." Victoria smiled sweetly at her husband. "Pray, don't be a killjoy, Stonevale."

The vicar and his wife stared in shock at Victoria. Lucas merely gave his wife another quelling glance and drank his tea.

The vicar, apparently sensing that he and his wife had accidentally stumbled into a mild bit of marital teasing, turned a bit ruddier and plowed forth gamely with a change of topic. "Far rather see a couple of harmless ghosts than that highwayman who's been plaguing the district for the past couple of months."

"Highwayman?" Victoria's attention was instantly riveted in a new direction. "What is this about a highwayman? Have you been robbed, Reverend?"

"Not I. And not any of the villagers that I know of. Daresay, none of them would be worth the fellow's time. But there have been reports of a couple of coaches stopped. The villain's a bit inept, I fear. On one occasion the driver of the coach pulled a pistol and sent the highwayman fleeing for the bushes. The second time the passengers fobbed him off with a few coins and a worthless ring."

"Highwaymen usually have a lair in the locality where

they conduct business," Lucas observed thoughtfully. "Do you think this man might be a local resident?"

The vicar shook his head a bit too quickly, looking more uneasy than ever. "I daresay not. Probably just someone riding through. I wouldn't be surprised if the fellow has quit the district by now. In his profession 'tis probably wise to keep shifting business locations." Satisfied that he had salvaged the social situation, the vicar fell back on a safe subject. "I say, Stonevale. Don't mean to be impertinent, but have you given much thought to the sort of crops you'll want to plant? I've lived around here for a number of years now and I have some notion of what does well in this soil."

Mrs. Worth was instantly alarmed. "Really, dear, I am certain his lordship will ask for advice if he requires it."

"Of course, of course." The vicar flushed a dark red. "Sorry about that. Horticulture is a hobby of mine. I fancy myself something of a student of the subject."

Lucas's head came up alertly. "Do you indeed, sir?"

The vicar coughed slightly again, but this time he looked a little more sure of himself. "Pleased to say I've had one or two papers published in the *Botanical Progress*. Working on a book on flower gardening at the moment."

"What do you know about buckwheat?" Lucas asked bluntly, all traces of restlessness vanishing instantly.

"Fine animal fodder. Good for your poorest soil, of course, but I'm more in favor of oats, wheat, and corn where possible."

"I have heard buckwheat can be eaten by humans in times of wheat shortages."

"Only by those who live on the continent. Doubt you'd get an Englishman to eat it unless he was frightfully hungry."

"I see your point. I have also become quite interested in marl as opposed to manure of late," Lucas said. "What is your opinion?"

"As it happens, I have done a bit of investigation on the subject," the vicar said, glowing with enthusiasm. "Tried marl out on my wife's rosebushes. Also peat, ground bone, and fish. Kept a detailed log. Would you care to hear the results?"

"I certainly would." Lucas stood up. "Why don't we go to the library where I have some maps of the estate we can look at?" He turned belatedly to Victoria. "You will excuse us, my dear?"

"Of course."

"Come along, vicar, I have several questions to put to you. Now, about manure. I must admit it has the advantage of being readily available."

"True. And when one does run short, one can always have it brought in from London. Several thousand horses stabled in London, you know. Something has to be done with all that manure. Have you by any chance read Humphrey Davy's *Elements of Agricultural Chemistry?*"

"No," said Lucas. "But I did get hold of a copy of Marshall's *The Rural Economy of Yorkshire*. Marshall is very fond of marl."

"It has its merits, I'll grant you. I shall loan you my copy of Davy's *Elements*, if you like. The man takes a very scientific approach to the subject of manuring. I believe you will find it most interesting."

"I would appreciate that very much," Lucas said.

The two men moved out of the room, talking intently.

Victoria looked at her guest. "More tea, Mrs. Worth?"

"Thank you, my lady." She gave her hostess an apologetic look. "Please forgive my husband. I fear he is quite impassioned in his studies of horticulture and agriculture."

Victoria grinned. "Believe me, he is in good company. My husband's interest has grown just as strong of late. You may have noticed."

Mrs. Worth relaxed. Her small chuckle was delightful. "I did. Imagine discussing manure in a drawing room. But, then, that is life in the country."

"It is not altogether different from life at my aunt's home in London. My aunt is very much interested in matters of intellectual inquiry and I fear I have followed in her footsteps. I quite enjoy such discussions."

The vicar's wife beamed enthusiastically. "Perhaps

you and Lord Stonevale would be interested in attending some of the meetings of our local Society for the Investigation of Curious Matters. We meet every week on Monday afternoons in our home. Quite a large crowd attends, I am pleased to say." The good lady suddenly flushed and began to stammer. "Of course our meetings would probably not be of great interest to you. I am certain you are already far ahead of us since you have had the advantages of being in Town."

"Not at all. The prospect of attending your next meeting sounds quite delightful. I shall look forward to it."

Mrs. Worth's smile returned in full force. "How kind of you. I cannot wait to tell my friends."

"You say you grow roses, Mrs. Worth?"

Mrs. Worth began to beam, and said shyly. "They are my passion, I fear."

"I would dearly love to discuss some plans for the gardens here at Stonevale. I cannot live without a proper garden and Lucas is far too busy with farming problems to help me. Would you care to examine the grounds with me?"

"I should be delighted."

"Excellent. And while we're about it, we can get on with our discussion of the most pressing charity needs in the area. In all truth, I am far more anxious to get started on that project than I am the gardens."

The vicar's wife smiled with genuine approval. "It is easy to see why the villagers are so eager to believe their Amber Lady has returned."

Victoria laughed. "You refer to my preference for a certain shade in clothing, I imagine. Pure coincidence, I assure you." She glanced down at her yellow and white afternoon dress with a wry smile.

Mrs. Worth was startled and then embarrassed that her hostess would think she had made such a personal remark. "Oh, no, madam, I was not referring to your lovely dress, although I will allow the color is stunning on you and does create a sort of amber effect. No, I was referring to the legend. It holds that the knight's lady was very kind and gentle."

Victoria wrinkled her nose and grinned. "Then it

cannot have been referring to me. I am certainly no paragon. Just ask my husband."

A week later Victoria sat in front of her dressing-table mirror while Nan finished preparing her for bed. Her maid was handing her a dressing gown when the connecting door between Lucas's room and her own was opened after a perfunctory knock. Lucas sauntered in with a proprietary air that Victoria was learning to expect from him. She glared at him in the mirror and nodded to her maid, who bobbed a small curtsy to Lucas.

"You may go now, Nan. Thank you."

"Yes, ma'am. Shall I have a tea tray sent up?"

Victoria met Lucas's sinfully amused eyes in the mirror and shook her head. "No, thank you, Nan. I will not be wanting any tea tonight."

"Very well, ma'am. Good night to you and yer lordship." She made her way quickly to the door.

Lucas waited until the door had closed behind the maid and then he moved with lazy menace to stand directly behind Victoria. He leaned forward and planted both hands on her dressing table, effectively caging her. His eyes continued to hold hers in the mirror.

Victoria could not repress a small thrill of anticipation. The man had a devastating effect on her senses. And she was learning the power she held over his physical reaction to her. She wondered if it would always be like this between them.

"I saw that a letter arrived from your aunt today." Lucas bent his head to kiss her nape. "What does Lady Nettleship have to say?"

"That it appears as though we are all going to brush through the scandal relatively unscathed." Victoria smiled ruefully, remembering the contents of her aunt's letter. "Thanks to Jessica Atherton, who has put it about that our hasty marriage is the great romance of the Season."

"Good old Jessica." Lucas ran his tongue along the sensitive rim of her ear.

Victoria shuddered. "I swear, Lucas, I do not like being indebted to that woman."

"Nor do I, but as a soldier I long ago learned to accept help from whatever quarter made it available."

"Obviously, or we would not now be in our present position."

"Shrew. You cannot resist such remarks, can you?"

"It is very difficult," Victoria admitted. Her blood was already heating just from the expression in his eyes and his closeness. It struck her that even if someone waved a magic wand and dissolved the marriage tomorrow, she would never be truly free of this man.

"Any other news from your aunt?"

Victoria saw the flicker of intensity in his eyes and knew it had nothing to do with the sensual assault he was launching against her. "Do you mean has she discovered any other objects marked with a 'W'? The answer is no. She also states she still has not found anyone claiming to have lost either the scarf or the snuffbox."

"Does she mention Edgeworth by any chance?"

"No."

"Just as well. Tell me, Vicky, what sort of letter did you write back to your aunt?" Lucas asked.

"I told her about my plans for the gardens and invited her to visit at her earliest convenience. I also mentioned how you and the vicar have discovered a mutual interest in farming techniques, horticulture, and manure. That was about all, I believe. Oh, and I asked her to send me some plant cuttings and seeds."

"What? No discussion of how you have nobly accepted your unhappy fate and have vowed to be a dutiful wife?" He kissed her neck. "No talk of how you have come to recognize that your womanly honor demands you submit yourself to your husband, even though the marital act is, naturally, quite repellent under the circumstances?" He nibbled on her earlobe. "No mention of how bravely you endure the performance of your duties in the marriage bed?" He kissed the curve of her shoulder. "No pathetic little commentary on how you have been made to pay the price of your folly and what a lesson this has all been to you?"

She shot to her feet and whirled around, pummeling

him unmercifully in the ribs. "Stonevale, you are a miserable, teasing beast of a husband and you deserve to rot."

"My leg, my leg. Cease and desist at once, madam, or you'll ruin me for life." Lucas retreated toward the bed, his laughter filling the bedroom.

"To hell with your leg." She continued her attack, closing in on him, forcing him back until he toppled onto the bed. Then she jumped on top of him, straddling him triumphantly. Lucas held up his hands in surrender.

"I beg for mercy, my lady. Would you continue to beat on a helpless man who is already down?"

"You may be down but you are far from helpless, Stonevale. You still have the use of your mouth and it seems to me that is what got you into trouble in the first place tonight. You could not resist taunting me in a most villainous fashion, could you?"

His smile was slow and filled with sensual promise. "Allow me to put my mouth to better use, madam."

He reached up with one hand and splayed his strong fingers around the back of her head. Then he dragged her face down to his and captured her lips with his own.

With a soft sigh Victoria gave herself up to the magic of her husband's embrace.

14

Lucas knew he had only himself to blame when the gossamer web of domestic harmony he was just starting to weave was ripped to shreds on the following Monday morning.

He should have seen it coming, he told himself. He should have been prepared. He, who always prided himself on his sense of strategy and planning, had been caught off guard, and there was no excuse.

But his wife's timing was as good as that of any field marshal who has studied the opponent well.

She breezed into the library, waving the newest letter from her aunt, just at the very moment Lucas was going through a detailed summary of her investments for the past three years.

"There you are, Lucas, I have been looking for you. No, do not bother to get up. I just wanted to tell you I shall be writing a fairly large draft on my account to cover an investment I plan to make soon. I assumed you would want to take it into consideration when you plan your own expenditures this month."

Lucas sat down again and looked up, his mind still

reeling from the shock of what he had learned recently about Victoria's investment habits. She smiled brightly at him from the other side of the massive desk, looking as elegant and vibrant as ever in a sun yellow morning gown.

"How large a sum will you be needing and what sort of investment are you considering?" he asked cautiously.

"Oh, I should think a few thousand pounds will be enough to get me into this particular investment."

"A few *thousand*?"

"Perhaps ten or fifteen." She glanced down at the letter in her hand. "Aunt Cleo says the group will be investing in some new collieries in Lancashire."

"Ten or fifteen thousand pounds? For a coal production project in Lancashire?" Lucas was stunned. "You cannot possibly mean to do anything so foolish. I cannot allow you to do it."

It was when he saw the light of battle flare in her beautiful eyes that Lucas knew he had just made a serious, tactical mistake.

"Our man of affairs, Mr. Beckford, has recently recommended the project very strongly," Victoria said. "Aunt Cleo writes that she intends to invest, herself."

"Your aunt is free to do as she chooses, but I cannot allow you to pour that amount of money into a coal pit in Lancashire. One can go through a fortune very quickly investing in collieries."

"I have a fortune, Lucas, remember?" she asked far too sweetly. "You married me for it."

Lucas tried to forge a path out of the mire in which he found himself. "Your inheritance is sizable, my dear, but it is not inexhaustible. Far from it. You are intelligent enough to realize that. You do not have enough money to warrant taking risks of ten or fifteen thousand pounds. Sums of that size should be put into acquiring land, not digging expensive pits in the ground."

"But I already own some properties in London from which I receive a very nice income. And," she added, with a challenging smile, "I am now a partner with you in owning a good-sized chunk of Yorkshire. I do not wish to acquire any more land, Lucas."

Lucas returned to the accounting summary and said, very matter-of-factly, "Then you can put the money into the improvements we will be needing here at Stonevale."

"You are busy enough as it is spending a great deal of my money on such improvements. This colliery project is a personal investment I wish to make on my own behalf."

"Vicky, trust me on this matter. Collieries are risky investments, especially when they are being run by others. If you are seriously interested in mining, we can think about having an engineer survey Stonevale. There is coal in Yorkshire as well as other minerals and there may be some worth going after on the estate. But I cannot allow you to throw your money into a distant project over which we will have no management control."

Victoria marched to the library desk and threw the letter down. "You are going to forbid me the right to spend my money as I wish?"

Lucas prayed for divine guidance but there was none forthcoming. He would have to deal with the devilish question on his own and he already knew he was damned either way.

He tried to choose his next words with care. "You have come to me with a large income that must be protected for the sake of our children and our grandchildren and their children. As your husband it is my duty to guide you in your investments."

"I thought so," Victoria announced grimly. "This is how it always starts, I imagine. One's husband begins by telling his wife that she is incompetent to manage her own affairs and that she must allow him to do it for her. From there he moves to take complete control, allowing her no say whatsoever in how her money is spent."

That angered him. Lucas gestured impatiently at the account book lying open on the desk. "To be perfectly blunt, my dear, I am not certain you should be making all your own decisions. You seem to have a tendency to take great risks in your financial affairs. You have been in deep water more than once."

"I have always come about," she shot back. "As you can plainly see if you look at my current income."

"Yes, thanks to your properties in Town. You see, Vicky? It is the investments in land that are most reliable. They are what shelter an inheritance such as yours. You have no business taking risks in the funds or in shipping and distant mining projects."

"No business taking risks? That is ludicrous coming from you. Before you married me, your entire income came from taking risks. What can be more risky than the battlefield or the gaming tables?"

The fact that she had a point only served to annoy him further. "Damn it, Vicky, I had no choice in how I made my money. I did what I had to do. But matters have changed. We both have a responsibility to manage Stonevale and the income you brought to this marriage as wisely as possible. Your days of taking huge risks with your capital are over."

She stepped forward and planted both hands on his desk. Her eyes shimmered with fury. "Say it in plain language, Stonevale. I want us both to hear you say it."

"I do not know how much plainer I can make it."

"Tell me very clearly that you are forbidding me to spend my money in any way I wish. Let us have the words plain between us."

His own temper leapt to match hers. "You are deliberately trying to set a trap for me, Vicky. You want me to choose between saying the words that will give you complete freedom and the ones that will damn me as just another tyrannical husband like the man who married your mother. Do you think you can manipulate me so easily, madam?"

"I am not trying to manipulate you. It is just the reverse. You are trying to manipulate me." Victoria's tone was unwavering under his severe gaze.

"I am trying to protect you from your own reckless nature."

"Reckless? You call me reckless? You, who made your living first as a soldier and then as a gamester? Hah. That is an excuse and well you know it. You want complete control of my money and you are telling me

you will no longer allow me any say in how I spend it.
What's next, Lucas? Will you force me to accept a small
quarterly allowance? Will I be obliged to buy all my
clothes and paints and books and the occasional horse
out of whatever you choose to allow me by way of an
income?"

That did it. He lost what was left of his temper.
"Why not? If you are going to play the role of a frivolous, spendthrift woman who doesn't give a thought to
economy, I shall have no choice but to treat you as
such. But we both know you are too smart to act that
way just to spite me."

"*Are you forbidding me the free use of my money?*"

"I am forbidding you to risk a vast sum on a project
you know nothing about except that your aunt's man of
affairs recommends it."

"I have made a great deal of money from some of Mr.
Beckford's recommendations."

"You have also lost money on some of them. I have
seen the evidence in your accounts. Mr. Beckford has
been far from infallible," Lucas said, flipping recklessly
through Victoria's business ledger.

"One must expect to take a few losses when one is
playing for important stakes."

"There are many men far wealthier than you who
have brought their families to ruin with that attitude."

"Say it, damn you. Say the words, Lucas. Tell me to
my face I no longer have any control over my inheritance."

Lucas gave up trying to salvage the situation. "Vicky,
I thought I had made it clear that just because I choose
to indulge you in some of your wilder notions, it does
not mean I will allow you to manipulate me whenever
you wish. One way or another you will learn that."

"Say it, Lucas." Her eyes continued to challenge him
boldly and her smile was deliberately taunting.

Lucas swore very softly. "Very well, madam, since
you are obviously determined to force this issue into a
full-scale battle, I will give you what you seem to be
looking for, namely an opponent. You are hereby forbidden to invest in the colliery project. I shall instruct
your bankers that you are to be given a small quarterly

allowance and nothing more unless I personally autho-
rize it."

She stared at him in stunned amazement, clearly
shocked by the extent of his retaliation. "I do not believe this. You cannot possibly mean what you say. To
forbid me to invest in the coal-mining project is one
thing, but to forbid me any use of my money at all
is . . . is unbelievable."

Lucas leaned back in his chair and studied her dispassionately. She really did look taken aback. This was
obviously not the outcome she had expected when she
had begun the skirmish.

"I can understand your surprise," he said gently. "I
am quite certain that when you walked in here a few
minutes ago, you were fairly sure you would walk out
the victor. You are too shrewd to have launched the
assault without first being convinced you stood a good
chance of winning. But you underestimated me, my
dear, and I fear you will persist in losing these skirmishes
if you do not stop doing that. A good field marshal
never makes the mistake of underestimating her opponent."

"You speak as if we are on a battlefield."

Lucas nodded bleakly. "I fear that is precisely the
situation you have created."

"And to think I actually thought you were going to
make a tolerable husband after all." She whirled around
and flew to the door. Not pausing to give him a chance
to get there ahead of her, she yanked it open.

"Where do you think you are going, Vicky?"

"Out." Her smile could have separated him from his
skin.

"Vicky, if you think you can fly off in a tantrum and
go looking for some mischief, you are sadly mistaken."

"Have no fear, my lord, I shall be in quite unexcep-
tional company. I am attending a meeting at the vicar's.
I'll wager that even you, with your newfound proper,
conservative airs and priggish ways, cannot find anything to say against my spending the afternoon in such a
gathering."

"What sort of society is holding this meeting?"

"One devoted to the investigation of curious matters," she retorted loftily.

"I might be able to find time to accompany you," he began carefully.

"Good gracious, Lucas, that is quite impossible. I am certain you are far too busy to join me. You have so many thoughtful, important decisions to make right here." She went out the door, slamming it pointedly behind her.

Lucas winced as the lamps shivered under the impact. He sat in silence for a moment and then got deliberately to his feet to cross the room and pour himself a glass of brandy.

He stood at the window to drink it and told himself morosely that it was going to be a long campaign. He had sadly deluded himself when he had decided the difficult part would be over once he got her to marry him. It was obvious the truly hard work came after the wedding.

Good God. Had he really turned a touch priggish under the weight of his newfound responsibilities? He wondered.

Victoria was still fuming by the time she reached the comfortable home of the vicar and his wife. But she managed a charming smile as she was shown into a pleasant, sunny room full of various members of the local gentry and their ladies. The welcome was gratifyingly warm and her ill humor faded quickly.

"Welcome to our little society meeting, Lady Stonevale. We have all been concentrating our attentions of late on trying to prepare an improved remedy for gout and rheumatic pains," Mrs. Worth explained after the introductions had been made. She waved to a table full of small glasses. Each contained a liquid. "Medicinal herbs and plants are a great interest for most of us. Sir Alfred, here, for example, is quite hopeful of claiming the Society of Arts' prize for discovering a means of increasing opium-poppy production in England. He has obtained a very high-quality product, indeed."

"How exciting," Victoria said. "You should feel quite proud of yourself, Sir Alfred."

Sir Alfred blushed modestly.

"And Dr. Thornby over there has been experimenting with various tinctures and decoctions that combine alcohol and other ingredients such as liquorice, rhubarb, and camomile."

It was Dr. Thornby's turn to be flushed with pride.

"Fascinating," Victoria murmured, examining the various glasses. "My aunt and I have attended many medical lectures on such matters. Have you had much success?"

"As you know," Dr. Thornby began with barely contained enthusiasm, "the combination of alcohol and opium in laudanum is quite effective for pain relief but tends to make the sufferer extremely drowsy. This is fine for certain ailments but not for more chronic problems such as gout or rheumatic pains or certain, ahem, women's ailments. Something is needed for these which brings relief but does not induce sleep."

"You want a pain-relieving concoction that will allow the sufferer to go about his daily routine," Victoria said with a quick nod of understanding. "Very important research. Very important, indeed."

"The farmers and laborers in my area of the country have achieved some success on their own through trial and error," remarked a plump gentleman in the corner. "They've developed some excellent remedies."

"The problem," said another, "is lack of standardization and analysis. Every family has its own remedies of course, but each recipe has been handed down for generations and is the result of tradition and folklore rather than proper scientific principles and study. Every housewife has her particular recipe for cough syrup, for example, but no two mixtures are quite the same."

"Obviously there are several aspects of the problem to be studied," Victoria noted.

"Quite true." Dr. Thornby approached the table. "But there is only one scientific approach to the problem.

We must conduct an experiment and take careful notes. Each of these glasses contains a particular remedy. Our goal today is to see which of them creates an immediately soothing effect without bringing on sleep."

"What about the actual relief of pain?" Victoria asked with deep interest. "How will you measure that? I am not, myself, suffering even a headache at the moment."

"We will have to do that in a second phase of the experiment," the vicar conceded. "Difficult to find five or ten people all having an attack of the gout or a headache at the same time, I'm afraid."

"As it happens," Mrs. Worth said helpfully, "I have a touch of rheumatic pain this afternoon."

"And my gout's been flaring up," another member of the group offered.

"I have been suffering from toothache all day," declared an elderly gentleman.

"I do believe I have a headache," Lady Alice volunteered.

The vicar brightened, as did Dr. Thornby and Sir Alfred.

"Excellent, excellent. We may be able to accomplish both phases of the experiment today." Sir Alfred's glance was both shy and distinctly hopeful as he looked at Victoria. "Understand you have an interest in this sort of thing, Lady Stonevale. Would you care to join us in our testing or would you prefer to observe?"

"Heavens, it is always far more interesting to participate in an experiment than to merely observe it. I should greatly enjoy helping you test your concoctions. It should prove most enlightening."

Sir Alfred was much flattered, as was everyone else in the room. Dr. Thornby stepped forward to take charge again. "Now then, I shall put the notebook here on the table and each of us must write a clear, concise description of our sensations as we proceed from glass to glass. I propose we each start with straight brandy first and record our reactions to it before we move on to the various tonic mixtures."

"Yes, of course," the vicar exclaimed. "We need to

be able to judge the differences between the pure
spirits and the spirits infused with other ingredients.
Very clever of you, Thornby."

Victoria frowned consideringly as a thought struck
her. "Might it not be best if at least one of us stayed
with the pure spirits for the entire experiment? That
way the reactions of those using the various concoctions
can be judged against the use of spirits alone at every
point."

There were several immediate nods of approval.

"Brilliant idea, your ladyship," Sir Alfred said. "You
are obviously quite conversant with such scientific investigation techniques."

"I have had some experience," Victoria admitted modestly. "As it was my idea and as I have no particular
physical complaint to alleviate this afternoon, I shall
volunteer to stick with the spirits alone."

"Very helpful of you, Lady Stonevale. Very helpful,
indeed," Dr. Thornby said. "Let us begin." He graciously extended a glass of brandy to Victoria.

Lucas was appalled at the sight that greeted him that
afternoon when he returned from a visit to one of his
tenants. A very unsteady Victoria was being assisted up
the front steps by her maid and two very concerned
footmen. Lucas threw his horse's reins at the groom
and hurried forward.

"My God, what is the matter here? Are you ill,
Vicky?" He peered at her with deep concern.

"Oh, hello, Lucas." She turned a beatific smile upon
him and nearly lost her balance in the process. "Did
you enjoy being a cautious, conservative prig all day? I
have spent my time this afternoon in a far more useful
fashion. I have been conducting a little . . ." She paused
to burp discreetly. "A little experiment."

A spicy cloud of brandy fumes wafted past Lucas's
nose. He glared at the anxious maid as the truth dawned
on him. "I will take care of her ladyship," he announced in a voice laced with steel.

"Yes, my lord. I'll run have cook prepare some nice
tea for her ladyship."

"Don't bother," Lucas growled as he caught Victoria around the waist.

He got her past the anxious gazes of the butler, two more footmen, and a couple of housemaids, and finally, he got her up the stairs and into bed. As she sprawled gracefully back on her pillows, Victoria smiled once more and regarded him with a dreamy gaze.

"Lucas, dear, you really must learn not to look so frightfully menacing. You do have a nasty habit of glaring, you know."

"What the devil have you been drinking?"

She frowned. "Let me see. Brandy, for the most part, I believe. Did I explain about the experiment?"

"Not precisely, but we can go into the details later."

"Oh, dear, does that mean another lecture?"

"Yes, I am afraid it does, Vicky," Lucas said grimly. "I will tolerate a great deal from you, my dear, but I will not have you coming home foxed in the middle of the afternoon, and that is final."

"I believe you will have to read me the lecture later, Lucas. I do not feel very well at the moment." Victoria turned on her side and grabbed wildly for the chamber pot under the bed.

Lucas sighed and held her head. She was right. The lecture would have to wait.

As it turned out, the lecture was put off until the following morning. Victoria tried to avoid it entirely by waking late and announcing she would take tea in her room. But a maid arrived shortly after nine with a request from Lucas that his wife attend him in his library at ten.

Victoria briefly considered the odds of getting out of the nasty business altogether by claiming to be still indisposed from the effects of the scientific experiment, but the pragmatic side of her nature interfered.

May as well get the thing over and done, she told herself as she got slowly out of bed. She scowled as a faint headache flared behind her eyes. At least her stomach was stable again. When her maid appeared with tea, Victoria drank the entire pot and felt somewhat better.

She chose the brightest yellow and white morning gown in her wardrobe and dressed as carefully as if she were going out for a formal visit before she headed reluctantly downstairs.

Lucas rose from behind his wide desk, scanning her face carefully as she entered the room.

"Please sit down, Vicky. I must admit you are looking none the worse for wear. I congratulate you on your excellent constitution. I know several men who would be in a much less viable condition after the sort of 'experiment' you engaged in yesterday afternoon."

"Scientific progress exacts a certain toll," Victoria said with dignity as she sat down. "I am proud that I have made some small contribution to the welfare of mankind."

"A contribution to the welfare of mankind?" Lucas's mouth twitched. "Is that what you call it? You came home thoroughly cup-shot in the middle of the day and you tell me it was all in the name of intellectual inquiry?"

"I have done far more risky things in the name of intellectual inquiry," Victoria retorted meaningfully. "Only consider the fact that I am married to a man who will not even let me spend my own money as I see fit. And all because I fell victim to the dangers of another sort of experiment."

His mouth hardened into a grim line. "Do not try to deflect me by hurling old accusations. It is your behavior yesterday that is under consideration here. What, precisely, were you doing at the vicar's?"

"Sampling medicinal drafts in order to log their various effects," Victoria informed him, her chin at a haughty angle. Just let him dare to find fault with such a pure, scientific investigation, she thought wrathfully.

"And those medicinal drafts were all based on brandy?"

"No, of course not. Some of the herbs were dissolved in ale and not a few were infused with sherry and claret. We were not certain which spirits mixed best with the herbs, you see."

"Good Lord. How many glasses of this experiment did you drink?"

Victoria massaged her temples. The headache was getting worse. "I do not remember precisely, but I am sure it is all carefully recorded in Dr. Thornby's book of experiments."

"The vicar and his wife were involved in this?"

"Well, actually, I fear Mrs. Worth dozed off quite early on," Victoria said placatingly. "And the vicar had a rather large dose of one of the concoctions and went into a corner to sit facing the wall for the duration of the experiment."

"I dread to ask what concoctions you swallowed."

Victoria brightened. "Oh, I stuck with pure spirits the entire time, Lucas. Mine was the standard by which the effects of the other mixtures were judged. It was a very important part of the experiment."

Lucas swore softly and fell silent. The ticking of the tall clock grew very loud in the room. Victoria began to get restless.

"I fear I shall have to lay down yet another rule for you, madam," Lucas said at last.

"I was afraid of that." She wanted to fight back but her head was hurting too much. She could not seem to generate any enthusiasm for the conflict. She just wanted to retreat to her bed and lie down.

Lucas ignored her morose expression, but his voice was surprisingly gentle when he explained the new rule. "Henceforth, you will not engage in any further scientific experiments without my approval. Is that quite clear?"

"As usual, you have made yourself excruciatingly clear, my lord." Victoria rose, her head high. "Marriage is a rather dull business for a female, is it not? No adventuring, no intellectual inquiry, no freedom to spend one's money as one sees fit. I wonder how women survive it for a lifetime without expiring from sheer boredom."

She got up and went out the door.

Lucas lay in bed that night and watched the moon

through his window. There had been no sound from Victoria's room since something large and heavy had been dragged in front of the connecting door an hour ago.

He had listened to her barricade herself in her bed-chamber with some annoyance. He did not like the idea of her pushing heavy objects around unaided. At the very least, she should have asked a servant to do the job. But she had no doubt been too embarrassed to have a footman or her maid participate in the small act of defiance.

On the other hand, the show of spirit was a good sign, he told himself. She was obviously feeling much better than she had that morning. Things were getting back to normal.

Normal, that is, if life with Vicky could ever be termed such.

Lucas shoved aside the covers and got to his feet.

The strategist in him knew that there had been no way to avoid the recent confrontations. Some battles were unavoidable, and when those arose, a man could do nothing except hunker down and fight.

Victoria had still not fully accepted the marriage. She was an independent, headstrong creature who had been allowed free rein for too long. Her own intelligence, her gentle instincts, and her desire not to jeopardize her aunt's position in Society had acted as controls until he had come along.

But now Lucas knew she saw him as the one who stood in her way, the one who threatened her independence. She was torn between her feelings for him and her anger at being trapped in the marriage.

Lucas remembered all the males who had danced attendance on her in London, and groaned. She was accustomed to keeping men in their place, accustomed to being the one in command.

But he sensed, even if she did not, that one of the reasons she had been initially fascinated with him was the very fact that she could not be quite certain of her ability to control him. She was a strong woman who needed a man who was even stronger.

Having found him, she could not resist testing him.

He was sorry open warfare had broken out. But Lucas knew that now that the battle lines had been drawn, he could not give in and allow Victoria her own way or there would be hell to pay in the future.

Life had changed drastically for both of them. He had to make her understand that. They had future generations to think about now, not just their own lives. An estate such as Stonevale was meant to be held in trust for one's descendants. It was an investment in the future, not just the present.

Those descendants would carry Victoria's blood as well as his own, Lucas told himself. She had as large a stake in this land as he did. Neither of them could continue to go on in the rather reckless fashion they had indulged before the marriage.

Good God. He really was starting to sound quite priggish.

For all either of them knew, the next generation of Colebrooks might be on its way. The image of Victoria growing round and ripe with his babe sent a savage thrill of satisfaction through him.

Lucas scowled again, thinking of how she had pushed a very heavy object in front of her door. He could not allow her to do that sort of thing, not now when she might be pregnant. She belonged to him and he would take care of her whether she liked it or not.

But first he had to find a way to breach her bristling defenses. Lucas thought of the cacti in Lady Nettleship's garden and smiled. Then he went to the wardrobe and took out a shirt and a pair of breeches.

Victoria saw him the moment he appeared on the ledge outside her window, a dark, dangerous, masculine shape against the silvered night. This was no nightmare image. This was Lucas. She knew now she had been waiting for him.

It was inconceivable that he would let a little thing like her dressing table lodged against the connecting door stop him. She sat up and hugged her knees as the dark figure on the ledge opened her window and stepped into her bedchamber. He was fully dressed.

"Ah, so it was the dressing table," Lucas remarked calmly, glancing toward the connecting door. "You really should not be moving heavy objects about like that, my dear. Next time ask for assistance."

"Will there be a next time?" she asked softly, aware of the challenge that hung between them.

"Probably." He paced forward to stand at the foot of her bed. "I fear we are destined to quarrel occasionally, my sweet. Given your reckless ways and my lamentably dull, plodding ones, it is inevitable."

"Dull and plodding is not how I would describe you, Lucas. I think the terms 'arrogant, domineering, and stubborn' suit you far better."

"And priggish?"

"I regret to say it, but yes, priggish is beginning to suit you nicely."

He wrapped a hand around the bedpost and smiled ruefully. " 'Tis a relief, of course, to know you do not think so badly of me, after all."

She tensed. "Lucas, if you believe for one moment that you can sneak in here in the dead of night and claim your husbandly privileges, you are wrong. If you try to get into this bed, I will scream the house down."

"I doubt that. You would not want to humiliate either me or yourself in front of the servants. In any event you sadly misjudge me, madam, if you think I would be so foolish as to deal with your temper in such a fashion. But, then, I have warned you before that you have a habit of underestimating me."

She eyed him warily. "What do you plan to do?"

He glanced away from her, looking back over his shoulder to where the open curtains rippled in the night air. "The night beckons, madam, and you have always been one to answer the summons. Have you ever gone riding at midnight?"

She stared at him. "Are you serious?"

"Never more so."

"You would take me riding at this hour?"

"Yes."

"This is a trick, is it not? You are trying to disarm me, trying to make me forget my anger at your high-handedness."

"Yes."

"You do not even deny it?"

He shrugged eloquently. "Why should I? 'Tis the truth."

"Then I should refuse your offer."

His wicked grin flashed in the shadows. "The question is not should you, but can you?"

He knew her far too well, she realized. She chewed thoughtfully on her lip. Going with him was no capitulation. She would merely be taking advantage of a glorious opportunity for adventure. *Riding in the moonlight.* It sounded wonderful. Besides, although her headache had disappeared several hours earlier, she had been unable to get to sleep.

"You will get the wrong notion if I choose to accompany you," she said.

"Will I?"

She nodded grimly. "You will think I have forgiven you for your recent treatment of me."

"I am not so foolish as to think you would forgive me so easily."

"Good. Because I will not."

"I understand," he said gravely.

"You are not to view it as some sort of surrender."

"You make yourself quite clear," Lucas assured her.

Victoria hesitated a second longer and then leapt out of bed and dashed to the closet to find the breeches she had worn on their midnight adventures in London.

"Turn around," she ordered as she tugged off her nightclothes.

"Why? I have seen you naked several times now." He lounged against the bedpost, arms folded across his chest. "And I have been curious to see how you go about getting into a pair of men's breeches."

She glared at him and carried her clothing across the

room to where the privacy screen stood. "You are no gentleman, Lucas," she announced as she went behind the screen and began struggling into the breeches.

"You would be bored by a gentleman. Admit it, Vicky."

"I admit nothing."

Ten minutes later, wearing an amber scarf around her throat and a hooded cloak over her breeches and shirt, Victoria stood outside the stables with a bridle in her hand and watched as Lucas quickly saddled her mare and a sleepy-looking George.

"I only hope I do not live to regret this," Lucas said as he handed her up onto her mount.

"It is too late for second thoughts." She picked up her reins, enjoying the rare freedom of riding astride. "And I like you best when you are going against your better judgment, Lucas. Let us be off."

"Slowly," he called after her as he swung up into the saddle. "It is the middle of the night, Vicky. Have a care where you guide your mare. Stick to the lane."

"But I would like to ride through the woods," she protested.

"I cannot be certain all the mantraps have been removed yet," he told her. "So we will stay on the road."

She was feeling too exhilarated to argue further. Just being out on horseback in the moonlight was ample adventure for now. She turned her horse toward the main drive and George fell good-naturedly into step beside her mare.

There was silence for several minutes as they walked the horses beneath the canopy of trees that lined the approach to Stonevale. Lucas spoke eventually.

"I have been talking to the vicar about planting some more trees. Oak or elm, perhaps. The timber would be an excellent investment for our children or our grandchildren."

"Lucas, I do not wish to speak about investments of any kind tonight," Victoria said rather forcefully.

"What about the future? Would you like to talk about that?"

Her hands tightened on the reins. "Not particularly."

His voice gentled. "Has it occurred to you that you might even now be carrying my babe?"

"It is not something I want to think about."

"Do you find the subject so terrifying, then? I am surprised at you, Vicky. You are no coward, of that I am certain."

"Did you bring me out here to discuss your heir, my lord? Because, if so, we may as well turn back now."

He was silent for a moment. "Do you hate me so much that you do not even want to bear my child?"

"*I do not hate you,*" she stormed, feeling pressed. "That is not the point."

"I am greatly relieved to hear that."

Victoria sighed. "I simply do not want to talk about your heir tonight or any other night until we have settled this matter that stands between us."

"The only thing that stands between us is your pride and your fear of losing your independence. Does it make you feel any better to know that you are not the only one who is no longer free?"

She slid him a sidelong glance. "You are referring to yourself, sir?"

"Yes."

"You seem free enough to me."

"Look around you, Vicky. I lost whatever freedom I enjoyed the day I inherited Stonevale. I am tied to this land and my responsibilities to our descendants for the rest of my life."

"And you are a man who will always fulfill your responsibilities, regardless of what comes." She studied the road between her mare's ears, thinking about her own words.

"I will do my best, Vicky, even when some of those responsibilities are not to your liking. But I would have you remember, even in the midst of our battles, that what I do, I do because I truly think it is best for us and for our future. I do not set myself against you lightly." He smiled. "Believe me, it requires far too much effort to do battle with you for me to waste my time and energy on minor skirmishes. I much prefer to indulge you whenever possible."

She was indignant. "Indulge me? You think you indulge me? You have a vastly overrated opinion of your own actions, my lord."

He motioned toward their midnight surroundings. "Look around you, my dear. What other man of your acquaintance would drag himself out of a warm bed at this hour merely to entertain you?"

She felt a grin tug at her mouth. There was something about being out with Lucas at this hour of night that always had a euphoric effect on her senses. At the moment she could no longer even summon up the hot anger she had nursed all day. "Well, as to that, my lord, I am not precisely certain just what other men of my acquaintance would humor me so. I have not had a chance to do a proper survey, you see. Perhaps if I started asking about, I would turn up one or two other noble types who would indulge me in this minor fashion."

"If I catch you doing such a survey, I will see to it that you do not sit a horse comfortably for a week."

Her amusement faded at once. "So much for your indulgence, my lord."

"I have limits, madam. And I fear you must learn to tolerate them."

"I have a dressing table I can continue to push in front of my door every night," Victoria warned.

Lucas smiled confidently. "The ledge that leads from my window to yours is wide enough to provide a safe path, even on moonless nights. But I warn you, madam, if you oblige me to use it in foul weather, I cannot guarantee to be in a particularly indulgent mood by the time I arrive at your window."

"But you will, nevertheless, arrive at my window?"

"You may count on that, my sweet. It is as certain as sunrise."

Victoria risked another sidelong glance and saw that he was watching her with eyes that reflected the moonlight. Her whole body responded to the irresistible power he held over her. He wanted her and he made no effort to hide it. It gave her a sense of her own power and it also made her light-headed with excitement.

At that moment her horse nickered softly.

"Lucas, I . . ."

"Hush." He reined in his horse and reached across to halt her mare. His sensual flirtation had turned to acute alertness.

Instinctively she kept her voice low. "What is it?"

"It seems we are not alone out here," he said. "Hurry. Into the trees."

She did not argue. Obediently she followed his stallion into the woods at the side of the road. They sat watching the moonlit lane from the shelter of the trees.

"Who are we hiding from?" she asked very softly.

"I'm not yet certain, but I can think of only one other person who might have business at midnight on this road."

"The highwayman." Victoria was suddenly breathless. "He has not left the district, after all. Lucas, how exciting. I have never seen a real highwayman."

"For which you should be very grateful, madam. I suppose I have no one but myself to blame for the fact that you might see one now."

Victoria heard the clip-clop of a horse's hooves in the distance. A moment later a dark figure riding what appeared to be a bulky-looking plow horse rounded the bend. The highwayman was dressed in a somewhat tattered-looking black cape. He had a scarf across the lower portion of his face.

As he came down the lane Victoria saw that he was impatiently kicking his horse's rounded sides. The rider's urgent voice carried clearly on the night air.

"Hurry it up, ye good-fer-nothin' nag. Do ye think we've got all night? That carriage will be here any minute now. Move, damn your fat sides."

The horse continued to plod stolidly along until the rider turned it and guided it into the woods on the opposite side of the road.

Victoria realized that she and Lucas were trapped on this side of the road. They could not move out onto the lane until the highwayman, or whoever he was, chose to leave the vicinity. Beside her, she thought she heard the softest of disgusted oaths from Lucas. But before she could catch his attention to see how he intended to get them out of this fix, the rattle of coach wheels shattered the stillness.

It seemed they were to be a witness to the local highwayman's latest piece of business.

A few seconds later the coach, a staid old vehicle pulled by an equally elderly team, rounded the bend in the lane and rumbled forward at a stately pace.

The highwayman urged his horse out of the trees and into the middle of the road. He brandished a large pistol.

"Halt," he yelled loudly. "Stand and deliver."

There was a startled cry from the coachman, who immediately began sawing on the reins to pull the slowly cantering horses to a halt.

"Here now," the coachman called uneasily. "What's all this?"

"Ye heard me, man. Tell your passengers to stand and deliver or it'll be the worse for all o' ye."

Lucas sighed. "Well, we cannot have this sort of nonsense going on around here. Stay right where you are, Vicky. Do not come out of these trees until I call you out. Understood?"

She realized he intended to halt the robbery. "I can help you."

"You will do no such thing. Do not move from this spot. That's an order, Vicky."

Without waiting for her response, he removed a pistol from his pocket and rode out onto the lane behind the highwayman.

15

"That'll be enough of that now. Hand over the pistol before someone gets hurt, lad."

Lucas's voice was the amazingly calm and overwhelmingly commanding one he used only rarely but always to great effect. It was definitely a tone that compelled instant obedience. Victoria was impressed in spite of herself.

The highwayman whipped around in his saddle. "What the devil . . . ? Damme, who are you? This is my coach. Go find yerself another one. I got no intention o' sharin' it with the likes o' ye."

"You misunderstand, lad. I don't want the coach. I'm in another line of work myself. Now hand over the pistol."

"Who be ye?" There was a quaver in the highwayman's voice now. "Who be ye, mister? Ye cannot be the ghost they been sayin' 'as come back. Ye cannot be."

"The pistol, if you please." Lucas sharpened his tone just slightly and the pistol was instantly dropped into his outstretched palm. "Wise lad. Now let us see to the passengers."

At that instant the coachman, no doubt under the impression he was suddenly facing two highwaymen instead of one, saw his chance and leapt from his box, sprinting for the bushes.

A piercing scream rose from the inside of the coach as one of the passengers apparently looked out the window and realized the coachman was abandoning his charges.

The team of horses started violently at the shriek of dismay and leapt forward, reins flapping wildly.

"Bloody hell." Lucas made a futile grab for one of the horses as the coach surged past him.

In that instant the highwayman saw his opportunity and drove his heels violently into his plump mount. The animal bolted in fright and broke into a heavy canter down the road in the opposite direction in which the coach was going.

Another scream soared through the open window of the coach. Victoria saw Lucas turn his horse to chase after the coach and she wasted no more time. The vehicle was much closer to her than it was to Lucas now and the highwayman was clearly bent on escape.

She urged her mare quickly out onto the road. "I've got it, Lucas. Don't let him get away." She cantered her mare up alongside one of the elderly coach horses and reached down for the reins. The animal began to slow immediately as if vastly relieved to be back under human control.

"For God's sake be careful," Lucas yelled. But it was obvious the coach had already come to a safe halt. He spun his horse around in the other direction and went after the lumbering plow horse.

Victoria patted the sweating neck of the coach horse and glanced back in time to see that it was going to be no contest between Lucas's blooded stallion and the farm horse. The highwayman did not stand a chance.

She collected the reins of the coach horses and pulled the hood of her cloak back up over her head so that her face was in deep shadow. "It is all right," she called to the missing coachman. "You can come out now. You are in no danger. Take charge of your team, if you please, my good man."

An elderly, diminutive woman wearing a turban stuck her head out the coach window. "Good heavens, you're a female, ain't you? Whatever is the world coming to allowing women to run around in the middle of the night in breeches? You should be ashamed of yourself, young woman."

Victoria grinned. "Yes, ma'am," she said in her demurest accents. "My husband holds much the same opinion as yourself."

"And just where is your husband, pray tell?"

Victoria nodded down the road to where Lucas was leading a dejected-looking highwayman back toward the coach. "That's him there, ma'am. He's caught your highwayman for you."

"Heavens, I don't want him." The woman leaned back into the coach and spoke to her companion, who appeared to be having a quiet fit of hysterics. "Martha, do stop that infernal noise and call John Coachman. I believe he ran off into the woods. One simply cannot rely upon staff these days."

"I be right here, ma'am," the coachman called, emerging hastily from the brush. "I was just waitin' me chance to get the bleeder." He glanced suspiciously at Victoria, who tossed him the reins. "You sure you ain't about to rob us?"

"No, I am not about to rob you."

"For pity's sake, does she look like a highwayman?" The elderly woman leaned her head back out the window and glowered at her coachman as he took control of the team. "She's a female dressed in men's breeches and she ought to be thoroughly ashamed of herself. Imagine a woman of decent breeding running around like that on horseback in the middle of the night. If her husband had any sense, he'd beat her."

Lucas rode up with his captive in tow in time to hear that last remark. "I promise you, madam, I will take your advice under consideration."

The woman switched her attention immediately to him. "You being her husband, I take it? What in heaven's name do you think you're doing letting her run about like this?"

Lucas smiled. "Trying to keep up with her, and I assure you, it is not easy. Are you and your companion all right?"

"Quite all right, thank you very much. We are late coming back from the home of friends. A mistake I shall not make again. What are you going to do with him?" She nodded toward the drooping highwayman, who was still wearing his scarf as a mask.

"Well, as to that," Lucas began thoughtfully, "I suppose I ought to turn him over to the proper authorities."

There was a whimper of protest from the highwayman, but that was all.

"Yes, yes, the proper authorities," the woman said briskly. "Do that. And when you've finished with that business, I suggest you do something about your wife. A woman who's allowed to run around in the middle of the night wearing breeches will come to a bad end, I can tell you that. Now, enough of this foolishness. Home, John."

"Yes, yer ladyship." The coachman heaved himself back up onto his box and flicked the reins. The coach lumbered forward and was soon out of sight around the next bend in the lane.

Victoria examined the highwayman. It did not take sophisticated powers of deduction to determine that the horse, at least, was probably from a nearby farm. "Surely a professional highwayman should invest in a faster animal. Who are you, lad? Are you from these parts?"

There was another whimper from the highwayman, who cast a frantic eye toward Lucas, as if he sought help from that quarter.

"Answer the lady," Lucas ordered softly.

The young man reluctantly reached up and pulled down his scarf. Victoria realized with a pang that he could not have been more than fifteen at the most. He stared first at Lucas and then at Victoria with a frightened expression. "Name's Billy."

"Billy what?" Lucas prodded patiently.

"Billy Simms."

"Well, Billy, I am afraid you are in a great deal of trouble," Lucas remarked, dropping his pistol back into his pocket. "The Earl of Stonevale does not approve of highwaymen operating in this district."

"Ye think I give a bloody damn what his 'igh-and-mighty lordship approves of?" Billy burst out. "I wouldn't be operatin' as a bleedin' 'ighwayman at all if the last earl 'adn't thrown Ma and me and my sis out of our 'ome. What was I supposed to do after Pa got taken off with the fever? We're livin' wi' me aunt and her family and there ain't enough room nor food to go 'round. Am I s'posed to watch all my womenfolk starve? Not bloody likely. I did what I 'ad to do usin' the pistol my pa left me. That's all."

Lucas regarded him in measured silence for a long moment. "You have a point, Billy. In your shoes I'd probably have done the same."

Billy eyed him in some confusion. "Ye look like gentry to me. Ye certain ye would have taken to the roads like this?"

"As you say, Billy, a man does what he has to do. But be that as it may, from what I hear, things have changed in these parts. There is a new earl in charge of Stonevale now."

"He won't be no better 'n the last one, ye mark my words. The bleedin' Quality's all the same. Out to suck the last drop 'o blood from people like me and mine. Ma says the new folks up at the great house are different and I heard what they're sayin' in the village about the ghosts reappearin', but I don't believe none of it."

"Is that right?" Lucas's horse tossed its head and he absently patted George's neck. "You thought I was a ghost at first, didn't you?"

Billy shot him a sullen look. "Ye took me by surprise, that's all. Ain't no such thing as ghosts." But he was staring at the amber scarf draped around Victoria's throat. The color had been clearly discernible earlier in the light from the coach.

"I'm sure you're right, Billy. But all that is beside the point. We have something of a problem here."

Billy wiped his nose with the back of his hand. "What problem?"

"Why, the problem of what to do with you, of course."

"Why don't ye just shoot me with yer bloody damn pistol and be done with it?"

"That's a possibility, naturally. And not an uncommon ending for a highwayman. What do you think, madam?" Lucas glanced at Victoria.

"I think," Victoria said softly, "that Billy should present himself at the stables of the Earl of Stonevale tomorrow morning and inform the head groom that he is to be hired. In the meantime I think he should go home and put his mother's mind at ease. She is undoubtedly extremely worried about him."

Billy looked up sharply. "What makes ye think I could get a job at the big 'ouse?"

"Rest assured, Billy," Lucas said calmly, "there will be a job waiting for you. One with more of a future than this one. It won't provide quite as much excitement as being a highwayman, but we have agreed a man does what he must. You've got womenfolk to see to and you cannot afford to be in a profession that's likely to get you killed this week or next."

The boy eyed Lucas suspiciously. "Is this a game yer playin' with me?"

Victoria smiled in the shadows of her hood. " 'Tis no game, Billy. Go home to your mother and in the morning report to the head groom. The wages may not be as high as what you can make out here on the road, but at least they'll be steady. And that's what your family needs. What have you got to lose? If things don't work out, you can always go back into this line of work."

Billy stared at her for a long moment, trying to peer beneath the hood of her cloak. Finally he shook his head in awe. "Yer them, ain't ye? The two o' ye be the ghosts. The Amber Knight and his lady. Look at that scarf yer wearin'. It's true what they been sayin' in the village. Ye come back after all this time t' ride the lands o' Stonevale at midnight."

"Go home, Billy. I think we have all had enough excitement for tonight," Lucas said.

"Aye, sir. Ye don't have to tell me twice. I ain't accustomed to makin' conversation with a couple o' ghosts." Billy tugged at the reins of his sturdy mount and kicked the beast into what must have been a bone-shaking trot.

Victoria watched as the boy vanished around the bend in the road. Then she threw back the hood of her cloak and laughed softly. "I must admit, my lord, that I always have an interesting time of it when you and I go adventuring at midnight."

Lucas muttered an oath. "Never a dull moment, is there?"

"Never. What shall we do next?"

"We could follow the suggestion made by that lady in the coach. I could take you home and beat you for being so brazen as to run around in the middle of the night in a pair of men's breeches. But it probably wouldn't do much good."

"Not a bit of good," Victoria agreed cheerfully. "In any event, tonight's adventure was all your idea in the first place, so it would hardly be fair of you to beat me."

"Ah, but you don't think me a fair man, do you, Vicky? You think I am high-handed and domineering and quite utterly ruthless, not to mention priggish."

She lowered her lashes. "Lucas, I . . ."

"Never mind, Vicky. It is past time we headed home. You've had your adventure for tonight."

He turned George's head back in the direction from which they had ridden earlier and Victoria had no choice but to follow.

Half an hour later she was safely back in her own bed and she was very much alone in it. But she was far from asleep.

She turned on her side and plumped a pillow, trying to get Lucas's words out of her head. *You think I am high-handed and domineering and quite utterly ruthless.*

And so he was, she assured herself for the hundredth time. Surely she did not need any more proof of that after their confrontation earlier in the day. She had known that sooner or later he would show his true colors and behave like any other so-called gentleman behaved after he married and took control of his wife's money.

But she also knew perfectly well that any other so-called gentleman of her acquaintance would have turned poor Billy over to the authorities and seen the youngster hung without a qualm. Either that or the gentleman would have shot the boy down on the road and thought himself a hero in doing so.

Yet from the moment she had realized they were dealing with a young local lad, she'd never had any doubts about how Lucas would handle the situation. She had known he would neither shoot the boy nor send him to the gallows.

The truth was, her husband was not at all like most of the gentlemen of her acquaintance and she had known that from the start. That was how she had gotten into this situation.

That did not mean, however, that Lucas was not excessively arrogant, high-handed, and domineering at times.

She turned over on her other side and gazed at the closed door that connected their rooms. The dressing table was still in front of it. Lucas had gone straight back to his own bedchamber after seeing her to her door.

Victoria had been anticipating that he would come to her bed after their night of adventure. The fact that he had not disturbed her.

She wondered if she'd gone too far by barricading her door against him. Perhaps she had dealt his pride an overly severe blow with that bit of defiance. He was her husband, after all. He did have rights.

Nor could she deny that as his wife, she had her obligations.

They were supposed to be partners in this marriage, just as they had been partners in sharing the night's adventure.

And right now she wanted to be with him.

Victoria gave up the useless attempt to get to sleep and slid out from under the covers. Her nightgown floated around her ankles as she went over to the dress-

ing table that blocked the door. She listened intently
for sounds from the next room that might indicate Lucas was having trouble sleeping, too, but she heard
nothing.

The urge to open the connecting door very quietly
and peek into his room to see if he was sound asleep
was overpowering. But the barricade was something of
a nuisance. She could move it back into its proper
position, but in doing so she would surely wake Lucas.

She glanced at the window and smiled. If the Earl of
Stonevale could get from one room to another using the
window ledge, then so could she.

Victoria went over to the window, opened it, and
looked down. From here the ground seemed very far
away and the ledge that led to Lucas's window did not
look nearly as wide as she had thought it would. Still,
he had managed to walk it even with his bad leg.

Victoria took a deep breath and stepped out onto the
ledge. The chilled air caught at her thin muslin gown
and she shivered.

Clutching at the cold stone of the wall, she edged
slowly toward the other window. It was not going to be
quite as easy as she had thought. She was discovering
the hard way that she did not have a head for heights.
Every time she looked down she got dizzy.

Halfway between the two windows Victoria came to a
complete halt. She knew she could not go on. Lucas
had made this ledge-walking business sound like a stroll
in the park. She did not know how he had managed it,
but she was forced to admit defeat.

It was when she tried to retreat back along the ledge
that she realized she had a major problem on her hands.
Going back was not going to be any simpler than going
forward.

This was ridiculous. She was appalled at her inability
to move. Shivering with cold, pressed rigidly back against
the stone wall, Victoria closed her eyes and tried to
think. She certainly could not stand out here all night.
She opened her eyes and realized that Lucas's window
was open.

"Lucas? Lucas, can you hear me?"

There was no immediate response and her heart sank. The thought of having to scream ignominiously for help until one of the servants heard her was too mortifying to even contemplate.

"*Lucas,*" she called, a bit more loudly this time. "Lucas, are you in there? Damn you, Stonevale, this is all your fault. Wake up and do something."

"Hell and damnation," Lucas said, appearing abruptly at the window. "I should have guessed you'd try something like this. What the devil do you think you're doing?"

Relief poured through her. "I just came out for a stroll," she muttered. "It would seem I have a slight problem with heights."

"Don't move. I'll come and fetch you."

"I'm not going anywhere." She watched as he put one bare leg over the windowsill and stepped out onto the ledge. "Good heavens, my lord, you're naked."

"Sorry to offend your delicate sensibilities. Would you prefer I went back inside and dressed first?"

"*No.* No, don't you dare. Get me off this horrible ledge before you do anything else."

"Yes, my lady. At your service, my lady. So glad to be of some assistance, my lady. Keep your voice down, my lady, or the servants will really have something to talk about in the morning."

She relaxed a little as his strong fingers closed around her wrist. "How on earth did you manage this earlier when you came to my bedchamber?"

"Be assured I didn't use this route because I enjoy running about on ledges. I used it because you'd shoved that damned dressing table in front of the door, remember? I take it the barricade is still in place and that's why you're out here?"

"I fear that is precisely the case." She followed him gratefully back to his open window. A moment later she was standing safely inside his bedchamber. She gave a sigh of relief and brushed off her hands. "Thank you very much, Lucas. I do not mind telling you, I was a trifle uneasy out there."

"And I don't mind telling you that I was a trifle

horrified to see you out there." His hands closed around her shoulders in a fierce grip. "I am, naturally, extremely gratified by your enthusiasm for my bed, but the next time you want to join me in it, try knocking."

She scowled at him. "You are assuming a great deal, my lord."

"Am I? Are you telling me you were out on that ledge because you were bored and couldn't think of anything else to do for the rest of the night except stroll from window to window?"

It was no good. She could not possibly deny that she had been attempting to get to his bedchamber. "Do not tease me, Lucas. This is humiliating enough as it is."

His smile was slow and deeply sensual. "What is so humiliating about admitting you enjoy what we find together in the marriage bed, sweetheart?"

" 'Tis not that. It is just that I have been furious with you all day and now you are no doubt jumping to the conclusion that I am here because I wanted you to make love to me."

"Isn't that precisely why you're here?"

"Yes, it is. But it doesn't mean that I have changed my mind about anything else, and of course you are bound to think that I have. Or worse, you will conclude that you can always bring me to heel by taking me for a midnight adventure. It is not that way at all."

He laughed softly. "There is nothing in any of this to shame you, Vicky. But if it will make you feel any less humiliated, I promise not to conclude that your presence here means I am permanently forgiven. Will that do? Tomorrow we can go right back to the battle lines you drew today, if that is what you truly wish."

"Lucas, you are incorrigible. You know very well that things will be different between us in the morning. How can I possibly continue to give you the cold shoulder tomorrow after you have made love to me tonight?"

"I don't know," he said, scooping her up and settling her into his bed. "How can you?"

She looked up at him through her lashes as he came down beside her. "Maybe I should be the one applying for a job in your stables instead of Billy Simms. That way, I could supplement the allowance you intend to grant me."

He kissed her throat. "Did you risk life and limb on that damned ledge just so you could continue our argument or did you come here so that I could make love to you?"

Victoria relaxed and put her arms around his neck. "I came here so that you could fulfill your husbandly duties and make love to me."

"I rather thought so." His hand closed over her breast and his mouth closed over her lips.

Sometime later Victoria stirred sleepily in the huge bed. She opened her eyes to see Lucas at the window. He had one foot out on the ledge. "Where in heaven's name are you going?"

"To shove that dressing table away from your door. Do you want your maid to know you felt obliged to barricade yourself in your room tonight?"

"No, of course, not. But be careful, Lucas."

"I'll be right back."

He vanished into the night and a couple of minutes later Victoria heard the heavy dressing table being shifted back into its proper position. The connecting door opened and Lucas sauntered back into his own room, dusting off his hands. Victoria glowered at him.

"Now what have I done?" he demanded as he slid back into bed beside her.

"I don't see how you can be so casual about wandering around naked."

"Who will see? Except you, of course." He grinned, throwing one leg over hers. "And you are every bit as naked as I am."

"Never mind." She paused. "Lucas, I have something to say to you."

"What would that be, my sweet?"

Victoria studied Lucas for a moment, choosing her words. "About our argument."

"Which one?"

"The one about my money."

"Can this discussion not wait until breakfast? I'm exhausted. Running about on horseback in the middle of the night, rescuing ladies from window ledges, and shoving heavy furniture around takes its toll on a man of my years."

"This is important, Lucas."

"Very well, then, say it so that we can both get some sleep."

"I just wanted to say that I am sorry, or at least somewhat sorry for most of the nasty things I said to you during the course of our discussion about money," Victoria said very gravely.

"*Most* of the nasty things? Not all of them?"

"No, not all of them, because I do not feel that I was entirely in the wrong. Nevertheless, I shouldn't have implied that you are like every other husband who takes control of his wife's money. The truth is, you are quite different from any other man I have ever met."

He touched the amber pendant where it lay nestled between her breasts. "And you, madam, are quite different from any other woman I have ever met. Since you have apologized for *most* of the nasty things you said, I suppose the least I can do is revoke my threat to put you on a limited quarterly allowance."

"Well, I should think so. Really, Lucas, you can have had no notion of how arrogant you sounded when you made that horrid threat."

He laughed and pulled her down across his chest. "I don't think you have any notion of how arrogant you sound when you set out to make me jump fences to suit your whims."

"I do no such thing."

"Don't you?" His thumbs traced the line of her cheekbones. "You are constantly testing me, Vicky, constantly pushing and probing to see how far I will let you go before I pull in the reins. And when I do reach my limits and refuse to indulge you in some manner, you retaliate by accusing me of being a typical, untrustworthy, domineering male who's only after his wife's money."

She realized he was perfectly serious. "Lucas, that is not true."

"I think it is true, sweetheart. And to be quite honest, I don't entirely blame you. You have good cause to be cautious about placing your trust in me. But I do not like it when you try to manipulate me."

She went still. "Is that how you see my behavior? As an attempt to manage you?"

"I think it is your way of proving to yourself that you are not at my mercy, that you can control me and therefore the situation in which you find yourself. It is a perfectly natural response on your part, but it does make for some awkward moments between us."

"It seems to me that you have tried to manipulate and control me right from the start," Victoria said quietly. "You even told me you were doing it that first night in my aunt's garden when you said I would be unable to resist you because you would give me what no other man ever had."

"So I did."

"Well? Aren't you going to apologize for that?"

"There's not much point, is there? I don't regret it." He eased her mouth down to his. "I would have done whatever I had to do in order to get you."

A small chill went through Victoria. Lucas had meant to get himself an heiress at whatever cost. There had been no love involved in the bargain, at least not on his side. He had been quite ruthless, right from the start. She had to keep reminding herself of that fact, especially when she lay in his arms. It was so easy to pretend that all was well between them at times like this, so easy to pretend that he was not plotting her surrender.

"Isabel Rycott once told me that weak men are more useful to a woman than strong ones because they are easier to control," Victoria mused against his lips.

"Look at me, my sweet. I am utterly at your mercy. A helpless slave to your wicked, carnal desires. How much more useful can a man be?"

"There is that. I must admit, you are not the least bit stingy when it comes to this area of our marriage." Victoria parted her lips and drew her tongue along the edge of his hard mouth.

Lucas groaned and set about proving just how willing he was to serve his lady in this area of their marriage.

Victoria awoke once more shortly after dawn, aware that Lucas was shifting about restlessly in his sleep. She put her hand on the ragged scar on his thigh and began to massage the taut muscles. He relaxed almost at once and fell back into a calm slumber.

She lay awake beside him for a few minutes, thinking that she had not been troubled with nightmares since her first night here at Stonevale. But the faint, nagging sense of unease had not completely vanished. Victoria could not completely escape the feeling that something dark and menacing was slowly closing in on her.

She cuddled closer to Lucas's hard, warm body and his arm went around her. She reached up and absently touched the amber pendant at her throat as she often did these days. A moment later she relaxed and fell asleep.

16

"You won't believe this, ma'am, but they're sayin' the ghosts were seen again last night. Fair gives one the shivers, don't it? Except that nobody around here seems to mind havin' these two particular ghosts runnin' about. But I reckon that's how country folk are. Peculiar." Nan finished fastening the bodice of Victoria's yellow-printed muslin gown and reached for the silver hairbrush.

Victoria watched her maid in the mirror. "Is this the Amber Knight and his lady you are talking about, Nan?"

"Yes, ma'am. So they be sayin' in the kitchens, at any rate."

"Are they saying precisely where the ghosts were seen?" Victoria asked carefully just as the connecting door opened and Lucas walked into her bedchamber. She was relieved to note he was fully dressed and even more pleased to see that he did not appear to be favoring his bad leg unduly.

" 'Mornin', your lordship." Nan dropped a quick curtsy and went back to work brushing Victoria's short curls into fashionable, casual disarray.

"Good morning," Lucas said easily. He met Victoria's

286

gaze in the mirror and smiled with lazy satisfaction. "Finish your tale, Nan. Where were the ghosts seen?"

Nan's eyes brightened. "Ridin' down one of the lanes, just as bold as you please. Can you imagine? What would a couple of self-respectin' ghosts be doing riding horseback in the middle of the night, I ask you? The tales some people come up with."

"I agree with you," Lucas remarked, his eyes gleaming as they continued to hold Victoria's in the mirror. "I cannot for the life of me imagine why a couple of intelligent ghosts would be out riding at that hour. Who saw them?"

"Well, as to that, I am not sure exactly, sir. I had the story from one of the kitchen girls who had it from a new stable lad. He just started work this mornin'. Don't know where he got it," Nan said.

"Probably made the whole thing up," Victoria said. "That will be all for now, Nan. Thank you."

"Yes, m'lady." Nan bobbed another curtsy and left the room.

Lucas grinned as the door closed behind the maid. "Ten to one Billy Simms has put a nice twist on the events of last night."

"No doubt." Victoria laughed. "It is getting to be a great joke, is it not, Lucas?"

"I fear it will not be quite so amusing when someone finally realizes that the ghosts are merely the current Earl of Stonevale and his hoyden of a countess. But we shall face that problem when it arises. Are you ready to go down to breakfast?"

"Yes, indeed. In fact, I find myself with an excellent appetite this morning."

"I cannot imagine why," Lucas murmured as he opened the door for her.

Victoria stepped forward and looped her arm into his. "Nothing like a little exercise to work up an appetite, is there? What are your plans for the day, my lord?"

"I am going to meet with the vicar to go over some ideas I have been studying for the new irrigation system. And your plans, my dear?"

She smiled serenely as they started down the stairs.

"Oh, I thought I would spend the morning going over the interest rates offered by certain moneylenders I may need to consult in the event I should ever happen to find myself placed on a strict allowance."

"Save your energy, madam. The day I allow you to go to a moneylender will be the day I have truly abandoned the fight and raised the white flag of defeat."

"An interesting notion. Somehow I cannot quite imagine you admitting defeat in anything, Stonevale."

"You are getting to know me well, Vicky."

The three letters arrived just as they were finishing breakfast. Victoria recognized her aunt's seal on one of them and Annabella Lyndwood's on the another. She tore Annabella's note open first.

> My Dearest Vicky,
>
> What a fine stir you have caused. Everyone is having a wonderful time discussing what is being termed the Great Romance of the Year. Lady Hesterly's daughter even went so far as to suggest that Byron scribble a verse or two to celebrate the event. That notion, of course, is reported to have sent Caro Lamb flying up into the boughs. It is well known she does not like being cast into the shade by someone more outrageously romantic than herself.
>
> Be that as it may, the rest of the gossip pales in comparison to talk of your marriage. Do hurry back, Vicky. I assure you that you will be heralded as a mythic goddess of love straight out of a classic tale of romance. And I must say, life has become rather boring without you. The only recent excitement is that I have succeeded in persuading Bertie to definitely refuse Viscount Barton's offer. He is presently moping (Lord Barton, that is, not Bertie) but shows every sign of perking up and turning his attentions elsewhere.
>
> Affectionately yours,
> Annabella

"So much for poor Barton," Lucas muttered. "Foiled by females."

"So much, indeed," Victoria agreed with relish. She opened her aunt's note next and scanned the contents quickly before giving a small shriek of dismay. "Dear heaven, of all the wretched luck."

Lucas looked up from the newspaper that had arrived with the letters. "What's wrong?"

"Everything. This is terrible. A disaster."

Lucas folded the newspaper and put it down beside his plate. "Has something happened to your aunt? Is she ill?"

"No, no, no, it is nothing like that. The disaster has happened to us. Oh, Lucas, what on earth are we to do? How do we get out of this horrible situation? This is intolerable."

"Perhaps I could be of greater assistance if you would give me a few more details concerning this intolerable, horrible disaster."

Victoria glanced up, her brows snapping together in a severe frown. "This is not funny, Lucas. Aunt Cleo writes that Jessica Atherton called upon her and suggested that it would be wise for you and me to put in an appearance in London before the Season ends. Lady Atherton has very kindly stated that she will honor us with a reception."

Lucas looked thoughtful. Then he shrugged. "Perhaps she's right. It might not be a bad idea. It would serve to enforce the notion that ours is a love match."

Victoria was appalled. "Lucas, are you listening? It is none other than Jessica Atherton who is proposing to give us this reception."

"Who better? As we both know, her position in Society is unassailable."

Outraged, Victoria stared at him. "Have you lost your senses? Do you honestly believe I will allow Jessica Atherton to assist us in this manner? Not in a million years. *I will not be indebted to that woman again.*"

There was a beat of silence from Lucas's end of the

table. "Again?" he echoed at last. "Are you by any chance implying you already feel indebted to her for having performed the introduction that led to our marriage?"

"Don't you dare tease me, Lucas. I am not at all in a mood to be teased. This is awful. What on earth shall I say to Aunt Cleo? How will we get out of this?"

"My advice," he said as he rose to his feet, "is that we do not try. Your aunt is quite right. It would be a wise move to make an appearance in the ballroom of a hostess such as Jessica Atherton before the Season is over. It would set the seal of approval on your marriage as far as Society is concerned."

Victoria could not believe her ears. "Never. I absolutely refuse. This is one issue on which neither you nor my aunt can make me change my mind. I have had more than enough of Jessica Atherton and her *generous, kind* assistance. I do not care if I never see the woman again as long as I live. I will not go to London if it means having to attend a ball in our honor given by her. It is unthinkable."

Lucas walked to her chair, leaned down, and kissed the top of her curls. "My dear, you are overreacting. The whole notion of letting Jessica give us a reception seems quite reasonable to me."

"It is the most unreasonable thing I have ever heard."

"We will discuss it later when you've had a chance to calm down. Now I must be off. The vicar is due to arrive shortly."

"I will not be budged on this, Lucas. I warn you." She glared at his back as he exited the breakfast room, and then, when she had finished fuming, Victoria reached for the third and last letter. She examined it curiously but failed to recognize either the handwriting or the seal.

Impatiently she opened it. A pamphlet, a newspaper clipping, and a short note fell out of the envelope. The note was unsigned and it was extremely brief.

Madam: Given your interest in matters of intellectual inquiry, the enclosed

should intrigue you greatly. It appears
the dead do not always remain so.

The note was signed with a single initial: a "W."

With a sense of dawning dread, Victoria picked up
the pamphlet and read the title: "On Certain Curious
Investigations into the Matter of Using Electricity to
Reanimate the Dead."

The newspaper article was a detailed account of how
a coffin which had recently been exhumed had been
opened and found to be empty. The theft of the de-
ceased was presumed to be the work of a ring of body
snatchers who were in the business of supplying the
medical schools with corpses. There was, however, some
speculation that a certain group of experimenters had
purchased the body for their experiments with electricity. The authorities were concerned.

For the first time in her life that she could remember, Victoria felt faint. She nodded sharply to the footman to indicate she wanted more coffee and watched
numbly as he poured it into her cup. The dark brew
seemed to fall from spout to cup in slow motion.

Very carefully, because she did not quite trust the
steadiness of her fingers, she picked up the delicate
china teacup and swallowed most of the contents in one
gulp. The light-headed sensation passed.

When she thought she could manage the act without
collapsing, Victoria got to her feet, collected the envel-
lopes and their contents, and went upstairs to her room.

Lucas was aware of being in an excellent mood as he
made his way across the hall and into the library. He
looked about him with satisfaction.

Stonevale was a far different place than it had been
when he had inherited it. Fine woodwork gleamed
once more under new layers of polish. Faded draperies
had been repaired or replaced. The old carpets had
been cleaned to reveal their subtle, beautiful patterns,
and the windows sparkled in the morning sun.

The house was fully staffed now and the domestic
routines were already well established. The footmen

wore their new livery with obvious pride and the food served at table was fresh and properly prepared.

Through the library window Lucas could see the progress the gardeners were making under Victoria's direction. The small conservatory she had ordered would soon be finished. Several trays of unusual plants were on their way from London.

Lucas knew that all the progress that had been made in and around the house itself was the direct result of Victoria's time and attention. Her money alone would not have achieved the miracle of turning Stonevale into a home. That feat required a woman's touch.

She had brought something infinitely more valuable than her inheritance to this marriage, Lucas acknowledged. She had brought herself with all her natural enthusiasm, intelligence, and generous nature. The staff and tenants adored her. The villagers were proud that she found their shops worth her patronage. The fact that the tradesmen's bills were always paid promptly did not go unnoticed, either. The quality of merchandise available in the village was already markedly improved.

He had chosen well, Lucas told himself as he studied the garden through the window. He had almost everything he could want in a wife, an intelligent lady for his days and a passionate creature of fire and spirit to warm his bed at night. What more could any man ask?

But the raw fact of the matter was that he was oddly unsatisfied. He had discovered of late that there were a few other things he wanted from Victoria. He found himself longing for the sweet, tremulous words of love she had withheld from him since the day of their marriage and he wanted her full and complete trust.

He probably did not deserve either her love or her trust, but lately he had come to realize he would not be able to rest until he had both. He did not care for her businesslike approach to her fate. This marriage was not just another financial investment for her, by God. He would not allow her to go on treating it that way much longer.

He glanced at the painting of *Strelitzia reginae* that

he'd brought downstairs earlier and propped on his desk. Every time he looked at it he remembered Victoria's glowing expression that night at the inn.

I think I have fallen in love with you, Lucas.

The door of the library opened just as Lucas was adjusting the position of the painting so that it would be visible from the chair on the opposite side of the desk. Reverend Worth was ushered into the room. He beamed at his host and brandished a magazine. "Latest issue of *Agricultural Review*," he announced. "Thought you might like to see it."

"Very much. Thank you, sir. Please sit down."

"My, there will certainly be a lovely prospect from these windows when Lady Stonevale finishes with the gardens." The vicar peered out at the ongoing work as he took one of the mahogany armchairs. "Your wife is a fine woman, sir, if you don't mind my saying so. A man could not ask for a better helpmate."

"I was just thinking something along those lines myself."

"You realize, of course, that in the village they've started calling her their Amber Lady on a regular basis?"

Lucas grinned. "I won't worry until the tenants start calling me their Amber Knight. I would not want them to think their landlord is a ghost. They might get the notion they can delay the payment of their rents until the afterlife."

"Rest assured," the vicar told him with a chuckle, "that they view you as altogether real and quite solid. Definitely not a ghost. You are a natural leader, Stonevale, as I'm sure you're well aware. And leadership is precisely what this land and the people on it have needed for some time. Which reminds me."

"Yes?"

The vicar arched his brows knowingly. "Word in the village has it the Amber Knight and his lady were running about again late last night."

"Is that so?"

"Seems a certain lad of the village reported seeing them. Personally I questioned what this particular lad was doing out at midnight himself, although I believe I

can hazard a guess. In any event, apparently his meeting with the knight and the lady changed the lad's mind
about pursuing an extremely dangerous career as a
highwayman. The boy has chosen to go to work in your
stables, instead."

"A much safer, if less exciting job."

"Yes, indeed." The vicar smiled. "The lad is basically
a good boy, and as he has the responsibility of caring for
his mother and sister, I am particularly pleased that the
knight did not deem it his duty to see the young man
shot down on the road or hung."

Lucas shrugged. "Perhaps the knight has already seen
far too many young men die senseless deaths. I imagine
even a ghost can get a bellyful of that sort of thing.
Now, then, vicar, I must ask you what progress you are
making on your gardening book."

The vicar gazed at him with piercing understanding
for a second and then blinked and smiled genially.
"Kind of you to inquire. I am working on the chapter
dealing with roses." He glanced at the picture propped
on the desk. "I must say, that's a wonderful rendering
of *Strelitzia reginae*. Quite perfect in every detail and it
seems to have a life of its own. Magnificent. How did
you come by it, if I may ask?"

"It was a gift."

"Was it, indeed? I am still looking for someone to do
the colored plates for my book, you know."

"Yes, I believe you mentioned you were inquiring for
a skilled watercolorist who also knew something of
botany."

The vicar continued to examine Victoria's painting.
"Whoever did this would be perfect. You do not happen to know the artist by any chance, do you?"

"In point of fact," Lucas said smoothly, "I do."

"Excellent, excellent. Any possibility you might arrange for me to contact him?"

"The artist is a woman, and yes, I think I can arrange
for you to talk to her."

"I would be most extremely grateful," the vicar said
happily. "Most extremely."

"My pleasure," Lucas said. "I will make certain you

meet her. Now, then, I want to ask your opinion on putting in an irrigation system for the farms that border the woods." Lucas spread a map out on the desk and indicated a section of land.

"Yes, indeed. Got to do something to increase productivity in that area, don't you? Let's see what you have in mind." The vicar leaned forward to examine the map and then glanced up one last time. "Don't mean to press you, Stonevale, but do you have any idea of how soon I might get in touch with the watercolorist you mentioned?"

"Soon," Lucas promised. "Very soon."

Two hours later Lucas saw his visitor out the door and then he headed for the stairs carrying his precious picture of *Strelitzia reginae*. He was feeling quite pleased with himself. The correct word might have been "smug," he admitted as he reached the landing and started down the hall toward his room.

Finding just the right gift for a wife who had brought considerably more money than her husband into the marriage was not the easiest task in the world. A man could hardly use the lady's own inheritance to buy her a diamond necklace.

Lucas rehung his picture with careful precision, stepped back to admire his handiwork, and then went over to the connecting door and knocked. When there was no answer from within, he frowned and tried again. He was certain Griggs had said Victoria was in her bedchamber.

"Vicky?"

When there was still no response, he turned the knob and opened the door to glance into the room. He saw her at once seated near the window with the three letters that had arrived at breakfast on the little rosewood secretary in front of her. She turned her head as he walked into the room. Her smile was wan.

"I am sorry, Lucas, but I am not feeling all that well. I came up here to rest."

An odd tension hummed through him. It was not unlike the sort of feeling he had known on the battlefield before the first shot was fired. "You were feeling well enough at breakfast."

"That was before I opened the post."

He relaxed somewhat. "I take it you are still annoyed at being obliged to accept Jessica's invitation?"

"Jessica Atherton is no longer of much consequence one way or the other."

"I am relieved to hear it." He went into the room and sat down across from her. He thrust his legs out in front of him, absently massaging his thigh. "What is it, Vicky? I have seen you in a variety of moods, but never one quite like this. I swear, madam, you leave me panting for breath trying to keep pace with you."

"I have never been in quite this position before and I admit I do not know how to deal with it. But 'tis certain something must be done or I shall go out of my mind."

"You are really not feeling well?" He grinned. "Mayhap you are breeding, after all, madam. Have you thought of that?"

"To be truthful, Lucas, being with child would be simpler than this business."

She was not carrying his babe after all. Disappointment shot through him. "I am sorry to hear that. Perhaps you had better tell me just what is troubling you, my dear."

She looked down at the papers on her little desk. When she glanced up again, her amber eyes were startling in their intensity.

"Lucas, do you believe it is possible to reanimate the dead through the use of electricity machines?"

"Reanimate the dead? Nonsense. I fear you have been playing too much lately at being a ghost, Vicky. I have never heard a single reliable instance in which such an experiment has been successful."

"But we do not know of all the experiments that have been done, do we? People all over England are playing with electricity these days."

Lucas looked doubtful. "I am certain that any successful experiment in reanimation would have been in all the journals and newspapers."

"Perhaps not, if someone paid the experimenter to keep quiet about the results."

He began to realize just how frightened she was and a cold anger swept through him. Without asking any more questions, he reached over and picked up the sheaf of papers lying on her desk. He immediately tossed aside Annabella and Lady Nettleship's notes. A glance at the pamphlet and clipping was sufficient to show that they were concerned with missing bodies and attempts at reanimation.

"Interesting, but I see no reports of successful attempts. Where did you get these?" He indicated the pamphlet and clipping.

"They were sent to me. They were in the third envelope that I opened at breakfast. Along with this." Victoria handed him a short note.

Lucas scanned it quickly and had to force himself to keep his rage under tight rein. " 'Madam: given your interest in intellectual inquiry the enclosed should intrigue you greatly. It appears the dead do not always remain so. Signed "W." ' " He tossed the note down on the table with a savage little flick of his hand. "Goddamned bastard."

"Lucas it is him, it is this 'W' again, the one who left the scarf and the snuffbox." Victoria was struggling for her self-control.

Lucas recognized the symptoms of shock and fear. He made a deliberate effort to keep his voice calm, much as he would have if he were dealing with a brave but frightened young officer on the eve of combat. "Calm yourself, Vicky. This has gone quite far enough. I will take steps to find out who is behind this and I will put a halt to it."

Her beautiful mouth trembled. "I know who is behind it. Samuel Whitlock. The man who killed my mother. He has come back, Lucas. Somehow he has returned from the dead and he is going to kill me or else drive me to my death the same way I—" She broke off and covered her face in her hands. "Oh, my God. *Oh, my God.*"

Lucas got up and reached down to pull her into his arms. She stood in the circle of his sheltering embrace, shaking. Although his hands moved gently, soothingly on her slender back, his rage was so cold now it could have frozen the marrow in his bones.

The shudders eventually ceased racking Victoria's body and she slowly disengaged herself from his grasp and went to her dressing table for a handkerchief.

"You must think I'm a witless little fool to believe in such things as reanimation of the dead," she whispered, keeping her back to him as she dried her eyes.

"I think," said Lucas, "that you have been very frightened and that someone has deliberately set out to accomplish that goal." He watched her face in the dressing-table mirror. "Who would do such a thing, Vicky?"

"I just told you. Samuel Whitlock."

"No, my dear, not Samuel Whitlock. He's dead. You have been so terrified by the signature on that note that you have not been thinking logically."

"It has to be him." She whirled around. "Don't you see, Lucas? He is not dead. Either he did not really die that night at the bottom of the stairs or else he has been brought back to life by someone with an electricity machine. One way or another he has come back and he is after me. Whitlock is the only one who could possibly have any reason for carrying out this horrible revenge."

Lucas studied her. "That brings up an interesting point. Just what is his reason for wanting revenge against you?"

Victoria's eyes clouded with an infinite sadness. "Lucas, I cannot tell you. If I did, you would be filled with such disgust for me that you would not be able to tolerate the sight of me."

In spite of himself, he felt his mouth twitch in a small grin. "Having led up to the grand revelation with a remark such as that, you most certainly will have to tell me the whole truth now. If you don't, I shall expire of curiosity."

"This is no joke. Lucas, you have no idea of what I have done."

He walked over to her and drew her tense body back against his chest. "I assure you that it is very unlikely you could tell me anything about yourself that would make me unable to tolerate the sight of you. I doubt there is anything to which you could confess that could compare with some of the small slices of hell I have seen on a battlefield. Tell me everything, my sweet."

"Very well, Lucas." Her voice was tragic. "But never say I did not warn you."

"I will never say it."

"I killed him." She went perfectly still in his arms, obviously bracing herself for his shock and disgust. "I murdered Samuel Whitlock."

"Hmmm," Lucas murmured. "I did rather wonder about that."

She jerked her head back to stare up at him. "You did? But what made you think such a thing? I have kept the secret to myself all these months. Even my aunt has no notion of what I did."

"It was nothing specific that you said or did. Just a few simple things that made me mildly curious."

"What simple things, for heaven's sake?"

"Well, there was the timing of Whitlock's death so soon after your mother's, and the fact that you were convinced he had killed her and would never hang for it. In addition to those two points, I have had occasion to get to know you rather well. Not as well as I would like, I will admit, but well enough to predict with some certainty that you would not let your mother's murder go unavenged."

There was a distinct pause and then Victoria spoke in a very small voice. "You do not sound particularly upset about this, my lord."

Lucas considered her words. "The only thing that upsets me is the thought of the risks you must have taken to get the job done."

She sighed. "I did not actually set out to kill him, you know. All I wanted from him was a confession. But I will admit I was not sorry when I realized he was dead. In fact, I experienced the most amazing sense of relief."

"I hate to be indelicate, but you did actually witness his death?"

Victoria buried her face in Lucas's chest. "Oh, yes. I witnessed it. And almost witnessed my own in the process."

"Good God. What happened?"

" 'Tis a long story. Are you quite certain you want to hear it?"

"I assure you I am prepared to listen all day and all night, if necessary." He eased her down into her armchair and resumed the seat across from her. "Talk, Vicky. Tell me everything."

She was twisting the handkerchief in her lap, but she met his eyes unflinchingly. "You must understand that my stepfather drank heavily. Sometimes he turned violent. His habits were no secret and I decided to make use of his weakness."

"Strategy," Lucas said approvingly.

She frowned. "Yes, well, I could not think of anything else, you see. I knew the house well because I had lived there for a few years before my mother sent me to my aunt's. It was a huge, old place with hidden passages and long halls with unexpected openings into certain rooms. I used that information to haunt my stepfather."

"You *haunted* him?"

She blew her nose. "Yes."

"Amazing."

"Really, Lucas, I'm sure you should not be looking quite so fascinated by all this. 'Tis rather reprehensible when you think about it."

"Let's just say I find it intellectually interesting. What's wrong with that? Surely no worse than trying to reanimate dead bodies. Pray, continue, sweetheart."

"I arranged to stay with friends who happened to live in a neighboring house for a week. Everyone knew I did not feel comfortable around my stepfather and these people had been friends of my mother's, so they were sympathetic to me. Several times during that week I slipped out of the house in the middle of the night and walked through the woods to my stepfather's house. I wore the dress in which my mother had been married and I began haunting Samuel Whitlock."

"You hoped that in his drunken stupors he would think he was seeing the ghost of his dead wife?"

Victoria nodded. "At first he thought he was having

nightmares. Then he began talking to me. It was eerie, Lucas. He ordered me to go away and leave him in peace. Then he told me about how he had never wanted to marry in the first place but he had to have the money and why could I not understand that? He pleaded with me to leave him alone. Finally, one night his nerve broke entirely. He came after me with a knife, saying he would kill me again and this time he would make certain of the job."

Lucas shut his eyes for a second, trying not to think of how close she had come to her own death. "That is when he had his accident on the stairs?"

"Yes. I was fleeing from him down the hall. I started down the stairs. He was directly behind me, holding the knife high in his hand and screaming about how he was going to kill me. He lost his footing about a third of the way down and fell all the way to the bottom."

"The servants," Lucas murmured. "Where were they?"

"There were only two in the house, an elderly couple with rooms far removed at the back. They were in the habit of retiring early and staying out of their master's way until morning. The screaming they may have heard that night was certainly not the first time they had heard such noises in that house. They had learned to mind their own business."

"I see. Did you check to see if your stepfather was truly dead?"

"No. I was so frightened that I ran. Perhaps the fall didn't kill him." She looked at the newspaper clippings. "Lucas, I do not know what to believe. Do you think he might have merely engineered his burial to haunt me as I once haunted him?"

"It is a possibility."

Victoria chewed her lip. "What has he been doing all these months if he is still alive?"

"Hiding, perhaps? Waiting to see if you would go to the authorities with your report?"

"He was dead. I know he was dead. I killed him," she said.

"You did not murder him, Vicky. You tried in a very clever fashion to extract a confession and you got it. In

the process, you almost got yourself killed, and that is
all there is to the matter," Lucas said very firmly. "As
to whether or not he is actually dead, that remains to
be seen. This business with the pamphlet and the note
certainly indicate there are some loose ends that need
tying up."

"Such as who sent me this note and the pamphlet
and clipping."

"Yes," Lucas agreed. "That is one of several questions I think we should get answered as soon as possible. There is also the little matter of that carriage that
nearly ran you down and the footpad who assaulted me
the night before you found the snuffbox."

"Lucas, this is making my head spin. I cannot go on
like this. I must have answers."

"I could not agree more wholeheartedly. As I said,
there are several questions that now must be answered
as quickly as possible. I think the best place to begin is
in Town, where this all started." He smiled. "Now we
have an excellent reason to go to London in addition to
the invitation to Lady Atherton's ball, don't we?"

Victoria gave a weak laugh. "Lucas, I swear you are
impossible. Even at a time like this, you are still plotting to get me to do precisely as you wish."

"Strategy, my dear. I'm known for it. Now, while this
will no doubt seem anticlimactic, I have a small surprise for you. Remember that picture of *Strelitzia
reginae*?"

"Yes, of course. What about it?"

Lucas flashed her an easy grin. "The vicar would like
half a dozen more watercolors on similar subjects for his
book on flower gardening."

The expression of shock on Victoria's face was extremely gratifying, Lucas thought.

17

Naturally Lucas had taken her horrendous revelation as calmly as if she had merely told him what Cook was preparing for dinner. What had she expected? Victoria was still asking herself that question a few days later as she stood with Annabella and Aunt Cleo in the shop of a fashionable London modiste.

Had she actually assumed, even for a moment, that he would have reacted as one would have expected any normal husband to react to such shocking news?

If there was one thing she had learned about Lucas by now, it was that he wad definitely not an ordinary sort of husband. While he was occasionally arrogant, high-handed, stubborn, and yes, a bit stuffy in certain matters, he was never at a loss.

And he always took care of his own. His dedication to his lands and the people of Stonevale proved that.

Still, even knowing what she did about him, she had not expected quite such a placid, pragmatic reaction. She was still a bit awed by his cool acceptance of her rather sordid past. Of course, she was dealing with a man who had once taken her to a gaming hell and a brothel, Victoria reminded herself, a man who took her riding at midnight.

"Is this not a lovely bit of silk, dear? Just your color, too." Aunt Cleo indicated a bolt of amber yellow stuff. "It would make a very nice evening gown."

"Oh, yes, Vicky. Absolutely perfect for Jessica Atherton's ball," Annabella declared. "You must be completely stunning for that great event, and your aunt is correct: the color is just right."

"Very pretty." Victoria reached out to finger the beautiful fabric.

"What do you think of the muslin, Vicky?" Aunt Cleo glanced at her inquiringly.

"Quite nice." Victoria forced herself to pay closer attention to the business at hand. The muslin was a deep yellow. She liked it at once.

"But not for Lady Atherton's ball," Annabella insisted.

"Perhaps a walking dress trimmed in aqua, then?" Victoria suggested, unwilling to let the fine muslin go.

The modiste, a tiny woman with a thick French accent, nodded emphatically. "Most charming, my lady."

"Very well, a ball gown in the silk and a walking dress in the yellow muslin," Victoria said decisively. "Now, as to the gown, I will want it in the height of fashion, do you understand?"

"It must be absolutely riveting," Annabella declared. "Perhaps something along the lines of this one." She indicated a fashion plate she had noticed earlier.

"A lovely gown, madam," the modiste assured her.

Aunt Cleo frowned as she peered down at the plate Annabella had pointed out. It showed a drawing of a woman in a dress that displayed a great deal of bosom. "Do you think Lucas will like that one, Vicky, dear? You know what he said last night at dinner. He distinctly mentioned that he did not want you getting anything with an extremely low neckline."

"Lucas is fond of saying things like that," Victoria explained. "But he really does not know all that much about fashion. This gown is for Lady Atherton's party, and Annabella is quite right: it simply must be as dramatic as possible."

"Yes, well, I shall leave you to explain it to Lucas," Cleo remarked. "He is your husband, after all."

Annabella giggled. "I am certain that by this time Vicky has molded her lord into an agreeable sort of husband who does not give his wife any trouble."

Victoria smiled serenely and decided it was not absolutely necessary to admit that there were still some rough edges on Lucas that needed a great deal more polishing before he would be molded into a perfectly agreeable husband. "He will be quite content with this gown."

"I swear, Vicky, you are an inspiration to us all," Annabella said in admiring tones.

Cleo Nettleship's brows rose. "Or an extremely dangerous example. Very well, then, let us be off. We have several more appointments to keep today."

A short time later Victoria followed her aunt and Annabella out onto Bond Street. The exclusive shopping district was crowded, as usual. Fashionable carriages, well-dressed women, and outrageously garbed dandies littered the landscape.

Aunt Cleo's carriage was waiting at the curb, but as they started toward it another carriage pulled up behind it and the groom jumped down to assist his passenger.

Isabel Rycott stepped out. She was dressed in a deep green that set off her eyes. A small, feathered hat was perched jauntily on her sleek, dark hair.

"Good morning, Lady Nettleship. So nice to see you."

"Isabel." Cleo inclined her head politely.

"And the radiant bride." Isabel smiled her mysterious smile as she turned to Victoria. "What a commotion you caused when you married Lord Stonevale. Quite romantic, I'm sure, although one wonders what your dear parents would have said about such a hasty marriage."

"As they are no longer around, it hardly signifies, does it?" Victoria remarked.

"Perhaps you are right. I had heard that you and your husband were back in Town. Lady Atherton is having a reception for you, is she not?"

"That is correct," Victoria said. "I hope you have been keeping well, Lady Rycott." She forced a smile.

"Very well, thank you."

"And your friend, Edgeworth? Is he in good health?"

Isabel's smile tightened fractionally. "I have not seen much of Edgeworth recently. I assume he is fine. Tell me, Vicky, dear, will we be seeing you tonight at the Foxtons'?"

It was Cleo who responded. "We are thinking of dropping in for a short time, although we will not be able to stay long. Vicky and Stonevale are in Town for only a few days and they have received scores of invitations. Impossible to accept them all, you know."

"I can imagine," Isabel murmured. "Now that Lady Atherton has given her opinion that it is the wedding of the Season, more than one hostess is anxious to have the famous couple grace her ballroom. Good day to you both. I trust I will see you this evening, and if not, then perhaps at the Atherton reception."

Victoria watched Isabel enter the modiste's shop and then she stepped up into the carriage, following her aunt and Annabella. "Really, that woman can be so damnably annoying. I cannot put my finger on it, but I know I shall never like her."

"Who? Isabel Rycott? I know what you mean. There is something about the woman that grates," Annabella agreed.

"Not on men," Cleo observed dryly.

Victoria grimaced and glanced back at the shop as the carriage pulled away from the curb. "Interesting what she said about Edgeworth, is it not?"

"He was not her first paramour and doubtless will not be her last," Cleo said. "Isabel always has a man or two trailing after her."

Annabella frowned thoughtfully. "Come to think of it, one does not see Edgeworth about much these days at all, not with Isabel Rycott or anyone else."

"Really?" Victoria could not wait to mention that little tidbit to Lucas.

As it happened, she did not get a chance to talk to her husband until she came down the stairs of his town house that evening. She had dressed with care for her first night out in London as a married woman. The yellow and cream gown fell in a graceful, slender line to her ankles. She had chosen to wear no jewelry except the amber pendant and a tortoiseshell comb in her hair.

Lucas was standing in the hall, waiting for her. He was dressed in starkly elegant black and white. His dark hair gleamed in the light of the chandelier. Victoria looked down at him from the third step and wondered if he would ever truly love her as she loved him. Perhaps the best she could hope for was his affection, companionship, and the protection he offered everyone toward whom he felt responsible.

She could hardly complain if that was all she ever received from him, Victoria told herself. It was a great deal more than many women were fortunate enough to obtain from husbands, especially those who had been married for their money.

Lucas bowed gallantly over her hand as she came down the last two steps. "You look lovely, madam. I consider myself the luckiest of men tonight."

She smiled. "I am feeling rather lucky myself, sir."

"Shall we go out and perform for the crowds?" he asked dryly as he led her out the door.

"That is exactly what it feels like, does it not? I would much rather go for a midnight ride with you, Lucas."

"Personally, I am looking forward to a relatively quiet evening of being squeezed and trampled and bored in a series of overheated ballrooms. It sounds positively restful compared to the adventures we always seem to encounter when you drag me out after midnight."

Victoria flashed him a berating look as he handed her up into the carriage. "Really, Lucas, the way you complain, one would almost think you did not thoroughly enjoy yourself on our midnight adventures. Now, then, I have been waiting all day for a chance to speak to you about Edgeworth."

"What about him?" Lucas asked as he sat down across from her.

"I ran into Isabel Rycott today on Bond Street and she made it clear she is no longer seeing him. In fact, I got the impression from what my aunt and Annabella said that he is no longer circulating much in the higher levels of the ton."

"Perhaps he has suffered some more losses at the gaming tables," Lucas offered mildly.

"Lucas, you suggested once or twice that he might have been involved in either the carriage incident or the footpad attack. Have you given any more thought as to whether he might have been the one who sent the pamphlet and note to me?"

"I have thought about it." Lucas studied the street outside the carriage window. "I do not doubt for a moment that he would not be at all concerned if I suffered an unfortunate accident. But I cannot see that it makes much sense to bother you. Not unless he was paving the way for a blackmail attempt."

"But there has been no demand for payment," Victoria said.

"I know. As I said, it makes no sense. Not yet, at any rate. Nevertheless, I intend to start my inquiries with Edgeworth. 'Tis as good a place as any."

"Shall we hire ourselves a runner?" Victoria asked, growing excited by the prospect. "The one I employed to track down information on Lord Barton was excellent."

Lucas met her eyes. "I would rather not get involved in hiring a runner if I can avoid it."

"Why not?"

"Because in doing so, I would run the risk of bringing up awkward questions about your stepfather's death, and those, in turn, might lead to awkward questions about you."

"Oh." Victoria sat back in her seat. "Yes, I see the problem. You are very clever, Lucas. Always thinking ahead."

"One tries."

"How will you go about tracking down Edgeworth?" Victoria asked.

"I shall start by making a few inquiries at my clubs. Someone is certain to know something about a man who gambles as much as Edgeworth does."

"An excellent notion."

"I am glad you approve. Because it means that you will be obliged to go straight home to bed after we have put in a few appearances this evening."

"What?" Her eyes darkened. "You cannot mean that."

"I fear so, madam. I cannot possibly sneak you into my clubs. We both know that. And since I do not want you running about at night without me, that leaves us with no option except to see you safely tucked up in bed at home."

"While you are out gathering information?" Victoria was incensed. "That is not fair, Lucas."

"It is not a question of fairness. It is a question of your safety. I will not risk any more runaway carriages, footpads, or ghosts who leave behind items marked with a 'W.' "

"But, Lucas, I will stay in Aunt Cleo's company or Annabella's. I will not be alone," Victoria insisted.

"Not good enough, Vicky. One cannot expect your aunt or Annabella to be on guard for a runaway carriage or a footpad, especially since they do not know they should be on guard for such things in the first place. No, I want to know you are safe at home while I am at my clubs."

Victoria's temper sparked as she sensed his implacability. "You cannot shut me out of this investigation. I will not allow you to do so. We agreed that the chief reason we would come back to London was to pursue this matter. This is my affair."

"I am not shutting you out. I'm simply ensuring that I know exactly where you are at a time when I cannot be with you. The danger lies here in London, Vicky. All the incidents occurred here. So while we are in Town, I want you under either my direct observation or lock and key," Lucas declared, his tone as definite as his words.

Victoria bristled. "Lucas, I must tell you that while you have made a tolerable husband in some respects, I do not like it at all when you assume the attitude of a superior officer and start giving orders to me. I am not under your command. I am your partner, remember? We are in business together."

"Above all, you are my wife, and as your husband I have certain responsibilities toward you. I am sorry if I offend you with the occasional command. I fear old habits are sometimes hard to break."

Victoria gave him a withering look. "Do not blame your old military habits. That is nothing but an excuse, my lord, and you are well aware of it."

"Well, then, to be perfectly truthful, Vicky, I must admit there are times when nothing else except a direct order will suffice in dealing with you. Tonight is one of those times. Now stop looking at me as though you would like to strangle me and try to look like a loving bride. I believe we have arrived at the Foxtons'."

"Lucas, I warn you I will not tolerate being treated like a witless child."

"I would not dream of doing so." He glanced out the window as the carriage drew to a halt. "It looks as if we have helped Lady Foxton draw a sizable crowd tonight. She will undoubtedly be feeling suitably grateful. Ready, my dear?"

"Damn it, Lucas, you are not going to get away with acting like this." She glared at him as he stepped out of the carriage and reached back to take her hand. "Just because you can seduce me virtually anytime you please does not mean I have become a weak-willed, fluff-brained female whom you can order about as it suits you."

His hand tightened roughly around her fingers and sudden laughter filled his eyes. "I do not believe I heard that properly. Would you care to repeat that, madam?"

"You heard me. Oh, look, there's Annabella and Bertie, now." She summoned up a brilliant smile. "I cannot wait to talk to them." Victoria rushed off, dragging Lucas along with her into the throng of people clustered on the front steps of the Foxtons' town house.

His wife's sense of timing was, as always, devastating. Lucas grinned ruefully to himself as he got out of the carriage in front of one of his clubs. Her admission that he had the power to seduce her at will was enough to make him want to carry her straight back home and take her to bed.

Instead he had been obliged to escort her into the Foxtons' ballroom, where he had been forced to spend his time fending off a lot of Victoria's old admirers. Every last one of them had felt it necessary to profess heartfelt anguish at the news that she had accepted another's hand in marriage. Victoria had enjoyed herself immensely and had flirted so outrageously that Lucas was determined to exact retribution when he returned home.

Just what form his retribution would take was a matter to which he intended to give considerable attention. But in the meantime there were other matters that needed his full concentration.

The first person Lucas saw when he walked into the club was Ferdie Merivale. The young man smiled in welcome.

"Congratulations on your marriage, Stonevale. Cannot say I was terribly surprised. Wish you the best and all that. You are a lucky man. Lovely lady, your new countess."

"Thank you, Merivale." Lucas poured himself a glass of claret.

"Come to play a few hands of cards?" Merivale inquired.

"Unfortunately, I fear my gaming days are behind me. I'm a married man now. Cannot spend all night playing cards anymore."

Merivale chuckled. "I expect Lady Stonevale would have a few words to say about that, wouldn't she?"

"My wife is rarely at a loss for words," Lucas agreed. "Any news of interest?"

"That's right, you have been spending the last few weeks rusticating in the country, haven't you? Since you had that bit of a scene with Edgeworth shortly before you left Town, you might be interested to know that he is rarely seen in the clubs these days. He was obliged to resign from this one, in fact."

"I cannot imagine Edgeworth giving up his gaming."

"Oh, don't think he has. But word has it he's carrying

on his business in somewhat less respectable surroundings. Heard he was seen in that same gaming hell you
rescued me from a while back. The Green Pig. Nasty
place. Rather suits him, though, don't you think?"

"I am sure he will feel very much at home there,"
Lucas agreed.

It was another two hours before Lucas walked into
the Green Pig. Nothing had changed since the night he
had brought Victoria here. It was still the same oppres-
sive, noisy place it had been when he'd deliberately
chosen it with a view to shocking Victoria into realizing
she did not really want to frequent gaming hells. Not
that it had achieved its purpose, Lucas thought with an
inner grin. Victoria had had a great time that night.

Edgeworth was sitting at a card table with a group of
well-dressed young dandies who were clearly deeply
into their cups. They had apparently set out to spend an
evening savoring the dregs of town life. Lucas got a pint
of beer from a passing barmaid and walked over to the
group of card players.

"Gentlemen," he said calmly, "I wonder if you would
all be so good as to allow Edgeworth and myself a word
in private."

One of the young pups looked up, scowling. "Here,
now, we were just getting into some deep play. You've
got no right to barge in like this."

But another young man was already on his feet, eyes
widening in belated recognition. "Your pardon, Stonevale.
Take your time. I believe we can all wait to continue
this particular game. Perhaps our luck will turn in the
meantime."

Lucas glanced at the man and smiled faintly. "The
only way your luck will come about is to find another
game. As long as you play with Edgeworth, you will no
doubt continue to lose."

"I'll have you know I won several hundred pounds
not more 'n an hour ago," the first man declared.

"Did you really? And how far down are you now?"

The man glared at Lucas. "That's none of your
business."

"I agree. But you may do as you wish. I assure you I

have no great interest in your losses. Now, if you will excuse me?"

"Come on, Harry," the second man muttered, dragging his friend away from the table. "You don't want to get into a brawl with Stonevale. Take my word for it. Friend of mine served under him on the Peninsula. Says he knows how to take care of himself."

Edgeworth watched the two young men disappear and then he turned to face Lucas. "I don't much appreciate your scaring off my lambs before they have been properly fleeced, Stonevale. Just because you have had the good fortune to marry money does not mean the rest of us must not continue to make a living."

"I am certain you will find other sources of income before dawn. You have always been quite adept at relieving the unwary of whatever they happened to have in their pockets. Tell me, Edgeworth, is there a bit more sport to be had in cheating foolish young men who have merely had too much to drink than there is in stealing from young men who are dead or dying?"

Edgeworth ruffled the cards on the table. "So you did see me that day. I wondered about it at the time. I should have slit your throat while I had the chance and made quite certain you were dead."

"Why didn't you?"

Edgeworth shrugged. "To be honest, I did not think you would live until sundown with that hole in your leg. Who could have guessed you'd make it, Stonevale? You do seem to have the most amazing luck."

"Lately someone has been trying to change my luck. I decided to consult with you to see if you might have any notion of who would want to do that."

Edgeworth smiled, his eyes glittering behind half-closed lids. "Someone who has lost a great deal of money to you at some point in the past, perhaps?"

"That list would include yourself."

"So it would."

Lucas paused. "Are you going to force me to kill you, after all, Edgeworth?"

"Rest assured, I have no intention of letting you call me out. Just how do you perceive your luck to have changed? It seems to me you have done very well for yourself lately."

"There have been one or two minor incidents. There is no need to detail them. If you truly know nothing about them, then the less said, the better. If you do have some knowledge of them, however, then you may want to see that they cease."

"Why should I care what happens to you? You have been a great nuisance to me, Stonevale."

"Let me put it this way. If there is another incident of any sort that I find, shall we say, disturbing, I shall come looking for you and we will discuss the matter in more depth. Perhaps at Clery Field? At dawn?"

Edgeworth's hand stilled on the cards. "Hardly fair if I am not the perpetrator of these incidents."

"Yes, but very little in life is fair, is it? I found that out for certain the day I watched you walk among the dead and wounded and take whatever you could find in their pockets."

Lucas got to his feet, turned, and walked away from the card table without a backward glance.

Victoria was standing at the window clad in her nightgown when she heard the connecting door open behind her. She whirled around. Lucas had changed into his dressing gown.

"There you are. Thank heavens. I have been so worried." She flew to him on bare feet and threw herself into his arms.

Lucas staggered a bit as his bad leg gave slightly under the impact, but he caught his balance quickly. His arms closed tightly around her. "I shall have to see to it that you get worried more often if this is the greeting I can expect."

"Pray do not tease me." She raised her head from his shoulder and frowned severely. "Where have you been? What have you been doing? Did you discover anything useful?"

Lucas caught her chin in his hand. "One question at a time, sweetheart. I have had a long night."

"Well, so have I. And I must tell you, Lucas, that I

will not allow you to order me to stay home again while you are out larking about in search of information. Sitting around waiting is very hard on the nerves. Now, just what did you do? Did you find Edgeworth?"

He released her and dropped into a chair. "I found him, for all the good it will do. I cannot tell if he knows anything about what is going on or not. But he does have some motive for wanting to cause trouble for me."

She nodded quickly, sitting down across from him. "Because you are more or less responsible for making him unwelcome in the clubs."

Lucas rubbed his leg. "Actually, it all goes back a bit farther than that."

She studied him intently. "Just what does it all go back to, Lucas?"

"To the day I got this damned hole in my leg. Edgeworth was there."

"You mean he also fought that day?"

"Not exactly," Lucas said. "Let us say he chose to watch the battle from a safe distance."

Victoria finally understood. "He broke and ran?"

"It happens in battle. Edgeworth was not the first, nor will he be the last. Who knows? If more men had the sense not to stand their ground and shoot at each other until there was no one left standing, we might have less warfare."

Victoria was astonished. "Lucas, you are not condemning him for his cowardice?"

"Not particularly. Cowardice under fire may not be considered an admirable trait—"

"I should think not."

"But I can understand it." He slid her a cool glance. "And forgive it. Fear is not easy to deal with and warfare is a remarkably unintelligent way to resolve problems. If I learned nothing else during my career in the army, I learned that much. The idea of a man choosing to flee from the scene of battle is not so difficult to accept. It almost seems rather logical when you think about it."

Victoria recovered from her initial shock and gave that notion some close thought. "You may have a point.

Never let your friends in the clubs hear you say such things, though."

He smiled. "I am not a complete fool. I only say such things to you, Vicky. You are the one person I know with whom I can talk freely."

She smiled at him, aware of a sweet warmth welling up inside. "That is the nicest thing you have ever said to me. I am very glad you feel that way, Lucas, because I have discovered I feel exactly the same toward you. I have told you things I have never even told Aunt Cleo."

"I am glad," he said simply.

Victoria smiled warmly. "But no matter how you feel intellectually on the subject of cowardice under fire, I know you would be incapable of behaving like a coward yourself. Edgeworth undoubtedly knows that, too. Is that why he holds a grudge against you? He knows you saw him flee?"

"That is partly it. The other part is that I saw what he did after the battle. He walked through the field and robbed the dead."

Victoria stared at him. "Good God, I can hardly credit it." Then another thought shook her. "Did he know you were lying on that field? Did he see you?"

"He saw me."

"And he did nothing to help you?"

"He assumed I wouldn't last long anyway and he was rather busy collecting jewelry, watches, and other souvenirs," Lucas explained.

Victoria leapt to her feet and raged back and forth across the room. She had never been so shaken with fury. "I will shoot the man the next time I see him, I swear I will. How dare he sink so low? How could he act in such a despicable fashion? To leave you lying there like that. It is absolutely unforgivable."

"I tend to agree with you that he sank to the depths that day. Nor has he conducted himself with much honor since," Lucas said grimly.

"No, he certainly has not. I wonder if Isabel Rycott found out about his habit of cheating at cards. Perhaps that is why she dropped him. She likes weak men, but she may draw the line at that sort of weakness."

"Perhaps."

Victoria whirled around and paced back the other way. "So you believe Edgeworth really is behind the incidents? That he holds a grudge against you because you know the truth about him?"

"It is possible. I cannot escape a certain feeling that he knew more than he was willing to say tonight. I warned him that if anything else happens, I will look to him first for an explanation, but . . ."

She eyed him carefully. "But you are not one hundred percent convinced he is to blame for what has happened to us?"

"I think there is more to the story."

"Because I was the target of some of the incidents?"

" 'Tis entirely possible Edgeworth selected you as a target because he knew it would annoy me," Lucas said.

Victoria sat down on the edge of the bed. "This is very frustrating. We are no better off than we were before you sought him out."

"That remains to be seen. If there are no more incidents, I will be able to assume I warned off the right man."

"True." She frowned, thinking about it. "But if the incidents continue, we must also consider the fact that my stepfather is alive."

"Regardless of the outcome in that quarter, I, personally, feel that I made tremendous progress in another area this evening," Lucas continued smoothly.

She looked over at him, intrigued. "How is that?"

"I was referring to your admission that I have the power to seduce you anytime I please."

"Oh, that." She felt the heat flood her cheeks.

Lucas got to his feet and came toward her. "Yes, that. A minor issue to you, perhaps, my dear, but a matter of overwhelming import to me. It gives me great hope, you see. One of these days you are going to take the last step and admit you love me."

She rose and backed away from him. "You probably should not read too much into what I said as we got out of the carriage, Lucas. I was very annoyed with you at the time and spoke without thinking."

He smiled. "Are you going to retract your words now? You cannot possibly deny them. I will not allow it."

She groaned and took another step backward. "You are going to assume far too much from this. You will see it as a form of surrender. I just know you will."

"Would surrender be so bad, Vicky?"

"Intolerable." She took one more step backward and found herself up against the wall. Her eyes widened as he stalked toward her.

Lucas's eyes were gleaming as he closed the distance between them. Very deliberately he caged her, flattening his palms against the wall on either side of her head. His mouth hovered bare inches above hers.

"Intolerable, hmmm? Very well, madam, why don't we call it a step toward a negotiated truce rather than a step toward surrender?"

She caught her breath. "In order for it to be a step toward a negotiated truce, we would both have to give up an equal amount of ground, my lord. You would have to admit I have the same power over you."

"Yes, I would, wouldn't I?"

Her tongue touched the corner of her mouth. "Are you admitting I can seduce you at will?"

"Madam, you can seduce me by merely walking across the drawing room or serving me a cup of tea. Every time I look at my picture of *Strelitzia reginae*, I am seduced."

"Oh." Then she smiled slowly. "Is this another example of your skill at strategy, Lucas?"

He did not answer that with words. Instead, his mouth closed over hers, hot, exciting and intoxicating. Victoria put her arms around his neck, glorying in the heat and strength of him.

He slid his hand down her side to her thigh and lifted the thin stuff of her night clothes up to her waist.

"Lucas?"

"Part your legs, sweetheart."

She moaned softly and, shivering delightfully, did as

he directed. His hand slipped between her thighs.

"*Lucas.*"

"Yes, sweetheart. That's it. That is what I want from you. Call it a truce or call it surrender. It does not signify."

She clutched at him as his tongue eased into her mouth just as he eased a finger into her moist heat. He began moving both tongue and finger in and out of her in a simultaneous rhythm. Victoria thought her legs would collapse.

She retained just enough self mastery to fumble with the opening of his dressing gown. She found him hard and heavy with his arousal. Her fingers circled him gently.

"Oh, God, Vicky."

He pulled her back toward the bed, dragging her down onto it. Then he was on top of her, kissing her breasts, her silky stomach, and the soft skin of her thighs. Without warning, his kiss became even more intimate. Victoria gasped, first in shock and then in wonder, as she felt his mouth on the most secret part of her.

"Lucas, this is outrageous. You cannot mean to . . ." Her fingers clenched in his dark hair and her whole body tightened unbearably. "*Lucas.*"

She was still in the midst of her searing climax when she felt him glide up the length of her and surge deeply, heavily into her body. Victoria's teeth sank into the skin of his bare shoulder. She clung to him as if she would never let him go as his hoarse, exultant shout echoed in her ears.

18

"I must say, you and Lucas have certainly contrived to brush through the entire incident quite nicely." Cleo raised her watering pot to reach a fuchsia plant that hung from a beam. "You were a great success at the Foxtons' last night. It is obvious you do not even need Jessica Atherton's public approval. The ton has decided you are their favorite couple, and the Season, one hopes, will be over before you can do anything to ruin that status."

"One hopes." Victoria grinned. "I believe Lucas is harboring the same sentiments. You and he must get together and share your concerns over my behavior."

"We would no doubt have a great deal to talk about, would we not?" Cleo smiled. "I did tell him once that one is seldom bored around you."

"Well, as far as I am concerned, it is not Lucas and I who contrived to escape the potential scandal, Aunt Cleo. You are the one who accomplished that. With a little help from Jessica Atherton, of course," she added in regretful honesty as she studied the half-finished painting of a cactus on the easel before her. Cacti were a nuisance to paint. All the little spines were something of a bother.

Cleo moved on to the next pot but she searched Victoria's face with concerned eyes. "I worried a great deal at first after Lucas took you away to Yorkshire. I could have strangled Jessica Atherton for showing up the morning of your marriage and causing such a stir."

"I had a few thoughts along that line myself. Lucas did, too."

"Not surprising. I am certain he could have done without her interference. The whole situation bordered on disaster, but I told myself that there was only one man of your acquaintance who could deal with such an imbroglio and you were with him. When I got your first letter requesting plants for his gardens, I knew the worst was over," Cleo explained.

" 'Tis true we have arrived at an understanding of sorts, Lucas and I."

Cleo's head came up sharply. Her eyes sparkled with laughter. "An understanding? Is that what you call it? You should see yourself when you are anywhere near him, my dear. You practically glow. I trust you are no longer worrying about following in your mother's sad footsteps?"

Victoria carefully mixed yellow with a touch of blue to create just the right shade of green she was seeking. "Lucas is no Samuel Whitlock."

"Good heavens, I should say not. Just as you are nothing like your mother, dear Caroline, rest her soul. She truly loved your father, you know. If he had lived, everything would have been much different. She would never have become an easy target for Whitlock's charms. But she was so hungry for love after your father died that she fell immediately for the illusion Whitlock was quick to offer."

"Love is a dangerous thing, rather like electricity, I believe. I think it is better to form a solid, working partnership with a man. That is what I am doing with Lucas, you know. We are making progress."

Cleo gave a start. "I beg your pardon? You are forming a business alliance with Stonevale?"

"It is the logical thing to do, given the circumstances under which we were married. There is no denying that Stonevale itself is an excellent investment. It is good land."

"I see." Cleo looked dazed. "How very fascinating."

"The arrangement works well, for the most part, although Lucas does have the lamentable habit of giving orders when he cannot get his way through reason and logic."

"Vicky, dear, this is quite interesting. Stonevale is going along with this partnership notion?"

"On the whole. I am meeting with some resistance in certain areas."

Cleo's eyes widened. "I can imagine. What areas?"

"He would still very much like to believe that I am in love with him and he never loses an opportunity to try to coax me into admitting it."

Cleo put down the watering pot with a small thud and stared at her niece. "Are you not in love with him? Vicky, I assumed from the start that your heart was charting your course in all this. Otherwise, I would never have insisted—"

"Of course I am in love with him. I would never have gone to the inn that first night with him if I hadn't been. But I am not about to give him the satisfaction of admitting it to him," Victoria declared.

"Why ever not?"

Victoria looked up from the painting. "Because, to be blunt, he is not in love with me."

"Good heavens, Vicky, are you certain? He seems inordinately fond of you."

"He is fond of me. That is one of the reasons the marriage is working. But he feels he cannot allow himself to love me because if he does, I will use the knowledge to run roughshod over him. He thinks I am something of a shrew, you see. Too independent and headstrong by half. Give me an inch and I will surely take a mile."

"Perhaps he is merely uncertain of you and cannot admit his love until he knows you love him," Cleo suggested.

"Why should he be uncertain of me? The man is married to me."

"What does that signify? How many married women of our acquaintance are head over heels in love with their husbands? More than one has resorted to a discreet affair, as you well know. And women such as Jessica Atherton, who would almost certainly never indulge in an affair, are testimonials to womanly duty, not womanly love. The thought of being married out of a sense of duty must give a man a few chills."

"Why should it? Lucas certainly had no qualms about marrying me out of a sense of duty. His goal from the start was to save Stonevale, not find a deep and abiding love for himself." Victoria dashed the brush fiercely across the paper and immediately had to blot up a long smear of green.

"Just because a man is forced to marry for the sake of his responsibilities does not mean he is not human enough to want to be loved. Lucas told me the morning of your marriage that he truly wished things had progressed in a far different fashion. He knows that because of that debacle at the inn, he never had a chance to finish the courtship properly."

"He finished it, all right. He concluded the matter with a special license, if you will recall." Another smear of green appeared on the paper.

"My point is that he is only too well aware of the fact that he did not have a chance to win your love. You did not marry him entirely of your own free will and he knows that. Later, when you found out he had begun his pursuit of you because you were an heiress, his position was further weakened. How can he possibly be all that certain of you unless you have assured him of your love?"

Victoria looked up, feeling pressed. "Just whose side are you on, Aunt Cleo?"

Cleo sighed. "I am not on anyone's side. I just want to see you happy, Vicky."

"You think I would be happy if I simply surrender completely to my husband?"

"Surrender? What an odd term."

" 'Tis the one he uses," Victoria muttered. "Except when he's trying to find euphemisms such as 'negotiated truce.' "

"Does he really? I expect 'tis because he spent so much time in the military and then devoted himself to gaming. Military men and gamesters have a somewhat similar vocabulary, you know. They are always thinking in terms of strategy and winning and losing. There is very little middle ground for them."

"Yes, I have discovered that for myself."

"Women, on the other hand, are capable of more flexibility in their thinking," Cleo continued.

"That is undoubtedly a weakness when it comes to dealing with men. It gives them a license to indulge their own inflexibility. No, I am married to a man who thinks like a soldier, and I must either break him of the habit or teach him to be content with the partnership we have managed to establish. The one thing I will not do is risk everything by giving him the surrender he wants."

Cleo considered her thoughtfully for a long moment. "What is it, precisely, that you would be risking?"

"My pride, for one thing."

"Is that so very important?"

"Of course it is."

"Well, he is your husband, my dear. You must do as you think best."

Relieved to be through with that topic of conversation, Victoria hurriedly switched to another. "Perhaps you would care to go shopping today? I mean to purchase some books on gardening and horticulture to take back to Yorkshire."

"I would be delighted. Are these for your library at Stonevale?"

"Some of them will go into the library but the rest are to serve as a gift to our local vicar and his wife. They have been most helpful. The vicar is writing a book on gardening." Victoria hesitated and then added in a rush, "And I am to the plates."

Cleo beamed. "Vicky, how marvelous. You are going to get your lovely botanical work published. I am so pleased. How did that arrangement come about?"

"Lucas arranged it," Victoria admitted softly.

Cleo's gaze sharpened. "How did he do that?"

Victoria flushed. "He showed one of my paintings to the vicar, who instantly asked to meet the artist to see if she would be interested in doing the plates for his book. Lucas swears he did not influence the vicar by telling him who the artist was until after Reverend Worth admired the picture. The vicar seems genuinely delighted to have me do the plates. I must confess, I am very excited about it."

Cleo leaned forward and admired Victoria's painting, musing thoughtfully. "Trust Stonevale to find a way to give his heiress the one gift she could not have bought for herself."

The amber yellow silk gown was stunning in its elegant simplicity. Victoria was pleased with the effect. The skirt fell in a narrow, graceful column to her ankles. The high waistline, topped with a small, artfully draped bodice, displayed a wide expanse of white skin and emphasized the gentle curves of her breasts. Her slippers were embroidered in gold thread and matched her long, elegant gloves.

The amber pendant hung in solitary splendor around her throat. With a last glance in the mirror, Victoria decided she was as ready as she would ever be for Jessica Atherton's reception. She picked up her gilded fan.

"I will take the black cloak, the one with the hood lined in gold satin, Nan."

"Ye do look wonderful tonight, ma'am," Nan breathed reverently as she carefully draped the long, flowing cloak around her mistress's shoulders. "His lordship will be ever so proud." She adjusted the hood so that the gold satin formed a deep, rich collar around Victoria's throat. "Wonderful."

"Thank you, Nan. I must be off. His lordship will be

waiting in the hall. Pray do not wait up for me. I will wake you when I return if I need any help."

"Yes, ma'am."

Lucas was pacing impatiently at the foot of the stairs, but when he saw Victoria draped in black velvet and gold, he halted abruptly. His eyes were full of gleaming, sensual admiration as he watched her come slowly down the staircase.

"Ready for battle, are we?" he murmured as he took her arm.

"Let's just say I do not want Jessica Atherton feeling sorry for me."

He laughed as Griggs opened the door. "She is far more likely to feel sorry for me."

"Oh, really? And why is that, my lord?"

Lucas tightened his hold on Victoria's arm. "She will know I must be helpless to resist my Amber Lady. She will undoubtedly worry that you are already in command of this marriage."

Victoria slid a sidelong glance at him as he assisted her into the carriage. "And are you helpless to resist me?"

"What do you think?" He climbed in beside her.

"I think you are teasing me again."

He reached for her hand and inclined his head gallantly over her gloved fingers. "Madam, I assure you that I find you utterly irresistible."

"I shall bear that in mind."

The streets near the large Atherton home were filled with carriages. Dozens of elegantly dressed people clogged the front steps. But Lucas and Victoria, as guests of honor, were quickly ushered past the crowds.

When Victoria handed over her cloak in the wide, brilliantly lit hall, the amber yellow gown was revealed in all its glory. Lucas took one look at the graceful expanse of his wife's throat, shoulders, and bosom revealed by the small bodice and he set his teeth.

"No wonder you kept that cloak wrapped around you until we got here," he growled. "This will teach me to examine your attire far more carefully before I take you anywhere in the future."

"Trust me, Lucas. This gown is in the height of fashion."

"It reveals more than a tavern maid's dress. You are practically falling out of it. If I had seen it before we left the house, I would have sent you straight upstairs to change."

"Too late for that now," she told him cheerfully. "Now do stop frowning so. We are about to be announced and you surely would not want Lady Atherton and her guests to think we are quarreling."

"You have won for now, madam, but rest assured, this discussion will continue at a later time." He led her toward the top of the stairs that descended into the glittering, crowded ballroom.

A hush fell over the throng of beautifully dressed people as the Earl of Stonevale and his lady were announced. And then a ringing cheer went up and glasses were raised in a salute as Lucas and Victoria went down the staircase to greet their host and hostess.

Lady Atherton's gaze held a trace of wistfulness as she smiled at Lucas. Lord Atherton, an austere man who was active in politics, inclined his balding head over Victoria's hand.

"So kind of you both to honor us with this reception tonight," Victoria forced herself to say as sincerely as possible.

"You look lovely, my dear," Jessica said to Victoria. "That gown is simply exquisite. And such an unusual style for a new bride. But, then, you have always been something of an Original, have you not?"

"I do my best," Victoria assured her. "After all, I would not want to bore my husband."

Lucas shot her a warning glance. His smile was full of menacing charm. "Boredom is not something I have suffered from much since the night I met you, my dear."

Lord Atherton smiled briefly. "And as I understand it, that momentous occurrence took place right here in this ballroom, did it not?"

"Lady Atherton was kind enough to introduce us," Victoria said politely.

"So I heard." Lord Atherton extended his arm. "Would you be so gracious as to honor me with the first dance, madam?"

"It would be my pleasure."

As she was led out onto the floor, Victoria glanced back over her shoulder in time to see a crowd of people close in around Lucas. He caught her eye over the heads of the throng and smiled faintly, a smile of possession, admiration, and sensual promise; a lover's smile.

Warmed by that smile, Victoria turned to give her attention to Lord Atherton, who was already starting to talk about politics.

Lucas kept an eye on his Amber Lady as the evening passed, but he had very little opportunity to speak to her. Just as well, he told himself. If he did get close to her, he would probably be unable to avoid bringing up the topic of the dress again, and since the damage was already done, it would be pointless to continue the argument.

A husband had to learn which battles were worth fighting, and he could not deny that the military strategist in him could not help but sympathize with Victoria's need to make a brilliant splash tonight in front of Jessica Atherton.

Nevertheless, he vowed as he caught sight of Victoria being led out onto the floor again, he would pay much closer attention to her clothes in the future.

"Your wife is cutting quite a swath through my male guests tonight," Jessica Atherton murmured as she glided up to stand beside Lucas. "I am gratified that she is enjoying herself."

"She deserves to enjoy herself."

"Yes. It cannot have been easy for her to come here tonight."

Lucas raised a brow at that bit of unexpected insight. "No, it was not."

"I know she must have been feeling somewhat battered by all that happened at the time of her marriage to you. And I did not aid matters by calling on her that morning before you left for Yorkshire. I am sorry about that, Lucas. I have wanted to apologize for it. My only excuse is that I was desperately anxious to know if you were going to be happy with her," Jessica said weakly.

"Forget it, Jessica. It is all in the past."

"Yes, you are quite right. It is just that I know you were angry with me that day and I expect I am trying to find out if you have forgiven me."

"As I said, it is over and done. Don't fret about it. Victoria and I have arrived at an understanding and we are both content with the marriage."

Jessica nodded. "I rather thought that is what would happen. She is, after all, an intelligent woman. She may be rather outrageous at times, but she is also a woman of honor and integrity. I would not have introduced you to her if I had thought otherwise. I was certain that when all was said and done, she would learn to accept her fate and fulfill her duty, just as you must."

Lucas realized he was starting to grit his teeth. He reached for a glass of champagne and took a large swallow. "Tell me, Jessica, have you had much pleasure in your marriage?"

"Atherton is a tolerable husband. That is as much as a woman can hope for from her marriage. I take satisfaction in knowing I am a good wife to him. One does what one must."

A tolerable husband. Victoria had called him that once or twice, Lucas reflected. He suddenly felt slightly savage. Was that all he was to her he wondered? *A tolerable husband?*

"Excuse me, Jessica. I think I just saw Potbury in the crowd by the window. I wanted to ask him a question."

"Of course."

Lucas escaped his hostess, but he knew he could not escape her words. As was frequently the case with Jessica Atherton, she might grate a bit, but she was not altogether wrong in her observations. She was right about Victoria being a woman of honor and integrity.

But Lucas did not want to think she was also right when she claimed that Victoria had no doubt accepted the marriage because it was the reasonable thing to do. He did not want to be merely a tolerable husband.

He could not bring himself to believe that when Victoria shivered and cried out in his arms, she was merely performing her wifely duty. She cared for him, he told himself. He was almost positive she could learn to love him again if she would just stop erecting defenses to protect her pride. Her damned female pride was all that kept her from the final surrender.

Lord Potbury smiled in genial welcome when he saw Lucas coming toward him. "Good to see you again, Stonevale. Must say your bride is looking positively radiant this evening. How are things in Yorkshire?"

"Very well, thank you. But I miss our weekly meetings of the society. Wanted to ask how the electricity experiments were proceeding. Heard of any more interesting work in that area?"

Lord Potbury brightened. "Grimshaw had a bit of an accident last week. Gave himself a terrible jolt. Thought he was done for at the time, but he is quite recovered now."

"I'm relieved to hear that. What was he working on?"

"Thinks he's got an idea for creating a smaller, more compact system for storing electrical energy. Have to hope he doesn't kill himself with the stuff before he finishes his work on the invention."

"I read something recently about more work on reanimation of the dead," Lucas said casually.

"Yes, yes, saw that bit myself. Quite interesting, but so far no one's seen any reanimated corpses walking about." Potbury chuckled.

"You don't believe that line of experimentation will prove fruitful?"

"Who can say for certain? But personally I'm highly doubtful."

"Yes," said Lucas. "So am I. Which means that we must look to the living for answers."

"Beg pardon?"

"Never mind, sir. Just making an observation to myself. If you will excuse me, I think I shall try and forge a
path over to where my wife is standing."

"Good luck. Quite a crush here tonight, ain't there?
And getting worse. More people arriving by the minute. Probably going to be the rout of the Season. There's
Lady Nettleship. Looks quite lovely tonight, doesn't
she? Believe I'll try to make my way over to her."

Lucas nodded politely and started off through the
crowd. Progress was difficult because nearly everyone
he passed insisted on stopping him long enough to
congratulate him.

He was midway in his journey across the ballroom
when one of the liveried footmen stepped into his path.
He held out a small silver tray on which lay a sealed
note.

"A man appeared at the door and asked that this be
given to you, my lord," the footman said politely. "I am
sorry for the delay. It took me a while to find you in the
crowd."

Lucas frowned and picked up the note, nodding
abruptly in appreciation of the service. He put a few
coins on the tray and the footman disappeared into the
sea of guests.

> Have information that
> should interest you concerning
> certain incidents. Very
> urgent. Am waiting outside in
> black carriage near corner.

Lucas crumpled the note and looked across the room
to where Victoria was standing in a group of chattering,
laughing people. He started toward her again, this time
not pausing politely when he was greeted by well-wishers.

"I wonder if I might steal my wife for a moment or
two," he said as he moved through the small crowd
around Victoria. It was a command, not a request, and
everyone stepped back immediately.

Victoria looked up in surprise and then smiled knowingly at the women in the group. "Men go through such

a change after marriage, do they not?" she murmured by way of apology. "Why is it they are always so accommodating and gallant before the wedding and so dreadfully dictatorial afterward?"

Lucas took her arm and led her a short distance away, aware of the laughter and giggles behind him. "I shall only keep you a minute, madam, and then you may return to your observations on husbands."

"Lucas, I was only joking, for heaven's sake. What is it? Is something wrong?"

"I don't know. I just got this." He showed her the note.

She read it with widening eyes. "Edgeworth?"

"It must be him. He probably does not have an invitation and could not get inside to talk to me. I am going outside to see what he wants. I came to warn you I would be missing for a while. I did not want you calling attention to the fact that I'm gone. I don't know how long this will take."

Victoria glanced around assessingly. "I think it will be perfectly possible for you to slip away unnoticed. Do you know, I believe we could both slip out. This crowd has gotten so huge no one would guess we had left. Anyone looking for us would just assume we were at the other end of the room or on the balcony or in the card room or even outside in the gardens."

"Victoria . . ."

Her expression brightened with anticipation. "Yes, I am certain we could both slip out. You go first and I will just sort of casually move out into the gardens, hop over the wall, and pop around the corner. You can meet me there."

"Are you out of your mind?" He was thunderstruck even though he supposed he should have been expecting something along this line. "You will do no such thing. I absolutely forbid it. You are to stay right here, Vicky. That is a direct order. Under no circumstances are you to leave this ballroom. Do not even go out into the gardens for fresh air. Do you hear me?"

"Very clearly, my lord. I assure you, you have made

your point. Honestly, Lucas, sometimes you have the most annoying tendency of putting a damper on something that particularly interests me."

"Forgive me, my dear, but sometimes you have the most annoying tendency of coming up with the most idiotic notions I have ever heard. Now go back to your friends. I shall return as soon as possible."

"I will require a full report as soon as you get back inside the ballroom."

"Yes, madam."

She put her hand on his arm and her eyes were suddenly very intent. "Lucas, promise me you will be careful."

"I am sure there is no danger in this," he said soothingly. "But I give you my promise." Then he scowled briefly at the décolletage of her gown. "The only real danger around here tonight is that you might catch a severe chest cold."

She grinned. "I shall try to keep warm by dancing. On your way, Lucas. Hurry back."

He wanted to kiss her full on her lovely mouth but knew that was impossible. Such a public display of affection would be quite scandalous. Absolutely unthinkable. Except that he could not seem to stop thinking about it.

"Vicky?"

"Yes, Lucas?"

"Do you still find me merely a tolerable husband?"

"Quite tolerable, my lord," she said cheerfully.

He turned and pushed through the crowd toward the windows. He took his time, not wanting to call attention to himself now. When he was satisfied no one would think it amiss if he stepped outside for a breath of fresh air, he did so.

And kept on going.

The Athertons' garden wall was no more difficult to climb than Lady Nettleship's. Lucas found a few chinks in the bricks, a handful of ivy, and a moment later he was over the top and safely down on the other side.

He found himself in a narrow alley that was nearly

pitch dark. It stank, as all London alleys seemed to do, but other than that presented no great difficulty. He walked around to the front of the house and moved through a group of lounging coachmen and grooms who were throwing dice.

He paused in the shadow of a team of horses and scanned the line of carriages. Near the corner, a little removed from the others, was a small, black vehicle of undistinguished lines. The coachman was on his box, apparently waiting.

Lucas circled around two other coaches that stood between him and the small, black one and came up on the far side of the vehicle.

"Were you by any chance expecting someone?"

The coachman turned around with a start and peered down at Lucas. "Yes, sir."

"Perhaps I am he."

"Never even saw you come out of the house," the coachman said with a touch of admiration. "Got a passenger inside who wants to have a word wi' ye."

Lucas glanced speculatively into the dark carriage and saw a man lounging in the corner. He reflected that being obliged to leave the party unobtrusively as he had, he had not been able to collect his greatcoat. There was, of course, no way to secret a pistol in his close-fitting evening clothes. Pity.

"Good evening, Edgeworth. Waiting for me, I presume?"

"I have something that I think will interest you, Stonevale. Do step inside for a moment, won't you?"

Lucas considered the possibilities and decided the prospect of getting some answers outweighed the risks. He opened the door and got into the carriage with some awkwardness, deliberately favoring his left leg more than was absolutely necessary.

He was not particularly surprised to see Edgeworth pull a pistol out of his heavy coat.

"I imagine you recall that day you should have died every time that leg of yours fails you, don't you Stonevale?"

"I do hope you will at least do me the courtesy of explaining what is going on before you pull the trigger," Lucas remarked, massaging his thigh as he sat down across from the other man.

"You may relax, Stonevale. I will not be pulling the trigger for some time yet. My associate has a few plans that must be carried out before I shall have that pleasure."

"Would the name of your associate be Samuel Whitlock, by any chance?"

"Whitlock? What an amusing notion." Edgeworth rapped twice on the roof of the carriage and the vehicle moved off. Then he looked at Lucas and broke into outright laughter. "Imagine forming a partnership with the dead. Most amusing."

19

The message reached Victoria on a silver salver just as she came off the dance floor with Lord Potbury. "Please excuse me." She smiled quickly at her escort as she opened the note.

"Of course. Nothing serious, I trust?"

Victoria scanned the brief message and hoped Potbury would not notice that her fingers were shaking inside her beautiful gloves.

> Come at once if you value
> your husband's life and honor.
> A carriage waits at the corner
> with the garments you will
> need. The driver will give you
> instructions when you arrive.
> Time is of the essence.

"No," Victoria said, smiling very brightly at Potbury. "Nothing is wrong. Just a short note from a friend to tell me she is going to take some air in the gardens. She invites me to join her. I suppose she felt it would be easier for one of the footmen to get the message to me in this crowd than for her to get through the crush. Will you excuse me?"

"Certainly." Potbury bent gracefully over her hand. "Enjoy yourself. Lady Atherton's gardens are quite extensive. Once again, my congratulations on your marriage. Good man, Stonevale."

"Yes, he is, is he not?"

Victoria unobtrusively collected her cloak from one of the footmen, explaining that she was going out into the gardens for a few minutes and found it cool outdoors. Then she made her way discreetly toward one of the windows.

A moment later she was deep in the unlit portion of Jessica Atherton's precisely manicured gardens. Several rows of clipped hedges and elaborately designed topiary shielded her from the ballroom windows. Jessica Atherton's gardens were rather like Jessica herself, Victoria concluded: beautiful, perfect, untouchable.

Climbing the wall took a bit of doing. She was obliged to hitch her gown up to her thighs in order to accomplish the feat and she thought fleetingly of what Lucas would have said had he seen her expose so much leg. The thought brought tears to her eyes and she dashed them away immediately. She would do something violent to Edgeworth as soon as she found him if Lucas had not already done so.

Victoria wrinkled her nose at the stench in the alley as she put on the cloak and pulled the hood up over her head. Then she walked swiftly to the corner.

A public coach was waiting. An obviously half-drunk coachman tipped his hat with mocking respect. "Expect you be the *lady* I been waitin' for."

Realizing he probably thought he was taking her to meet a lover at a secret rendezvous, Victoria said nothing. She shrank deeper into the cloak and climbed quickly into the coach. The vehicle jolted forward before she was properly seated and she nearly lost her balance.

When she reached out to brace herself, her hand touched a sack. She knew immediately it contained the clothes she had been told to wear.

Even as she pulled the breeches, shirt, and boots from the bag her stomach turned over with a sickening realization. This was no coincidence. Whoever had sent the note must know that she was in the habit of wearing men's clothes at night. If that same person knew that dark secret, he might know others.

A ghost would know such things, she reflected, or a man who trailed her like a ghost the way she had once trailed Samuel Whitlock through the corridors of his own home. Victoria shuddered.

But she could not think about that now, she told herself as she changed quickly into the male garb. Indeed, she must not think about it. The only thing that mattered was rescuing Lucas.

Her stomach felt distinctly queasy again as the coach pulled up outside the Green Pig. The choice of destination could not be a coincidence either. Someone knew everything.

With shaking hands, she put her cloak back on over the masculine clothing and pulled up the hood. Then she quickly rolled up her gown and the rest of her discarded clothes and stuffed them into the sack.

"Third room at the top o' the stairs," the coachman muttered as she stepped down from the cab. "Trust you'll 'ave fun. Quality usually does, unlike the rest o' us that's got to work for a livin'." He did not even bother to look at her as he took another sip from his flask, flicked the reins, and drove off.

Victoria watched the carriage roll out of sight and then she removed the cloak and put on the high crowned hat that had been provided. Taking a deep breath and squaring her shoulders, she walked boldly through the front door of the gaming hell.

Everything was different this time, she thought nervously, and she knew that was because she did not have Lucas by her side to make it all seem a grand adventure. The red glare from the hearth illuminated the rough crowd of Green Pig patrons, making them look like demons from the underworld. The coarse, drunken laughter was unnerving. She had the feeling a violent brawl could break out at any moment. As she started toward the stairs one of the barmaids sidled up to her.

"You don't want to be goin' up there alone, now do ye, sir? You'll be wantin' a lady friend and it just so 'appens I'm free at the moment."

Victoria thought frantically. "Thank you, but there is someone waiting for me."

"Ah, so that's the way of it, eh?" The barmaid winked. "I saw your *friend* go up earlier and I ain't one to pass judgment on that sort o' thing. Besides, the bloke already paid for the room. Good luck to ye, I say. But if ye decide you'd rather have a woman, ye just give old Betsy a shout, hear?"

Victoria stared at her in confusion. "Yes, thank you very much, I'll do that."

Betsy roared with laughter. "Ye can always tell the well-bred coves. They remember their manners even in a place like this." She sallied off into the crowd, still chuckling.

Victoria went grimly up the stairs, the sack containing her dress still clutched in one hand, the cloak draped over her arm.

At the top of the stairs she found herself in a dark hall. She could hear obscene laughter and groans coming from the rooms as she passed two doors and stopped at the third.

She hesitated a moment at her goal and then tapped cautiously on the third door. It opened immediately.

Isabel Rycott stood framed in the doorway, looking even more exotic in men's clothes than she did in a ball gown.

"Lady Rycott. What a surprise." Victoria struggled to sound calm and cool and almost detached, the way Lucas always managed to do when he was facing a startling situation. At least she was not dealing with the reanimated corpse of Samuel Whitlock, Victoria told herself. "Where is my husband?"

Isabel Rycott smiled with a terrible satisfaction and revealed the pistol in her hand. "Won't you come in, Lady Stonevale? I have been waiting for you."

Now that she was over her initial shock, Victoria told herself she must stay calm. She would be no help to

Lucas if she had hysterics. "Is Edgeworth with you?" she asked as she stepped into the room. "I cannot imagine you have managed this entire business by yourself. You are accustomed to using your male acquaintances, are you not?"

"How very astute of you." Isabel backed away from her. Her eyes were feverishly bright. "But, then, you always were a very clever girl, weren't you? Too clever by half. And now you are going to pay for it."

Still clutching the sack of clothing and the cloak, Victoria wandered over to the fireplace to lean negligently against the mantel. The blaze on the hearth cast a sordid glare over the small, shabby room. "You don't mean to tell me that all this is because you hold some sort of grudge against me, madam? What on earth have I ever done to you?"

"You killed him. That's what you did," Isabel hissed. "You killed Samuel Whitlock and ruined everything."

Victoria went still. "Perhaps you will be good enough to tell me just what it was I ruined for you?"

"I had it all planned, you stupid little bitch. Whitlock was going to marry me after he killed your mother. It took me months to work him up to the point where he had sufficient nerve to see to the business of murdering Caroline. *Months.*"

Victoria almost collapsed against the mantel. "You prodded him into murdering my mother?"

"Do you think he'd have done it on his own? He hadn't the guts to do it without being pushed into it. He saw no need. Kept saying he had the use of her fortune anyway, so what did it matter if she was alive. But I did not have the use of that fortune. So I made it clear to Samuel that he could not have me unless he got rid of her, and he wanted me very badly, Victoria. Very badly, indeed. He finally arranged the riding accident."

"I *knew* it was murder, even before he confessed."

"Yes, you guessed that immediately, didn't you? Less than two months later he started acting very strange. Kept saying he was seeing your mother's ghost. I was afraid he was losing his mind, that he would get himself sent to Bedlam before he could marry me. So I decided to see for myself what was going on at his house at night."

Victoria's fingers tightened on the sack. "You were there that last night when he came at me with a knife, weren't you?"

"Who do you think put the knife in his hand? I told him he must kill Caroline again and this time she would stay dead. He was so crazed with drink and the notion that Caroline had come back to haunt him that he did as I told him."

Victoria's pulse was racing, driven by savage anger and a terrible fear. "Where is my husband? What has he to do with any of this?"

"All in good time, Victoria. All in good time. He will be here, never fear. Edgeworth is going to bring him."

"So Edgeworth is involved."

Isabel tightened her grip on the pistol and laughed softly. "Oh, yes. It was Edgeworth's idea to finish the matter in this particular fashion. He has a score of his own to settle with Stonevale, you see. I agreed to do it his way so long as I could be certain of your death."

"You cared so much for my drunken sot of a stepfather that you wish vengeance on me? I am appalled by your taste in men, Lady Rycott. But, then, I suppose I should not be so astonished. After all, you took up with Edgeworth and he certainly is not an admirable specimen of manhood, either, is he? Perhaps you like men who are as low as you yourself?"

"I told you once I like men who can be controlled. Men who are weak and therefore easily manipulated. It makes everything so much easier, you see. Whitlock was completely in my power. Edgeworth is now, too."

"How did you happen to select Edgeworth as your assistant?"

"I heard the talk that there was ill feeling between him and Stonevale. When Stonevale began pursuing you, I decided a man who disliked him as much as Edgeworth did could be of use to me."

" 'Tis a bit late to murder me," Victoria pointed out. "My husband has legal control of my money now. In the event of his death, the inheritance goes to our remaining relatives, including my aunt. You will never see a penny of it."

Isabel's eyes sparked in anger. "Don't you think I know that? You deprived me of any chance of getting hold of your fortune the night you caused poor, stupid Samuel to fall down those stairs. You ruined all my plans and now you will pay."

"Why have you waited so long to take your vengeance? Why did you go to the continent after Whitlock's death?"

"Because I was afraid you would realize I had been involved. You were so damn clever that I could take no chances. I had no way of knowing how much you knew or how much Samuel told you that night he tried to kill you. I fled the night of his death because I feared you would put the entire tale together. But you never did."

"No. But for the past few months I have had the oddest feeling that there was something left unfinished." The nightmares had begun shortly after she had been introduced to Isabel Rycott, Victoria realized with a chill.

"I did not care for life on the continent," Isabel continued coldly. "Oh, it suited me well enough at first, but there were problems after I became involved with a young Italian count. His mother, you know. She was afraid her precious son would marry me and she could not bear the notion of the family fortune falling into my hands. She contrived to have me cast out of the higher circles of society, ruining all my opportunities. Most unpleasant."

"So you decided to return to England."

"It is here I have the best chance of securing another fortune. And mark my words, I will find another Samuel Whitlock, and soon. I have gone through my first husband's money and I find myself in need of more. Quickly. While on the continent, I had kept track of you through friends. After several months I realized I was safe, so I returned to London."

"And decided to make me pay for ruining everything for you?"

"Precisely. But I also wanted you out of the way

because it was simply good policy to tidy up after oneself. There was always the chance that you would put it all together, you see. Since I must be free to stay in England, I could not take the risk that you would eventually figure out that I had been involved in your mother's death."

"It was you who put the scarf and the snuffbox where you knew I would find them," Victoria said evenly.

Isabel glanced down at her breeches and boots and smiled strangely. "You are not the only one who has learned to enjoy the freedom of men's clothing. I owe you for that, by the by. Do you think there will ever come a time when women will be free to wear breeches in public?"

Victoria ignored that. "You followed me about at night."

"Oh, yes. I kept very close watch on you for weeks before I made my plans, learning your habits and your ways. When you took up with Stonevale, it all became vastly easier. You began taking so many risks, you see."

"Yes." Greater risks than even Lucas had imagined, Victoria thought. "Who was it who nearly ran me down that night outside this tavern?"

"That was Edgeworth. I told him I only wanted you frightened, but I do believe the fool saw his chance to get rid of Stonevale in the process. I was very angry with him afterward."

"And the footpad who attacked my husband?"

"Edgeworth hired him for me. Again, you were supposed to be frightened, perhaps nicked a bit with the knife, but that was all. Something went wrong, however. You did not follow your usual pattern that night. Stonevale went to fetch you from the garden as usual, but you did not return to the carriage with him. The dolt of a footpad attacked him anyway, figuring he had to earn his money somehow," Isabel said.

Victoria remembered that had been the night when she had summoned Lucas to the garden to tell him she wanted to begin a love affair with him. She had not planned to go adventuring that evening, so she had not gone back to the carriage with him.

"Why the haunting tactics, Isabel? Why the business with the scarf and the snuffbox and the pamphlet on reanimating the dead?"

Isabel's eyes brightened noticeably. "I got the notion from you, of course. Don't you appreciate the irony? I wanted you to be scared out of your wits and to know there was no one you could turn to. After all, who would believe Whitlock had come back from the grave to kill you? My original plan was to terrify you into believing you had lost your wits. Everything would have been so simple if you had gotten yourself committed to a madhouse. Imagine yourself chained to a wall to rot for the rest of your life. A sane woman trapped in a world of madmen. It would have been a most piquant ending. And a safe one for me."

Victoria nodded. "You would not have had to risk your own neck by resorting to murder."

Isabel paused, considering Victoria's words. "True. I do not like this business of having to do one's own killing. However, once you married Stonevale and left Town so abruptly, it all got very complicated. There was always the chance that if you confided in Stonevale he might decide to make an investigation. That was when I began to agree with Edgeworth that you both must die."

"You still have not answered my first question, Isabel. Where is my husband?"

"Edgeworth is bringing him here so that you both may die together in this room. It will all be excessively tragic and very romantic, I assure you. We should not have much longer to wait."

Victoria smiled coolly. "I fear you have made a mistake in sending Edgeworth to fetch my husband. Stonevale will be here soon, of that I have no doubt. But it is my guess that Edgeworth will not survive to accompany him."

Isabel walked over to the window, gazing at the dingy alley that ran alongside the Green Pig. "I fear you have a great deal of misplaced faith in your husband's abilities, Victoria."

"I have a great deal of faith in his knowledge of strategy, madam."

    *   *   **

From the dark confines of Edgeworth's carriage, which was parked in a lane near the Green Pig, Lucas watched Victoria alight from the coach and go into the gaming hell. His hand tightened into a fist.

"You have just sealed your own death, Edgeworth. You should never have involved my wife in this business," he said icily.

"Your wife was involved before I was," Edgeworth said with a thin chuckle of satisfaction. "Her death is as important to Isabel as yours is to me."

"What is your plan?"

"I suppose there is no harm in telling you now. You are known for your ability to plot tactics and strategy, Stonevale, so you should be able to perceive the cleverness of my scheme."

Lucas did not take his eyes off the front door of the Green Pig. He could feel Edgeworth's tension filling the coach. The man smelled of it. "You are a coward and a fool, Edgeworth. The combination means that whatever you have planned is bound to end in failure."

Edgeworth raised the pistol slightly, his smile of satisfaction turning to a snarl. "You will see, Stonevale. This time your luck has finally run out. It is not only your life you will lose tonight, but your precious honor. Tomorrow morning all London will be talking about how the Countess of Stonevale left Lady Atherton's reception to carry out a secret rendezvous with an unknown lover in the upstairs room of a gaming hell. They will delight in saying how you followed her and discovered her in bed with another man."

"Who is this other man?"

"No one will ever know because he will have mysteriously escaped while you were busy killing your wife."

"And my own death? How will it be explained?"

"Very easily. What else could a man in your situation do except put a pistol to his own head?"

"Tell me, Edgeworth, was it you who notified Lady Nettleship of Victoria's whereabouts on a certain evening?"

Edgeworth smiled dryly. "I followed her from the ballroom that night, as usual. When I realized you were taking her to that inn in order to seduce her, I thought I saw my chance to enjoy a most agreeable vengeance against you. I was certain that when you were discovered, your reputation would be in shreds. I thought you would be shunned by Society afterward and cast out of the clubs. But you moved too quickly and married the lady within hours. And once Lady Nettleship and Jessica Atherton made it clear they approved the marriage, there was nothing to be done."

Edgeworth motioned with the weapon in his hand. The movement was jerky, betraying the man's anxiety. "I think we've given my associate enough time alone with your wife. Isabel has the instincts of a cat, you see. She wanted to toy with her victim a few minutes before she delivered the deathblow."

Lucas started to step out of the carriage. He stumbled in the process and grabbed at the edge of the door, stifling a groan.

"Damn you, Stonevale." Edgeworth moved back hurriedly, the pistol coming up sharply as he made a grab for his own balance.

"Sorry. My leg, of course. It has a habit of giving way at inappropriate moments."

"Shut up and get out of the carriage," Edgeworth said nervously.

Lucas obliged, moving cautiously. He watched Edgeworth alight behind him.

"There is a flight of stairs at the back. We will use those," Edgeworth said. "I don't intend to have you try to escape in the tavern, where there would be witnesses if I was forced to shoot you."

"Very farsighted of you." Lucas started into the dark alley that led to the back of the building that housed the Green Pig. The shadows suited him well. All that running around at odd hours with Victoria had paid off, he thought wryly. He had become quite accustomed to moving about in the deepest part of the night.

He did not make his move until they reached the stairs. Then, in obedience to Edgeworth's command, he started up the steps ahead of his captor.

"Hurry," Edgeworth muttered, his voice quavering and anxious now.

"This must be exceedingly difficult for you, Edgeworth. Your nerve was always somewhat weak, was it not? I can just imagine what a strain this must be on you."

"God damn you, Stonevale. You will soon pay for that, I swear it. *Hurry.*"

Lucas waited until he was on the third step before he deliberately let his bad leg go out from under him again. He started to reel backward, flailing wildly.

"What in hell's name are you . . . ?" Edgeworth instinctively tried to get out of the way, but the stairs were narrow and he wound up having to grab at the shaky railing as Lucas's full weight hit him. He fought to get the pistol back in line to fire but it was too late.

The struggle was brief. Both men rolled together down the three steps. Lucas paid attention only to the pistol in Edgeworth's hand. Edgeworth's finger began to tighten and Lucas used both hands to force the man's arm across his body.

Edgeworth heaved frantically, just as the pistol exploded. He cried out as the bullet went into his own chest at point-blank range.

Lucas felt the shock and the sudden, terrible limpness that went through the other man. He was vaguely aware of a ringing in his ears caused by the noise of the pistol. Then he felt the unmistakable sensation of warm blood pumping over his fingers.

"God damn you to hell, Edgeworth." He levered himself away from the dying man.

"He did that a long time ago. The day I turned and ran on the field of battle." Edgeworth's eyes were already closing. "You never told anyone about that."

"Each man must see to his own honor."

"You and your bloody damn sense of honor," Edgeworth said, his voice strained and not much above a whisper.

"Which room is my wife in, Edgeworth? Do not go to your maker with murder on your conscience along with everything else."

Edgeworth coughed and choked on blood. "Find her yourself, Stonevale." He fell silent.

Lucas got to his feet, certain the man was already unconscious. He dried his hands on Edgeworth's coat and picked up the pistol.

He had just turned to start back up the steps when Edgeworth spoke one last time.

"Should have slit your throat that day when I saw you lying on that goddamned battlefield, Stonevale. Should have killed you when I had the chance. You have haunted me ever since like some damned ghost. And now you have had your vengeance."

Lucas said nothing. There was nothing left to say. He bounded up the stairs as fast as he could without jeopardizing his balance.

At the top he found himself on a narrow landing. There was a door at one end which opened onto a dingy hallway. The grunts and groans and laughter that came from behind the closed doors told him where he was.

He could start throwing open each door as he came to it, but that would cause alarm and give Isabel Rycott too much time and warning. Lucas reluctantly stepped back out onto the outside landing and eyed the narrow ledge that ran beneath the windows. It was a lucky thing he had a head for heights, he decided.

Victoria was still leaning against the mantel when she caught the trace of movement outside on the window ledge. She knew immediately who was out there. Relief soared through her. Lucas was here and everything was going to be all right. She redoubled her efforts to keep Isabel talking and to make certain the other woman's attention did not stray to the window.

"Tell me, Isabel, do you think you will be able to give up the habit of going about in men's clothing now that you have discovered the freedom associated with it? I vow, I will have a hard time resisting the temptation. It is a marvelous sensation, is it not? Think how much better off the world would be if all women felt free to wear breeches when it suited them."

Isabel shook the pistol menacingly. "Shut up, Victoria. You will not have to worry about that particular temptation after tonight."

Victoria smiled and used the toe of her boot to poke a small stick back into the fire. "Edgeworth will let you down, you know. Weak men may be useful on occasion, but I fear they cannot be counted upon in a crisis. I shall be the first to admit there are difficulties in dealing with a strong man, but I have learned that at least one can depend upon them. Have you ever met a man you could depend upon, Isabel? I have come to the conclusion that they are a rare and valuable commodity."

"I told you to shut up, damn you. Edgeworth will be here any minute and then you will not be feeling so talkative," Isabel hissed.

Out of the corner of her eye, Victoria saw a booted foot slide along the ledge. She put down the sack of clothing and absently fiddled with the cloak that was still draped over her arm. "The thing about talking is that it will help to pass the time until Stonevale gets here."

"Your husband is not going to rescue you, Victoria. You might as well get that notion out of your head."

"Nonsense. Lucas is the most amazing man, you know." She smiled very brilliantly and in that second Lucas came through the window in a shower of glass and shattered wood.

"*No.*" Isabel Rycott screamed in fury and swung her pistol toward the window.

But Victoria was already whipping the cloak out in an arc that caused it to settle over Isabel's head. Isabel screamed again. There was a shriek from under the cloak and then the pistol skittered along the wooden floor.

Lucas looked at Victoria as he straightened and brushed off his clothes. "Are you all right?" he asked quite calmly.

"Amazing." Victoria ran into his arms. "I knew you would get here. Where is Edgeworth?"

"In the alley. Dead."

Victoria swallowed. "Somehow that does not surprise me. What will we do with Lady Rycott?"

"A good question." Lucas released her and picked up Isabel's pistol. Then he yanked the cloak off his victim,

who glared at him with her glittering, gemlike eyes.
"We don't have a great deal of time to make the decision. We must get back to the ball before we are
missed. I suppose the easiest thing to do is simply kill
Lady Rycott here and now. The proprietor of the Green
Pig is already fated to discover one body in the morning. He might as well discover two."

Victoria was horrified. "Lucas, wait. You cannot simply shoot her dead."

"I told you, we cannot afford any time to think about
alternatives. We must be gone from here as quickly as
possible."

Isabel stared at him, her eyes full of fear. "You cannot just shoot me in cold blood."

"I fail to see why not. The proprietor will no doubt
see to it that both your body and Edgeworth's are
removed from his premises and dumped into the river.
There will be no questions asked."

"No," Isabel choked on a scream. "You cannot do
such a thing."

"Lucas, she's right," Victoria said.

"You care what happens to her?" Lucas asked.

"Of course not. But I cannot allow you to shoot her
down like this. Not only will it go against your sense of
honor, but I do not want you to have to endure yet
another act of violence. You have had far too much of
killing in your life as it is."

"You are, as usual, much too softhearted, my dear. I
assure you my honor is not offended by the thought of
killing the woman who was going to kill you, and one more
death on my conscience will not make much difference."

"It will to me," Victoria said quietly. "I will not allow
it."

"Then have you any other ideas?" Lucas asked a bit
too casually.

Isabel's eyes widened in horror.

"Well," said Victoria, thinking quickly. "I don't see
why we could not just leave her here and let her find
her own way home tonight. In the morning, she can
begin making arrangements to return to the continent."

"The continent?" Isabel looked momentarily startled.

"But I cannot go back there. I will be penniless. I will starve."

"I doubt it," Victoria murmured. "Lucas, make her leave the country. It will serve our purposes just as well as killing her."

"Yes," Isabel said slowly, taking another look at the pistol Lucas was idly pointing at her. "Yes, I will go back to the continent. I give you my word I will leave the country at once."

Lucas considered that. "I suppose it is a possibility."

"*Yes.*" Victoria spoke at the same time Isabel did.

"You will naturally want to leave Town at the earliest possible time," Lucas remarked. "And you will not return for a very long while, if ever."

"No, no, I won't come back at all, I give you my word."

"Because if you do decide to return, you would very likely find yourself tried for murder."

Isabel's mouth fell open. "But I have killed no one."

"I fear you are wrong, Lady Rycott." Lucas smiled. "You see, in a fit of jealousy, you followed Edgeworth to this tavern tonight, where you suspected he was meeting another woman, and you shot him."

"But I did no such thing."

"Unfortunately for you, madam, there will be a signed confession saying you did precisely that. That confession will be produced under appropriately dramatic circumstances should you ever return to England."

Victoria looked at Lucas with fresh admiration. "How very clever of you, Lucas. What an excellent notion. It is the perfect answer. We shall keep the confession and have it handy in case Isabel returns."

Isabel's gaze swung from Lucas's calm, implacable face to Victoria's delighted expression. "But I have signed no such confession."

"You will before you leave this room, Lady Rycott," Lucas said.

20

"Hurry and get those damned breeches off. We have no time to waste if we are to salvage both our reputations." Lucas opened the sack that contained the amber yellow ball gown. He tugged out the rolled-up silk as the public coach he had hailed a few minutes earlier worked its way through the crowded streets.

"I am doing the best I can, Lucas. There is no use snapping at me. It is not my fault men's breeches are difficult to get off."

"If you think I am snapping at you now, you may rest assured it is nothing compared to what I am going to do to you when we get home tonight."

Victoria stopped working at the breeches, her head jerking upward in consternation. It took her a few seconds to realize he was furious. "Lucas, what's wrong?"

"You have the nerve to ask me that? After what has happened tonight?" He peeled off her waistcoat and shirt, seeming not to notice her bare breasts in the shadows. He was too busy trying to stuff her into her gown.

"Be careful or you'll tear my gown." She thrust her

arms through the small sleeves. "I really wish you wouldn't yell at me just now. I have had a most upsetting evening."

"Your evening has not been any more upsetting than mine, and I would like to point out that I am not yelling at you now. I will save that for when we are in the privacy of our own home. Good God, we forgot your petticoat."

"Never mind. No one will know I am not wearing it."

"I will know it. I am not about to let you go back into Lady Atherton's ballroom without a petticoat."

"Yes, dear." She struggled obligingly with the petticoat. "Lucas, I was so worried about you tonight."

"How do you think I felt when I saw you get out of the carriage in front of the Green Pig. You would have been in no danger if you had done as you were told. Here we are. Put on your cloak."

She slid her feet into her slippers and pulled the hood of the cloak over her head. The next thing she knew, Lucas was opening the carriage door and hurrying her out onto the street.

A few minutes later he led her back into the alley outside the Athertons' garden wall.

"I will go first." Lucas found a toehold and hauled himself up to the top of the wall. Then he leaned down to pull Victoria up beside him. "I think breeches are a better idea for climbing walls," he muttered as her skirt hiked up above her knees.

They dropped down onto the graveled walk on the other side. Lucas rubbed his leg and glanced around the dark, empty corner of the gardens.

"The worst is over," he announced. "If we are seen now, the most anyone can say is that the Earl of Stonevale was dallying with his bride in the darkest section of the garden. Not exactly proper, but hardly scandalous. Let's get back into the house."

Victoria ran a hand through her short curls, brushed a few creases out of her skirts, and put her gloved fingertips on her husband's proffered arm in a graceful gesture. She could not repress a small grin as he walked her back toward the lights and laughter of the crowded ballroom.

"There is nothing funny about this, Vicky."

"Yes, my lord."

"I ought to paddle your backside," he said.

"Yes, my lord."

"You have implied before now that I have turned into a conservative prig of a husband, but by God, madam, you have not seen anything yet. Henceforth I intend to show you just what a conservative prig I can be."

"Yes, my lord."

Before Lucas could utter further threats, a familiar figure caught sight of them from the terrace.

"Oh, there you are, Vicky," Annabella Lyndwood called cheerfully. "Enjoying the gardens, I see. I want you to meet Lord Shipton. Bertie says there's a chance he will be offering for me one of these days and naturally I wanted to get your opinion on the man."

"My wife is no longer in the business of hiring runners to investigate her friends' marriage prospects," Lucas said. "She has decided that the time has come for her to start acting in a more refined, conventional fashion."

"Oh, dear," said Annabella. "Are you hoping to turn her into another Jessica Atherton or a Perfect Miss Pilkington? How depressing."

"Yes, Lucas," Victoria asked, turning innocent eyes up to meet his grim expression. "Would you like me to model my behavior after that of Lady Atherton or Miss Pilkington?"

"I don't believe we need go quite that far," Lucas muttered. "If you two ladies will please excuse me, I believe I see Tottingham standing with Lady Nettleship. I want to see if he has read anything interesting lately on manure. For some reason the subject is uppermost in my mind tonight."

Victoria watched Lucas saunter into the ballroom and then she turned to smile at Annabella.

"Lovely party, isn't it?" Victoria remarked as she removed her cloak and started toward the open windows.

Annabella grinned. "Lovely. But, then, one can always depend upon Lady Atherton to give the perfect

soirée. And I think if we are very careful to stay close
together once we are inside, I can arrange for the skirts
of my gown to hide the dirt stains on yours."

Three hours later Victoria sat on her dressing-table
chair and watched her husband pace back and forth in
front of her. She had never seen him this angry. His
voice was low and dangerous and his mood was precarious. It was clear that he had been pushed as far as he
intended to be pushed tonight.

"Why in God's name did you fail to follow orders,
Vicky? Answer me that, if you can. I told you not to
leave the ballroom under any conditions. But no, you
could not be bothered to obey a few simple instructions
designed to protect you. You must go gallivanting off
into the night at the first opportunity."

Victoria frowned. "What could I do after I got that
note saying you were in danger?"

"You could have done as you had been told, that's
what you could have done."

"Would you have stayed behind in the ballroom after
getting such a note?" Victoria said in an effort to defuse
his anger.

"That is beside the point. You should never have left
Jessica Atherton's house alone and you know it."

"I am sorry, Lucas, but I must tell you in all honesty
that if I had it to do over again, I would do it exactly the
same way."

"And that's another point. For a supposedly intelligent woman, you do not seem to learn much from your
mistakes. As soon as one adventure is concluded nothing will do but for you to start looking forward to the
next. Well, I have news for you, Vicky. You have
climbed your last garden wall."

"Please, do not make rash statements now in the heat
of anger, sir. Give yourself a chance to cool down. By
tomorrow I am certain you will see that I acted in a
reasonable manner, given the circumstances."

"Your idea of a reasonable manner is totally opposite
from my own."

"I do not believe that, Lucas, not entirely. I know I

am too headstrong as far as you are concerned and that you think me rash on occasion, but—"

"On occasion?" He rounded on her with an incredulous glance. "More like ninety percent of the time, madam."

"Really, my lord. Surely I am not such a bad wife?"

He stalked past her. "I did not say you were a bad wife. You are a disobedient, wayward, reckless wife who will almost certainly wear me out before my time if I do not teach you some respect for your poor, harried husband."

"I do respect you, Lucas," she said very earnestly. "I have always respected you. I do not always approve of your actions and sometimes you annoy me no end, but be assured I have the greatest respect for you."

"Yes, you find me *tolerable*, do you not?"

"For the most part."

"That is, of course, vastly reassuring," Lucas said through his teeth as he turned and stalked back across the room. "I shall remind myself that you have the greatest respect for me and that you find me tolerable the next time you willfully defy me."

"I have never actually willfully defied you, my lord."

"Is that right?" He swung around and came back to her, stopping directly in front of her. "What about what you did tonight? Was not that an act of defiance? Of disobedience?"

Victoria straightened in her chair. "Well, I suppose it could be viewed as such if one were to put the worst possible construction on my behavior, but I never meant—"

At least have the grace to admit you did it because you loved me."

Victoria's eyes flew to his and a great stillness descended on the bedchamber. She hesitated a moment, cleared her throat delicately, and nodded. "You are quite right, my lord. That is, of course, precisely why I did it."

"My God, I don't believe it." Lucas looked stunned for a moment and then he reached down and hauled her to her feet. "Say it, Vicky. After all I have been through tonight, I deserve to have the words at last."

She smiled tremulously. "I love you. I have loved you since the beginning. Probably since the night we met at Jessica Atherton's party."

"That was the real reason you rushed off to rescue me tonight, the real reason you would not allow me to kill Lady Rycott as she deserved. You love me." He tightened his arms around her, crushing her close. "My dearest wife. I have waited so long to hear you say that. I thought I would go out of my mind waiting."

"Do you think there will ever come a time when you will be able to say those words to me, Lucas?" Her voice was muffled against his dressing gown.

"Dear God, I love you, Vicky. I think I knew it the night I took you to that inn and made love to you. I certainly knew then I would never desire another woman the way I desired you. But everything went to hell the next day when I walked into the conservatory and realized Jessica Atherton had told you why she had introduced us. All I could think of was that she had cost me far more than she would ever realize. I wanted to lash out at anyone and everyone. I knew you would never believe I loved you after that."

"I was not in a mood to hear a declaration of love just then. But you could have told me later, Lucas."

"Later you were too busy telling me that you would graciously condescend to form a business association with me. You made such a point of painting our relationship as a partnership that I grew desperate. The only thing that gave me hope in my darkest moments was the fact that you never removed the amber pendant."

She looked briefly startled. "The pendant? I never removed it because there were times when it was the only thing that gave me hope."

" 'Tis your own fault for being so stubborn," Lucas said.

Victoria fingered the pendant around her neck. "You could hardly expect me to tell you I was in love with you after learning you had married me for my money. Besides, you were very busy letting me know that you were not about to give an inch lest I take advantage of your good nature and try to manipulate and control you. You wanted my surrender, Lucas."

"I may love you to distraction, my dear, but I also understand you, at least somewhat. You would not have been above using any leverage you could get in our small war and I could hardly have blamed you for doing so. You have my utmost respect as an opponent, but I would much rather have you as a loving wife, Vicky."

"Very nicely put, my lord." She hugged him fiercely. "Oh, Lucas, I do love you so."

Lucas kissed her warmly. "And while we are on the subject, there is another point I would like to clear up. I did not marry you for your money. I started courting you for it, I'll admit, but I wound up marrying you because I could not imagine being wedded to anyone else. Good God, woman, I had to be in love with you. Why else would I have gotten myself leg-shackled to a female who was almost certain to turn my life into a series of near disasters?"

"I suppose that's true enough. Let us not forget you did have a choice. There was always the Perfect Miss Pilkington to whom you could have turned in a pinch."

He shook her gently. "Are you laughing at me, wench?"

"Never. I would not dream of laughing at my husband. I have nothing but the highest respect for him." She lifted her head from his shoulder, her eyes sparkling. "Does this mean you are going to cease reproaching me for my actions tonight?"

"Do not look so pleased with yourself, madam. I have not finished with you yet."

"Really? What is next? Will you have me hauled before a court-martial? Shall I be stripped of my rank and privileges?"

"I think," Lucas said, "I will simply take you to bed and strip you of your nightclothes. Then I shall make love to you until you have been brought to a full realization of your erring ways."

Victoria put her arms around his neck as he picked

her up and carried her to the bed. She smiled up at him through her lashes. "That sounds delightful."

His laugh was husky with passion as he settled her down onto the turned-back bed. "As usual, we are very much in accord in this area of our marriage."

He removed his dressing gown and came down beside her, already fully aroused. He fumbled briefly with her nightclothes and then he tugged her down across his body. The amber pendant dangled from her throat, brushing the crisp hair of his chest.

"Tell me again that you love me, Vicky."

"I love you. I shall love you always." She cradled his head between her palms and kissed him with all the emotion that was in her heart. "You are the only man on this earth I could have married. What other man would discuss the merits of manure with me during the day and climb my garden wall at midnight to take me to a gaming hell? You are unique, Lucas. Now tell me again that you did not marry me entirely for my fortune."

His hands tightened on the back of her head as he brought her mouth close to his once more. "It does not really matter why I married you, my Amber Lady. I am so deeply enmeshed in your coils now that I will never be free. I love you, Vicky. I will put up with any amount of wall climbing, ledge crawling, or midnight adventuring if you will just give me your word that you will love me for the rest of your life."

"You have my most solemn vow, my lord."

She no longer saw ghosts in his eyes, Victoria realized as she gave herself up to his kiss, only moonlight and love, and a passion that would last a lifetime.

Lucas woke once during the night, aware of a familiar ache in his leg. He thought about getting up for a glass of port, but before he could slide out of bed Victoria put her hand on his thigh and began to massage it gently. Lucas closed his eyes again and a moment later he was asleep.

The following spring Lucas went in search of his wife. He found her, as usual, in the conservatory, where she

was working on a painting of an odd little lily she had
just recently received from America.

She had returned to her watercolors immediately
upon rising from childbed the previous month. She had
been greatly inspired, she said, by the news that Reverend Worth's *Instruction in Methods Guaranteed to Create a Beautiful Flower Garden* had sold out the first
edition and gone into a second printing.

The vicar had been adamant that the plates, etched
and hand-colored from original paintings by Lady Victoria Stonevale, had ensured the book's overwhelming
success. He was most anxious to get on with a sequel,
this time on the subject of exotic plants for private
gardens.

A baby's happy gurgle greeted Lucas as he made his
way down the aisle of luxuriantly blooming exotic plants.
He paused by the cradle which had been set next to the
easel and grinned at his healthy baby son. The babe
seemed symbolic somehow of the now-thriving lands
that surrounded the great house.

The gardens outside the windows were lush with
blossoms and the fields beyond were rich and green
with the promise of excellent crops. It was going to be a
good year for Stonevale, the first of many, Lucas vowed
to himself.

He leaned down to kiss his wife, who was busy
mixing colors with her brush, and noticed a spot of
orange on her nose.

"What have you got there, Lucas?" she asked, glancing at the leather-bound volume in his hand.

"A small gift, madam. I had a copy of your book
bound for you."

She blushed with delight as she reached for it. " 'Tis
not precisely my book, you know. It is Reverend Worth's
book."

"I shall let you in on a little secret, my dear. Your
aunt Cleo says people are buying the book as much for
the lovely plates as they are for the vicar's excellent
treatise on gardening."

Victoria examined the book, running her hand over
the leather.

"Oh, I doubt that."

"It is quite true."

"Thank you, Lucas." She looked up at him, her love in her eyes. "Aunt Cleo was right about one thing. You do have a knack for being able to give me gifts I could never buy for myself."

He smiled his slow smile. "And you, my love, have given me far more than I ever bargained for when I went hunting for an heiress."

"Do you know," she murmured, idly touching the pendant at her throat, "I think it is about time for the Amber Knight and his lady to make another midnight appearance on the grounds of Stonevale."

Lucas groaned. "And you only a month out of child-bed. Forget it, my love." He glanced significantly at his son. "Besides, you have other things to do at midnight these days."

"Well, perhaps not tonight, I grant you. And mayhap not tomorrow night, either. But soon." She laughed up at him, her eyes brilliant. "You know how you like to indulge me, Lucas."

"Why is it," he asked as he brushed his mouth lightly, lovingly across her own, "that I still ask myself which of us did the surrendering?"

Victoria's answer was lost in the kiss, a kiss that held the promise of a lifetime of glorious midnights.